Acknowledgements

We acknowledge with a lot of gratitude the inspiration and help we got from Hester Ross with whom we began this project of collecting short stories but who had to leave for Scotland before the project was completed. Her suggestions and material contributions have helped to make this anthology a reality. Many of those who have contributed to this volume urged us on in moments when our zeal for the project faltered and the task became too much to squeeze in between our normal official duties. If you have any joys in seeing this work come to fruition, then they are definitely shared with us. To Ndikufera Malekano and Jane Sulamoyo, who helped in the typing of some of the stories in this anthology, we feel deeply indebted.

The publisher would like to thank the following for giving permission to use their material: all the writers who submitted their works, Malawi Pen for the following poems from *Malawian Writing Today*: Lupenga Mphande's 'Why the Old Woman Limps', Francis Moto's 'Songs from the Clouds', Steve Chimombo's 'Modern Advertising', K L Phiri's 'Chameleon', Jack Mapanje's 'Another Fools' Day Touches Down: Shush', and Edson Mpina's 'Monkey Bay'; WASI publications for extracts entitled 'Feeding' and 'Beading' from Steve Chimombo's Breaking the Beadstrings; NECZAM for Felix Mnthali's 'Songani Lookout', 'My Uncle E P Mtungambera Harawa', 'The beauty of Dawn', 'Waiting for Rain', and 'Remake the World' from *When Sunset Comes to Sapitwa*; and Heinemann for David Rubadiri's 'African Child', 'Thoughts After Work', 'Yet Another Song', and 'An African Thunderstorm' from *Growing up with Poetry*.

Most of the works in this anthology were received from individual authors. However, if one knows of a piece included without permission, we will be grateful for the information so that we can correct the mistake.

Contents

vi

INTRODUCTION

This anthology of stories and poems from Malawi is written by a wide spectrum of literary artists. The purpose of the anthology is to meet some of the requirements of the MSCE Literature in English syllabus. At MSCE students are required to develop an understanding and appreciation of the four main genres of literature. Going through this anthology will equip the students with all the skills, knowledge and attitudes necessary for them to take the MSCE literature examinations. Essential aspects of literature have been defined and discussed.

Another helpful feature of this anthology are the questions after each story or poem. These questions are intended to assist both the teacher and students in exploring crucial areas of a given story or poem so that they can achieve the greatest literary benefit. Some poems have no questions. This has been done in order to give teachers an opportunity to form their own questions for discussion in class.

The short stories which we have selected for this anthology are only those that have not appeared in an anthology before, though they may have appeared in newspapers and magazines within Malawi or elsewhere.

The following are the themes and areas that have been covered by the short stories and poems in this anthology:
- Politics, democracy, chaos, lies, seduction, and disillusionment;
- Beautiful Malawi, Places, People, and the environment;
- Education, Determination, Achievement, and Frustration;
- The youth, Life, Living, HIV/AIDS, and Suffering;
- Gender, Exploitation, Conflict, and freedom of expression;
- Love, Beauty, Friendship and Affection;
- The sun, Rain, Seasons, Disasters and Poverty;
- Death, Sorrow, and Comfort;
- Home, Traditions, Values, Beliefs, and superstitions.
- Drug and alcohol abuse, inheritance, greed, murder, regret and broken promices.

We offer you this treasure of stories and poems and hope that you will enjoy reading them just as we enjoyed working on them.

PART 1
POETRY, DRAMA AND FICTION: SOME SIMILARITIES AND DIFFERENCES

Although literature encompasses many genres, there are only three principal genres in the world. These are poetry, drama and prose fiction which is sometimes simply called prose or fiction. Poetry, drama and fiction can be traced to ancient times. However, societies have at one time or the other revived each one of them at various times whenever their needs dictated. This section shows how these three genres are similar and different.

For hundreds of years history had dominated literature. In ancient Greece, for example, there were written records of wars between Athens and Sparta before many other peoples started keeping their historical records in writing. Some histories, however, are solely devoted to the lives of individuals and these are called *biographies*. If one writes a book about his/her own life, it is called an *autobiography*. Normally autobiographies are based on entries of a diary. As a result when not formally re-written, autobiographies remain diaries. A good example is the *Diary of Anne Frank* which was written by a young Jewish girl in the 1940s when she and her family and friends went into hiding from persecution by Nazi Germans.

There is also another literary genre that takes the form of prose and this is the essay. This genre is normally historical and intellectual. It is a short composition devoted to a philosophical discussion based on one or more topics of interest. These days, essays may appear in the form of magazine articles or as feature columns in newspapers. For example, in Malawi, there is "My Turn" in the *The Nation*

The major difference between histories, biographies and essays on the one hand and poetry, plays and fiction on the other is that the former are usually deductive while the latter are connotative. This means that essays, histories and biographies seek to present direct and explicit facts. Poems, plays and prose, however, communicate an emotional and intellectual impression that cannot be reduced to a single meaning. The meaning they present is highly suggestive and ambiguous. These genres do not usually mean exactly what they say. In other words, they involve the imagination so much that they probably provide the most fulfilling pleasure that can be obtained in the study of literature.

In view of the preceding discussion, great works of literature can be understood in at least three ways, the first is biographical, the second is historical, the third is interpretative. The interpretative approach is regarded the most difficult though ironically it is also the most rewarding because it involves close attention to the work itself free from biographical or historical distortions. The power of great literature lies in its ability to tell the reader what authors from other times and places understood about life's problems and solutions. In other words literature which has value in our lives should enable us to understand ourselves and the world that we are living in.

POETRY

This genre of literature comes to life mainly through being read aloud or recited. It is difficult to fully appreciate a poem without hearing it read aloud or recited. There are three main forms of poetry:

LYRIC POETRY

This is a brief musical expression of the thoughts and feelings of a speaker. It is named after a Greek stringed musical instrument called a *lyre*. No wonder the word lyrics also refers to the words of a song. Lyric poetry includes many humourous and witty types of light verse as well as serious works.

NARRATIVE POETRY

This is a type of poetry in which the author or persona tells a story.

DRAMATIC POETRY

Dramatic poetry normally takes the form of dialogue, common in drama. However, it is not intended for performance. Normally there is more than one speaker present. When there is only one speaker, the conversation is called dramatic monologue.

DRAMA

Plays are unique among the principal literary forms in that they are meant to be performed like music rather than read like fiction. The word drama is derived from the Greek word for action. Plays that are read can only be enjoyed partially. A play can be best understood and appreciated when it is performed. In modern times dramatic arts include: musical comedies, pantomimes, television plays and movies. A play can be transformed into other literary genres such as novels and viceversa. Drama is more versatile than the other two principal genres because it can be used in a variety of ways to suit the needs of audiences and different historical eras.

While drama is versatile, one needs to pay close attention to the following in order to fully appreciate it. Firstly, as in poetry, one has to pay attention to the language used. Secondly, attention should go to plot, character and setting just as in fiction. Thirdly, attention should dwell on drama's unique qualities including lighting, stage design, interpretation of roles and the organisation of actions by the director. Though these qualities are well perceived during performance, written plays may also depend on the use of these qualities and it requires one's imagination to recognise and appreciate their influence on the play.

KINDS OF PLAYS

Plays are of three types depending on their plots.

TRAGEDY

This is a presentation of admirable heroes or heroins who fall from good to bad fortune because of some weakness arising from their best qualities. This weakness is called "a tragic flaw". Though the hero or heroin is defeated we still recognise him/her as a noble person but we sympathise with him/her. We blame the person and wish that he or she had been a bit more careful with his/her good characteristics to avoid self-destruction.

COMEDY

Comedy presents laughable yet sympathetic characters and leads up to a happy ending. We watch a play whose characters make us laugh before we finally see them triumph and make us feel happy. For example, we may watch a play on an abused slave who acts stupidly before finally beginning to fight for his/her freedom and achieving it. We may sympathise with the abuse but we may laugh because he/she may not recognise the abuse until something happens in his/her mind. When he/she gets his/her freedom after a brave fight we may feel happy and relieved and we may want to identify with him/her. In all comedies therefore the comic actions of simplified characters in an ideal world have relevance to real-life situations.

TRAGICOMEDY

Dramatic tragicomedy is a relatively modern combination of the two discussed above. In this case events which apparently head for a catastrophic ending as in tragedy actually have a comic or ambiguous ending. Tragicomedy therefore manages to combine the entertaining qualities of comedy with the serious issues of tragedy.

USEFUL TERMS IN DRAMA

ACT: One of the major divisions of a play. Many plays of the past had five acts, but many modern plays usually have three acts. Other plays may have only one act.

SCENE: A unit within an act of a play, usually indicated by a change of setting or by a brief action or blackout.

CHORUS: Group of people on stage that comments on but does not participate in the dramatic action. The chorus was an essential part of ancient Greek drama, which consisted of masked dancers who sang or chanted on or behind stage.

COMIC RELIEF: A humourous story or character inserted into a serious play to release tension briefly and to intensify tragic emotions by contrast. Shakespeare uses comic relief to this effect with the grave diggers in *Hamlet* and the drunken gatekeeper in *Macbeth*.

ASIDE: An aside is a brief comment made by an actor on the stage but intended to be heard only by the audience and not the other characters.

SOLILOQUY: This is an extended speech by a lone character on the stage, in which he/she often reveals truths not admitted in the presence of other characters.

FICTION

Today prose fiction is probably by far the most popular of the three principal literary forms. Originally, the word fiction included any imaginative creation with a story whether in poetry, drama, or prose. In modern times, however, the term fiction is usually used to refer to prose such as the short story and the novel.

Poems and plays are governed by strict conventions such as metre and structure. In contrast, prose fiction is less confined by conventions and is the most natural and informal kind of literary presentation. In a story, the narrator speaks and provides an account of imaginary events for the entertainment of an audience.

Since the 1700's, literary fiction has branched in many directions. Some writers have explored the past. Others have explored particular settings, while still others have chosen to explore the emotion of an individual. Many writers have concentrated on the social relationships of their own times. There are also particular types of stories called "genres of fiction". These include the Gothic novel, detective stories, satirical fiction and science fiction.

In all fiction, appreciation hinges on recognition of four principal elements. The first is plot, or the order of events in a narration. These events are not always presented in chronological order, but the cause and effect reletionship between different events in a story is often crucial to a full understanding of it. The second element is character and characterisation. The third element is setting: time and place of the story. Attention to the setting and its influence on the story's outcome may help illuminate the writer's ideas and purposes in writing the story. The fourth element is the teller of the story. Some stories are told by an objective third person narrator who knows all the circumstances and thoughts of all the characters. Many others are told by a subjective fourth person narrator whose knowledge and understanding of the story is limited. The great power of fiction is that it can let a reader exprience events in another time and place and discover how similar, yet how much different other people's lives can be.

KINDS OF SHORT FICTION

FABLE: Brief story, often featuring animals as characters, intended to illustrate a moral lesson.

FAIRYTALE: Short narration that is generally fantastic and is today read or told principally to children.

FOLKTALE: Anonymous story tied to a single cultural group and handed over orally before being recorded in writing.

TALE: Short story, slightly unrealistic in character and event and related to the longer prose romance.

SHORT STORY: Brief prose narrative designed to be read in one sitting describing a limited number of characters involved in a single major event. Descending from the forms described above, the modern short story has become increasingly realistic in the hands of modern writers.

LITERARY DIVICES IN PROSE, POETRY AND DRAMA

Prose fiction, poetry and drama have devices which are used to enhance meaning. Ironically, these divices may make one unable to understand and enjoy these genres. This problem, however, is more prevalent in poetry than in the other two genres. Thoughts that are conveyed through poetry are difficult or sometimes impossible to be paraphrased fully in prose. The language of poetry is normally compressed hence it requires closer reading than prose. It is not strange to see a poem changing before the reader's eyes as different aspects of its language unfold. Specially, poetic language requires the active involvement of the mind because it usually includes imagery, visual expressions of thought and feeling. The problems arising from the use of poetic language complicate with the use of figurative language which expresses complex thought. Similarly, poems may use symbolism by including things that represent a variety of associations rather than a single meaning. For example, the eagle is a symbol of power in some parts of the world and it requires such knowledge for one to interpret a poem where the eagle is featured without any explicit explanation. However, though these devices are more prevalent in poetry, they may also be found in plays and fiction. Nevertheless, poetry's unique quality is its use of rhythm and sound. Poets use the rhythm of the language to enhance their meaning. Some of poetry's sound effects are rhymes, alliteration, and the use of words with the same consonants.

There is a special use of visual effects in poetry which cannot be shared by drama and prose fiction. For example, poets may write acrostics poems in which the first letters of each line spell out a word or a name. There are even some picture-poems in which the lines form the shape of the object that they describe.

From this discussion of the use of literary divices in poetry, prose and drama we may conclude that though poetry shares some of these elements with the other two genres, it need not be taken for granted. Poetry is a special reading experience in which the style of expression is as important as the content of the words.

Because of its rhythm and sound, most poetry is best read aloud so that its language can be appreciated unlike prose. The language of drama can also be appreciated better if performed than read silently. However, this does not mean prose fiction may not pay attention to sounds and rythms. There are prose writers who have adopted a poetic touch in their prose. For example, Alan Paton, author of *Cry the Beloved Country* opens his novel with a very poetic description of the land on which the story is set.

PART 2

UNDERSTANDING SHORT STORIES AND POEMS

Good short stories like other genres of literature are not written anyhow. Rather writers write them using expertise, knowledge and skills. So it is only those readers who have at least basic background and/or skills of how short stories are written who can fully understand and enjoy the short stories that they read. This section discusses those elements of the short story which writers take into consideration when writing their stories. It is expected that the reader will read the elements with the aim of mastering them so that he/she may understand and enjoy the stories in this collection. Most of these elements are also true to the novel in general.

PLOT

A complete short story is made up of events or actions which are arranged in a particular way. This sequencing of events or related actions is called plot. Plot in other words is the arrangement of events that enables the reader to see and understand what happens at point A so that action at point B should take place. Therefore within the plot there are actions which happen at particular times. Plots are of three kinds: Firstly there is what is called comic plot. This presents events which have a sad beginning and a happy ending. Secondly, there is tragic plot. This presents events which have a good beginning and a sad ending. Finally, there is tragicomic plot which combines the characteristics of tragic and comic plots as the name suggests. The plot of the short story borrows many of its characteristics from drama, therefore it is advisable that the reader turn to part 1 for further information on this subject.

CONFLICT

Conflict takes place within the events of the plot. Conflict means a situation in which two or more opposing forces meet one another. Conflict can either be psychological, or physical or emotional. A person can feel two opposing forces in the mind. He/she may be presented as being in the middle of deep thought but failing to make a decision. Physically, a person may find himself/herself in conflict with a fellow human being. For example a father may be involved in conflict with his son or daughter.

CLIMAX

Usually, events in a story move from one stage of tension or conflict to another. Normally the situation is that as the story progresses the conflict becomes bigger until it reaches the highest point. This point of events in a story is called climax.

RESOLUTION

After the climax we see the final outcome. Things may be resolved or may take another trend altogether. This final outcome of events is called a resolution.

FLASHBACK

Plot may however not always be as straightforward as discussed above. There are cases when the writer uses a technique called flashback. Flashback presents events of the past in the midst of a story in the present. It is the reader's task to put the events into a chronological order as he/she reads the story.

SUSPENSE

In some cases the story may not have a definite resolution. The reader may end up being left without really being told the final result of the climax. In this case the writer has used a technique called suspense. In some stories one may meet the use of suspense right at the beginning. Writers do this deliberately so that they may keep the reader interested in reading the story. Where suspense is used properly the story is usually very interesting. Normally, mature readers do not enjoy stories which have all events neatly tied up together.

DILEMMA

Some writers instead of using suspense as discussed above may introduce what is called dilemma. In this case they present the characters of the story in a situation in which it is difficult to make a decision, because the options available to them are equally bad.

SURPRISE ENDING

There are also other writers who may not necessarily use suspense or dilemma but may instead use what is called surprise ending. The story may end abruptly or not, but in whichever case the story ends at a note that surprises readers because they did not expect it would end that way. The surprise ending can be a happy or sad one.

FORESHADOWING

Suspenseful plots often contain foreshadowing, clues that hint at later events in the story. This enables the reader to predict forthcoming events. Writers use foreshadowing to make surprise endings believable, but a good surprise ending is one which is believable even in the absence of foreshadowing. Some writers are particularly known for startling their readers with surprise endings.

CHANCE AND COINCIDENCE

The readers' expectation is that a short story will resemble real life. Therefore some writers think that, because in life things sometimes happen by chance or coincidence, they should present activities which happen by chance or coincidence. This however is viewed differently by those who think that a good short story should not allow things to happen by mere chance or coincidence. Such critics believe that a successful writer should be able to create a problem for his characters and in the end provide convincing solutions. Readers should be satisfied with what has been done to solve a problem. In short story writing as well as in other genres of literature such as the novel, the use of chance or coincidence to explain why things happen is technically called *deus ex machina*.

CHARACTER AND CHARACTERISATION

Characters are actors in a story. They could be human beings, animals, plants or ghosts. Characters are inseparable from plot because they are the ones who move the plot. A simple plot is normally associated with characters which are simple to understand. Similarly a complicated plot is associated with characters who are difficult to understand.

Characters can either be flat or round. Flat characters are those whose behaviour can be easily predicted by the reader. They normally have one major character trait which can either be in form of a strength or a weakness. They are static in nature hence readers can easily understand them. On the other hand, round characters are those whose behaviour is unpredictable. They always surprise us as to how they behave. A story with well controlled round characters is more exciting than that with flat characters. However a fair representation of both flat and round characters in a story may represent life in a better way.

Characters have character traits. These are qualities of their personality. In this case readers can study characters and conclude that they are either good or bad, intelligent or foolish etc. However the study of characters is not done anyhow. One can learn more about characters by using one or more of the following ways:

Firstly, one may look critically at what the characters do and how they do it. Remember it is said that action sometimes speaks louder than words. Some people may not be good speakers but their actions may speak a lot about them.

Secondly, one may consider what characters say about themselves and others and how they say it. For example we may know that a person is cruel by looking at how he shouts at a servant when it is possible to send the same information without shouting at all. The message, and how it is expressed, is very crucial to the understanding of character.

Thirdly, one may understand character by comparing and contrasting two or more characters in the same story or in another. Characters may mirror one another.

Finally, the author may describe the characters as to who they really are. However, this does not mean that the reader should accept the description. It is wise to study the characters using other means to confirm the stance of the author. This is why it is reasonable to combine two, or more of the methods discussed above.

Related to the character traits of the characters in a story is what is called characterisation. This is the character's personality or the method by which the writer reveals this personality. Therefore by studying characterisation we may understand the characters of a short story better.

When writers state what characters are like, they are using direct characterisation. When they show you what the characters say and/or do, they are using indirect characterisation. To enjoy and understand a story which employs indirect characterisation, the reader must make inferences about the character's personality. Inferences are those guesses which one makes basing on information that has been given. Inferences allow the reader to use the known to understand the unknown.

MAJOR AND MINOR CHARACTERS

Characters in a story play different roles. However, whatever the case, characters may either play a major or minor role. As a result characters may be broadly grouped into major ones and minor ones depending on their roles.

Major characters are those who play great roles in a story. They are the ones on whom the story revolves. These are the ones about whom we learn many things. They are the ones who dominate the story. In a well written story, they are the most fully developed of all characters because the author makes special effort to make them come as alive as possible. The major character in a story is called protagonist or a hero/heroin. The major character whom the protagonist comes into conflict with is called an antagonist.

THEME

Writers normally have a message or several messages which they intend to send to the reader. They want to communicate some ideas to the reader. The central idea that is conveyed by a story is called theme. This communication may be done in two ways.

Firstly, the author may state the theme directly. This kind of theme is very easy to identify and understand. Secondly, they may just suggest the theme to the reader. It is the duty of the reader to consider what the story may be saying about the nature of people or life to identify the theme.

MAJOR AND MINOR THEMES

When reading the short story, one may realise that some themes are more prominent than others. The more prominent ones are called major themes while the less prominent ones are called minor themes. In good short stories more space is devoted to major themes rather than minor ones.

A theme which is only implied may also be expressed through a sentence that may be deliberately designed to suggest it to the reader. This sentence is called a key statement. Where there may not be a key statement the reader must infer what the theme may be.

SYMBOLS

A symbol is an object, an action, a word, or an idea that stands for something other than itself. For example a dove is a symbol of peace in most parts of the world. The olive branch is the symbol of unity worldwide.

In a story a writer may either use symbols that are familiar to most readers or those that occur in the story alone. Whatever the case writers usually emphasise or repeat the symbols or place them in strategic places in the story. The symbol's meaning depends on its context. Readers who are able to recognise symbols as well as understand what they mean are more likely to identify and understand the theme(s) of the story and enjoy their reading as a result.

IRONY

In a short story, as in a novel or a play, the writer may use irony within the plot. Basically irony is a form of humour, or an indirect way of conveying meaning, in which one says something in such away that people realize that he/she is joking or that he/she really means the opposite of what is said. There are three main forms of irony:

VERBAL IRONY

This is the simplest type of irony. Its major feature is that the speaker says the opposite of the things which are intended. There is a discrepancy between what is said and what is meant.

DRAMATIC IRONY

In this type of irony the contrast is between what a character says and what the readers know to be true. The value of dramatic irony is in the comment it implies on the speaker or his/her expectations.

SITUATIONAL IRONY

In this kind of irony the discrepancy is between appearance and reality or between expectations and fulfilment. The situation is not what would seem appropriate.

SETTING

The setting of a story is the time and place of the action. In a short story the setting is usually presented through brief descriptions. In some stories the setting may play crucial roles. It may affect what happens to the characters and how they respond to life. In some stories the setting is not explicitly stated by the author. The author instead expects the reader to infer the setting by using the clues given in the story.

In stories in which the setting is clearly defined, the author may make the story come alive by using vivid details to describe the setting. These descriptions are called descriptive details and they may allow the reader to feel that he/she is at the place where the story is taking place. Good readers should be able to analyse the effect of setting on the plot and of the aspects of the story.

As already mentioned above, setting includes the time of the events in the story. In some stories, the time period is important for the understanding of the story. The time period may be represented by the character's dress, customs, actions, and beliefs. While most stories take place in the past, some may take place in the present or even in the future. Science fiction stories usually take place in the future.

Some stories may be set in a real place within history. Where a story is accurate in the way the place, times and historical events are described, it is said to have a historical setting. Good authors are careful to include only details that describe a place and time accurately if they want their historical setting to be true.

ATMOSPHERE AND MOOD

The atmosphere or mood of a story is the overall emotional feeling created by the details that the author provides. The atmosphere may be a sad one, a frightening one or a jovial one. It may be created through descriptions of settings, characters, and events. Good writers choose their words carefully so that they may affect one's emotions in the way that they want. This may make readers identify themselves with characters or disassociate themselves from them. Similes and other similar devices such as metaphors may also be used to create atmosphere.

POINT OF VIEW

In its most basic sense, point of view means the way the story is told. The point of view shows from whose eyes the story is told. To know this, it is helpful to ask questions such as: Do you see the events through the eyes of one of the characters or not? If yes or no, how is this done? An author may tell a story directly or may let one of the characters tell it. Sometimes the author shows the story unfolding as if he/she is just watching. There are three main points of view from which a story can be narrated.

THE OMNISCIENT POINT OF VIEW

Through this point of view, the story is told by the author using third person pronouns. The narrator has unlimited knowledge and powers over his/her characters. He/She knows everything that takes place in the story including what happens in the minds of the characters. He/She is like a god. The omniscient point of view is flexible and permits the widest scope of the story. On the other hand, there might be too much telling instead of showing events and leaving the readers to make conclusions for themselves. Authors who use this point of view may literary say that their characters are either good or bad instead of leaving the readers to make their own conclusions.

LIMITED OMNISCIENT POINT OF VIEW

Through this point of view, the author tells the story in the third person but tells it from the view of one character in the story. The author looks at the events of the story through the eyes and mind of this character. Unlike in the omniscient point of view discussed above, the author only knows everything about one character. He/She tells readers what the character sees, hears, thinks and feels. He/She may also go further to explain or interpret the experiences of this chosen character. He/She knows all the other characters through this chosen one.

FIRST PERSON POINT OF VIEW

Through this point of view the author tells the story as if he/she is one of the characters. The story is told in the first person using the pronoun 'I'. As a result it is also called the I - narrator point of view. Rarely do authors use the pronoun "we". The character who uses this point of view may either be a major one or a minor one; a protagonist or an observer.

When this point of view is used, the story sounds more realistic and immediate. Furthermore this point of view offers excellent opportunity for dramatic irony to be achieved. One can easily see discrepancies between what the narrator perceives and what he/she does not know.

Through this point of view, the author disappears into a kind of camera that roves around, but can record only what is seen or heard. The narrator cannot comment, interpret or enter a character's mind. It is like the reader is watching a play as it unfolds without the help of a commentator. It is this resemblance with a play that makes this point of view to be called dramatic.

LANGUAGE IN THE SHORT STORY

Language, especially how it has been used, is one of the major aspects of the short story. Writers write differently. Some may use very simple language while others may use difficult language. It is easy to understand a story which is written in simple language. However writers may have their own reasons for using a particular kind of language. This could be determined by the purpose of the short story or the intended audience. Let us for example say that the author wants to teach English to foreign students through short stories. This may influence him/her to choose words which may have to be learned by the readers.

But differences in the use of language do not lie in the choice and use of words alone. There may also be differences in the way the words are used to form sentences. Some writers may use short, active sentences while others may use very long descriptive sentences. Some writers may go as far as writing a paragraph comprising of one long sentence broken into parts by commas, semicolons and colons. The kind of sentence patterns that authors use may affect the way the reader reads and understands the story.

The other factor that may influence language usage in a short story is the kind of social, professional or educational background of the writer. A scientist may use more technical words than a nonscientist. It is therefore important to know the background of the author in order to understand his/her use of language. However it is also true that the use of language may reveal the background of the author where it has not been stated explicitly.

At another level, the use of language may be regarded as formal or informal. This may be determined by the setting of the story or the kind of characters involved. This is done to reflect real life situations. For example, if the story takes place at an official meeting of government ministers discussing important matters, the language used may be formal reflecting the setting and the characters involved. On the other hand, if the same group of ministers meet at a holiday resort on a Christmas holiday their language may be informal, reflecting the casual interaction that the ministers are involved in. It is therefore possible to say that the setting or the atmosphere can influence the language that the author may use in the short story.

Depending on the cultural context in which the story is taking place and/or the reasons why it is written, authors may use what is generally regarded as obscene language. Some cultural contexts, however, do not allow the writer to use words anyhow no matter what the purpose may be. The author may use other forms of language to express the offensive idea. This use of language is called euphemism. Readers are expected to discover the meaning behind the euphemistic expressions.

Some short story writers may use language which may sound more or less like poetry. The reader may feel a rhythmic pattern of words and sounds as he/she reads the story. This makes the story sound interesting in most cases. Writers who are also poets are likely to use poetic language in their short stories. This may be the case because they deliberately do so or it may be due to the fact that it is a skill which is within them.

The choice of words may also make the story move fast or slowly. Short sentences normally allow for more and quick action while long sentences are winding, descriptive and make a passive presentation of ideas.

Whether style is a matter of choice or not, it may affect the readers' way of reading and understanding of the story. Unfortunately, not all writers can write in the the the same style.

FANTASY

A fantasy is a non-realistic story and goes beyond the bounds of known reality. The story is so fictitious that it conjures up a strange world full of marvellous things. In such a world ordinary laws of nature are suspended. The characters do those things which the readers cannot believe. Even the landscape of the world is strange too. The characters may be ghosts, dragons, wolves and other animals which may be presented with the characteristics of both human beings and animals.

PART 3
THE TEACHING OF LITERATURE

The introduction of Literature in English as an elective subject in the secondary school curriculum is a welcome development. The study of Literature is very important for the development of values and aesthetics, which are well articulated in the secondary education objectives of the syllabus under such headings as ethical and socio-cultural skills, and creativity and resourcefulness skills. Apart from the affinity there is between Literature in English and English as a subject, the main reason why the study of Literature was attached to English was to make sure that, through English which is a second language and a compulsory subject in Malawi, Literature also is studied by all the pupils in secondary schools. There was, however, a problem with this arrangement in that time devoted to Literature, since it had to share the periods allocated to English, was limited.

Now, apart from Literature, the curriculum has incorporated many other subjects, affording pupils a wide choice. With problems of inadequate supply of teachers and textbooks, many pupils could be forced to drop Literature, or schools may not offer it. This could work against the perceived advantage of introducing Literature in English as a separate subject. There are, therefore, challenges posed to the Government, the publishers, and the teachers: to the Government the challenges are to provide sufficient funds for purchasing literature books and to improve teacher education in Literature and English, so that more are qualified in these fields; to the publishers the challenge is to increase the publication of Malawian Literature, because it is this that can facilitate proper grounding of pupils in Literature; and to teachers the challenge is to teach the subject in such a way that it becomes not only academically rewarding, but enjoyable as well. For poetry, generally believed to be difficult, teaching it so as to increase enjoyment and aesthetic appreciation is particularly important.

In the syllabus the verbs commonly used in the objectives of the teaching and learning of the poetry genre are: identify, describe, define; and the higher level ones are: discuss, explain, analyze, and evaluate. It seems clear from the objectives that the teaching of poetry should aim to foster the development of knowledge at different levels of Bloom's taxonomy. The broad headings of the content to be studied in poetry are: the origins and types, such as lyrics, epics, and narrative poems; the setting, such as in political, socio-economic, cultural and historical situations; the story in the poems, which leads to the examination of such things as the presentation and development of the experience, in the beginning, middle and ending part; the types of characters, such

16

as the persona, addressee and subject; the language and style, which examine such things as sound effects, and figures of speech; the themes, which cover values, visions of life and the world, and issues and concerns such as love, politics and good governance, culture, growth and development, HIV/AIDS, and gender; the performance of poetry, such as reciting, dramatizing, singing, dancing, beating rhythm, and storytelling; and how to critically evaluate aspects such as setting, story, character and characterization, language and style, themes and performance. Given this range in content, the teachers or schools will need to choose anthologies with poems that cover most if not all of these aspects.

Under teaching/learning activities or experiences, the syllabus recommends such classroom activities as reading aloud, reading silently, reciting, dramatizing, singing, beating rhythm, brainstorming, discussing in pairs and groups, debating, classifying, storytelling, analyzing, evaluating, composing, value-voting, and hot-seating. The activity of hot-seating is done in this manner. Choose a person to represent a character in literature. Seat the person in front, facing the rest of the class. Tell members of the class to ask him or her questions about what he/she did, why, how, and what he/she will do to correct the situation. The person should imagine that he/she is the real character in the situation as presented in the literature text, and answer questions from that position. There are many poems in which hot-seating can be done. For example, in 'Whose Responsibility', by Steve Chimombo, one pupil can be Minister of Information. Questions from stanza 2, and other questions about why Kamuzu's grave has been neglected, and what the government is going to do about it can be asked. The other types of poems in which this interesting activity can be done are the many narrative poems such as Dotolo, by Zondiwe Mbano, and the panegyric such as 'My Uncle E P Mtungambera Harawa', by Felix Mnthali. This activity, if well conducted, can generate a great deal of fun and also clarify certain things that some learners found difficult to understand; moreover, the teacher can also use this activity to assess how much learning has taken place.

The syllabus recommends that the short story and the novel be tackled in Form 3, while the poetry and the drama come in Form 4. This is a general guideline meant to assist teachers to balance their teaching so that they do not spend too long on one genre to the detriment of the teaching of another. It is clear why the short story and the novel should go together because they are closely related and cover almost the same area in terms of content. The problem with following this arrangement strictly would be that the poetry and the drama strands would end up being so squeezed in the short teaching time available in Form 4 that pupils would not learn sufficiently well; and yet among the four genres, people consider poetry to be more demanding, and drama has aspects of stage and production, which involve practical work that cannot be done in a hurry. The same reason given for putting the short story and the novel to follow each other in Form 3 can be used to justify separating them. If the short story, for example, is put at the end in Form 4, coverage will not be jeopardized by the shortage of time since the relevant literary content would have already been covered through the novel. On the contrary, the tackling of the short story towards the end of the final year will not only introduce the genre, but also enhance revision of the aspects of the novel already covered. The other way would be to tackle two genres concurrently in each year; for example, teaching the novel and the poetry in the Form 3 and the drama and the short story in Form 4. This way, more time saved from the short story could be committed to the drama, and perhaps some of the stage and production aspects of drama could even go into extracurricular activities of term one or two.

In terms of planning the work a pertinent question is: how should the teacher tackle the content specified in the syllabus, and examine fifty or more poems from the chosen anthology? This question seems important even when considering the planning of the work in the other three genres, and therefore the teacher will have to think carefully about this. While many strategies could be identified, perhaps these could generally fall between two extremities. One strategy would be to plan to deal with the origins and types of poetry, and discuss the broad terms as meaning and experience, structure and conventional form, language, and judgement. After defining these terms clearly, then the teacher can deal with specific content given in the syllabus, before examining individual poems from the books. This would ensure that pupils have a general knowledge of the content and technical terms of poetry before they delve into actual poems; and this seems a prudent and systematic way to proceed in a new area. Such an approach could even influence classroom teaching where the procedure would be first to define terms theoretically without showing how these ideas work in actual poems. In the teaching of grammar, such a deductive approach was employed in schools up to not long ago, and even to date many teachers in Malawi could be found using such an approach. The argument is that pupils need conceptual frames for examining language and organizing the various aspects of it before plunging into it; and that such an approach provides a necessary shortcut to learning. However, it is known that such an approach often leads pupils to simply memorizing terms, definitions and examples from books; and yet they fail to demonstrate their knowledge in real performance given practical situations. Moreover, in the teaching of poetry it would appear purposeless to teach terms and definitions outside the context of actual texts of poetry. It is doubtful whether such an approach can really facilitate the development of relevant skills for independently reading and understanding poetry.

The second strategy for planning the teaching is to tackle individual poems directly, and define and apply the technical terms in the course of examining the poems. In each poem or group of poems various poetic devices employed can be analyzed so that pupils understand how these are employed to build the overall experience and meaning. For this to work well the teacher may need to group the poems according to poetic devices he/she wants to deal with, or the content or themes being covered. In this way the teacher would avoid too much repetitions or the going back and forth on the same content; thus the schemes and records of work would look more orderly. Such a strategy in planning will mean that in classroom teaching and learning the pupils will directly be involved in the discussion of the relevant elements of poetry. This has the advantage of teaching ideas within the context of actual poems. Perhaps, the other advantage is flexibility in that the teacher can plan to start the teaching from any poem; although a good teacher would still know that the best is to start with those poems that are more accessible before going to the more difficult ones. The problem is that even after going through a number of poems, pupils may not easily develop a clear conceptual frame for organizing and examining various elements of poetry. Furthermore, without clear guiding principles, pupils will not know technical terms for communicating their aesthetic appreciation; and yet these technical terms are needed as frameworks on which to mount such knowledge. Moreover, for examination purposes, the candidates will be required to demonstrate their understanding and appreciation of different poems by discussing technical aspects.

As can be seen, each approach of planning the work has advantages and disadvantages. The teacher should aim to maximize on the advantages of each approach and work to significantly reduce the disadvantages of each. It seems therefore that the way to proceed is by embracing an eclectic approach. In this way the first approach will be useful to start from, and then move quickly to the second approach; the first approach will provide the necessary conceptual frames and the second will make learning both meaningful and enjoyable. The other way is also possible, where most poems are studied using the second approach; and later, building on the knowledge pupils have gained, the teacher intervenes to teach the elements themselves and shows how each works in the poems already studied. Similarly, the schemes can marry the two approaches by making the literary elements from the syllabus visible and the context for teaching them are actual poems from the chosen anthology. The actual classroom teaching, guided by the topic objectives, should practise activities suggested by the syllabus; in this way pupils will develop literary appreciation and enjoy learning poetry.

This anthology aims firstly to provide a variety of poems in terms of levels of difficulty, and range of subjects, themes and styles; and secondly to demystify poetry by compiling beautiful poems written by Malawians, not people from distant places or times. Most of the writers are teachers, and amongst these many of them teach or have taught in secondary schools. Among the poems are those of Malawi's prolific and accomplished poets, such as David Rubadiri, Steve Chimombo, Jack Mapanje, and Felix Mnthali. At the end of most poems, questions have been provided to guide the discussion. While in the short story section they bemoan the dearth of female writers, poems from as many as seventeen female writers have been included in this section.

Another important feature of the anthology is the inclusion of different levels of question. The questions avoid too much use of technical terms so that pupils can use them on their own without the guidance of a teacher. Extra questions at the very end give opportunity to review and compare themes and styles of a number of poems. It is not, however, possible to design questions that exhaust important aspects of a poem; so the questions serve to start the process of examining the poem. The teacher should therefore feel free to add to, and modify or re-organize the questions to suit his/her lesson.

It was stated earlier on that the perceived advantage of introducing Literature in English as a separate subject would be lost if schools fail to offer it, or if many pupils do not opt for the subject because they feel it is difficult or simply boring. It is important for the teacher to aim at high standards of teaching so that the learning of poetry becomes not only academically rewarding, but enjoyable as well. The challenge seems great in the teaching of poetry because there is a general belief that poetry is inaccessible except to a coterie of savants called poets.

There are proverbs in our local languages that state that there is no tree too tall for monkey to climb. This is true because every tree grows from the ground, and canopies of different trees in the forest combine to form one vast canopy where branches cross. To climb a tree monkey either starts from the ground or crosses from another tree; and he does not always need to climb to the highest twig of every tree. Similarly, poets use human language and human experiences to produce poems. Therefore poetry cannot really be incomprehensible. Let this be our conviction as teachers of Literature, as we confidently strive to give pupils the necessary skills for the enjoyment of this art of great beauty and refinement.

Zondiwe Mbano

HOW POETRY DIFFERS FORM OTHER LITERARY GENRES

The similarities and differences of the literary genres and the key elements of literature have been well discussed in part 1 and 2 of this book, but this has been done from the point of view of the novel and short story. There is need therefore to focus on poetry and discuss elements that distinguish it from the other genres, and also discuss whatever the teachers and pupils will need to know about this selection of poetry. To achieve this, I have endeavoured to define key elements of poetry and draw examples of these from the poems in this anthology. Although some examples may appear far-fetched, this approach has the advantage of making the ideas clearer because of the familiar local examples; and furthermore, this is expected to help pupils gain confidence as they see that Malawian writers also employ the poetic devices to good effect.

Comparing items of content under the scope and sequence chart of the syllabus of Literature in English can show areas in which poetry differs from the other genres. For example, it will be seem that the rest of the content is basically similar except the headings, Language and style, and performance, and what comes under these headings. While the content under performance - reciting, dramatizing, singing, dancing and beating rhythm - may not be very significant in a discussion of how poetry differs from other genres, it does show that there are musical and dramatic effects in poetry. The main difference, however is in the items under language and style, and these are: structural elements or form such as stanza, lines, syntax, meter, and rhyme; sound effects such as assonance, consonance, euphony, cacophony, alliteration, rhythm, and also meter and rhyme; and figures of speech or tropes such as imagery, metaphor, simile, symbolism, irony and paradox. Other genres also use these elements; and whenever they employ these skilfully, the writing has noticeable poetic effects such that, whether it is a play or a novel, it reads like poetry. However, it is only in poetry that these elements are used with such a high intensity that the text produced becomes concentrated in thought, expression and aesthetic effects; and this is so much that even after extracting external aspects such as structure or sound effects, there remains texture that calls for deep analysis.

TYPES OF POETRY

Occasional, Epic, Panegyric, Narrative, Lyrical, Dirge, Sonnet, Dramatic, and Idyll

Classifying poetry can be a difficult task. The syllabus identifies seven different types, and these are occasional, lyrical, panegyric, epic, dirge, sonnet, and narrative poetry. **Occasional verse**, according to C Hugh Holman and W Harmon (1986) <u>A Handbook</u>

to Literature, New York, Macmillan, refers to poetry written for a specific occasion such as a social, historical, or personal occasion; and such type of poetry tends to be written by celebrated poets commissioned to write for the commemoration of an event, or sometimes the poet himself/herself may decide to write for a personal event. In Malawi, the closest example to occasional poems one can find are perhaps the pieces read on functions such as political gatherings or published in newspapers on national occasions, which usually tend to be written in a hurry. In this anthology, perhaps 'Vipya', a poem written to commemorate the sinking of a passenger vessel on Lake Malawi in 1946, would be the nearest example of occasional poetry. The epic, the panegyric and the narrative are similar in that they use the narrative mode. **The epic** is long, in elevated style, and presents the adventures of a legendary or historical figure. Some examples of epic poetry are Chimombo's long poem entitled Python! Python!, and the long narrative texts about Mbona in his play, The Rain Maker. It is important to note that, although the syllabus does not mention plot amongst elements to be discussed in poetry, narrative poems do have a clear plot. In poetry, as well as in the other genres, two elements need to be distinguished in the area of plot; and these are the plot itself and story or storyline. The plot is a result of the skill of the artist to recast the source material, such as an anecdote, in line with his/her thesis, and highlight aspects of cause and effect by employing such devices as in medias res (Horace's, starting in the middle of action), flashback, characterization, and narrative summary and narrative moment (terms used in Harvey S. Wiener and Nora Zisenberg, Great Writing: A reader for writers; New York: Mc Graw-Hill Book Co.). In narrative summary the writer zooms out over a long period of time by skipping some events in order to give a broad picture; while in narrative moment he/she zeroes in on a short time frame in order to depict moment by moment incidents. The story or storyline differs from the plot in that it is simply action in time sequence from beginning to end.

The other type of narrative, **the panegyric**, is a poem praising or eulogizing a person who is either living or dead. Perhaps most Malawians will remember the songs women sang for the Ngwazi, which if one presented them as poems would be examples of panegyric poetry. In the anthology we have Mnthali's 'My Uncle E P Mtungambera Harawa' as an example. The ordinary narrative poems tell a story or report an event, such as in Mbano's 'Nyumbani's Tale' and 'Dotolo'. **Lyrical poems** are short, subjective and imaginative such as the poems of love in this anthology. Note that poems such as 'My Man' and 'The way' are translations of traditional songs, and can be sung to the accompaniment of a zither, the instrument locally known as bango or bangwe. The dirge is a kind of lyrical poem which is written to commemorate death or to be sung at a funeral. Another lyrical poem is the sonnet which has an elaborate structure of four-

teen lines arranged in patterns of 8 and 6 or 4+4+4+2; and the lines are in iambic pentameter, which means five metric feet of the basic pattern of unstressed followed by
stressed syllable. This form of poetry is traced back to Petrarch of Italy who wrote during the Renaissance, and the form was developed later by such poets as Shakespeare.

Other types, although not among the examples in the syllabus, are the **dramatic poetry**, which has elements of drama, and the **idyllic poetry**. Dramatic poetry is character-
ized by the use of dialogue or monologue portraying a conflict situation through,
among other things, the use of vigorous diction. In other respects this type of poetry is
similar to the narrative ones except that here the characters are more visible before us
as they talk directly. Nazombe's opening lines in 'Exorcism' are abrupt and highly con-
frontational, May I not see you again...I have met you before. There is a similar confrontation in Mnthali's 'Remake the World', and we find dialogue in Chimombo's 'Who
is Responsible?'. The idyll is descriptive, narrative or pastoral, and usually depicts rural
life from a nostalgic point of view. Examples are Kusauka's 'Village Life,' and Chiwindo-Chirwa's 'Chikanda Beach'; and Mpina's 'Monkey Bay', Mbano's 'Sunset over
Mparayi' and Rubadiri's 'Thoughts After Work' which go beyond mere nostalgia for
rural life. So far these are some of the types of poetry found in the anthology. It must
be observed that such a discussion can by no means exhaust the classifications of poetry; there are other types of poetry not mentioned here. While classification is a good
intellectual exercise, it must be observed that good poetry is usually elusive to toxon-
omy.

FIGURES OF SPEECH : TROPES

**Image, Metaphor, Simile, Apostrophe, Synecdoche, Metonym, Symbolism, Irony,
Paradox and Proverb**

Apart from the structure, perhaps the main difference between poetry and the other
genres can be seen in the concentrated use of tropes. A **trope** is a figure of speech in
which words are used in nonliteral sense; that is to say, there is what is called a 'turn'
or change of the sense. In a *chilangizo* ceremony where newly-weds are instructed in
how to live, a woman from Thyolo warned the couple to be very careful because, as
she put it in Chinyanja or Chichewa, *'Dziko lamwa tamiki'*, which can be translated to
'The world has drunk termic'. (Termic, a black powder used to kill rodents, is a deadly
poison which people take to kill themselves.) Here is an interesting use of images or
metaphors from one of our local languages. The main idea being expressed is an appeal
to uphold chastity, or a warning against promiscuity in the face of HIV/AIDS. This in

technical terms would be in the realm of what is called the *tenor*. The visual images as objective and concrete realities are the person (male or female), the poisonous termic powder, the action of the hands and the mouth as the person throws the powder into the mouth, and the water washing it down. The sense experiences evoked are of the sound of swallowing, of the taste of termic in the mouth, and the general feelings or atmosphere of the whole process, such as sadness or shock at the sight of a person taking in what he/she knows is going to destroy his/her life. The significance of this action is that the person is committing suicide. In technical terms,the whole of this would be in the area of what is called the *vehicle*. And the tenor and the vehicle together make the figure of comparison called **metaphor.**

The other figure of comparison is the **simile**: which, unlike the metaphor, is identified by linguistic clues such as the words like, as and others with a similar function. These can be found in almost every poem, for example in Zimba's 'Dear Lord' there is *My love is / Like a cloud.../ But your love / Like the sun...* These work at literal level by, in the first stanza, transferring fickle qualities of a cloud to the idea of human love; and in the second transferring the constant and abiding qualities of the sun to divine love. This way the writer shows how unreliable human love is. Similarly in Mambo's 'Love', the lines, *Nothing is good without you / For you refresh like sleep / Full of sweet dreams* express comparison in form of simile; while the following two lines, *You are a gentle wind / Sighing from fresh roses* work as metaphors. These figures of comparison transfer the qualities of peaceful sleep, sweet dreams, gentle wind and the fragrance of roses to the notion of love. By employing these figures of comparison the writer brings out vividly her experience of love.

Rubadiri's 'An African Thunderstorm' employs many similes such as: *Like a plague of locust...Like a madman chasing nothing...Like dark sinister wings....* It will be noted that the similes here help to depict a vivid sensuous experience of the storm; and at the surface level this is a sincere description of an African storm, consistent with our experiences of storms. But the similes also take us to a deeper level where they progressively suggest disaster, confusion and death. When we carefully read the repeated bending and waving of flags to the wind, the fired smoke (from guns), and the picture of exploitation of women, forced to expose dangling breasts, we see that this is not an ordinary African storm: it seems to be a powerful devastating force, like the onset of imperialism and colonialism.

There are also examples where the writers use words with such strange combinations that the reader is forced to seek meanings at a deeper, figurative or nonliteral level. In

Rubadiri's 'African Child' there is: *African child/ Your wings will grow...* We know children do not grow wings, and so we have to seek the meaning of wings at nonliteral level. In 'Remake the World' Mnthali makes a strange combination of familiar images of *snakes* and *sneeze*. While the alliteration of the sound *-sn* - in both words brings a dangerous hissing, the experience of snakes sneezing, especially in the heat, not cold, is unusual. In the other lines the images of owls *chant(ing) eerie dirges / over corpses yet to be born / while hyenas heap(ing) their dung / on graves yet to be dug.* are puzzling. If owls wait for corpses of people who are not yet dead, and hyenas in anticipation mess up places where graves have not even been conceived, then there is grave danger and the future is terrifying. In 'Beauty of Dawn' Mnthali says *no longer at ease / among our own people / clutching their shadows.* The combination of the visual image and sense of touch in clutching, a very strong way of holding something, and shadow, an intangible thing, cannot be resolved at literal level. We are forced to think that either the people are so dulled by doing meaningless things that they start holding on to some ephemeral things, or they are so frightened that while walking they make sure they leave nothing behind them, not even a shadow!

In Chimombo's Feeding, there is, *may their* (water and flour from maize and millet) *mingling slake / our thirsting spirits.* The combination of slake, thirsting and *spirit* is unusual. It will have to be understood at nonliteral level. It seems therefore that the experience here is of offering libation or of a ritual performed to bring about peace. In Modern Advertising, there is *The soul erosion exorcised truth / And replaced it more permanently with: / 'Life is richer with Leonex'* The combination of soul, a disembodied entity, with erosion, an environmental degrading process makes us think deeply as we seek clues to the interpretation of the poem. We see that the poem works at three levels or more. The first level is of reporting the experience of advertising Leonex products, the visual and sound effects used at surface level. The second level of the experience is deeper in that it shows the advanced skill of advertising which has the effect of converting people to believe in the merit of a product beyond what it can really offer, as is stated in: *Life is richer with Leonex'* . This also reveals how gullible people are in pandering to specious claims. The third level of the experience is an overall commentary on the society where there is degradation of spiritual values and promotion of aggrandizement.

In the syllabus there is a list of key themes that Literature in English must deal with. What are called themes here relate to important issues in Malawi such as HIV/AIDS, gender, growth and development, good governance and conflict resolution that Literature needs to tackle. In Part 2 the concept of theme is well elaborated as 'the central idea that is conveyed...what the story may be saying about the nature of people or life...'. This goes deeper than the issues above; it is in the area of what is sometimes called the thesis, a statement or message that the writer is positing through the experience presented. We have seen how in Chimombo's 'Modern Advertising' what ushers the experienced reader to the second or third level of experience or meaning is the understanding of the tropes. Other interesting examples are in 'The New House" where he writes: *We came home to this:/...Nightmares chasing each other / on our pillows jolting us awake;* and in 'Zomba Mountain' where there are the lines: *I too, laden with a packetful of poems / under each arm..* In this poem, we meet another trope. The direct address to Zomba Mountain, referred to as a divine being, or as Makewana, in such lines as, *I read your visage like verse... and in, This you will never surrender to man.* goes beyond personification - it is in the area of **apostrophe**; a figure of speech in which an abstract quality or a non-existent personage is directly addressed as though present. Other examples of apostrophe, are in 'Earth' by Longwe, and 'Dear Mother' by Makhala-Nyamatcherenga. Besides apostrophe, there is craftsmanship in Chimombo's use of other poetic devices such as alliteration, consonance, assonance and internal rhymes as in, *played and prayed ... hurted and hunted...lived and loved;* and also rhythm, balance and wit in

They blasted.../ smashing myths to smithereens
They graded.../ mashing watermaids under wheels
They pulverized.../ flattening out their sighs and songs.

The use of tropes is well represented in poetry in this anthology. We find more examples in Moto's 'Songs from the Clouds', *and heard songs from the clouds / Songs bathed in blood.* The combination of song and bathed in blood has to be understood at figurative level. The other examples are in Iphani's 'Drifting Scum', *winds from the western hills / Blow morals afloat into the air;* Bvalani's 'My Beauty' *Your presence perfumes my day;* Banda's 'Pillars of Love', A pillar of love / *Towering over / Jeers taunts...;* Mbano's 'Songs of Sorrow', *Its still far across time / How can I sing / ...when my heart / is sinking in many a tear;* and in Maideni's 'Love' in which the second stanza mentions gold, rivers, honey and milk, and ends with the question: *But where can I find love?* This suggests that love is more precious than the preceding things, including gold, and yet closer to milk, that nurtures human life.

In Pungulani's 'Leaders of Tomorrow', *Can you find happiness / In sex drink and smoke / The very horns of death.;* death is presented as a wild goring bull. This takes us to another trope, called synecdoche, where the mentioned part, horns, signifies the whole, bull; or it could be vice-versa. Other examples of synecdoche are in Saidi's 'Chasing Pages' in the lines: *This madness of chasing pages / Where can one find a cure for it.*

Here chasing pages stands for reading books, which in turn stands for pursuing education. In Nazombe's Aunt Mao, the lines, *This ear now hard of hearing / Has seen many tobacco rolls.* the image is of a village woman who has stuck a tobacco cigar between her ear lobe and head, as is usually done; and the mention of the ear is to represent the whole woman, Aunt Mao, whose age is determined by the number of tobacco rolls she had smoked. Closely related to synecdoche is another figure of speech, called **metonym**, in which a term naming an object closely associated with a thing or person is used, for example a hoe can be used to represent the farmer. In Mnthali's 'Waiting for Rain' are the following lines, *...sing and ululate / for Land and Range-rovers / Mercedes Benzes ... / with multicoloured flashlights.* These are vehicles that ordinary people sing and ululate to represent ministers and the police coming in pomp, as forerunner to the presidential motorcade. It is as if the very symbols of obscene extravagance in a poor country are there to endear the oppressors to the masses.

Symbolism describes the use of symbols in literature, and a symbol is described as something that stands for another thing, or a word or words that evoke an object, which in turn suggests a meaning. In this sense therefore the words we use, such as mango, Mulanje, people or poem, are symbols because while they can stand on their own, they also mean something outside themselves. There are many poems in this anthology that use symbolism; amongst these is Mwase's 'Song of a Car' which at literal level can be understood to describe a car that is abandoned after having been used, and yet this, well understood, presents the experience of an abused person. Mnthali's 'Songani Lookout', describing the feat of scaling the precipice of Songani View at Zomba Plateau from Songani below, is another example. It presents the hurdles some people in Malawi have to go through in order to succeed in any important venture, such as education; and the important message is that somehow such people do manage. Other poems are Zenengeya's 'Shire River', that looks majestic and gentle, and yet it has rapids and crocodiles; and Jobe's 'Serpent', which is a common symbol for the Devil, but in this case it is a symbol of education that lures you only to throw you into servitude.

The following examples involve **irony**, which says one thing when the opposite is intended, such as expressing happiness when anger is intended; and **paradox**, which involves expressing an apparent contradiction. There is irony in Matewere's 'The Spear' in the lines, *A rich man wastes in a posh ward / Nourished only by drips and penicillins..* The whole of Chimombo's 'Formula for Funerals' is satire, a form of irony in which a serious subject, such as criticism directed to society, is presented with humour and wit. There is paradox in Rubadiri's 'African Child' where the child asks questions too silent, and in 'Thoughts After Work' where the combination of shroud and peace in the line Gracing in all a shroud of peace seems contradictory; and in Matope's *'Lord, hear our Cry'* in the lines, *At the end of the day / The coffin seller / Has a happy profit* . In Mbano's 'Why, oh Why' each of the following pairs of lines shows a paradox:

Dressed in colours of flowers / To meet a blind suitor...

Elected an impotent slave / To marry the chief's daughter...

Danced the victorious mgubo / To welcome a famished runaway...

The **proverb,** a sentence or phrase that is concise and memorable, and is usually handed down from the past, has the characteristics of figures of speech because it uses such devices as metaphor and paradox. Examples of proverbs are Mbano's 'Train to Balaka', *For days are so many / Fewer the hairs of a bull;* and Nazombe's 'Aunt Mao'

The riddle that makes/ The dutiful cock crow

Yields its knot to fingers/ That knead the earth

It is possible that each of these writers translated a known proverb from a local language, or attempted to construct his own proverb from the knowledge of other proverbs. What is important is to note how the proverb uses tropes.

STRUCTURAL ELEMENTS

Syntax, Caesura, Enjambement, and Meter

The other elements listed in the syllabus, apart from the tropes discussed in the preceding paragraphs, are those that have to do with structure or form, and sound effects. Some of the structural elements are stanza, lines, syntax, meter, rhythm and rhyme. Elements such as stanza and line do not really need a definition. **Syntax**, the organization and connection of words in a sentence or phrase, is important because it affects the structure of stanza, the rhythm, and the meaning; and as we have seen, certain combinations of words form tropes. Another element called **Caesura**, for example, occurs where within a line a meaningful group of words is marked by a pause in form of a comma, semi-colon, colon and fullstop; and **enjambement** is where the end of line does not mark a natural pause in the syntax. There are many examples of these in the anthology and one of them, having both examples, is in Nazombe's 'The Last Act':

Beloved, I desired you that moment

But you would not come; and

I sat on this rock, throat burning

Another example is in Mapanje's 'Another Fools' Day touches down: shush' where caesura is built into even the title:

A Ph. D., three books, a baby, three and half years -

Some feat to put us...Shush. Such frivolities no longer

Touch people here. 'So you decide to come back, eh?'

Note that in this case caesura, effected by commas, fullstops, dots, and the word, shush, has been used skilfully to guide the reading so as to bring out a slow rhythm, consistent with the mood of fear in the poem. Enjambement has been used in the second line in that both the sentence construction and the sense proceeds into the third line. Other examples of enjambement and caesura are in Mpina's 'Monkey Bay', *I'll return to this harbour to / live my life; I have lived all my / life for others in the past ; and in Phiri's 'Chameleon', Basically, he started lean / and weak. Moths facelifted / him. Up one branch,;* The opposite of enjambement is end-stopped lines, which too is common amongst the poems in the anthology. One example is in 'Nyumbani's Tale:

Trappist went to the river
In the heat of early afternoon

There he came near a burrow
With footprints of monitor lizard

Since all the lines are end-stopped, although the second line is an adjunct of the first line, the poem flouts orthographic rules by omitting commas and fullstops. The other example is 'Lake Kazuni'.

Meter refers to regular rhythmic patterns in a line of poetry. This depends on the number of feet, or number of syllables that possess rhythm in a line, as in octosyllabic (8 syllables), decasyllabic (10), and Alexandrine (12), as exemplified in Desmond Graham (1968) <u>Introduction of Poetry, London</u>: OUP. Poetry in which rhythm depends on a number of feet - where a foot is a unit of stressed and unstressed syllables or viceversa, like in the old English versification - has five basic patterns as follows: iamb (iambic), with an unstressed followed by a stressed syllable; trochee (trochaic), with a stressed followed by unstressed syllable; anapaest (anapaestic), with two unstressed followed by a stressed syllable; dactyl (dactylic), with a stressed followed by two unstressed syllables; and spondee (spondaic), with two stressed followed by an unstressed syllable. The common meter patterns, combining the preceding feet, were the tetrameter, four feet long, like in most old English hymns, and the pentameter, five feet long, like in the sonnets of Shakespeare. **Rhythm** is achieved by using these patterns, and also by using repetition, such as the use of *anaphora*, where the same words or syntactical arrangements are used at the beginning, such as, *Do you know why the old woman...* in Mphande's 'Why the Old Woman Limps'; *I see him now... I see him again,* in Mnthali's 'My Uncle E P Mtungambera Harawa'; *I sat at... I sat on ... Sitting on..* in Moto's 'Songs From the Clouds'; and *Machine of men with...* in Mbano's 'Silence

Returned' The other way to achieve rhythm is by skilfully using a combination of caesura and enjambement as in Mapanje's 'Another Fools' Day touches down: shush'. We have an example of the use of meter to effect rhythm in 'Lake Kazuni', where there is an experiment with couplets based on tetrameter, with the first line beginning with a trochee and ending with a trochee and the second line beginning with an iamb and ending in an iamb, and each line containing nine syllables, as follows:

`Lap and `listen to a` widow `wailing
Her `man cap`sized by the `battering `storm

Note that the syllables marked (') have stress, while the unmarked ones fall under unstress.

SOUND EFFECTS

Rhyme, Assonance, Consonance, Alliteration, Euphony, and Cacophony.

Sound effects are also used a great deal in poetry to effect beauty and enhance the experience, by indirectly contributing to the meaning. Among these, assonance, consonance and rhyme are closely related. A **rhyme** occurs when the words, usually at the end of lines, have the same sounding vowel and consonant, and the vowel is stressed; in other words, the words have the same nucleus and margin. Where only the nucleus is the same, there is assonance; where the margin is the same there is **consonance**; and where the nucleus and margin are the same but fall under unstress, there is feminine rhyme, which is considered weak, and therefore not very much preferred. This explains why the trochee, especially when followed to the end of the line, is not popular. **Alliteration** occurs where the words following each other have the same initial cluster or consonant, called the onset. In this anthology there are examples of poetry that follows a rhyming scheme, one of these is Kalimbakatha's Fiery Ball. Mbano's 'Why, oh why' follows a partial rhyme scheme. It must be noted that rhyming, still popular in children's poetry and rap music, is a convention of the past which is not very much used these days. The formal or external elements have the problem of making the poem sound contrived, and this often works against meaning. Modern writers experiment with devices that enhance undercurrent effects so that the poem flows naturally, like a river flowing through a deep forest at the bottom of a mountain.

The other sound effects used, such as onamatopae, in which the sound of the word suggests its meaning, can be seen in Mapanje's use of the word shush, the sound of which suggests that it is a request to someone to be quiet. **Euphony** occurs where the sound of a word or group of words have a pleasing effects, and **cacophony** is the opposite of this. Although one can say the statement, *your presence perfumes my day;* or *May their mingling slake / our thirsting spirits; or Canoes quietly sail on the blue / Sheet swaying up and down*; have a pleasing effect, it is difficult to say why this is so. Perhaps this depends on the overall pleasurable experience one gets from reading a poem, and obviously this is tied to understanding the poem.

The main aim of this essay was to discuss elements that distinguish poetry from the other genres, and present whatever the teachers will need to know about this selection of poetry. I have endeavoured to offer some definitions of key elements, and to give examples from the poems in the anthology, as a way of proving that these elements are not difficult to understand and use. It is possible that some of the examples will appear far-fetched, but I feel for a beginner's course in literature these examples are better than those from poetry written by people from lands and times so remote from the present Malawian pupil. I hope that the discussion of tropes, which are central to poetry, and the use of examples from the language of a village woman and many poems by both accomplished and amateur poets will prove that poetry flows in Malawian blood. The confidence gained from this course should adequately prepare our pupils to tackle the Okigbos, Soyinkas, pBiteks, Eliots and Shakespeares when they continue in the study of poetry in the university. It was stated that the main difference between poetry and the other genres is not so much in the literary devices or elements used as in the intensity of use which makes poetry concentrated in thought and expression.

B. Z. Mbano, Zomba,

PART 4: Short Stories

A SMALL MATTER

Andrew Kulemeka

TWO UNCERTAIN knocks, a brief pause... and then the door was being pounded with what felt like a sledge hammer. Mandala instinctively crouched, protecting the maize porridge which was still warm in his stomach. He looked at the frail door shaking in its frame. It had to be one of the women. Who could come so early and knock so aggressively? One of them was here to humiliate him in front of his family. He could see her drenched with dew having walked on the narrow red clay path from the village across Namilulu stream. Her broad bare feet cracked and covered with dew and mud. She would sit on the verandah, wrapped in a wet chitenje, and refuse to go away until he had paid for the beer he had drunk on trust ten years before. And he was supposed to remember how good the beer had been that distant afternoon as he had sat on a mat, chatting with his friends who were unusually happy because he had taken upon himself the task of filling their stomachs with this woman's beer, promising to pay for it when the cheque arrived the following week. When she had come to see him the next week, the mail had not arrived due to the rain and the muddy roads. The following week, yes, Tuesday, would be fine. But when she came on Friday instead, he had screamed at her for not keeping appointments. He had spent the money on food, she would have to come at the end of the month, yes on the last day of the month.

For Mandala the end of the month arrived in a blink of an eye, and the woman was there. He couldn't pay her then, his sister was very sick in the hospital. He had to go and see her, perhaps the end of next month. When she came at the end of that month, Mandala was gone to a far away town on some official business, his wife said. At that very point in time, Mandala had squeezed his tiny frame under the uneven bed and could hear his wife smoothly lie to the village woman.

For many months he had invented one story after another, until one day Mandala's own six year old son told the woman that his father was dead.

"Had a burial taken place?"

"Yes."

"Where was he buried?"

"Hhmmm? Where is he buried? At school." The young boy lowered his gaze, turned and stared at the bedroom window. The woman was disgusted and decided she was wasting her time and had better just forget what Mandala owed her. That was how she had stopped coming, until today. What had provoked her? Mandala couldn't understand it. It had to be hunger, or a husband, yes a husband insisting they had to get what he owed them. Shameless beings! They were as tenacious as desert camels.

More pounding and a distinctly male voice shouts, "Open, open, we know you are there!" Mandala jumped in his skin. Whose voice is that? He did not recognize it. What could he want? It had to be her husband brought along to scare him. That was not necessary. He had a family. They shouldn't treat him like that... after all he was a teacher. Noiselessly, he stood up and tiptoed to the door. He squatted, and without touching the door, peeped through the key hole. The unmistakable trousers! So this is it! It's Khweya. And what gave him the right to knock like that? Just because they drank together does not mean he can thrust himself on him like this. Mandala was filled with rage and was just about to wrench the door handle open when he was paralyzed by another thought. His right palm froze above the door knob and it slowly retreated: that was not Khweya's voice.

Slowly, he parted the curtains and blinked, and blinked again. What he was seeing couldn't possibly be true. But Khweya wouldn't go away. He stood on his old two feet in the same tight and faded green jacket with cotton padding showing on the shoulders. His navy blue polyester trousers stiff and metallic shiny with ironing as if snails had smeared their slime on them. The knot on the stringy necktie dug into his neck below the bulging Adam's apple. The necktie hang onto his neck like a snake. But it was regulation necktie and he had to wear it. Everyday.

It had to be a mistake or a particularly bad dream. He hoped it would be, but Khweya would not go away. He stood drab and expressionless like a wet garbage bin. His puffed stodgy hands handcuffed and held in front of him. On his either side was a fat looking man. Mandala felt a strong urge to run, but despaired on seeing that at least eight armed policemen had formed a semi circle in front of his house and each one was coldly watching him. Besides, he noted mentally, his house had one door: this one. The windows were so narrow that he could not pass through them. He trembled. He was a rat on a bare cement floor watching a club swiftly descend on its head without an escape hole anywhere in sight.

The evening was cold and wet as the rain ceaselessly pattered on the rusty iron roofs. It had been like this for a week now. The frozen June winds whipped the cold rain round the slender bluegum trees, whose dead leaves lay soggy and matted to the red clay. Dedza town and its mountain had disappeared shrouded by the fog and the dense poisonous vapours from the flooded pit latrines.

At the bus station were a number of charcoal stoves made from old petrol containers. They were producing little amounts of heat and tiny wisps of black smoke under the blanket of fog. The wanderers huddled around their little stoves, helplessly trying to keep warm. The wanderers lived here. The cold and damp bus station under the gloomy gum trees was home. Here they lived where the travellers cursed the bus for being late; where everybody was in great haste to leave. Home was surrounded by rotting banana peels, the yellow mango stones, thrown away chicken bones, and the acrid ammonia from the damp urinals and the deathly vapours from the fifty latrines surrounding the bus station on three sides. They were all filled up and overflowed in a thick greenish scum which covered the floors like an expensive carpet.

Thirty years before, on the eve of independence and before the scum had reached the thresholds, an overzealous party youth had pinned special edition pictures of the Founder in each of the filthy latrine huts; to remind users of the goodness of the Leader. Over the years, as heat, fermentation and more shit had made the latrines impossible to use, the only face to continuously witness the progress of decay in the fifty latrines has been the Founder's. He wears a bold fly stained smile, pointing resolutely to a future rich with putrid smells and the mass of squirming white maggots forever feeding on old human faeces whose pestilential odour hangs over the bus station like the drizzle.

Khweya and Mandala came out of the decayed mini-bus. It had not been an easy ride with all those people and the bags of potatoes, cabbages, and fish bags all squeezed into the rusty mini-bus whose doors were held closed by rubber strips cut from old car tubes. The mini-bus was so full that it had been impossible even to make the slightest change in position. Thus, Khweya had found himself completely crushed behind a rather full woman. Her warm perfume aroused him as he allowed her ample behind to settle in front of him. She was alarmed at him, and then upset as she felt his breath on her neck. She struggled to wriggle out of the position, to get her neck from his face, but it was impossible. She tried to stand sideways with her back to the door, but there was absolutely no room for such a simple move once the door of the mini-bus was closed. To close that door the driver and the conductor had shoved and heaved together against people's backs, almost crushing their ribs to fit them all in the tiny mini-bus. And when the door was closed, the mini-bus looked distended and full from outside like a grilling pork sausage. It was a wonder that the mini-bus moved at all.

But it did move. With a loud grinding of gears, prolonged revs on the accelerator, and squeaks and clouds of dark smoke belching from the exhaust, the mini-bus had shuddered violently and jerked forward. It paused..., jerked forward and paused again. There was a more piercing revving accompanied by a violent shuddering of the mini-bus. A dense spurt of pitch black smoke emerged and whirled heavily around the bus. Then it began to crawl slowly, tilting dangerously to one side as if the road were slanted. It screamed, coughed and hesitated as the driver changed gears, but it resumed crawling with both of its front wheels wobbling so much that they looked like they would detach any moment and just roll away leaving the old mini-bus stranded in the middle of the road. In that slow and crab-like-manner the mini-bus had completed its journey from Bembeke Thanofu to Dedza bus depot.

"Why did he have to pack us like that?"

"I guess they like to make the best of each trip. Common sense to me," Mandala said with a smile.

He did not seem to worry so much, but accepted things in his stride, so to speak. In spite of his possessing a solid certificate to teach in the primary schools, he had always survived like a peasant. His pair of shoes was of the most ordinary, by the cheapest shoe manufacturer in the country. The sweater he wore now had a few noticeable holes in it. There was a big hole close to the right armpit which should have stopped him from wearing it, but not Mandala. He seemed not to care about it. Sometimes, though, he was seen trying to cover it with his left palm.

Mandala was of average height, with rather narrow shoulders and a prematurely curved back. He had a plain face with an upper front tooth which stuck out between the lips like the blade of an axe. It was impossible to cover that tooth, so it stood exposed, gathering dust and mildew. Mandala's skin, however, was beautiful. It was soft, silky and dark. It made him look much younger than his age. Most people thought that he should not have a stooping back, but he knew that he deserved it at the very advanced age of thirty five. In five or six years' time, he knew he would be dead forever. It was just the way it was.

In contrast Khweya, who was younger, looked more decrepit. Although his head of hair was intact and there was not a single white strand in it, the man had a puffy appearance about him. He looked sickly and bloated like a rotting fish filled with water. If you touched him, you left dimples in his skin. It was as if beneath his skin there were inflated pockets of air which made him look swollen and fat in a sickly way. His skin was scorched and gray. As the elders say, "His grave lay yawning ready to receive him."

A discoloured red patch on Khweya's lower lip showed that he drank large quantities of the potent maize spirits. Regardless of time of day, his breath was the smell of kachasu. He spoke hurriedly in short, incoherent sentences. With each utterance, his face twitched and contorted like he was swallowing quinine or pure castor oil. He finished every sentence with his tongue licking his lips and when he was silent, his upper teeth bit the lower lip repeatedly. Although he tried to hide it, his hands shook all the time as if he was anxious or nervous about something. Those who knew, recognized the signs of an advanced alcoholic.

Khweya and Mandala walked abreast past Joni Fly restaurant, which stood at the corner of Market Street and the pine-lined Wenela Avenue. The tiny tea-room now looked old and was boarded up closed with pine planks. They used to serve wonderful cocoa in there, Mandala recalled with a deep sense of nostalgia. He remembered the time when he was a secondary school student and used to come here. He would sometimes come with his cousin Loyi. Under the benign gaze of the Savior of the Nation, they would sit down on the unpainted white pine chairs with their backs to the open wooden shutters. Often it would be in the afternoon with the sun warming their backs and bidding farewell before it disappeared behind the mountain in the west. They would order very hot cocoa poured from a large black kettle which Joni Fly, the owner, kept perpetually boiling on a log fire behind the canteen where the scones were baked. The scones they drank the cocoa with were hot, long, puffy and delicious. They drank the cocoa slowly, savouring each mouthful, the tongue mixing cocoa with scones, both coursing warmly down the throat into the stomach. At other times, Mandala would bring his girlfriend to Joni Fly.

Mandala and Khweya were now approaching the market. They crossed the open stinking gully, which carried animal blood, cow dung, hooves, fish guts and scales, rotten fish and tomatoes from the market to the river beyond the hospital graveyard. Now they were face to face with this old structure with the name 'Sitizeni' written in red on the lintel. Khweya scraped the sole of his shoes on the upturned hoe planted next to the steps to the building. There was already a pile up of sticky red clay all around the tiny hoe. The rain continued to fall. Mandala followed suit and carefully scraped the mud off his soles. The two trudged into the low ceilinged restaurant where an ancient "radiogram" was screeching an old "high life" song. Centrally positioned in a gold frame on the front wall, the President's eyes stared into the future with invitation and promise.

The restaurant was narrow and long, and the ceiling could barely be touched with the tips of the fingers. The lime washed cloth ceiling was uneven, and sagged heavily in many places. From the ceiling came the squeal, rumble and bounce of rats as they chased each other in their little heaven above there.

Three naked bulbs hang from the ceiling casting a dim orange glow on three rows of tables. Each of the square, rickety tables could barely seat four. They were made from some unknown cheap wood, perhaps light pine or wet blue gum wood, and had been hastily painted in bright plastic green, yellow, red and white. The gaudy colours shot through the tattered plastic sheets that served as table covers. Sitting at the center of each table, were greasy white shakers, one with the label salt and the other pepper scrawled carelessly on the side as if by a child learning to write. The pepper looked the colour of brick powder.

The queue at the front of the room was long and winding. Khweya shifted on his puffed legs and smiled wearily at Mandala behind him. Mandala smiled back and scratched his beard. The "high life" song stopped with a long screech, and the radio came alive playing the president's music, which if interrupted and this was reported to the Party could lead to many years of detention without trial. And so the drooling sycophancy continued with the women from Dedza villages praising the president for development which allowed them to drink coca-cola on independence day at his palace. Khweya and Mandala moved forward, the service was fast. The menu was not elaborate. It was permanently painted on the front wall. It consisted of fish and chips, or rice with meat and salad, or nsima with meat or fish and salad, or potatoes with meat or fish and salad. Next to the eternal menu was a painting of a man sitting at a table across from his woman friend. He had worn shoes with thick soles and huge heels. In his left hand, he held a big fork with a square chunk of red meat poised to enter his never closing mouth full of chalk white teeth. Under the painting was the caption: Welokamu. Sayini, Minija ofu Sitizeni.

Now Khweya was the third on the line. He thought that he should not be here, but he needed to save money. These official trips were the only occasions that he came close to making enough to look after his family. The responsibilities were enormous: his four children all growing so fast and needing new clothes almost every two months. His daughter at fourteen was the most worrisome and overly conscious of herself. Sometime he had watched her with pain in his heart, seeing her pulling at her dress as if to stretch it. Her budding breasts were flattened by the tight dress. He felt angry, but he was impotent; trapped in a situation he barely understood. Everybody seemed to blame him for his incomprehensible poverty, as if he willed it on himself and his family.

"Can I help you?" The voice of the waitress rang out.

"Rice, meat and salad," Khweya answered mechanically.

"What plate size?" She creased her lips to attempt a smile under a face drenched with sweat. The huge pot with yellow rice was placed on a low black table in front of her; it was steaming and smelled of Asian curry powder.

"Give me a din..., a big plate."

Next to the rice pot, was a large pot of meat. The meat floated in warm water thinly flavored by the meat and a few rinds of tomatoes. The waitress had big arms. She served a mound of rice and poured two spoonfuls of a thin sauce on it with perhaps three pieces of meat scattered on the rice. Khweya was not impressed.

"Could I have more meat. I'll pay for it."

Another three pieces fell on the mound of rice, and more lukewarm sauce was poured so that the plate was flooded and the rice totally immersed. One of the pieces of meat was certainly sinew with suet on its side. It was obvious that the pieces would not add up to much.

Khweya moved from the queue to look for a table, and then saw what he had never thought possible. A mass of rags, shiny grime was slowly and quietly advancing into the restaurant through the doorway. It was moving with its back

38

bent forward. The entire figure was encrusted with dirt the colour of soot. The eyes looked like new ice in the face of indescribable filth. All at once, a profusion of smells hit the restaurant: the heavy smells of rotting beef or milk; the acrid and penetrating smell of ammonia from accumulated adult urine. Floating, almost apart from these other smells, was the repugnant odour of a mouth full of decaying teeth.

Khweya dropped his plate next to the billy-can and dashed out of the restaurant. He jumped over puddles where the Zambian women were huddled, drinking "chibuku" beer, laughing loudly, trying to get men who would take them home for the night. But men were afraid, the new disease was widespread in Zambia.

He found Mandala across the street, laughing and pointing at "Sitizeni" restaurant. Khweya was too preoccupied with the incident in the restaurant to laugh. They decided to drink a few beers and forget.

This morning Mandala's mouth felt as if he had eaten ashes. There was a bile taste on his tongue. He recalled with a shrug of the shoulders the quantities of beer he had drunk the previous night with Khweya in the township. Having decided they would not spend money on a resthouse room, the two had attempted to stay awake the whole night by moving from "Whayo Bar" to "Dedza Hotela", and then to "Che Brown" and back again to "Whayo" and so on and so forth, endlessly. They had been forced to drink to stay awake. It was while they were at "Che Brown's" for, perhaps, the third time and feeling rather hungry, that they each bought two boiled eggs to eat. Khweya was cracking his egg against the concrete pillar when Mandala noticed this other man. A silent man who was obviously listening to their conversation, although he tried hard to appear not interested. Mandala had wanted to warn Khweya about his suspicions, but his drunk mind drifted away to something else before he could do it. Meanwhile Khweya spoke with the brevity and profound conviction of a drunk that he saw absolutely no point in giving the president money gifts when the later's salary was probably a million kwacha a month. This was theft. It was theft. What did he do with the cattle, goats, chickens and thousands of kwachas that he forced people to give him. Wasn't he ashamed to steal from the poor? What kind of person is this who always receives, even from the very old? Women in their eighties have to give him presents or face detention. Is this freedom? What kind of freedom. Khweya had gone on for a while, until Mandala had remembered about the silent man and whispered something in

Khweya's ear. That stopped him instantly. Like a movie in reverse, Khweya tried to undo the damage. He started to lavish praise on the President for the development, for the schools, hospitals, fertilizer, clothes and roads. He started a praise song which competed with the music from the "radiogram". Khweya fished out his party card which he made a point of showing everyone in the bar. At this point the silent man walked out of the door into the rain and the darkness outside.

They had continued to drink. And soon forgot about the silent man as they danced to East African rumba and kanindo. "Che Brown" offered the best variety of music even though the dance floor was old and full of holes.

Soon after, Khweya landed on a woman whose behind completely filled the light pink floral patterned skirt. She was about average height, neither tall nor short with a tiny voice and eyes which tended to look down, giving her an air of innocence which she probably did not deserve.

"Do you have children?" Khweya asked and put his arm around her shoulders which were so narrow compared to the fullness in the skirt.

"No. I just finished form four last year." She obviously lied because when he touched her breasts, they were not firm and cupped like a tennis ball. They were long, thin and flaccid; a definite sign that she either had several children or had been pregnant several times. Khweya had the strong suspicion that she was a veteran prostitute, which pleased him under the circumstances. He would not have to worry of having corrupted an innocent school girl.

The record Wazazi (parents) came through the speakers. The Kiswahili musicians were strumming vulnerable chords with their appeal to kindness to an orphaned child. Khweya and his woman, whose name turned out to be Lozi, floated to the dance floor, to join the thronging multitudes of couples who were fused together and barely moved. Khweya held his woman similarly. His practised right hand immediately went to work, massaging her waist. And then his hand felt one buttock, moving up and down feeling the skin beneath the thin skirt. He discovered what he expected: Lozi was completely naked under the skirt. His loins caught fire.

Later that evening, as he entered an ancient cave without challenges, as he struggled to touch the walls which seemed weak and unresponsive, he had to focus his mind elsewhere to complete the journey. When he emerged, he quickly left the tiny room behind the bar to look for Mandala. He found him slumped in a corner and snoring with his mouth open. It was dawn, they had to go and wait for the bus to take them home.

Mandala disliked Khweya's lust for bar women. Especially with the killer disease so widespread, it was bound to cost his life one day. But Khweya was fatalistic. He always responded with the title of a famous song Zonse ndi nthawi basi "everything has its time". It was worthless to argue against him when he said that.

Suddenly, Mandala remembered the silent man. He trembled with fear of the special branch. He assured himself though that he was safe, especially considering that he had personally thanked the president on a certain occasion by giving him his entire one month salary. He was sure that people would remember that and not consider him disloyal. Besides, he bought his party cards every year for all his children. He also had the president's picture framed and hang in the living-cum-dining room. In this picture, the Life President is shown sitting in an enormous chair holding a pen and writing in a big book open on a large brown table. To His Excellency the Life President's left is a small globe with the map of Africa and Europe clearly visible. The lines of concentration on His Excellency the Life President's forehead indicate deep concentration. All around the picture are cloud like formations which suggest that the Father and Founder of the nation descended from the heavens to fulfill this onerous job of ruling his people.

It was all Khweya's fault, Mandala concluded as he contemplated the frightening prospect of detention and death. The fool liked to indulge in the deadly game of politics whenever he was drunk. Perhaps, for my own good I should stop drinking. His armpits felt cold and wet with fear.

Mandala moved the tip of his tongue against the roof of the mouth and felt stabbing pain run the length of his tongue; he had a raw blister on the tip of the tongue. He smelt his own breath and it was foul.

He needed to clean his mouth now. He went to the window and pulled aside the square faded green piece of cloth which covered the rattling four panes in the window. Outside was a sheet of gray, the rain was falling. It had been pattering relentlessly for the past full week. This is Saturday, it should stop, Mandala asserted with a distinct hate for the cold, and never stopping rain. It did not come as a huge down-pour, but grudgingly and forever like an old woman's tears. In his mind Mandala saw the cold rain streaking down the robust gray gum trees that tower over his house, keeping the surrounding and his house perpetually damp. Things in his house always felt damp and soggy. Mildew flourished on everything including shoes, clothes, blankets, food, paper, and even toothbrushes had mildew growing in the bristles. The mildew was as inescapable as the rain and the poverty. The children always coughed as if they also had mildew growing in their lungs, but it was probably TB.

Mandala moved from the window and the rain. But his mind was concentrated on the incessant rain which seemed like a punishment for a mysterious crime his family, only his family had committed. He seemed always to be just at the boundary of abject poverty; always not having enough to feed his eleven children. Mandala wondered bitterly about the cruel fate which always appeared to place him at the periphery of things. It seemed as if he was condemned even before he was born to live this hard life. He looked at his mattress where the wife was sleeping. He wondered about the joke he had perpetuated these many years of using that mattress. The cotton mattress gave as much comfort as rocks and bricks of different sizes and shapes laid out on the bed. But he had clung to the idea, the idea of sleeping on a bed with a mattress was important. The mattress was like the snake necktie and the threadbare faded green jacket he was forced to wear everyday. Everything about him was a pretence, a facade to mask the grim poverty and sordidness of his life. As a teacher, it was important that he did not sleep on the floor, but on a bed because teachers stood for the new era of prosperity and must be seen to sleep on beds. His back, and his wife's had paid the price of many years of clinging to the illusion of success spawned daily by the radio.

Why should it rain on a Saturday? How does one go to Galioni's to drink, drink, drink and play at being the well to do teacher? Deceive everybody, except oneself, about the fruits of independence and an education. He picked up his toothbrush and a bar of Lux soap from the old shoe container. Quietly, he walked out of the bedroom, skirted the small pine table where remnants of last night's food were still in a plate. The small pine table doubled as a dining table and as a place where things were kept. There was an assortment of things here. A huge bottle of Shell Vaseline body ointment, old free magazines from South Africa like Panorama which lied with glossy pictures of smiling Africans about how wonderful life was for black people in the Republic. There was also the family mirror on the table which could fit in one palm.

Mandala heard some noise from the boys' bedroom. Pitala emerged, his stomach swollen and lined with veins as usual. The skin on his face clung to his skull making his eyes look sunken and pale. There was a vacant stare from his pale eyes as he slowly looked around trying to see what he might eat. Mandala knew that until the porridge was ready, there was nothing the children could eat. Oh well, unless they wanted to eat the beans which their mother would not allow.

Pitala's shorts hang heavy on the sisal string threaded through the belt loops to hold them around the waist. The seat was torn again in spite of the dense and intricate network of patches, patches and more patches with thread upon thread criss crossing like a fish net. There were blue patches, khaki patches, yellow patches, white patches: any colour was there. Pitala's big navel had worked a hole through the mosquito net T-shirt. Really what remained of the T-shirt were the collar and the shredded front.

"How have you woken up son?"

"Fine." The young voice was croaky with sleep and the morning cough. He moved his hard and cracked feet in the small room which combined as a sitting, dining, and store room. He kicked against an earthen pot. Full of red beans, Mandala instinctively knew. Pitala turned the long key in the door-knob and was gone into the gray rainy morning. The smell of dampness came into the house. Mandala moved quickly and slammed the door shut.

He will get wet, and might even catch a cold. Mandala thought. But what was to be done? Two umbrellas had been lost in that latrine; falling in through the hole and sinking. When they had lit the torch down there, all they saw were the different shapes and sizes of people's faeces on a steaming dark greenish bed.

Shivering from the rain, Pitala came through the doorway. Mandala then realized he needed a bath. He walked out of the house with the faded threadbare orange bath-towel barely covering his shoulder. He was brushing his teeth vigorously. He took a sip of water from the metal cup in his left hand. He swirled the water in his mouth several times before spitting it out. It came out in a white jet and landed on the grass on the path to the bath fence. On reaching the bath fence, he put his shirt over the doorway and eased himself sideways into the fence. He carefully stepped on the bricks before putting both of his feet on the huge uneven stone which formed the floor to the bath fence. When it had rained so much, Mandala knew, the stone tended to rock rather dangerously. On a number of occasions, he recalled, he had been thrown off balance on stepping on the rock and found one or both of his feet in the dirty water beneath it. That water left you smelling like the sewer the entire day. Today, he was extra careful. The trick was not to resist the motions of the rock, but to go with it until it settled down. So for, perhaps, a full second, he let himself roll with the rock. As he was rocking, on this stone island surrounded by the heavy and faecal water, Mandala felt a sense of entrapment. He had a vision of himself always confined to stony soil and completely pervaded by decay and filth. The rain continued to fall, beating him at the back when he bent down to scoop water from the basin. His clothes were getting soaked at the doorway. He needed to hurry up, but there was this matter of balancing on the rock. So he took as much time as the rock needed before he emerged from the bath fence dressed in wet clothes which would dry up on his body.

When he returned to the sitting room it was full of his children. Each one had a bowl of maize porridge that they were quickly polishing off. After which they would return to their crowded bedroom to try to spend the day because outside there was the rain.

He put sugar on his porridge and ate it silently. He was thinking about how he was going to go to Galioni's bar to drink and try to forget when there was a knock on the door. He rose up, parted the dirty curtain and saw Khweya standing on the other side. Khweya's face is frozen. Mandala opened the door. He sees that on Khweya's either side are beefy looking men. They are clean shaven and smiling in blazer, black blazer jackets with shiny metal buttons and the President's face on the lapels. Khweya has his hands together in front. Oh Lord, he is handcuffed.

"Are you Mandala?" one of the fat men asked.

"Yeees". Mandala's voice was faint and rather hoarse when it came out. He looked at Khweya, but Khweya was looking down, expressionless. He had heard about arrests, but never thought it would happen to him or his friend Khweya. Somehow he had thought that his poverty made him invisible to the special branch police. He had known that the police were often after educated university professors whom they considered a distinct threat. As for himself, Mandala couldn't see how anyone could be interested in his life which was really a lice infested bundle of rags. But here they were. Special branch police!

He must have drawn attention to himself, even as he scavenged like a cockroach among the refuse at the bottom of the human heap. Perhaps the very stench of his poverty had annoyed the great leader.

"We've a small matter we would like to talk to you about at the division office." The same fat man said, visibly happy as he smiled flashing his white teeth. When Mandala looked at the fat man's eyes, they were the colour of ashes, dead and cold like the eyes of a frozen fish. For a brief moment Mandala thought the fat man regarded him like a housefly buzzing helplessly in a window screen.

"I must... I must... tell my..my..wife." The wife was standing right behind him. Her arms folded across her chest; each hand clasping firmly to the opposite shoulder. Behind the narrow door, twenty two eyes had popped out in fear and were trying to make sense of the obscenity.

Mandala was turning... turning to face his wife and do what only he alone - a man with eleven children and a pregnant wife on the brink of being abandoned - could have imagined. The two fat men grabbed him by the shoulders and shoved him towards the Jeep. He careened forward like a stuffed doll and fell with his face in a puddle. When he stood up, his face was covered with water and sticky red mud. He was handcuffed and led to the Jeep. Behind the narrow door, twenty two tiny eyes mourned and cried for their father whom they would never see again.

There was a full moon. In this part of the river, the water is slow and has formed a deep pool. Forever circling and barely visible above the tranquil water surface are numerous pairs of tiny nostrils. Beneath the water surface the giant crocodiles waited patiently for the usual evening feed. Soon enough wriggling bound bodies hit the water surface and were instantly shredded to pieces and gobbled by the enormous jaws. The tiny red coloration where the bodies had fallen quickly dissipated. The pool became serene once again as the river continued to flow downstream.

The End

Questions

1. Who does Mandala think is knocking on his door?
2. Mandala sees his friend standing outside. What had he come to do?
3. The story seems to suggest that there has been little development, if any, since the country became independent. Identify three cases that show this lack of development.
4. What is Mandala's profession?
5. Mandala and his friend are not really old people, but there are signs of old age on their bodies. What are these signs?
6. Why is Mandala arrested? Explain with examples from the story.
7. Why do you think the President's portrait is hang in almost every building?
8. Do you think what happens to Mandala and his friend is justifiable? Explain your opinion with evidence from the story.
9. The author describes poverty using images and symbols. Make a list of these images and symbols and explain what effect they have on the plot of the story.
10. Mandala has eleven children and yet his wife is pregnant. As somebody who went to school, Mandala should have known the advantages of child spacing. Discuss.
11. A flashback presents events of the past in the midst of a story in the present. Andrew Kulemeka uses flashback to relate events that took place at a bar in the past to an event this morning. When does the flashback start and end in "A small matter"? What is the effect of flashback on the plot of this story?
12. One of the character traits of Khweya is that he is fatalistic, one who believes in destiny. Prove him right or wrong according to the events that take place in the story.
13. The picture portrayed in this story is that of a country trapped in a dictatorial type of government. List down the disadvantages of such a government and relate them to how they have led Malawians to appreciate a democratic kind of government.
14. Describe the appearance of Mandala and his home.
15. When Mandala is being arrested, the author says 22 eyes instead of 11 people looking at him. Why do you think he has decided to use the former rather than the latter? Explain.
16. The last paragraph of this story is the most tragic. Discuss.

THE SYMPOSIUM

Evance Hlekwayo Moyo

UNTYPICAL OF a June morning, that Saturday at 9 am, it was bright and warm. The sun was shooting down its fiery rays, producing sweltering heat and making the misty atmosphere stuffy.

Mrs Malango Gundo was now through with her ablution. As her gleaming self made its way into the living room, her sweating husband who was busy arranging cutlery and other items in the display cabinet quickly turned in her direction. The room was filled with a strong odour of the over-applied Eau-de-Cologne so that the poor man could hardly breathe. He forced a smile and remarked "You smell nice and you look cute honey, very cute."

The wife paid no attention. Her eyes were keenly surveying the general appearance of the living room. Apparently satisfied, she invited her husband for a kiss.

"Well done. But the cloth should not completely cover the stereo. Make the front a bit visible," she advised as she quickly checked the rest of the room.

"All right darling," the husband said, "you will find everything in order when you come back from the symposium. By the way, you look a bit tired, darling. You overworked last night."

"I know. There was all the need to work hard because today's symposium has drawn delegates like Dr Malaki, Professor Silungwe and others. To raise a point one needs to have all the elbow grease one can afford."

"All the best, darling," said the husband. Once inside her posh Camry, she glanced at her Paris made Les Must de Cartier wristwatch and then at the car digital watch. Both registered 09.05 hours. Too early! The symposium was scheduled for 10.30 hours. She could start off even at 10.15 since the auditorium in which the symposium was to take place was less than 10 minutes drive from her house.

To pass time, she took her documents and started going through them. She was feeling so giddy with the previous night's work that it was quite an effort to go through the documents again.

The car park outside the auditorium seemed fully parked. Only a few spaces reserved for the notables were available. She parked her Camry at the space reserved for her and briskly walked inside. All the other delegates were already seated in their designated seats and she would have been late. The female delegates wore grave and serious faces. Some were still clasping their files under their armpits rather protectively as if they were under strict instructions never to part with whatever was in the files.

However, the male delegates looked relaxed. Some were even puffing at their cigarettes unmindful of the many non-smokers in the auditorium. This appalled Mrs Gundo but she sat down quiet, thinking that she would raise the point when her time to speak came.

The Chairperson of the conference entered the room from the side door and the delegates rose. She gave a flamboyant smile which filled her over-powdered face. Her smile matched well with the long artificial curls of her hair and the full-length floral chiffon gown she was wearing.

The gown was a trace too transparent to a keen observer and those who knew her well- they said she was a nympho- could swear that she had done that on purpose as she was clearly aware that she would be the cynosure of all the eyes and who knows, one man could have it in his burning head to try his luck!

She majestically made her way down the aisle to the high table, coursed by two other women both of whom were wearing tie-and-die cotton gowns with matching headkerchiefs.

When the three women reached the high table they simultaneously made slight bows. The delegates bowed as well and the Chairperson signalled them to take their seats. She herself remained standing. She smoothly whisked away from her sleeves something out of place though not conspicuous to any other person. She then read a 20-minute opening speech after raising the official gavel.

"I, Jane Cholinga, Attorney-At-Law, President of the Association of Women, presiding chairperson of this August meeting, hereby declare this symposium open." She said at the end of her speech. Her voice was small and it came from her giant self.

The woman on her right, Ms Catherine Masangano, President of the Total Rights of Women Union - TORIWU - rose immediately after the Chairperson sat down.

"Ladies and gentlemen, you are cordially welcome to this debate session otherwise called symposium. It is the first of its kind in the history of this country.

48

This venerable symposium has the theme: "Power for Women Today, Why Not?" There was hand clapping and cheers.

"All delegates will be invited to express their views on whether the recognition of a woman's worth is imperative and if it is, how it can effectively be implemented.

"Research findings by reputable groups have shown that 90 to 95 percent of women in this country are of the view that a woman is denied her full rights because of the mistaken belief in male superiority, male chauvinism. It is believed by women that the majority of men are obsessed with this repulsive paternalism which makes them feel more human and that a woman is here to be led and not to lead".

"These women argue that in this present era, a woman is in pursuit of excellence which, irrefutably, is a worthwhile goal towards the attainment of all rights due to her. Ladies and gentlemen, you will therefore be invited to focus your views upon these research findings. Thank you very much." She mopped her forehead with a handkerchief and sat down amid hand clapping from the delegates.

The chairperson, still wearing her flamboyant smile, stood up.

"The floor is now open for contributions, ladies and gentlemen," she said.

She had hardly finished her sentence when Mrs. Gundo the director of Women's Lobby Association, WOLA, a shrewd and the only afro-haired lady in the auditorium, raised her name plate high up.

She was in her early 50s but at a glance one would say she was 30. She was a strong supporter of "equal opportunity" and rumours, which were true, in fact, had it that her husband who was 15 years younger than herself, was completely under her control.

"Yes, Mrs Gundo," the Chairperson said. Mrs Gundo grimaced at her fellow female delegates and then barked with a voice befitting a man.

"The hour has come!" the women echoed in chorus.

"The hour has come for a woman to deride her segregators and discriminators!"

Mrs. Gundo said as she made flirting movements with her eyes.

"The hours has co.."

"Point of order, Madam Chairperson." Dr Malaki stood up. He was an Associate Professor of Sociology at the University. He was six-feet five inches in height and at the age of 48, he was still single. When asked by his students why he was still single, his answer was "Not all guys are foolish, some are single." It was rumoured that he maintained his bachelorhood because he vehemently abhorred women for reasons which stretched back to his teenage, but best known to himself alone.

"Yes, Dr Malaki?" the Chairperson gave a go ahead.

"May the distinguished speaker be reminded that this is neither a political rally nor a 'pamtondo' gathering for women. We, the male delegates are not particularly eager to hear 'the hour's done this or that' hullabaloo. Could we please, with your permission, Madam Chairperson, be spared that stuff?"

As he sat down, he took out a cigarette, pressed it in between his thick lips and started for a lighter.

"I second that point of order," shouted Mr Chibwana. He was a representative of the ruling party. He stood up without asking for permission or even bothering to raise his name plate. He sounded angry and his voice was many octaves higher than that of Dr Malaki.

"We are here not to be told what the time is. I am sure we all have wrist watches and in case there are some who don't have one, there is a wall clock there!" he pointed to the wall clock and sat down, gnashing his teeth.

"I need your protection, Madam Chairperson," whined Mrs Gundo.

"Yes, may all the distinguished delegates be reminded that this symposium will not entertain insults or comments directed at persons," the Chairperson warned.

"Now, ladies and gentlemen," Mrs Gundo continued, "I, in my capacity as director of WOLA, stand to agree with the points raised by the honourable secretary, Ms Masangano.

It is true that we are living in a country of monopoly. All the best opportunities, be it in the political or economical realm, are monopolised. I wonder why these men continue to live with the wrong belief that they are to rule and the woman is simply to follow.... I wish to remind the symposium that the days of suppressing women are gone. This is now the era for women to work along side men and vice versa."

"Hear, hear! Bravo, bravo!" the women cheered.

"Yes, this is the time to have female rulers. Viva all women! Viva a female ruler! Viva women's rights! Viva a female president!"

"Point of order!" This was James Mponda, a tall and handsome political science student at the University.

"Yes, Mr Mponda," the Chairperson gave him the floor.

"I wish to observe that the last speaker's contribution to this symposium is biased towards politics. As far as I am and my knowledge is concerned, no one is barred from any political race on the grounds of sex. All one has to do is make it officially known that he or she is aspiring to contest for political position this or that." He did not sit down when he finished speaking. He stood stooped in front, both his hands on the table.

"Indirectly women are barred," this was Mrs Gundo again. "Customary and social norms in our society pronounce a woman inferior and incapable of any positive leadership acumen. But women have now realised that these customs and social norms are biased against them. Between a man and a woman there must be gender equality," she specifically emphasized the last two words.

James Mponda smiled. He was now standing upright. "Point of correction!" He was given the floor. "Their is no such thing as gender equality and never shall there be. May the learned leader of WOLA be in the know that equality basically means equal or same in all respects. If this distinguished delegate meant to raise a view of equal favours and fairness to both sexes, she should have used the term gender equity." He sat down smiling and feeling victorious.

"My good lord! What ever happened to respect!" Mrs Chawa, the Secretary General of WOLA, who was sitting next to Mrs. Gundo lamented. "That is now a personal attack."

Mrs Chawa was a beautiful lady of about thirty and a strong advocate of gender equity. She had been divorced for claiming to be an equal to her husband, the last one whose name she was now using.

"Protect me, Honourable Madam Chairperson. Far from being a personal attack, mine was a simple point of correction. I believe in being respectful and using the very best of the normal etiquette. I make my apologies if the honourable director of WOLA is insulted," Mponda said.

"Apology accepted," the Chairperson said. "Now since it seems that many delegates here wish to discuss politics, I don't have any objections to hearing views on it."

Several name plates shot up. She gave the floor to Anthoinette Benga, a social science student at the University. Benga was a coy but very intelligent girl.

"I wish to express my gratitude to Mr. Mponda, first for making that important observation of the difference between equity and equality in gender issues and I will use that in giving my views."

"Naturally, a woman is a busy person by comparison with a man. It is irrefutable to say a woman looks after 80 percent of a child's welfare even if she is employed elsewhere just like her husband. Now, if these two were contesting for the same seat, say a parliamentary seat, you will find that the man would have more time for campaign than the woman since he doesn't breastfeed. This, coupled with the psychological belief of the local person out there that a man is superior, automatically puts him at an advantage. This is where equity comes in. If fairness and equal favours are to be implemented, these aspects should be put into consideration. What I suggest is that the minimum vote percentage required to be declared winner be lower for the woman than for a man."

"I am for that suggestion!" shouted Mrs Chawa even before Benga had sat down.

"I stand to second it!" shouted Mrs Zibilo, a director of a local newspaper.

"I'm totally against it!" This was Professor Emmanuel Silungwe from the Faculty of Law at the University.

"And I am another one against it!" shouted Chibwana.

The Professor frowned and then said: "If such political lunacy as propagated by Miss Benga were implemented, where then do we put democracy? To slumber?" He stopped for the words to sink in. "Where genuine democratic polls are concerned, it is the contester who attains the majority votes who emerges and is declared and accepted as a victor. Therefore, Miss Benga's imploration is

politically, economically, and democratically an unattainable concept which
would enshrine injustice and unfairness unless someone wishes to redefin
these terms." He slowly sat down.

After a long cheer of support from the male delegates, Mrs Chawa stood up
"But that same democracy which Professor Silungwe wishes to protect, tend
to favour certain individuals, mostly men. By practice, not by definition
democracy means an equal chance to contribute within a framework of goal.
and a structure of rules established purportedly to favour all, but actually in
support of favouring the selected few since that is in accordance with positions
Those individuals in high position are entitled to far much more and better
favours than those on the lower end. Therefore, democracy tends to favour
those individuals with better positions. And who are these favoured few?"

"Men!" an excited delegation of women chorused.

"Of course," continued Mrs Chawa, "and this is because men monopolise,
almost all opportunities by pretending that they know better. Yet it is simply
because they are protected by a psychological hindsight. There is no equity in
the Professor's kind of democracy."

"Point of information!" This was Dr Malaki speaking while pulling his goatee.
"Lest we forget, Baroness Margaret Hilda Thatcher was once a prime minister.
Did she have to first introduce that equity some delegates are crying for?"

"May the distinguished speaker be reminded that we are in Africa, not in
Europe." This was Mrs Gundo shouting above the cheers of the men.

"And what about the continental difference?" Mr Chibwana asked, panting.

"Here chauvinism is the order of the day!" Benga answered.

"Point of view Madam Chairperson," this was Dr Juliana Ofatsa, a Lecturer in
the Department of Theology at the University. She had not uttered a single
word until just now. Most people respected her for her mature views once she
spoke. The auditorium was silent. She was given the floor.

"Personally, I feel that a woman could be equal to man in competence if and
when she was given a chance to do so. If you want proof of this just go and
check in the women Who is Who. I tell you women have performed miracles.
And even right here at home the few women we have in authority are not by

any means lagging. Therefore, in the political sphere, I find that the greatest problem is not the system of deciding the victor but that a woman is not allowed to contest. If a female is featured as a candidate by a good political party, I see no reason for her failing to win popularity. But the existing parties are all in favour of male candidates, maybe because they are founders of the parties. Thank you Madam Chairperson." She quickly sat down.

"True," Mrs Zibilo took over. "The existing parties are unwilling to balance sexes in party representation. Hence I conquer with what Dr Wofatsa has spoken. Now is the time for women to unite and form their own political parties if this monopoly and gender inequality is to be checked".

"Pooooint!" Mrs Gundo and Mrs Chawa shouted simultaneously.

"If men are willing to join they should do so on the understanding that they are to be where they really belong; on the same level as women!"

"Even below!" Mrs Gundo said now standing up.

"I wish to contradict Madam Chair..." Dr Malaki could not be allowed to finish his sentence as Mrs Gundo shouted: "The hour!"

"Has come!" the other women finished.

Her face was bright as she started jubilating followed by most of the women.

"Women want change! Women want change!"

The commotion was so big for the male delegates that they started walking out; Dr Malaki in front followed by Mr Chibwana, then Professor Silungwe trailing behind in a file. They looked angry.

"That Malango Gundo has an insane mind. She has spoiled the symposium," Mr Chibwana said.

"She is very dangerous and a very shrewd feminist," Dr Malaki observed.

"I hate that lady. She can't make a good leader. But I adore that nymphomaniac, Mrs Cholinga. Did you people notice the over-transparency in her dress..."

Inside the auditorium, Mrs Gundo read the women into another chant; "Aluta continua - Aluta! Aluta continua - Aluta!..." She stumbled over a chair which fell with a very big noise. She looked and saw her husband knocking at the car window.

"I thought you had already gone darling. You'll be late, it's 10:20 hours now,"

54

her husband said looking at his wrist watch. She checked hers as well while rubbing her eyes. She had fallen asleep in the car.

Wryly she picked up the papers which were scattered on her lap. Then she turned the key in the ignition hole, engaged into gear, waved to her husband and started off for the symposium.

She just had about enough time to cover the distance to the auditorium. She wondered whether her dream was a kind of prophecy.

"I wish it were real!" She confessed aloud to herself.

The End

Questions

1. When we first meet Mrs Gundo, what is she doing? What is her husband doing? What does this indicate about the relationship between the husband and the wife?
2. What things in this story show that Mrs Gundo is well-to-do?
3. Why do you think the female delegates wore serious faces whereas the male ones were relaxed? Give your answer in not more than two sentences.
4. "The hour has come for a woman to deride her segregators and discriminators".

   (a) What do the following words mean: 'deride'; 'segregation'; 'discrimination'?

   (b) Do you agree with the statement above by Mrs Gundo? Give reasons.
5. All the girls in the story were selfish. Do you agree? Write a brief paragraph to support your answer.
6. Mrs Gundo is described as "very dangerous and a very shrewd feminist". Is this observation correct? Whatever your answer, support it with evidence from the story.
7. From the way the 'Symposium' ended, what does gender mean for
   (a) women and (b) men?
8. Describe the techniques used for telling this story and explain how they affect your understanding of it.
9. Sometimes people claim that they want to understand each other but they do not do enough to achieve it. How far true is this in this story?
10. What is the difference between feminism and gender equality or gender equity?

WHY THE DOG CHASES THE CAR

Duncan N. Mboma

ONCE UPON a time the Cow, the Goat and the Dog lived together in one kingdom. They called themselves the 'Big Three'. One day they were invited to the coronation ceremony of Mr Lion as the new King of the Forest. He lived on the other end of the kingdom at Mthunzi. The big three received the message late so they decided to try *matola* instead of walking to the venue of the ceremony. The three stood by the side of the road to wave down a lift. Fortunately soon one came by and they got in. The driver told them to pay K2.00 each for the journey.

The Cow paid the fare of K2.00. The Dog gave the driver K5.00 because he didn't have already changed money and asked for change. The driver said he would give him his change afterwards. The Goat promised he would pay afterwards on the way.

When they reached their destination, the Goat jumped out of the car and ran away without paying for the journey. The driver was angry and tried chasing after him. But the Goat being a fast runner, managed to escape. The driver failed to get him. On return to the car the driver found the Cow and the Dog impatiently waiting since they were late for the function. The Dog wanted his change of K3.00. But the driver coming from the chase, tired and angry, did not pay any attention to what the Dog was saying. He went straight into his car and drove off. The Dog chased after him but failed to catch the car. He came back to the Cow very angry. They proceeded to Mthunzi for the function. They found the Goat already there.

Since then, whenever the Cow sees a car, she does not move away fast from the road because she feels he owes the driver nothing, having paid her full fare. She does not fear a car. The Goat on the other hand will run away on the sound of the car fearing the driver will stop and ask for the fare he did not pay. The Dog is still looking for his change and will chase after the car hoping to get it from the driver.

The End

Questions

1. In groups, narrate folktales to explain why certain things happen as they do in the present.
2. Write your own folktales that explain the existence of some things in your community such as a river, a hill, or a cave.
3. Name the events that move the plot foward.
4. What is the climax of the story?
5. In your opinon, is the conflict that arises between the characters solved by the resolution that they made concerning the grudges which each had against the other?
6. If you were to retell the events of the story to somebody who has never read it, how would you sequence the events? Write them in point form and number them in their logical order.
7. Folklorick stories of Malawi normally start with the phrase "Once upon a time there was..." However, modern stories though based on folklore may not start with this phrase. Write a paragraph which does not start with "Once upon a time there was..." but should present the ideas that are presented in the first paragraph of this story.
8. What moral lessons can you learn from this story?

THE ROAD TO LUNZU MARKET

Felix Mnthali

IT WAS the dance of forgotten things. The sighs and the sounds became so familiar that they bred drowsiness. In the north and east loomed Zomba Mountain and all along the road mangoes and tomatoes formed a guard of honour to motorist and pedestrian alike. Then the drone of the engine and the language of the birds completed in sound what the landscape had done in colour. It was a festive occasion in the natural world but we did not applaud the performance. We saw and did not see it.

We spoke with our minds and lost ourselves in the echoes of unfulfilled dreams and the threatening return of half-forgotten nightmares. And the echoes and the nightmares revealed paths that led to nowhere and flickers of light which were so short as they were sudden. For the mind has jungles, as the earth has and it is not always safe to remain too long in the jungle.

We were half-way between Lunzu and Nyambadwe when Kizito Kanonono burst in an affected cough followed by a long sigh, "Hmm." He had left his jungle, and we, good followers that we were could not waste a minute more in ours. We stared at Kizito attentively.

Before us stretched the road to Lunzu Market. In the drowsy and twittering haze of a sunny morning it seemed we were destined for the North Pole and not for a popular market, ten miles out of Blantyre. To the north and east of us stood Zomba, serene, blue and rather misty - alone among lesser gods and goddesses of the land.

"Hmmm..." began Kizito, "I suppose you gentlemen were out again last night - grooving it up at The Sunnyside Groove Night Club! I wished I were there too, but, you know as they say in the city, 'the month has reached a sharp corner.' Still I don't regret my absence - what turned out of the old box of mine more than compensated for the grooving."

We murmured something to the effect that we hoped it had, especially as we had also failed to go to The Sunnyside Groove. Kizito cut us short and went on as if we hadn't murmured anything. We had learnt to put up with this irritating habit of his but always gave back as much as we got by mocking Kizito's world of remembrances and anecdotes.

> "Old papers can be fascinating - especially if they bear the stamp of loneliness and nostalgia. Here, for example, is one which you gentlemen may wish to publish when I am dead ..."

"Don't worry, you are still around," someone said, but by that time we were already at Lunzu market.
When we were ready to return to Blantyre someone bowed to Kizito and said mockingly:

"Now, my Lord KK, and I am not saying that one of the Ks stands for Kesare, we shall hear the will in that crumpled and yellowing piece of paper which you were going to read to us."

Kizito returned the mockery. "While the will is read, the multitudes shall follow the road to the North until every comma of the will has been read."

We had nothing in particular to do and that following the road to Lunzu Market beyond Lunzu was as good an activity as any on a day like that.

"Begin, O wise and puissant One," we shouted mockingly as our car turned its back on Blantyre and headed north.

Kizito began, reading his crumpled piece of paper. "I woke up with the urge to search for truth - just truth as such - not the truth of mathematics or that of philosophers. Just truth. I literally roamed the wide valley of Rome, climbed some of the hills and munched my lunch on a rock. Truth seemed hard to find but something else intruded on my lonely search..."

"A woman," exclaimed an irritated voice at the back of the car.
"Music," exclaimed another.

"Neither," Kizito continued quietly, 'had had' musical interludes' every Sunday and sometimes every Saturday afternoon. (My radio and I were inseparable). What intruded was not a woman either. While searching for the truth, you see, I discovered happiness. It haunted my waking hours and blessed my dreams. It hovered on my desk as I took notes from lecturers. It lingered on my window long after I turned in. It ran my life for me. I shall never forget the day during that long train journey between Mafeking and Bulawayo when a heated discussion took place in the compartment, the topic being, 'Power or the love of a woman, which of these is the most exciting?' I could hardly restrain myself before blurting out, 'Happiness, of course,' whereupon an embarrassed silence gripped the compartment until I went out for some fresh air.

I had found happiness, but my problem increasingly became one of finding exactly on what the happiness was based. I consulted my friends on psychology and they said I was becoming a 'manic-depressive' by which they meant that at certain times I become filled with overwhelming joy and other times I was in a frighteningly depressed mood. I consulted the philosophers and they reasoned that I had found something to live for - which is what my question had implied in the first place although the problem was what that thing worth living for was. My literary friends quoted the Bible and spoke of 'the peace that passeth understanding.' The economists were convinced I had received some money from home and the geographers argued that the geographical formations of Lesotho had affected my physiology! The historians felt I must have lost my sense of history, going on like that in that part of Africa where the historical imperatives admitted of no effusion of happiness. My friends in the physical sciences simply gave me up for a lost cause. 'That comes of reading too many anthropological books,' they would say.

I went on like this for a whole academic year. Where poverty had worried me to the point of distracting me from my studies, I now saw it as a merit to possess only one suit (reserved for Sundays and dance-parties!). Where I had always longed to spend a day in the city shopping and window-shopping, I now enjoyed the company of my small radio so much so that I went on from the appreciation of pop music to the enjoyment of Beethoven, Mozart, Bach and the whole gallery of the white man's geniuses.

It was at the beginning of the year when the doctor who freely helped the University with its medical problems beckoned me back after I had finished my check-up. Come again next week, it's nothing but I want to be sure of one or two things which seem to be quite normal. When I came again I had to be flown to Barafwanath Hospital. Yes, indeed, there it was cancer of the bones."

Kizito seemed strangely affected by his early attempts at writing. We all were. Someone, the driver, I think, said in a flat voice, "we need petrol." We drove back for a while and had to walk to the nearest station to get petrol for fear of losing the last pint at an awkward turn in the road.

The road to Lunzu Market beckoned us forth-shimmering grey, somewhat long as if it wasn't taking us to Blantyre but to the South Pole. We spoke with our minds and lost ourselves in the echoes of unfulfilled dreams and the threatening return of half-forgotten nightmares.

And the echoes and the nightmares revealed paths that led to nowhere and flickers of light which were as ephemeral as they were sudden. For the mind has jungles as the earth has and it is not always safe to stay long in the jungle. Due south came the blue presence of Soche Mountain not alone among the wonders of beauties of this land. In the sunshine like a plate dried up to the meat from Lunzu Market gleamed the City of Blantyre.

The End

Questions

1. Find in paragraph one an expression that means 'lined up along'.
2. The word 'jungle' in paragraph two may imply 'being lost' or being 'surrounded' by an environment that causes fear. What do you think might have led the characters to feel that they were in a 'jungle'?
3. Why do you think the characters felt like they were headed for the North Pole?
4. Explain in your own words the meaning of the expression 'the month has reached a sharp corner'.
5. The story seems to be dealing with a person's attempts to understand life or aspects of it and the difficulties encountered in the search for understanding. Which paragraph of the story captures this most accurately? Explain what the paragraph is all about.
6. In his quest for truth, Kizito Kanonono found something else. What was it? What was the significance of this discovery on Kizito's life?
7. What is the setting of the story?
8. Explain how the author employs of characterisation to spice up the details of the physical setting.
9. What paradoxes does the author present in the first and last paragraphs of the story? What contribution do these paradoxes make to the major theme of the story?
10. Suddenly, the characters in the story change their minds and start heading north instead of south. What is the significance of this action in relation to the major theme of the story?
11. The activities of the story move very fast. However, this does not make the story simple or folklorick. Look at the language that the author has used and explain how he has handled the use of language to achieve this.

BALEKILE

Norah Ngoma

IT HAD been a busy day at work and Patricia felt exhausted. She locked the office and started for home. It was dark and the idea of walking four kilometres to Segelege Township where she lived worried her. Drivers were gone as she had not alerted any to wait around to take her home after work. It was well over seven o'clock and the buses had long stopped operating. So she had to walk home. As she strode through the deserted streets, a few kilometres away from her office, she saw something dart from the left side and stop in the middle of the road. A gust of wind blew across her face making her feel cold. Though the street lights were on she could not see far. She paused and looked around to see if there was anything peculiar. When she came close she noticed that it was only a squirrel trying to cross the road. She ignored it and quickening her pace this time, she proceeded.

Upon reaching her house, Patricia hastily opened the door and stopped awhile at the doorway to make sure there was nobody following her or something amiss in the house. She strode into the house closing the door behind her. She dropped her handbag on the table and threw herself on her new sofa. She heaved a sigh of relief. She had reached home safe.

Patricia wanted to rest awhile before retiring to bed. She was in no mood to make supper that evening. As she relaxed, she was startled by a knock on the door. "Who can that be?" she wondered nervously. The loneliness and the silence in the house made her tremble. She was all alone in the house. The house-girl and her seven year old son, Mufo, had gone to Zomba to see some family friends and she did not expect them back that evening.

She thought it was the Inkatha, a group of thugs in Kabula City at her door step. With the coming of democracy and the flopping of the economy, robberies had become more frequent in the country, particularly in Kabula City. People were being robbed and murdered in broad-day light. She had, in fact, once witnessed her friend, Natasha, being robbed and stabbed. Patricia wondered why there was so much unrest in the world more especially in Africa. She remembered her uncle, Kajiso, who was murdered in Zaire where he lived. What a living! She was thinking about this when the knock on the door was repeated. This time it was stronger. Patricia froze with fear and she stood motionless.

She was in a dilema. Should she answer the knock or not? She finally gathered some courage and tiptoed to the window. She parted curtains and peeped through. Uh! she couldn't believe it. It was just a woman holding a plastic carrier bag in her hand. With darkness outside, however, Patricia could not recognize the stranger. She opened the door. Who was she? What did she want at that time.

"*Muli bwanji?*" Patricia greeted her while standing on the doorway. Silence.

62

"Muli bwanji?" Still silence.

"Tikuthandizeni nanga?" She asked trying to figure out who the woman was.

The silence scared her. Then the stranger squeaked, probably trying to say something but no audible word came out. She covered her face with her ragged chilundu.

"What can I do for you at this odd hour then ... uh?" Patricia said perplexed. Still the stranger did not utter a word. Convinced, by the looks, that she was either a mad woman or a beggar, Patricia fished out some one kwacha coins from her pocket and pushed them onto her hands.

"You beggars are becoming a bore! Visiting people's homes even at night!" she said while retreating into her house with disgust, slamming the door behind her.

She wondered why there were so many beggars in town, mostly disguised as mad people, while in the village, her home for instance, nobody went about begging in people's houses unless one was mad. Nonetheless, Patricia felt sorry for this particular stranger. She looked sick and miserable. She picked up her handbag and disappeared into the bedroom switching off the lights at the sitting room.

Thirty minutes later, Patricia felt so hungry that she decided to get something to eat. Should she go to the kitchen or make herself a cup of coffee right in the bedroom? She decided for coffee and was soon finished and ready to go to bed. However, she checked her khonde to make sure the stranger was gone. Alas! the uninvited visitor was still there; she had not moved an inch.

Patricia was now worried. She could not imagine what she could do to drive her away and she certainly was not going to give her a place to sleep in. She decided to confront her and if possible threaten her away.

"What do you want from me?" she asked as soon as she opened the door. But as she looked closer at her unannounced visitor she discovered that the woman was crying.

"Who are you?" Patricia asked with exasperation. "What do you want from me?"

"It's me, mama, it's me, Balekile."

"What? Balekile?!"

"Yes, mama, it's me, I have come to apologize?" the visitor announced while trembling and was now holding her hand across her face.

Patricia stood motionless and confused. Her mind raced back to her past. A past she had abhorred, and wanted to remember no part of it any more. The mischief and misery she had suffered in all those years came back to her. She remembered clearly how she had struggled bringing up Balekile.

She had been thirteen years old when she got pregnant. She was in form three then. Everything turned upside down. Her parents disowned her. The man who made her pregnant denied responsibility and later 'disappeared'. She went about looking for him but could not find him. She wandered in town for some time before deciding to go to her grandmother in the village. Life in the village was not easy. Living there for the first time made it even more difficult. The child was born in the village. She immediately engaged herself in menial jobs to earn some money for a living. She bought bananas, sweet potatoes and sugarcane from the wages received from the piece jobs, for sale on school premises.

When Balekile was two years old, Patricia got a job as a data clerk with a Construction Company which was building a road through her home village. It was a chance in a life time. Later she left the child in her grandmother's custody and went to town for greener pastures. It was in the city.that she met and later fell in love with Lusungu Kambuwa, the Foreman of the company she worked with. After a few months of courtship they got married. It was one of the happiest days of her life. She did not hide that she had Balekile because she did not want to live with the secret. Thus, Balekile was brought into town soon after the marriage and Lusungu adopted her. She was eight years old then.

Balekile grew up into a quiet and lovely juvenile. She was humble and well behaved. People liked her. She was hard working at home as well as at school. She successfully completed her primary education and went to Katawa Girls Secondary School from where she was selected to go to the renowned Chilunga University at the age of fourteen. Patricia was all excitement.

However, problems started when Balekile came back from College for the first semester vacation. Patricia noticed that Balekile had changed in the short time she had been there. She behaved not like before. The low grades for the semester served to confirm her suspicion. She learnt later that Balekile spent much of her time in college with boyfriends, attending parties and discos. She was often drunk. Patricia felt bitter and disappointed. She decided she would talk to her.

"This is democracy and I thought you would respect my personal and private feelings," was the answer Patricia got back. She was lost for words. Her heart burnt with fury especially when she remembered the suffering she had gone through in her life because of Balekile.

When Balekile came for another holiday, the situation was worse. She was rude and showed no respect for Patricia. To her surprise, Lusungu, her husband seemed to defend her. He advised her to avoid poking her nose into children's affairs. "She is a big girl and in college, what more do you expect her to do; go ratting, chasing monkeys? She is past that age now, and moreover this is a new ge-ne-ra-ti-on." Patricia felt helpless.

Much as Patricia was dismayed when Lusungu took Balekile out to parties, she was not shocked. He had grown fond of the girl and since he approved of her behaviour in college, it could not be strange that he took her out. However, she was disappointed to see them come back drunk. She kept quiet for some time believing it wouldn't go on forever. One day, however, when Patricia was look-ing for some paper in Balekile's bedroom, she picked up photographs of Lusun-gu and Balekile taken while at the lake. There were also letters and postcards from Lusungu to Balekile. There was no doubt that they were in an affair. A love relationship between daughter and father. She could not believe it. When she asked Balekile what all this meant, Balekile retorted: "I know you hate me. I know you don't like seeing me with Lusungu." She addressed her father by his name. Patricia realised that she had lost her child.

Later that evening when she tried to mention the letters and photos to Lusun-gu, he was defensive and explained them away. "What is wrong with you?" She is my daughter as well as yours. What do you think I can do with her!" he explained.

When, Balekile overheard the conversation, she cut in, "I think it's too late to change anything now. I am two months pregnant and Lusungu has promised to marry me." Patricia charged as if to beat her up but Lusungu stood up and chal-lenged her.

"Look here, my dear," Lusungu said. "Balekile is not my child! There is nothing that can prevent me from marrying her. One thing you ought to know is that Balekile has made me happy while all you do is nag, nag, nag." Lusungu took Balekile's hand and walked out, banging the door behind them.

"It's taboo," Patricia tried to call at them, "It's taboo!"

She cried as she sank into the sofa. It was a stab in her back. She searched to see where she had gone wrong. At first, Patricia thought it was a joke. But it was never to be. Balekile never went back to school. Three years went by without hearing anything from them. She accepted her defeat and started afresh. At thirty-two, she decided not to get married again. She moved into a one-bed-roomed house in Segelege Township and changed jobs as well.

"I am sorry, mama," Balekile said, bringing her back to the present. I wronged you. I did not know what I was doing. I was tempted by the devil. I want to go back to school, mama.... Lusungu left me for someone else. He used to spend most of his time drinking and sleeping out. When I asked him, he shouted abuses at me and called me names. He threw me out of his house and accused me of killing my own son. The child died three months ago now," she said between sobs. She could not hold her tears any more.

"Yes, ...yes... I..." Patricia didn't know what to say.

"Now I am all alone and I have nowhere to go. For five days I have been wandering about without any food. If you chase me I am going to die, mama. I am to blame for all this misery but I still ask for ...!" More tears rolled down her cheeks.

Patricia looked at her. She was blank and confused. "Oh what a day!" Patricia sighed. She shook her head and went back into the house without saying another word. Balekile followed and shut the door behind her.

The End

Questions

1. Why did Patricia not feel like preparing supper when she returned from work?
2. What happened when Patricia gave the visitor some coins?

3. Explain in your own words the main request that the visitor made to Patricia.
4. What is the relationship between Patricia and Balekile? How was this relationship affected by Balekile?
5. Do you think the visitor's request was granted? Give reasons for your answer.
6. Imagine you were Patricia, would you have granted the visitor's request? Why?
7. Compare the plot of "Why the Dog chases the Car" and "How Mice began eating books". Specifically check the sequencing of the major events that move the story.
8. How fast does the reader arrive at the climax of the story?
9. In your opinion do you think the events of the story have successfully presented what can take place in real life?.
10. What are the major themes in the story?
11. What are the minor themes of the story?
12. Although Patricia says nothing but allows Balekile to enter her house, do you think the conflict which was there has been resolved? Explain.

I MISS YOU MOTHER

N Bisani

HE HEAVED his body out of the minibus. The journey from Zomba had been quite interesting. He stretched as he went down the steps leading to the bus-stand where he was to take another bus that was to lead him to Nguludi Turn Off. From Nguludi Turn Off he was to take *matola* that was to drop him off at Mikolongwe. The five kilometre walk from Mikolongwe to his mother's home worried him. But he was more concerned about finding his mother than walking the distance. He missed her.

He took advantage of the holiday that fell on Friday to stay away from books and visit his mother. "He is my first born son," he once heard her say, very proud of him and his achievements so far. He had just finished secondary school then. Now he was about to graduate from the university with a degree. He thought he would brief his mother about the prospects of employment once he finishes exams which were due in a month's time.

As usual, getting into the bus at Limbe was never an easy undertaking. The bus to Nguludi arrived and was followed by a sudden massive motion of people gathered along the shop verandahs. The swarming of people on the bus door and the struggle to get a ticket nearly suffocated Mlada. His shirt was drenched in sweat by the time he got into the bus. Since he could not get a seat, he had to stand all the way to Nguludi Turn Off.

Mlada stamped on the foot of the man standing next to him as more and more people pressed in, causing him to rear off balance. He was startled to notice that it was his cousin he had stepped on.

"Oh, are you closed this early?" Kambani, a cousin asked.

"No, I just want to see people over the weekend," Mlada gave a warm answer.

"You are stepping on my foot!" Somebody close to Mlada screamed as a woman cradling a baby, with another one at the back squeezed through.

"If you want comfort, you should go and get a taxi," the woman said. People fanned their faces relentlessly as heavy air filled with stinking sweat filled the overcrowded bus.

"Hey, conductor! the bus is full!" a man yelled out in a harsh voice. Mothers, filled with wrath, tried to silence their crying babies.

Mlada felt restless as he asked Kambani about home news. "Where are you coming from?"

"I came to buy some plastic shoes and a pair of trousers. I've just sold a bag of pepper which I harvested this year," Kambani answered, taking freezits.

"Oh, that is wonderful. How is your wife?"

The driver accelerated before engaging the bus into gear. The bus jerked back and forth following a gear shift.

"You don't look similar to your brother, Damiano. Even your behaviour and general perception of life is quite different," Kambani flattered Mlada, ignoring his question.

"We can't look similar since we are from different mothers. Having the same father cannot make us behave alike either," Mlada retorted.

"You can't believe it. Damiano has just run away from hospital with his newly born son. He says that he fears the doctors might kill the child with regular injections."

68

"Really?" What was the baby suffering from?" Mlada asked.

Streaks of showers came through the open windows and some holes on the roof of the bus.

"Close the windows, please. We are getting wet here," the man in a blouse lamented.

"I am getting fresh air from here," was a soft reply from a middle aged woman taking a yellow bun.

"If she is suffering from high blood pressure, we can get an ambulance for her." A roar of laughter swept through the back of the bus following the remark from a boy carrying school books.

The thought of missing his mother struck Mlada much. The link between them was so strong that some people joked that she was his close sister.

"This is what happened," Kambani continued with his story. "Two weeks ago Damiano and his wife came to Namita with their sick child. In fact, the child is regularly sick. If you could remember well, the child was born at a village women's maternity clinic. It falls sick now and again and in this instance, the sickness was very unbearable."

"What was the child actually suffering from?" Mlada asked as the bus took Midima road. It hit a pot hole.

"Driver, there are women with young babies on this bus," the man wearing a blouse yelled. A murmur of confirmation swept through the bus as two women relentlessly tried to silence their babies.

"Do you have a ticket?" the conductor asked randomly as he squeezed through the standing passengers, sending others off balance.

"Hey conductor, there is no more space left in this bus," lamented a passenger as the bus stopped at the first stage.

"We are getting off here," answered another passenger as he pushed through the crowd.

"When your brother came to Namita with his sick child, your mother gave him money and a car to go with the child to Lenga Private Clinic. On the night following this, the child could not sleep. It cried the whole night and your mother, with Damiano's wife, watched over it," Kambani said. The bus swerved as it gave way to an oncoming car that could not leave the narrow tarmac. The passengers that were standing were sent off balance and they swore bitterly.

"In the morning, your mother went to Namita government clinic with the baby. There, it was discovered that the baby was suffering from meningitis. The clinical officer suggested that the child should be sent to the Central Hospital for effective treatment." The bus hit a pothole again. Mlada felt its impact deep down in his heart as Kambani got interrupted.

"These politicians of ours are liars. During the campaign period they promised they would repair all the bad roads. But look, it is three years now since and the roads are getting worse." lamented a passenger.

"Yes, he promised that he will fix a bridge where there is no bridge. These potholes are big enough for bridges ...," the man in a blouse commented.

"Don't laugh, some of us are going to Nguludi hospital with sick children and by the time we reach there, they will be fainting," the woman carrying two children said.

Mlada felt very annoyed with the interruptions. He had begun developing an interest in the story. "So my brother and his wife ran away from Queen Elizabeth Central Hospital with the baby?" Mlada asked.

"No, your mother, together with Damiano's wife returned with the baby. When your brother heard about the infection, he directed that his beloved son be treated at a private hospital. This meant that the medical document had to be readdressed. While the clinical officer was doing this, the child fainted.

"Oh, let us pop out fast and board that pick-up," Kambani said when they reached Nguludi Turn Off.

The boy standing close to the pick-up truck yelled on the top of his voice, "Malowa, Mikolongwe, Tchoda, Nkando, Mulanje, we're now leaving!" Mlada reached for the hanger of the body of the pick-up truck, pulled himself up and sat on the railing close to the hanger itself. He promptly recognized a car going in the opposite direction. It was Bagodo. His mother was sitting next to Bagodo looking preoccupied with the urgency of the journey. Bagodo drove by without taking any interest in who was in the pick-up.

"I hope they return fast. I have to go back today. Oh, mother why didn't you look this way. I was coming to see you." Mlada thought while taking note of the time which had reached half past twelve.

"Hey, you, put your suitcase on top of the cabin and the one standing should hold it. And you four don't sit. You would rather stand and hold the hanger to give room to your friends," the driver directed. The backward pushing of the car sent other passengers off balance. They clung to one another while others got pushed to the edge.

"He has packed us like charcoal bags," a passenger complained.

Mlada felt very low but, there was an interesting story to listen to. "So what happened after the child fainted?" He managed to ask.

Kambani pulled himself before answering. "Your mother was called from the shop and Bagodo was left to attend to the customers. She decided that the child be taken to Namita hospital since it is a few metres away. Your brother and his wife rejected this, saying the child is already dead and there is no need to bother. At this your mother snatched the baby, jumped into the car which had just arrived, and drove to the hospital."

Kambani suddenly stopped speaking as the car swerved while trying to avoid two potholes. The fifteen year old boy standing close to Mlada lost balance and fell on Mlada's legs. Mlada didn't seem to feel the pain but still he was very irritated. The thought of missing his mother was greater than the pain the boy caused.

"Hey, driver, remember you are carrying people and not bags of maize." The man in a blouse yelled without bothering whether the driver heard it or not.

"The roads are really bad," Kambani commented as he continued. "They set off for Nguludi mission hospital right away. That was two weeks ago and the couple returned two days ago with their child. They say the injections were just too much. As I was leaving, I heard that they want to go to a traditional medicine-man to find out about the one bewitching their son."

The earth road that followed was better than the potholed tarmac. Twenty minutes after disembarking the bus, Mlada and his cousin took a side road that led to Namita. Mlada was contemplating the five kilometre walk when all of a sudden a lorry emerged from a corner in front of them. The lorry stopped as the driver shouted at them to jump in.

"I am going to Sakata and I will be back soon. It is better to reach home late than walk all the way." It was Hiwa, Mlada's uncle.

Kambani decided to walk on since he had almost reached his home as Mlada jumped into the lorry. The lorry roared as it moved up the road. Upon reaching

Mikolongwe, Hiwa geared down and turned into the direction which the pick-up truck took. Hiwa seemed to enjoy driving his car. He talked less, fixing his eyes in front. He seemed to enjoy pumping the clutch pedal three to four times before changing into another gear. The hitting of a bump sent Mlada rocking forth. He felt a sharp pain as a piece of metal scratched the small of his back.

"Sorry for the broken seat. You know, the problem with our African cars is that they are far below standard," Hiwa said while clearing his throat.

"It's alright," Mlada answered.

As the lorry took a right turn three kilometres away, the rear left tyre gave a hissing sound. Its twin tyre was already deflated. Since the car had no spare wheel, it meant removing one tyre from the rear right side. Hiwa's apology about African cars gave no solution. "Mum," Mlada thought, "I have to be back to college tonight. How can I see you?"

The arrival of a man on a bicycle gave relief. Mponda, the assistant shopkeeper, was coming from Sakata where he went to deliver an important parcel. The feel of a bicycle carrier made Mlada appreciate that he was indeed home. Mponda's whistling and fast riding amused him. Numerous questions, which Mlada asked about home seemed to bother him. But still, he managed to answer them all though in short phrases.

The sight of the pick up at the house made Mlada realise that his mother was back. He promptly entered the house in which he met his father, stretched in a sofa. "Oh, glad to see you!" His father explained. "Come and sit here on this seat," his father said pointing to the seat next to his.

Mlada had a lot to discuss with his mother. The first thing was to tell her about his job prospects. Then he may discuss his plans to marry the girl from college. "Your mother is in a hurry. She is going to chair a ladies' meeting at the church," the father explained in answer to Mlada's enquiries after her. Mlada felt a cold shrill pass through his spine. The mother emerged from the bedroom fastening her head gear.

"Oh, it's you Mlada. Have you just arrived? she asked. It's good to see you back home. She was zipping up her handbag.

"I am alright, mother and ...?" Mlada was answering when his mother disappeared into the kitchen. He had not sat down yet.

"I am sorry that I have to leave for the church. I will see you in the evening."

She was speaking from outside the house.

"I have to go back today. I just came around to see you," Mlada was speaking to an empty kitchen.

Mlada felt very low as he sat next to Bagodo who was driving him to the trading centre. As the car hit the potholes, he felt the pain of missing his mother.

The End

Questions
1. Where was Mlada going?
2. What was the purpose of the trip?
3. Name three important people who travelled with Mlada in the minibus.
4. What evidence is there that there is a transport problem to Mlada's destination?
5. It appears Mlada is being prevented by certain forces or misfortunes to see the person he wanted to see. Do you agree? Give reasons.
6. Briefly explain the story that Kambani was telling Mlada on this trip.
7. In what way did this trip have a sad ending for Mlada?
8. In this story there are vehicles and a bicycle which are used for transport. How do these modes of transport affect the movement of the events that carry the plot.
9. In your opinion, do you think the events of the story are predictable or not ? Explain.
10. From the title, the major theme of the story is the love that may exist between mother and child. However, there are also sub-themes in the story which are related to this major theme. Explain how this is done.
11. The story contains two plots. What are they? Explain how they affect each other.
12. Dialogue may control or may be controlled by the plot of the story. Explain the role that is played by dialogue in this story.

THE GOAT

Zondiwe Mbano

HE SAW it clearly now. It was a he-goat, standing in a shrub, within the distance of a whisper. Its odour was heavy in the air. He saw its head with horns pointing backwards; then he saw part of the body disappearing into the shrub. What was it doing there? From the way it looked at him, it seemed interested in him; perhaps it was waiting for him to drive it to its pen. But he was not particularly interested in it, so he walked on looking ahead. A brook snaked through the forest to avoid big rocks; but further down, a rock imposed itself on the course, spreading to the right and left, so that the water had to leap over it, like angry horsemen, and on the other side spread out with effervescence. He saw all this, and his keen ears picked up the music of the water. This music woke up solitude in him, his only faithful companion for all the years he had lived on earth.

Now he remembered the two brooks at his home, far away up the country. One was Msambayifa: the place where death bathes. This was where people went to take a bath after burying their dead. Otherwise, no one went there alone because, apart from the many graves there, the place was said to be infested with snakes of all descriptions: some of them as long as the brook itself, and with a body that flows like the water; and others with a long body that divides into two or three and rejoins. There were also stories of witches seen bathing there under the devouring eye of the sun. The other brook, where girls went for a bath, was called Msambazintombi. It was here - in the wild abandon that comes with the removal of clothes, fetters on the body and mind - that girls waggled their waists, splashed water on each other, and ran about giggling as they exposed their naked beauty to the sun. It was this name, Msambazintombi, that he decided to give this brook that he was looking at. Now solitude left him, and immediately poetry came. The water sang a poem of love and beauty, untouched by claws of selfishness.

The goat was not in the least amused by this response to its presence. It looked angrily at him for a long time, showing him its goatee; then, it emitted a sound similar to that of a rutting goat. He heard this sound and wanted to turn and look at it again, but he fought hard against this. There was intense debate within him for some time, and then someone inside him spoke.

"Surely, you need to look back."

"No!" he answered abruptly; then, as an afterthought, "Why?" he queried.

"Look back," the voice pleaded. "You may be in danger."

"Danger! No, not from a goat!" he challenged, although somewhere inside him, he was not completely without anxiety; for this goat was a bit strange. He remembered how he had grown up looking after goats and cattle, and how some big he-goats would sometimes butt a cow; and in one incident, a goat knocked off the horn of a cow.

"Perhaps you can read its intentions" the voice persisted.

"Its intentions?"

"Yes! You can read from its eyes."

He pondered over this. What intentions would a stray goat have, apart from wanting to go home? He saw the whole idea as obviously foolish. His mind turned back to the brook; then, to poetry: he drank in the music of the water, so lovely. The song was in praise of feminine beauty, and accompanying it was the chorus of the wind in the trees.

Suddenly, he felt warmth around the backside of his legs. Something seemed to be breathing close to his left thigh; or, was this not a trick of his anxious mind? He decided he was not going to turn and look back, for - what would the goat think if he did this? Would it not think that he was interested in it? Yet the need to turn became greater as the warmth on the thigh increased. He could no longer resist; so he decided to turn, trying to make sure that the goat did not notice. He stealthily turned his head; and, just as his chin was reaching his right shoulder, "Mayoo!" he screamed, as he leapt sky-high, and ran to stand behind a big tree. What was the goat after; grinning at his leg like that? Surely, its intentions were not friendly. Meanwhile, the goat stood exactly where he had been, and looked at him with arrogance. Now, satisfied with what it had done, it walked jauntily to a shrub nearby; and turning towards him, it maintained a sneering look at him.

A serene wind blew. Birds twittered in the tree with a thick canopy spreading across the Msambazintombi and casting a shadow that made the otherwise shallow little pool near him look deep. The Msamba resumed purling. Everything was calm. The only sound that was out of tune with the calm rhythm around was that of his heart-beat. For a long time he stood there, waiting for his heart-beat to normalise. He looked at the shrub again; the goat was not there! Where could it have gone within this short time? Was it behind him again? His heart-beat was now a pounding noise. He looked around him, and back to the shrub. How had he lost sight of it? It was still there; but now crouching, chewing something, and not looking directly at him.

He now wanted to go. He wondered why this goat thought it could detain him like this. After thinking about this for some time, however, he decided that it was all foolish to think he was standing here because a goat had detained him. How? Even now, if he wanted, he could simply walk away. But the voice came back, with another suggestion.

"Take some stones and chase it."

"Yes, that's a good idea... but..."

"It'll run away."

"Yes, it will...but..."

There were many stones around. He bent and picked three, but soon dropped them. The goat might just be frolicking after all. Or, perhaps, it was lost, and wanted to sniff at him to check if he was its master, as dogs do. He was not going to throw stones at it, this would be outright savagery; and, who knows, this very action might make it aggressive!

He decided to walk away. However, he was not going to do this carelessly; he was going to walk backwards until he covers a certain distance. It was a matter of prudence, not fear. He had to keep looking at it; perhaps, from its eyes, he could discover what its intentions were. So he walked slowly backwards along the brook, at one point stumbling and landing on his hands, behind; but he pressed on until he reached another small pool, and stopped to wash his hands. He noticed that he was sweating. Could this be due to the start he had had? Perhaps not. Walking up and down the brook for a man working for a busy corporation, who spends from Monday to Friday - and sometimes Saturday too - either on a desk with files and two digital telephone receivers and a cellular, or in a Peugeot 505 estate, can cause such sweat. He thought of drinking some water, cool and clear water flowing mellifluously from the plateau, but he quickly changed his mind; cold water from the plateau can sometimes enervate you.

Now the goat had been left far behind. He therefore crossed the Msamba and walked slowly up another ascent, all the time listening for footsteps. He was no longer walking backwards, for obviously the goat had stopped following him. Before he could assure himself about this, however, he saw it ahead of him, facing away, but its horns pointing at him in a way that seemed to signify danger. What showed clearly from that position were its hind-legs, which were dark and thin; also prominent between the legs was the male pack, which was obviously not very light, for the legs looked rickety from carrying it. How, with such legs, was it able to fulfill its impish whims. From the way it stood, he could tell that it had not seen him; therefore, he turned left and walked towards the brook. Although he had long stopped walking backwards, for this had not served any purpose, he walked softly, making sure he did not step on anything that could crackle, while time and again checking behind him. He had to be careful, for this goat was proving a bit elusive; or, perhaps, was this not a different goat?

He walked on, passing bramble bushes which bear *nthona*, yellow berries, like strawberries: walked on thinking about the movements of the goat until he reached where the Msamba was joined by another brook, almost of the same size. He stopped and looked around. Pink, purple, and blue flowers and others of other colours, grew on both sides of the bank, as if to mark the confluence. The area directly in front of him was steep, and therefore he walked on to a gentler bank. From here he saw the whole lay-out of the place: the two brooks joining to form a V-shape, the colourful flowers, the ferns and grass spreading out greenery from the banks, the rocks rising from the ground, the clear water purling, and the blue sky with white clouds. All this, he drank in. And now his mind started to perceive a feminine figure emerging from this lay-out. Oh, how lovely it was to be here and see it developing! At first it was the general form, and then details started emerging: the head, two erect breasts, the navel, two legs.... And all the details came, just like that. Now he understood why He that created the woman had to cause deep sleep in the man while He created her, otherwise the man would have snatched her from the Creator before he finished His work. Imagine the Creator putting in final details: painting black the nipples and the surrounding area that would be touched by saliva from sucking lips, tucking in the navel, pushing modest parts to dark background, and then parting the thighs and stretching them a bit, so that they do not look like drumsticks - could the man have mustered enough patience to watch to the end? Surely it would have been beyond the endurance of man.

He would have gone on musing about this, but somehow he perceived that he was being checked. Fear started mounting: a fear so distant at the moment, but so real. He remembered the goat. It must be standing where he had left it; or, perhaps, could it not have traced its way home? But suddenly a terrific force charged at him from behind. He quickly jumped into the water, and dashed to the other side, almost falling into the mud while climbing the other bank. Hearing no splash behind him, he turned to see - and, indeed, it was the goat! Standing exactly where he had been, it revealed no impishness: it was serious. Its black hoofs, mouth, nose and eyes revealed dark intentions. The horns were short and thick, but they were sharp; the only good thing was that they pointed backwards. He walked on and sat on a rock, directly facing the goat. His trousers, below the knees, and his socks and shoes were sodden and soiled; water dripped from the trousers into the shoes. He tried to take off the shoes but failed because his hands were trembling. He sat still for some time, all the time looking at the goat, and feeling a mixture of self-pity and anger. After some time, his hands were a bit steady, so he slowly took off his shoes and socks. He felt the skin of his feet, which was cold and soft, although wrinkled. As if this was what it had been waiting for, the goat sauntered away and crouched under a shade.

The more he looked at it, the more he grew angry. He felt an urge to register his anger, and therefore he spoke. But the words, when they came out, did not have the urgency and direction he had intended for them.

"Why did it want to butt me?"

"Are you certain it wanted to?" was a prompt question in answer to his.

"Why are my trousers, and socks and shoes soaked then?" he asked, rather angrily.

"Standing on the edge of a slippery bank is dangerous, especially if you are wearing shoes. Better with bare feet," replied the voice, preaching.

He remained quiet for some time; he was disappointed with his effort to register his anger. But this did not go on for long, for he felt he should press on; now, however, his talking was not so much for registering anger as for a deep inquiry into himself.

"Why is it that it keeps on disturbing me?"

"Disturbing you from doing what?" queried the other voice.

"I came here to pummel myself and draw in eternal strength."

"That is impossible when the noise of the body is so loud, paralyzing the soul and drowning the spirit," came the voice, preaching again.

"The noise of the body..." he was going to say something, but the words escaped him, and so he said, "But why should it be so much interested in me?"

"Are you sure you are not more interested in it yourself?"

"Interested in it?" he rose in agitation, "How?"

"Beware of delusion!" came down the final knock of the hammer, clinching the point.

Delusion. Could this really be the problem? If so, what was its source, and in what way did it manifest itself? How was he deluding himself? Or was somebody else deluding him? He sat down and started thinking deeply about this, again and again scratching his head, as was his habit in such situations. Much as he thought about this, however, he did not come close to understanding anything and all these things that clouded him now. Everything was vague. But for the time being, one thing seemed clear enough: the fear of the goat. Although, even now, if he started thinking about it - removing the cloud around it to see what there was at the centre of it - it disappeared. He noticed that this fear was not as distant as it had previously appeared to be; and although it seemed directly linked to the goat, it had been there even before he saw the goat.

About the goat, he saw that it would be safe to regard it as mad; therefore, he now resolved to keep an eye on it, even if it meant watching it every minute. To occupy his mind with poetry and beauty had proved dangerous in this territory of the wild goat. There were, however, safer things to contemplate while the sun was shining, and he was sitting on the rock, which was broad and elevated. He therefore turned and faced away from the goat. He was sure he had done this to show that he was brave, goat or no goat. But his critic would have seen cowardice in this very move. Between the goat and him was the Msamba, which could warn him if the goat tried to cross to his side. But behind him shrubs were so close that if the goat came from this side it could reach him without his noticing it; therefore, it was this side where vigilance was important. Faced with such a riddle of the goat, he could not say with certainty whether his action was brave or cowardly? Whatever the case was, he knew he needed to look away from the goat; perhaps, this way, he could shatter its rude presence. While his eyes frequently stumbled on it, he could not hope to successfully keep away from it.

Hardly had he drawn the last strands of his thoughts into himself, to see how they would weave into a pattern and shape that would show him clearly the nature and extent of the delusion, when he felt some fear rising in his heart. He turned and looked under the tree. The goat was not there, and there was not even a sign to show that it had ever been there: the grass was straight, just as it was everywhere around, and even the odour was gone. Obviously, the goat must have gone away some time back. However, the goat had shown enough of its dark intentions - or, was it devilry? - to make him act quickly. He therefore rose and walked around to make sure the goat was nowhere around, hatching another 'operation blitz'. He saw that it was nowhere, and somehow he felt a bit disappointed to think that it had gone, which meant it was not really interested in him. Slowly, he walked on. This walk took him down the Msamba to a place where there were no bushes close by, and the few *msuku* and *chiyombo* trees around were not close to each other. A flat rock overlooked the water, and he decided to sit on it. Long ferns grew between the rock and the water, and on the water black beetles swam, leaving a trail after them. The late afternoon wind sighing in the trees announced the approaching cold season, and a dove cooed its song in one of the trees; a song which, although he liked listening to, expressed an opinion he greatly opposed:

Koo koo-ho! Koo koo-ho!
Better a string trap
It simply catches you
And you can flap about.

Koo koo-ho! Koo koo-ho!
The weight trap is bad
Even before it pounds you
You are already dead.

The sun stole out into full view, and then slowly set behind velvet clouds with yellow, orange and pink layers that had gone up to welcome it. He saw all this because the canopies of trees were not thick around him. Then he thought of going home, and this filled him with much anxiety. He had invited her for supper at 7:30 p.m. Surely, it was rash of him to have invited her. True, she was irresistible, and her youthful looks made people think she was twenty-three; but by using the formula: *True Age equals Declared (or Apparent) Age plus Seven*; - where seven is the error factor on every girl or woman with declared age of between eighteen and forty - he reckoned she was about thirty. She had recently joined the corporation, on the side of the professionals, and had a rather difficult surname - no wonder she liked being called by her first name. He had several times seen her in town with a small girl of between four and six. This little girl was obviously her child, for she resembled her so much. One day, talking on the phone as he went into her office, he had heard her saying: "There are mistakes you make in your teens for which regrets or blame will not help; it is better to understand yourself and live."

This is what he knew about her. For her part, she seemed to have done good research on him; and, on the strength of this, was making determined effort. Through beating chance into a desired shape - although not in a Machiavellian fashion, for in this case the beating was pleasant to both the beater and the beaten - she was succeeding in getting him increasingly entangled in her net; and it was from this net that he found himself inviting her, against what everyone who knew him well expected of him.

Some years back he had decided that he was not going to pander again to this uncertain thing called love. He had tried it, invested everything in it. However, the whole thing ended in a titanic disaster: the crew had done their best to save the ship, but to no avail. Looking back later, he thought it was good that that love ended when it did, before it brought too much agony. For what kind of bridge would the flimsy hand of love - or is it infatuation, as often tends to be between a man and woman - build across a chasm that had been deepening and widening over more than a century of hate and distrust between their peoples? When between them was a battle front, how could their hands extend and pull them together and roll them into an embrace that makes the two one; roll them into one solid ball, knocking obstacle after obstacle down the path of love, the path of life? It was impossible. Even the old book records how such love once ended into disaster, into misery. Samson and Delilah.

So it was, having experienced the titanic disaster, he had built a cocoon around himself, and for a long time, he lived safely. Now there was no more safety, and all this was because of her. She had come, walking through all the gates well manned by fierce-looking guards. And immediately he saw her, that combination of fear and joy overwhelmed him; and in the poetic rapture that followed, he said to himself:

Daughter of the land
The music of your body
And sunshine in your soul
Lighting up your radiant eyes
Wake me to a morning dance.

From then her smile followed him everywhere: he could close his eyes, and still see her smile. Her eyes expressed what her heart said; and this is what her heart said: "I love you. Now use your voice, man of my heart, to say these same words to court me". This was repeated every time they met, and each time she was getting more certain that he was going to obey the command of her eyes. Whenever she said anything to him - a greeting, a comment on the weather, a question about work - her pleading tone expressed something different. It said, "Look at my body, trim and ready; look at my hair, long and sleek; look at my dress in flowers of love; listen to my stiletto heels, singing my journey to you. And, above all, smell the dear scent, feel the oil-smoothness of my dark natural skin, and look at my eyes with love welling over in tears. Now tell me what it is that I have not done, and I will do it in a special way for you. I do all this because of you. I open all the treasure of my heart to you. Why don't you say the words that you know must be said, now?"

All this had started at a farewell party. Before they sat down for the main meal, there was a long time of chatting while drinking. Whether it was due to some borrowed western manners, or some remorse that any human being, however selfish and cruel, must feel when face to face with innocent defenceless people he has always victimized, he could not say. But he noticed how the big bosses tried their best to show that they also were human beings, and, as such, were interested in at least every human being who attended the party. They moved about, and tried to talk to everyone. Such occasions only heightened loneliness in him; for the more these people talked to him, the more he realized that he was not one of them. Their love for the Mercedes, for the most expensive three piece suits, for frequent parties, and the way they grinned at you; all these and many more made him feel lonely during such occasions. He was not one of them, and that was why, despite having better qualifications, obtained after years of study, within the country and outside; and despite serving the corporation for many years, he could not head the section. Someone from the right region, and area, and family had to be brought in to head their section, even though all that the man could do was to read newspapers while slowly sipping coffee from a pot that never ran dry - sign one or two documents, even before reading the contents, and time and again dash off to various plots where people slaved at building his mansions.

These were the people he had to smile to in response to their lies. Being what they called a member of senior staff, he was obliged to attend these functions. He hated these functions. For this one, he had calculated that he would show up, and as the noise grew louder with more glasses being emptied, he would sneak out. Unfortunately, things did not go according to plan; for immediately he had walked in, a white circle seemed to have been described above his head, and a bird followed this through the crowd. It hopped and hopped till eventually it came to him, and - oh, the pert little thing, how it decided to confront him and confuse all his plans for that evening!

From then something haunted him. It was not some weird figure lunging in the dark, seeking poetic justice for some wrong committed or right omitted. What followed him everywhere, even to his bedroom and robbed him of all sleep, was her smile, her eyes, and her voice - these three together, that have formidable power to break through all masculine fortifications. He could not believe this new excitement; he believed he had successfully buried such excitement in his twenties. Now, moving towards forty, why the teenager excitement? He could not even sleep after the encounter; his whole body was cooked, his thoughts could not rise above the jelly, melting at the centre, sprawled on the bed. A long night of torment.

And when in the morning he goes shopping absent-mindedly at the superrette, picking a detergent and putting it back after remembering that he bought some only two days before, and doing this for several items, and then going to the till to pay for bread and a few other items, who does he see waiting for him outside if not her? And how he starts and almost drops his groceries. But she is composed, and sees such craven reactions that just confirm expectations, without showing that she has seen. She well knows that waiting for such men to speak first can be agonizing; they are so inhibited by some old-fashioned considerations.

"Ha-i!" she says with all warmth and a broad smile, while directly looking at him as he walks towards her; and almost clashing with his slow response, she adds: "I saw you while I was at the till."

He mumbles something, confused, avoiding looking directly at her face; and yet, to make sure she notices his interest, he comes to stand near her. She is alone, without the small girl. For a moment she is quiet, and this gives him time to compose himself a bit and think what to say:

"I didn't see you," he says apologetically, as if this is a serious crime; then adds: "I shouldn't have taken such a long time."

"No, I did not wait for long. Besides, where do I have to rush to on a Saturday," she kindly says, her words both reassuring and indicating that this chat will go on for quite a few minutes.

Many people pass by and raise a hand to greet him in a way that would not unduly disturb. Although somehow he really enjoys her company at such an awkward place, he feels he must go. But when he tells her that he is leaving for the market, she says she too is going there. His critic, whispering sneeringly to his self-conscious mind, tells him that he has deliberately invited her to the market, and that he would have had a whole weekend of disappointment if she had left him at that moment.

There is no time for internal debates. They go to the market together. Inside the market, amid the confusion that comes with so many sellers calling you to buy their commodities, she knows all the fruits and vegetable he wants to buy, chooses the best quality, and the right quantities to be divided between them; and he has to resist rather strongly to stop her paying for most of them. At the end of the shopping, he escorts her to her car, a little Toyota, looking almost new; and after furtive glances at her while she is putting the stuff she has bought in the boot and walking towards him as if she intends to gather him up in a farewell embrace, he still does not find what to finally say to her. She is in control of every passing minute, and after starting the engine, she reckons now is the time to release him from the tension of a sweet moment, by shouting, "Bye!" and slowly driving off, with a smile and waving of the right hand.

Such were the first meetings, and now he had even taken the bold step of inviting her to his house. What a commitment! It was inevitable because if he had not, he knew she was going to invite him, which would have been worse. And surely she must be busy preparing for coming now. While the prospect of her coming titillated him, there remained a deep-rooted anxiety that nothing seemed able to uproot. But whatever his feelings, he had to go now. For what would she think if he was not there? Of course she was the determined type that would wait for you, either in the car or inside the house if the servant opened the door; the type that would welcome you to your house with no show of disturbance. Now he started rehearsing what he would say to entertain her the time she would be there, although he knew she was likely to be the one entertaining him much of the time. It was again this fact that worried him. She seemed so confident in whatever she did, while so far he had simply drifted along. Because of this he was sometimes afraid of her, and shaking himself he would sometimes ask himself: where are you? He now imagined her entering the sitting-room; which chair would he show her? One furthest from him? No, she would not accept it; she would simply ignore his offer, and choose the most strategic position towards him. By inviting her for supper, had he not called for a final devastating blow, which would no longer leave him flapping about, like a pigeon in the trap? For imagine, at very close range, the combined effect of her smile, her eyes, and her voice!

He had indulged himself for too long. Now a coldness started pervading him. It was not the coldness due to exposure, although the sun had just set. He realized now that he had been mistaken; this brook was not Msambazintombi. There was fear in the darkening shrubs, in the dark serpentine water that no longer mirrored the sky; there was fear in the shrilling winds, the piping insects, and the whistling night birds. No, this brook was not Msambazintombi, where girls found enough peace to dance naked. This brook was Msambayifa.

Suddenly, he heard fast hoofs galloping to the rock. There was no time to turn and look. He leapt off the rock, crossed the brook, and dashed to the other bank. The goat was close behind him, charging with all its madness. He noticed that he was running without shoes on. This, however, turned out to be to his advantage, for his feet were fast and accurate: he could dart through the undergrowth, through the brambles, without getting entangled or scratched. He felt a certain unity within him: his whole being was wrapped in one thing, and by one thing - running, running still. Although he had had to apply effort when starting, now everything went on without any effort. His mind was clear. He even remembered his car, which he had left near some buildings on the road, after a girl of not more than fifteen years, carrying a baby in her hands, and a man of over forty years, who suddenly emerged from servants' quarters, after he heard his wife exchanging greetings with a man driving a car, had assured him it would be safe; and, although the couple had not asked for any payment, but were happy to be entrusted with looking after such a great item of property, he thanked them with a twenty kwacha note, which was more than four times what the husband earned in a day. And now he wondered why, after running for so long in what he believed was the right direction, he did not reach the place where he had left the car.

Meanwhile, a white Toyota 1.3, was slowly moving into his yard, slowly moving into the parking area; and after a reverse and forward movement with hard revving, it stopped, and a lady confidently emerged and stood beside the car. She was smart in a slinky, knee-length suit of light blue with faint vertical lines of red, orange and yellow, which made her look taller than she really was; and her sleek hair was pulled back and secured by a pin with a wide, hand-size blue flower, matching her suit and low-heeled shoes. A male servant ran out and in several times before coming to usher her into the house, at the time her patience had run out and she was already walking towards the door on her own. She had deliberately come thirty minutes before time in order to catch him just before he was ready for her.

"*Moni mayi,*" the servant greeted her, squatting near one of the armchairs, a respectful distance away from where she was standing, looking at photographs in a picture-frame, amongst which, prominently positioned, was that of an elderly woman, obviously his mother. *Bwana* has gone away, but he should be coming any time now," he told her after the response to his greetings, which she gave without very much looking away from the pictures. Although this was somewhat disappointing, she was determined to wait for him even for two hours; so she picked some magazines from the bookshelf and sat on one of the armchairs facing the gate. It was a large sitting-room and she noticed that the armchairs and the sofas were far apart. Meanwhile, after going out and closing the door to the corridor, the servant kept passing behind the door, to get as close as possible to the scent of feminine refinement, which filled the whole sitting-room - a rare blessing in this house.

Running in the forest, the goat was still behind him, chasing with ferocity. He had run for a long time now, but he did not feel any tiredness. It was getting dark, and yet the furious hoofs were still after him. Now and then he got a glimpse of the red eyes burning in the dark, close behind him; but he was still running. At first, his running seemed to follow a steady, but powerful rhythm, like that of reggae music of Bob Marley; or like the rhythm of *hlombe* clapping by Ngoni women, as men wielding clubs and shields dance the glorious *ingoma*, stumping the ground with a thud that can shift the earth. But now, with the relentless hoofs very close, the running followed a frantic rhythm, like that of *gule wamkulu*, the great dance, as bare palms break the skin of the *mbalule* drum. And running along the Msambayifa, with strong brakes in his knees, he was now skirting round a dark pool while saying to himself: "Goat of the wild, how many times have I run alone in the forest, run across brooks, skirting deep pools with slippery sides? And I am still running, running in the dark, running even for the whole night; running, for - why should I fall into the dark pool? Why should I be knocked down and trampled upon". The goat was close behind him, furiously chasing.

The End

Questions

1. Identify the physical features that form the surrounding of the meeting place of the person and the goat.
2. Copy the sentence from paragraph 1 that indicates that the sound of the water made the person feel lonely.
3. What signs are there that the goat does not have friendly intentions towards the person?
4. What is the normal occupation of the man in this story? How do you know?
5. The man observed one good thing about the goat. What is it? Why do you think this was a good thing?
6. It appears there are two voices inside the man. What type of advice do they usually give him?
7. Explain in your own words the meaning of the following phrase, "... the noise of the body is so loud, paralyzing the soul and drowning the spirit."
8. "... it is better to understand yourself and live." What signs are there in the story that this man does not really understand himself?
9. What do you understand by the term 'delusion'? What in the final encounter between the man and the goat shows that the man was under a delusion?
10. The story has two plots. One of them is presented in the form of flashback. Explain how it matches with the other one.
11. There are two major conflicts that take place in the story. What are they? Explain how they contribute to the climax of the story.
12. This story has a very deep kind of suspense. How is this achieved?
13. The major human characters of this story have no names. Instead the author

has just used pronouns for their names. Furthermore, one of the major characters is the goat. How does this technique affect the plot and the atmosphere of the story respectively?

14. Writers may use different styles to express themselves and Mbano has used a unique style in terms of the type of sentences and paragraphs which he writes. Critically look at this element and give your opinion as to how it affects the way you read the story and how the plot unfolds.

15. In your opinion, can this story take place in real life? Explain your answer giving concrete reasons.

DESPATCHED

Patrick Nyirenda

SHARP THRILLS of laughter in the rain woke me up. I was cold and shivering - the body felt like it was freezing. I sat up and pulled the remaining strands of the blanket to myself. The floor felt much harder and smelt more terrible than usual. I was pulling my feet closer when I knocked a bucket. It rolled over, spilling the contents on the already moist floor. A strong offensive odour of urea greeted my nose, threatening to suffocate me.

I got up on my feet and pulled out the shirt that I had plugged into the hole to keep the rain out. It was the only hole in the wall. It was there to serve as a window. It was barred by steel wire, although not even a baby's head could pop out. I raised my nostrils onto the hole and took a long deep breath of fresh air. Then I peeped out only to be greeted by darkness. The security lights in the fence were on. I must have been sleeping for more than four hours.

Various songs by creatures that delighted in the rain drew my attention. I was picking out the croaking of frogs and sifting the meaning of their hoarse tones when the door creaked open. It must be ages since it was last oiled; the hinges were getting rusty, I thought. A pair of large black boots filed the doorway announcing the arrival of one of the most dreaded moments of my life at Minga Prison. Sunday night was a time when every inmate was visited by a man calling himself Scorpion. Scorpion generously donated harsh doses of embarrassing pain. I wished I could sublimate.

"How is the day?" he asked.

"Bad," I snorted the reply.

"Bad? Why bad?" He sounded irritated by my rather frank response. I was surprised by his response because it was not the first time to tell him this truth. In any case, he never cared. Now I failed to see why my innocent and fair assessment of the day should irritate him at all. It made me panic.

"Ea a I... I... mean... the rain... eh... I am terribly cold sir... its awful here," I hesitantly fumbled an explanation.

"Hm mm!" he mumbled.

Silence followed. I longed to have a look at the man's face but I was never permitted. I believed no one was. Scorpion was a peculiar sort of person. He often laughed at scenes nobody saw humuor in. I sometimes felt he was only trying to pretend sanity in his sadistic life. His silence now made me remember the night when he had asked me to hold his 'thing' in my hands. I was sneezing badly then and each time I lifted the hands to my face it was his thing bobbing there! He went on to urinate in my palms and laughed his lungs out. Now I dreaded to think he was formulating another act of torment. His actions were aimed at reducing a person to nothing but a shred of muslin cloth!

"You must be very very ungrateful Mr. Kameta." He said breaking the silence.

I remained silent. Fear took charge of the corners of my body. I imagined him striking his famous "Venomous Blow." Although I did not know what it was but the way he boasted about it was enough to cause terror. "That will be the end of you." I recalled him saying. According to Scorpion nobody ever survived the blow. Whatever it was I could not imagine what would happen if it was unleashed on me.

"Look you buffoon! You have the best accommodation at this place, you get the utmost treatment and maximum respect. Have you ever danced naked before school girls?" He asked in a tone that suggested I was about to dance. I felt scared. My stomach seemed to melt at the idea of an adult: some of them fathers and others grandfathers, parading before a bunch of school girls who would be screaming with laughter.

"No," I promptly said.

"You have the largest room here and the choicest food available yet you say it's awful here! Perhaps you should be transferred to Wing B so that you can have friends around you." He suggested. The suggestion made me uneasy. I started feeling unthankful to Scorpion.

"No! Please don't," I protested but the door creaked shut and darkness swallowed the strange figure of Scorpion. He was gone. I was now alone staring at the darkness while strange imaginations of Wing B whizzed in my mind. I revisited tales about the place which I heard when I was entering the life of Minga. My knowledge has been updated since I was locked up in cell X639.

I settled down on the floor. I no longer felt the heavy odour of urea. My thoughts lingered on the accusations Scorpion had levelled at me. My reasoning was coming into line but I failed to accept the privileges that Scorpion said I had. He knew that I ate only once in two days. The meal itself was prepared for pigs and only diverted to my cell. My thoughts returned to the impending transfer. Going to Wing B made me feel scared. I felt like jumping over a cliff to die and forget about the whole ordeal or drink the contents of the bucket in my cell to poison myself to death. I picked up the bucket quickly, raised it to the mouth and waited for the contents to flow in, but no single drop did. It was empty! I fumed at myself for having overturned the bucket in the first place. I was putting it down when it occurred to me that I could jump off the bucket and break my legs. I tried to stand on the inverted bucket but my head hit the roof before I could stand straight. Hopeless and helpless I retreated to my corner waiting for Scorpion to do as it pleased him.

But the man did not return. I gave up waiting. My mind wandered off into the time I had been in this prison. I slowly flipped through memories of the very first days. Upon arrival I was told by inmates that I was not going to walk out of cell X639 breathing. Thus, when I went in, I was already dead. I had no hope of survival. But I began to gather hope of living on after four years in the cell.

The sound of a lady's shoe in the corridor alerted me. I heard the key turn and the door creak open. I was called out for the first time in four years. It was scaring. I knew I was leaving never to return to my beloved place again. I quivered my way out while putting on the wet shirt. I was astonished to meet a sturdy half naked woman. She only wore a mini-skirt and a brassiere! Her navel was in the open. I stepped back unsure of the sight before me. She saw my discomfort. She took me by hand and led me out assuring me that nothing was amiss. I followed reluctantly. Years had passed since I was last treated to such an onerous occasion - feasting my eyes on a woman's figure bouncing before me. Strong currents rose from various parts of my body almost jamming the body system.

"I know you are afraid but I want to assure you of no harm from me!" She said turning around to show me a broad smile.

Deep down I was perturbed but I chose to maintain my silence, unsure of the strange happening. My voice was safely stacked away in dungeons of suspicion and disbelief.

"I want you to have a good time with Nelisa. Feel free please." She was drawing close, I panicked. Her left hand stretched out giving my beard a soft stroke. I noticed for the first time that my beard was in dire need of a shave. I felt ashamed.

All sorts of fears rammed into my mind. I thought she was plotting my fall. On the other hand I felt she was only helping herself on inmates and it was now my turn. But the thought that Scorpion was hiding somewhere watching me fall into his trap made me powerless and helpless. I gathered courage and spoke out.

"Woman, who are you?"

"What a question!" she retorted

She looked at me searchingly before pronouncing her name. "Nelisa."

"Nelisa," I repeated the name to myself trying to figure out where I had heard such a name. I looked at her.

"What do you want from me?" I asked remembering to be suspicious.

"You are not a child, are you?" She was not amused by my probing.

"Woman I know you!" I declared much to her astonishment. She looked at me stunned.

"Yes, I know you have been sent. You are working for Scorpion," I went on.

"You don't know me," she said calmly adding that I should stop the stupid behaviour I was engaging in. She assured me that all she wanted was to give me a nice time, to make me forget the troubled times of prison life. She embraced me but I told myself to stand frozen. For a moment I did, but nature

took charge, passionate currents surging in my veins obliterated all reason. M
arms moved and took their natural place around her waist. I was lost in the he
of the moment when the door burst open. A furious Scorpion stared at us. M
heart ceased. I grew cold, all the charged muscles slithered into death. TI
world was a crucible. Tears rolled down my cheeks as I was dragged away.

Though Scorpion said nothing I could hear him swear at me. He shoved m
against a door and my forehead bumped into its woodwork. Above was writte
Punishment Cell. I turned my head to see what Scorpion meant. Surely he w
not posting me to my death that early. He opened the door violently and pushe
me in, asking me to find a chair to sit on. I stumbled on it in the darkness. I
switched on the light and asked me to prepare for my death. "This is the famo
electric chair," he boasted. He ripped off my clothes and burst out laughir
before forcing me to go into the room.

I braced for my death and sat still in the chair, just to show Scorpion that I w
no longer scared of death. Satisfied that all was ready he closed the door behir
him, leaving me alone. He switched off the lights. I could see Nelisa peep
me through a glass in the door. I could not make out what was on her mind, y
I chose to believe she was praying for my safe journey to heaven. Scorpior
voice boomed through the darkness.

"Elton Kameta. Good bye." He began to count down and told me to close r
eyes when the count reaches 1. I wanted to cry out for help but the urgency
a prayer dashed in. I rushed through a prayer and said "Amen". When the cot
was at 3. I sat frozen. I could hear my breath no longer and then tried to op
my eyes. Nothing happened. I didn't hear the count stop. I eased myself in t
chair but there was no current. Impatient. I struggled out of the chair. I f
strapped hands and legs. I tried to get up. I stumbled into a bucket spilling t
contents over my worn out blanket. I was still in cell X639.

The End

Questions

1. Where do you think the contents of the bucket that is knocked over in pa
   graph 1 came from?
2. Who is Scorpion? How do you know?

3. "You must be very very ungrateful Mr. Kameta." What does Scorpion mean by these words?
4. What do you think were the real intentions of Nelisa?
5. Where was Kameta taken to by Scorpion after Kameta's encounter with Nelisa and why?
6. In groups, prepare a sketch based on the events in this story and perform it to your class.
7. One of the characteristics of a good short story is its use of figurative language. Identify examples of figurative language in this story and explain how it has been used.
8. This story is characterised by its intensive use of suspense. When does the suspense reach its highest intensity? Give examples of occassions which represent this suspense.
9. At some point the author hints that the major character who is also the prisoner is going to get into more trouble through his interaction with Nelisa. Find the hint that foreshadows this trouble.
10. We are not told whether the prisoner was convicted or not but it seems the writer is interested in showing the evils of prison life. List five examples of such evils and explain why they are evils.
11. Malawian prisons were known for their illtreatment of inmates during Dr. Banda's reign. Find out more from people who have ever spent their lives in prison or those who know something about life in a Malawian prison and compare your findings with the illtreatment of prisoners in this story.
12. The author uses the first person point of view to narrate the story. Why is the first person point of view effective for developing the plot of this story?

WHISPERS

Max J Iphani

THAT IS what he normally did. He cleaned the chalkboard before greeting them. They wondered why he did so all the time. Did he have to do it? After all, he rarely wrote anything on the board. However, nobody could dare ask him why. It was not worth the risk. You had to be careful with what you did or said during his lessons. He could easily humiliate you.

Before they entered the classroom, they often gathered outside and discussed the impending ordeal. "The course is too difficult," they would say, "and the lecturer is a bore," was their consensus. They complained that the course demanded too much of their attention, what with the reading lists which were given out at the end of each lesson and the writing assignments which they had to turn in at the beginning of each lesson. All these coupled with the behaviour of the lecturer made their life difficult.

Today, it is the same. They watch him push the duster across the board in quick circular motions with his right hand. He has not spoken yet. He is wearing a large shirt and a tight fitting pair of jeans. He has a digital wrist watch whose chain is rather too big for his thin hand. As he cleans the board, the chain of the watch makes a clinking sound.

In his absence, especially when he has missed his hour, which he rarely did, some courageous students sometimes imitated his manners, exaggerating a bit here and there and in the process drawing a lot of laughter from the other students. Doing this was not only a source of fun and joy but also satisfaction. They felt heroic.

Often, during a lesson, what attracted their attention was not so much what he said as his appearance. They never really got tired of looking at him. He had a small pea-shaped head. His ears, eyes, and nose were all small. His hair, was short and stunted. It looked so tough that the students wondered whether he did not find combing it painful. One young man in this class often commented that the hair looked like a swarm of small flies riding on the lecturer's head. The comment was repeated so often that it should have long lost its appeal had it not been for the very unusual shape of the lecturer's head.

The instructor was tall and thin. He looked rigid and stiff, with wiry hands and legs. Because he was so small, there was disagreement among students as to the size of his heart, of all things. The majority said that the heart must be really small, otherwise, they argued, how could it fit in that small trunk. Those who opposed this view claimed that human nature was such that the smaller the person, the larger the heart. Another feature of special interest to the students was the lecturer's big mouth, which he was in the habit of keeping wide open.

Now the instructor has finished wiping the chalk board and is looking at his

94

students with his small eyes. His eyes have a certain peculiar quality which, when they fall on you, make you feel that something terrible is going to happen to you. So when he looks at them like this, they avoid his eyes. Some students look down. Others look outside through the window at no specific object. After greeting them, he straight away starts delivering his lesson.

"Now ladies and gentlemen, last time I was telling you that character portrayal cannot be done with any verisimilitude. In a short story, you need to be economical, terse, direct, lucid ..."

"Excuse me sir, I've got a question."

"This is the greatest difference between a novel and a short story. The ..."

"Excuse me sir, I've got a question."

"The things you look for in a short story ... anybody wants to comment?"

"No, it's a question."

"OK, what's your question?"

"What's vere.. versim.. the word you just mentioned in your explanation?"

"This is difficult to believe. I didn't expect that question from this class. Such questions should not drag us on our progress with the syllabus. This is a university, you know."

"But sir, we've never..."

"The point I want to emphasize here is that you can't meaningfully talk about character portrayal in a short story. You can't say this character is flat or round or indeed trapezoid." He breaks the outflow with a metallic laughter that jerks his whole body. And then he continues.

"These are just basics which you should be familiar with. You did literature in form four, didn't you?"

"Yes, but that doesn't..."

"That's fine, then. You will find these things easy. Studying these novels will be much easier than the short stories we have just covered. OK. Now that we've clarified that, let me tell you that in this course we shall mostly depend on the phenomenological, existentialist and the archetypal approaches to study our novels. I'll assume that you have come across and fully studied these terms in your own reading. And ..."

As the lecturer is about to continue, a few of the students hiss in anger. Somebody whispers to himself: "who'd have the damn interest in these damn terms anyway."

But the learned instructor is excited about impressing his students, the lazy lot. The whispers that he hears are a sign that he has won their hearts.

"And I will not waste your time and of course my precious time defining these terms for you. OK. We'll also do structuralism and Freudian studies of the last three novels. That should take us to the end of the semester."

One or two people whisper in disbelief. One of the students sitting at the back whispers to the one in front of him: "Does he himself believe what he is saying?" "Where will this lead us?"

His friend whispers back: "No one knows. The guy is insane, you still didn't know?"

The lecturer has noticed the blankness on the faces in front of him. They are faces which show no understanding at all. He inwardly feels happy that they find the material tough. It shows that now they know that he mastered difficult stuff. It is important that they should know this, if they are going to respect him.

"Ladies and gentlemen. I'm amazed, really shocked. Honestly, I'm amazed. You look at me with blank expressions on your faces. Your lack of knowledge of the most basic facts, theories and principles amazes me."

He pauses a little to let the statement sink into their heads. But this time they are exchanging whispers. The two students who always sit together at the back and rarely speak in class are whispering as well. One of them says: "He should be more amazed that after his teaching us all this time, we still do not know the most basic,... whatever he calls them."

"Have you done any psychology?"

Someone answers, "no", and is about to ask of what relevance psychology is to literature, when the others murmur, almost loudly, things of which the gist is something like: "did he come here only to ask us what we don't know and not to teach us?"

"Yes, I can see from your faces. You have no idea at all what psychology is all about. But it's high time you did some in-depth psychological studies. Then you'd find interesting the works by our theorists in this course, Carl Jung and Sigmund Freud. Characterisation in stories is really a matter of psychology. If

96

you haven't been trained in psychology, the novels we want to study in this course will not make much sense. A bit of knowledge about Gestalt, behaviourism, classical conditioning and Pieget would help you a lot."

The students stare at the lecturer and hiss under their breath.

"Has anybody here heard about Gestalt? No, nobody? Then it's easy to find this course difficult."

"By the way, you also appear to me to have no idea what philosophy is. Do you ever spend anytime reading philosophical works? Because to understand... to appreciate the theme of the first novel we will deal with, you need at least to read Russell, Kant, Hobbes, Hegel or even Fueuberch. These are not dispensable. The technique which Ngugi uses is one that Joseph Conrad and Thomas Hardy used heavily. So to understand Ngugi fully you could also have a go at the novels by these two authors. I expected students at this level to have read these masterpieces by great writers."

As he speaks, his thin hands go through many swishing motions. He stands erect and straight. This actually makes his stiffness more pronounced. His small eyes stare at the students and become even smaller as he talks. The students wonder, and have always done so, whether with such small eyes he can really see well. One student stands and says:

"It seems, sir, you don't know our problems."

"The truth is you'd do yourself some good if you read these works I've just mentioned. Otherwise ..."

"Excuse me sir, we just don't have the time to read such books. Anyway, the books you have mentioned are not available anywhere in this country."

The students are becoming more courageous, as another student whispers almost too audibly: "And I just don't have any speck of interest in his great writers. Thomas Hardy bores me like snails."

"What? No time? You must be joking my friends."

There is another whisper just near the lecturer. Somebody says to his neighbour: "I didn't know we were his friends."

But this learned lecturer is too absorbed to hear the remark. "If you had known how I struggled to get my second degree. I sweated. I..."

Another whisper, again from the one in front: "He is talking about his second, this is only our first."

"Anyway, the novel we will deal with first resembles the latest novel by Kwakuvi Azasu. It would be an interesting study to compare this novel with Azasu's *The Stool*." Has anybody here read *The Stool* by Azasu? When the instructor gets no response, he goes ahead.

"You are not up to date fellows. What do you do with your book allowance? You can't afford a Drumbeat once a month?"

More whispers: "Does he give us any allowances?"

The student who sits in front and near the instructor stands up: "It's just too little. We cannot afford all the important books. And sir, it doesn't necessarily follow that when you buy one book per month, you will buy *The Stool*."

The lecturer, for the first time this morning, walks to the back of the room without once looking back or sideways, and then walks back to the front, still very stiff and erect.

"No, ladies and gentlemen. You are being unrealistic. With the same amount of money I could buy a lot of things. Why? You people are just thoughtless."

At this, the whole class boos and murmurs. They are now getting less careful about what they are saying. So many of them want to speak at the same time. If he had been more attentive, the learned lecturer would have heard things like "The fellow is insane," "look at the big mouth,"; "if I had my catapult, I would have slotted a stone or two in that yawning hole,"; "no, I would smash the bean on his neck,"; "with a razor, I would enlarge his eyes". Everybody is excited and a powerful noise results.

After sometime a student who is normally silent stands up to address her lecturer. The class quietens to listen to what she is going to say.

"Sir, with your permission, I would like to share with you my opinion about you and the way you have conducted this course. If you can allow me, sir, I want to let you know that you personally offend me, and I believe everybody else here, when you treat us like illiterates. Your boasting about your great learning is really uncalled for and without foundation. You give us endless lists of reading and writing assignments, not because you want to help us to learn, but because you want us to suffer in this college. This is malicious. When you come to this lesson you mention many terms, theories and books with the sole intention of dazzling us. This is sickening, at least it nauseates me. Your view of life is the narrowest that I have ever encountered. You fail to see ..."

There is a lot of handclapping and whistling from the students. They never thought she could speak so well. The lecturer did not expect that things could come to this and he is visibly shaken. He looks at his digital wrist watch. There is still fifteen minutes to go, but the obvious signs of an impending commotion cannot be ignored.

"OK. Ladies and gentlemen, for today, let's stop there." He goes out of the room in quick rigid strides. His walk out is greeted with victorious cheering and jeering by students.

"For the first time in my life, I enjoyed this man's lesson. You really reduced him my friend." The silent girl who had spoken is being congratulated and just manages to resist being carried shoulder high.

"Now you have told him what we think. I feel great."

Another student says: "The fool thinks that each one of us wants to get a masters."

Another one adds: "He has the most jaundiced view of life. I just want my first degree and then I will go and struggle for a job, that's all. That's why I don't want to read like a Ph.D. student."

"I agree with you. I particularly loathe the way my essay comes back from him, completely mutilated."

"You are better off, comrade. He writes his own essay and superimposes it on mine. I can't write what's in his head, you know. So he writes it for me."

"As for me, I don't like this course at all. My favourite courses are discourse analysis, demography and literary theory."

"That's a queer combination. No wonder you find this course difficult."

One by one, the students walk out of the classroom, feeling a deep sense of victory and satisfaction. It was like they had just conquered the Ngwazi himself.

The End

Questions

1. What did the lecturer usually do when he entered the classroom?
2. What did the students do in the absence of the lecturer?
3. Explain why the students never really got tired of looking at their lecturer.
4. What is the hair on the lecturer's head compared to?
5. In what way would you say that the lecturer's physical appearance is related to his manners?
6. What do you think the lecturer should change in order to become a good teacher?
7. Conduct a debate on whether the students' conduct was good or not.
8. In what two main tenses is this story told? Which parts of the story is each tense used to tell?
9. The narrator uses the third person point of view. How does this affect the way plot unfolds?
10. Tension develops between the lecturer and the students. Mention the stages of this development. How does the third person point of view affect the development of this tension.
11. What is the general atmosphere in this short story?
12. Though there are many people in this story, one can say that there are two major characters. Explain how this is the case.
13. The story is dominated by the use of dialogue between the class and the lecturer as well as between students. This is an acceptable style in modern literature. In your opinion what does the dialogue contribute to the story as a whole?

THE DEADLY SPEAR

Mike Sambalikagwa Mvona

NACHAWE HAD no alternative but to go back home. His failing to get back would plunge his clan and indeed the entire village of Likhula into chaos. After his father, it was he who could patch up things together. The letter had said so. Although he was not the first born in his father's family, who also happened to be village headman Likhula, Nachawe was considered an automatic heir to the throne.

This brought jealousy from his brothers. Although no one talked to him openly, Nachawe knew his life was at stake. There was anger and tension generated from all corners of the family. That is why without telling anyone, even his beloved father and mother, he fled to South Africa. He never wrote any letter home to tell them where he was or what he was doing.

Nachawe settled in fast in this foreign country. He received rapid promotions on his job with a mining company. He then married a woman from there, a Sotho by tribe. All was well for him and his family and he forgot about his home. He forgot about the miseries of his home village and the hatred of his brothers.

As time went by, he began to see his father in his dreams asking him why he had left home without a word. The father was asking him why he was not sharing with his home what he had found. Nachawe struggled to make a decision on what he should do. He gathered courage and wrote his parents telling them where he was and the job he was doing.

Two months passed and then he got a letter in reply to his. It was a fat envelope with enclosures from his friends and relatives telling him that they were all excited to hear that he is a big bwana on his job. His parents told him how they celebrated when they received his letter. They brew beer and cooked to celebrate that he was still alive and on an important job. Songs were composed and sung in his honour. However, none of the letters mentioned about his wife though he had introduced her in his letter. Not even his father said anything about her.

Nachawe began to think what that meant. He knew that by the customs of Likhula, no one was allowed to marry outside his village let alone another country. He was sure they had just postponed talking about it and their next letter would condemn him. However, at least for now he had the chance to think more seriously about his decision. By the customs of his village, he was a traitor.

Nachawe felt that no one had the right to dictate his life. No one had to decide for him what he was to do or whom he should marry. Actually, this is one of the reasons that made him leave his village in the first instance. He wanted to be left alone and live in peace. If it were not for the appearance of his father in his dreams he would not have written home. But even now, should they attack him for his marriage, he would never write them again.

Time passed on very fast. Nachawe was now getting old. He had been promoted several times again and was now in an administrative post at the company headquarters in Johannesburg. He was very successful. They had three children with his wife. He began to think how he could take all this wealth and his children back to his home country and village. He wanted, when he got home, never to have anything to do with his father's estate but live on his own wealth. He didn't want to fight with his brothers and relatives. Of course his father was rich. He had inherited the wealth from his uncle who served in the Kings African Rifles in Seychelles and India. Much of this wealth was hidden. Not even Nachawe's mother knew how much money there was or where it was being kept.

It was while he was thinking of going back home that he received another letter from his father. It read:

My Son,

It was time you came back home to put things together. I have very little time left to live now. If you fail to come, Likhula will fall apart and your brothers will rise against each other. When you come, share the assets I am leaving behind with your brothers and sisters. If you don't want to become chief, still come to distribute what I am leaving behind. In a separate note I have given you the directions on how to find where the money is. Destroy this note after reading it in case...

The note said,

'Dig at the far right hand corner of my private hut. You will find two boxes stacked with money. The box marked X should be shared between your brothers, your mother and sisters. The box marked N is yours. As chief you need this. I love you my son.'

Likhula

Nachawe had no choice now but to leave immediately for home. Not that the money he was going to inherit meant much to him but to receive the final blessings from his father before he died. He wanted him to see what grandchildren he had produced for him. He will definitely be excited to see the grandchildren.

He decided he would just share all the money among his brothers, sisters and mother and would take nothing himself. He had enough to keep him and his children for the rest of their lives. He would not be worried with his father's money. He would give the largest share to his mother.

He picked up his belongings and together with his first son, he started for home in his car. He would drive through Zimbabwe and Mozambique.

After three days of driving, he was at the border to enter his country. He felt excited. After the border formalities, he was heading to Likhula. In the blazing sun on this dry weather road, he drove his automatic BMW as people on foot waved to him though they didn't know him. He couldn't tell if they were waving at the car or at him. Children stopped playing to see such a beautiful car they had never seen before. They marvelled.

Eventually, he pulled up at his father's house and the crowd that was gathered there parted to give room for the car. Men wore somber faces and inside Likhula's house crying could be heard. Could he be dead? When did he die? He asked himself hoping strongly that he was alive. There was excitement and people especially the elderly, gathered around the car to see who this important person had come to a funeral in their village.

"It's Mbwiye," some whispered immediately they had recognized him. "Mbwiye Nachawe," some sobbed as others cried the name out. Some women cried louder as others smiled broadly. Some came out to hug him.

Twelve years was long enough for one to forget the village and its people. Nachawe was taken to the Chief's official house where his father lay dead. The young man grieved uncontrollably.

Later, he was taken to the Chief's private house where a band of elderly men and women were waiting for him. Amongst them were his four brothers and two sisters.

Nachawe was ushered to the far corner where the letter from his father had disclosed the fortune was buried. One elderly woman rose and handed him a chicken bone. As per custom, Nachawe rubbed the chicken bone with both hands and then handed it back to the woman. This ritual was meant to quieten the spirit of the dead. The spirit in turn examined the purity of the one to perform the ritual. There was total silence. No one coughed or said anything. When nothing happened, they proceeded with the ceremony.

"Is it well where you are coming from my son?" One elderly woman, the sister to the deceased said, inquiring on behalf of the group.

"It is well," he answered. "When I received the letter from my father ...," he continued, "I said I should not delay but go quickly. Fortunately, the car we used did not give us any problems on the way. However, from the dreams I had on the way, I felt not all was well here or back where I was coming from. When I entered the village, I noticed Likhula weeping and knew that the dreams were correct. A sad situation indeed."

"It is bad indeed," everyone chorused.

Many were happy with the fact that he had not forgotten the traditions. His wise sayings echoed what he had been taught from youth. "He has not forgotten the ways of the tribe though he left while he was only a toddler. Yet he lives right inside their city eating with the white man, speaking his language," an old man that had been quiet all through the ceremony mused afterwards. However, his elder brother was not amused at all. He hated every single bit of the moment and wondered why Nachawe had decided to come back now that the father was dead. He was particularly annoyed when Nachawe said that the father had written him before he died. He wondered to himself what he had written about. He remembered that no one knew for sure where the money was hidden and how much of it there was.

"Well, your father died of asthma," the aunt continued. "He was never free from it any way. Only that there were times he felt better. This season after the harvest, as the sun crept across the Muleya, he said this to your mother, 'Remind Mbwiye when he comes back home from the gold mines what I said to him'. Is that not so you who were there," she asked for confirmation. "You are right," two gentlemen sitting next to Nachawe spoke together. "Actually he wished he spoke to you in person. He always hoped you would come back home before he died," the aunt said. "It is good sometimes to visit home even if you want to stay away from home. But we understand. Now that we have said all this, let us go out. People are waiting for us. We have taken too long in here. Let us go and bury the dead."

A spear and a shield were given to Nachawe to signify that he is the heir. The youthful member of the group was asked to go and beat the drum to show they were ready for burial rites. But before the man could go away, the elder brother asked if they would not have the child that Nachawe had brought with him purified since he had foreign blood in him. "Has it become part of our tradition to simply accept anything that comes into our village. This blood is not the pure blood of Likhula unless we purify it," he said with emphasis. Nachawe seethed inside. He knew his brothers would be out to discredit him and frustrate anything that sought to elevate him as an heir to the throne.

No one answered the brother's call. One man stood and started out and the rest followed with Nachawe holding the spear and the shield as a warrior. He advanced into the dancing arena when the drum sounded as demanded by custom. There was ululating as the mjiri dance started. It was the custom of the village that if the Chief's body is being buried there must be a mjiri to mark the exit of the old chief and entry of the new one. It was a handover ceremony. The other relatives joined in after the drum signalled their time after which the coffin would be brought out to join the throng which would then turn into a procession to the graveyard. The new chief would lead the procession to the graveyard. Before the coffin could be picked up from inside the hut to come out, there would be the sound of a horn from the top of Muleya hill and at that sound, all the dancers would throw into the air their spears with a loud shout and in that moment, the coffin would be quickly brought out to join the dance.

The horn was sounded and a loud shout went forth as the spears went up in all directions. There were clicking sounds in the air as some of the spears clashed in mid-air. Some spears did not go up into the air. No one noticed except Nachawe. But it was too late. In the twinkling of an eye, the spear landed and he screamed. It came from the hand of his brother. It dug in and he fell down as people ran to pick him up. He sprawled full length on the ground and there was wild crying. Women tore on themselves as men tried to save the situation. He was rushed into the house where within seconds of examinations, he was pronounced dead. No one wanted to say who had done it. Suspicions and silence.

After burial of the two chiefs, which was not accompanied by the mjiri and the usual funeral rites, the elder brother searched through the luggage of his brother for any valuables. He didn't find much except the letter. It said there was a note explaining where to find the money. He rummaged through the luggage again but could not get it. No one could help. He felt depressed and hopeless and wished he had not killed him.

The End

105

Questions

1. "Nachawe had no alternative but to go back home." Where was he?
2. Why did Nachawe leave his village?
3. What prompted him to go back home?
4. Why was Nachawe's brother not happy to see him back?
5. Who do you think killed Nachawe? Why do you think this person killed Nachawe?
6. Explain why it was a great mistake to kill Nachawe?
7. Do you like this story? Give reasons.
8. Though the story does not start with "Once upon a time..." the plot of this story is folklorick. Do you agree? Explain from the story itself.
9. From what you have read what are the character traits of Nachawe?
10. What is the setting of the story? Support your answer with evidence from the story.
11. Because of its folklorick nature, the story presents some activities which are not realistic. Give as many examples of these activities as possible.

A PARTY FOR THE DEAD

Steve Chimombo

I WAS going over the guest list for the hundredth time when Sokole, a work-mate and friend, walked into my office. His corrugated forehead made me sit up.

"Mtunduwatha is dead!"

"What?!" I was paralysed. Mtunduwatha was one of the up-and-coming young executives.

"Car accident."

It had to be a car accident. Mtunduwatha was in his mid-thirties, as healthy as they come. It was only yesterday, I had been sprinting to catch another colleague in the corridor when I bumped into him.

"Oh, so you're still strong enough to run?" he had said as he joined me for a few steps.

"I can marathon you to hell and back," I cracked breathlessly as I rushed past. I was a good fifteen years older than him.

"No! It can't be true!" I said hoarsely.

"I actually saw the car being towed in by the police." Sokole's shoulders convulsed.

"But I saw him yesterday afternoon, before knocking off."

"It happened last night."

"Where?"

He told me.

"What are the funeral arrangements?"

"We don't know as yet. We're waiting for the boss to tell us."

Sokole's footsteps echoed mournfully in the corridor as he walked out. I slumped in my seat.

My wife and I had both liked Mtunduwatha. We had invited his family over several times for dinner or drinks. They were coming to the party on Saturday, too.

"We'll have to cancel our party," I said to an empty office, helpless.

Suddenly the full implications of Mtunduwatha's death hit me, and I was overwhelmed by conflicting emotions.

It had taken us a long time to organize the party. I remembered the long list of guests, inclusions, exclusions, deletions, arguments with my wife on doubtful names of the people we didn't exactly like or know, but who for some reason or another we had to invite.

The party was going to be a big social event, with friends from all over the country meeting after long separations. We had spent a lot of money too, to make sure everyone enjoyed themselves. It was to be the party of the year.

Although it was one in a series of other Christmas festivities, we had selected this particular Saturday because it was not too near Christmas to compete with other parties. It was just close enough to Christmas to be part of the season's spirit, but far enough to be an independent event.

And here was Mtunduwatha dying on us just three days before the big occasion. Three quarters of our guests would be going to the funeral.

"Will you go to his village for the burial?" my wife sobbed when I phoned her.

"I'll have to. He was like a brother."

My minor prayer had been that it wouldn't rain on Saturday, to make the party a wet and muddy affair. The house could not accommodate the more than one hundred guests. That is why I had arranged for the whole garden to be used for clusters of guests to sit around, leaving the lounge free for dancing.

My major prayer had been that my old, ailing aunt would not die during the week. She had been in and out of hospital during the past four months. I would obviously have had to cancel the party if she had died. She hadn't, but Mtunduwatha had. I had not anticipated the sabotage coming from within my office.

I settled down to do some phoning. I had to ring some one hundred numbers before knocking off.

"Hello?"

"You got your invitation?"

"I've got it right in front of me. My wife and I are looking forward to ..."

"Exactly. We've had to cancel it."

"What happened?"

"Mtunduwatha is dead."

Dead silence. Then, "It can't be." My reiteration.

"I know several people are dying all over the place," one of them said, "and it's cruel to say it but he was one of those young men you don't imagine dying at this time."

It was the same ritual for the other names. Well, with slight variations.

"I've been told already," one guest said.

"Oh?"

"He happens to be a cousin of mine, so they told me early."

The most difficult ones were those not on the phone.

"This telephone is temporarily out of order." I wondered why. Unpaid bills? Had they gone out of town and disconnected to prevent the servants from using it? How was I going to get in touch with them before Saturday? For one family, I had to leave messages in three different hotels I knew they frequented, on the off chance they would get one.

I drove round personally to those in town. I sent messages to others by word of mouth, or left notes. By lunch time I was in a daze.

"He's messed up our party," I said at table.

"Think of the mess his wife is in," my wife reminded me.

Mtunduwatha had left two kids: ten and twelve, a boy and a girl.

We ate in silence. I was thinking of the several kilos of pork, chicken, peanuts; litres of beer, wine, and spirits, in various parts of the house.

"When are we going to eat the cake?" one of my kids asked. We had left the huge cake on the dining table for lack of space in the kitchen.

"We can start right now," my wife said. "Otherwise it will go bad."

She took off the foil. My stomach turned as I saw all the almonds and dried fruit embedded in the cake. I looked away.

"What are we going to do with all the food?"

"Put it in a freezer. It can keep for at least three months."

"We haven't got a freezer that big."

"We've got friends who can help us out."

"What are we going do to with it during the three months? We can't have chicken and pork everyday. They'll start clucking and honking through our ears and noses within a fortnight."

"We're still going to hold the party, aren't we?"

"The earliest I can think of is in the Easter vacation. Say Good Friday?"

"I don't approve of parties on Good Friday. In any case, it's too far away. We can still have it in January."

"It's anticlimactic to hold a party after Christmas and the New Year. People are fed up with everything."

"They may be bored, but not fed up. People love parties. After all, we're asking them to come and wine, dine, and dance at our own expense."

We leave the house of the deceased in a very orderly manner.

It is not far to the graveyard, as we discover before long. However, it seems further as, every minute or so, brown hands stop all progress to relieve the bearers carrying the coffin. Some of the brown hands I recognize as belonging to the guests who were supposed to be coming to our party this evening. Instead of holding wine glasses or snacks they carry the brass handles of the coffin in tight, nervous, sorrowful grip, staring gloomily ahead. Instead of swaying to the rhythm of dance music, they march the slow measured step of grief, with funeral hymns punctuating each step as the cortege nears the graveyard. Instead of the noisy chatter and guffaws of the inebriated, it is the sobbing, wailing, choking, nose-blowing that mix with the mournful melodies surrounding me. I shake my head again in disbelief.

Bare brown feet toast in the hot dry dust of the pathway. The sun is so hot even the rubber shoes I am wearing do not protect me. Sweat pours down from every imaginable pore. It makes me think ahead to the weekend at the lake I am taking my family to between Christmas and the New Year. Just to get away from the bouts of elation and sorrow we seem to be alternately wallowing in.

"What are you celebrating?" I had asked Sokole in the staff room. He was buying a round of drinks for the accountant, executive secretary, and administrative officer, all sitting at a corner table.

"We're organizing the staff Christmas party."

"I hope it's not for this Saturday. That's reserved for mine."

"Don't worry!" Sokole had grinned. "We all know about your big party. Nothing could disturb that one. This is for next week."

"There seem to be too many parties this year."

"It's to compensate for all the funerals we've been attending lately."

We had both laughed, although it was no laughing matter. We had lost four staff members: two from mysterious causes, and two because of car accidents. A party or two would surely console some depressed souls.

We enter the graveyard, recently cleared of a tangle of grass and shrubs for the new inmate. I see mango, cassava, and sugarcane peels, snacks for the grave diggers, hastily scattered to disguise the fact that there had been a feast before our arrival. It reminds me of an initiation song:

The nalimvimvi is not fat from birth.

He feeds on funeral food.

At the rate we are losing our young men, some of the regular grave diggers would be putting on as much weight as the corpulent insect of the song. It's only the earth, as another song goes, that doesn't get fat from feeding on so many corpses.

It is an extensive graveyard. The more than mile long procession is easily contained in the spaces between the mounds, concrete slabs, and passages where more bodies will eventually be buried. It is also an ancient graveyard, judging not only from some of the now indeciphered writings on the stones or crosses but also from the gnarled trunks and branches of some of the trees shading the graves. The mourners gratefully flee from the pitiless sun to the shade of the old trees away. Even the reverend in his robes with his entourage retire to the nearest tree after his dust to dust, ashes to ashes, to wait for the mountain of earth to be returned to the hole once the coffin has been lowered.

"What are you celebrating?" my friends had kept asking upon receiving the invitation.

"Can't I hold a party without celebrating something?" I kept retorting.

"Most people organizing parties ask their friends to contribute some money first and then invite them as guests. Here you are inviting half the country to wine, dine, and dance for free with you. It can't be for the fun of it."

"We haven't had a party for years. We've been dining, drinking, and dancing at other people's parties free of charge for too long. It's our turn to return the compliment."

The explanation had satisfied some but it had not convinced me. The more I thought about it the more I became persuaded that I was really paying tribute to my ancestral spirits. I had not been to my father's graveyard for some time. My relatives had held a commiseration for him a few years ago, but I was abroad. My mother had died when I was out of the country, too. I visited the subsiding earth mound three months later. The prayer that I had uttered at the graveyard had choked in my throat. Then there had been my uncle before him. And my grandmother. My kid brother, too. And little nephews and nieces. I felt they were all out there pressurising me to do something. The party was to appease all these hungry spirits who had died before me and before their time, I realized.

But here was Mtunduwatha denying me my resolve to expiate my sins of omission. In dying, he was preventing me from sacrificing to my ancestral spirits. What right had he? If it came to that, what was he a sacrifice to? He had not died a natural death of old age. He had been in his prime. A target for sacrificial rites for the gods or the spirits. They did not want him to live to come to my party. They did not want me to hold my party, either. What did they want? I remembered the carcass of the pig. Dismembered parts: trotters, snout, entrails, the disembowelled navel, lying bleeding on the hanging scales. I imagined Mtunduwatha squashed up in the driver's seat under the bridge. His bones smashed up. Some limbs hacked by the metal. They had to remove him by cutting him out to separate him from the metal. What was he really a sacrifice to? Did he too have some sins of omission or commission to expiate?

"Shall I bring a brandy?" I remember Mtunduwatha asking me when I had handed him the invitation card. I had just laughed.

It is now time for laying the wreaths. The reverend does not spare the young widow. Her fresh wreath must grace her husband's mound until flowers wither, crack, and in turn change to dust. She takes her wreath from one of the elderly church women. We feel her heart tearing and wrenching in its mooring. We cannot see her face, her whole head and shoulders are covered by a back hood. We see her trembling hands as they lay the wreath at the head of the mound. We feel her knees wobbling as if her legs will give way, go earthward to join her husband underneath. Luckily, she does not collapse. Her helper supports her with strong arms and carries rather than walks her away from the source of her anguish. She collapses at the edge of the crowd, where her supporter also sits to wait for the long procession of wreath-layers to follow her example in grief.

"We have now reached the end of the ceremony," the reverend announces after the ordeal-by-wreaths. "Before we return to the house, is there anyone who would like to say something?"

No one has the heart to say anything more after all the speech-making we had at the church and the house. The reverend does not really expect any either. He asks us to return to the deceased's house for the closing rites.

2nd January

I resumed work today with no fanfare. I was still in a holiday mood though, so I spent the day with the list of invited guests, phoning them to remind them of the 4th January, when my postponed party would be held. I emphasized to them that the 4th was a Friday, not a Saturday as some confused friends thought.

"Don't miss it!" I ended each chat before putting the phone down.

I firmly pushed thoughts of funerals out of my mind. I wanted to enjoy this party after all the series of funerals I had been to last year. The new year was for pleasant thoughts only.

I checked with some of my guests that they had their favourite numbers on tape, ready for the dancing. I wanted them to enjoy the party too.

3rd January

I spent the morning out of the office collecting drinks and depositing them in the cold room to stay overnight. By mid afternoon the next day, they would be well chilled. I had blocks of ice ready also, just to make sure they would stay like that for the rest of the party.

I checked that everything was on schedule and in place: food, music, furniture, appetites. It would take minimum effort tomorrow to activate the whole house and garden to an all night binge.

In the afternoon, I worked hard in the office clearing my desk. I felt a little guilty for not having been in the office in the morning. However, I felt absolved from grievious sin since I was entertaining a good three-quarters of the staff, if not the country, tomorrow. I had to make sure everything would work this time.

I was preparing to go home at 4.45 when the shy knock of the messenger interrupted me.

"From the boss," he announced as he walked in and dropped an open memorandum on my desk.

I could not think what the boss would want at that hour, when there was the whole of tomorrow to deal with any matters concerning me. I pulled the memo towards me and sat up with a jerk as I skimmed the few lines:

MEMORIAL SERVICE

Mtunduwatha's memorial service will be held at 4.00 p.m. tomorrow, Friday 4th January, in the staff room. Since you were a close friend of the deceased, the staff have unanimously decided that you should do the first reading. Please accept the honour.

Signed: S. Mfitizalimba, Director.

I relaxed again. The service would only take an hour or so. There would still be time to revive our spirits for the conviviality in the evening.

4th January

Friday morning came with the riotious chirping of birds in the trees in my garden. Last night's rains had washed the air clean. As I opened the bedroom windows, I could smell the dew evaporating from the greens of the blades of grass and leaves in the heat of the sun, rapidly rising in a cloudless sky. It was a glorious day.

I was dressing for work when the phone rang. Who could it be at this hour, before breakfast?

I lifted the receiver and said hello to the blank wall opposite.

"It's Mavuto."

I detected the agitation in my cousin's voice. My hand chilled on the receiver.

"Our aunt is dead."

The End

Questions

1. In the first paragraph of this story, we meet the main character reading a guest list. What was this guest list for?
2. Describe briefly what happened to affect the guest list.

3. Why was he disappointed?
4. Why do you think the author remembers the funeral song about nal-imvimvi?
5. Give evidence from the story which shows that Mtunduwatha's wife has been deeply affected by grief.
6. Write a paragraph explaining briefly why you think the title of the story is appropriate.
7. One of the conspicuos features of this story is its use of dialogue. From this dialogue describe the character traits of the narrator.
8. The point of view of this story is the first person point of view. Looking at the theme of death and its consequent inconveniences do you think this point of view is appropriate for such a story? Explain your answer.
9. In your opinion, what is the mood or atmosphere of this story? Give examples of the vocabulary which expresses this mood.
10. There are two dominant tenses in this short story. Read the story carefully and explain the relationship that is there between each of the tenses and the events that it is used to explain.
11. In this story the author is one way or the other exploiting some common religious and/or traditional beliefs of Malawi. Mention as many such beliefs as you can from the story.
12. Names of characters may reveal some of the themes discussed in a piece of writing especially if they are connected with the events of the story. Consider the following three names and say how they relate to the theme of death in the story:
    (a) Mtunduwatha
    (b) Mfitizalimba
    (c) Mavuto

HOW MICE BEGAN EATING BOOKS AND CLOTHES

Duncan N. Mboma

ONCE UPON a time there lived a man called Ndavutika in the interior of a dense forest. He had a big family of two wives, six daughters and three sons.

Ndavutika was both a farmer and a hunter. He had extensive farms of cassava on the edge of the forest. However, for some time his crops were being destroyed by wild animals. The most destructive were the warthog and wild pigs. They ruthlessly uprooted the cassava and ate the tubers. He had tried to scare them away many times but he failed to keep them away completely.

Seeing that all his plans had failed to stop the animals from destroying his crops, he decided to go and ask for advice from a wise old man in the neighbourhood. He thought the old man would help him with ideas to protect his crops.

"Oh! Welcome my son," said the old man to Ndavutika as he approached him.

"Ah, good father, how are you, tata?" Ndavutika greeted him.

"Not so fine my son. I have fever. I know I don't have long to live. I am dying soon. I am old my son. Anyway, what can I do for you in this early hour of the morning?" asked the old man.

"I thank you my father. Please don't say anything about dying. God forbid that you should die now. I have come to seek for your advice with my problem," he said after brief formalities. "Wild animals are destroying my cassava plantation and it seems I will not yield anything from it. I have tried to chase them away, but my efforts have been in vain. What can I do?"

"Well my son, you need not worry too much about it," he answered in a very calm manner. "Go and dig a trench two metres deep and two metres wide along the trail of the animals to your farm. Sharpen some sticks, about forty, and stick them up in the trench with the sharpened end pointing up. Then cover the top of the trench with some grass so that it is not possible to tell that there is a trench. The animals will now fall in the trench and get pierced by the sticks. They won't reach your farm to eat the crops."

"Thank you father. I will do as you have advised me. May God add more days to your life. Good-bye father."

Ndavutika went home delighted and determined to make the trap. Early the following morning he started digging the trench, helped by his three sons. By noon they had finished the whole task. He told everyone in his family not to go to the farm until the following day.

On the following morning, Ndavutika went to see what had happened in the night. When he reached the trench he heard the groaning of an animal. There was no grass at the top of the trench. He trembled with joy as he thought that the old man's plan had worked. He drew nearer and looked into the trench. His eyes met with those of the lion. The lion was in great pains and pleaded with Ndavutika to pull him out of the trench. Ndavutika was filled with fear but at the same time he was sympathetic. He felt pity for the lion though he distrusted him. He thought that if he pulled the lion out of the trench, the lion would kill him. The lion said that he would not do any harm to Ndavutika because he knew that the trap was not meant for him but the warthog and pigs. Ndavutika then pulled the lion out of the trench.

Once out of the trench, the lion said he would kill him for making him fall into a trap. Ndavutika pleaded with the lion. He apologised but the lion insisted that he would kill him.

While they were still arguing, the mouse which was passing by heard the quarrel and came to greet the lion, saying, "King of the Beasts, I salute you," and asked why they were quarreling. The lion explained what had happened. The mouse asked Ndavutika to explain his part as well. He told him that the trap was for the warthog and wild pigs which were destroying his crops and not the lion.

The lion got angry and shouted, "Don't you know that this is my path when I go to catch the wild pigs which I eat?"

The mouse tried to cool down the lion and asked Ndavutika to make up his trap again. In no time the trap was ready again. The mouse then said it might have been the lion's fault that it fell into the trap. The lion got furious. He told the mouse to try to walk over the trench. The mouse agreed and walked over without falling in. He walked over it twice and nothing happened. He then asked the lion to try it again and assured him nothing would happen. The lion agreed and as soon as he stepped on it, he fell in and was pierced by the sharp sticks which went deep into his stomach. The mouse told Ndavutika to finish him off.

Ndavutika was very thankful to the mouse for saving his life. He asked the mouse what he could do for him in return. He offered to give him part of the farm or a daughter for a wife. The mouse refused all these offers but asked Ndavutika to keep him in his house. Ndavutika accepted this without objections. The mouse immediately gathered his family and moved in to stay in Ndavutika's house.

The mouse told Ndavutika that they preferred eating nkhoko to any other food. As time went and the size of the mouse's family increased, there was less and less food available and no nkhoko were provided to the mouse. The mouse and his family began to starve. The mouse then turned to eating anything they found in the house, clothes, pieces of paper, soap, flour, plastic ware to stay alive. Ndavutika could not chase the mouse out because of the promise that he would keep him in the house despite that he was not able to give them food anymore. This is why mice will eat anything they find in the house.

The End

Questions

1. What problem did Ndavutika have on his farm?
2. What advice did the old man give to Ndavutika?
3. Describe the problem that arose following the old man's advice.
4. How did he solve this new problem?
5. Ndavutika made a promise to the mouse. Describe this promise in your own words.
6. In groups, narrate other tales involving mice and other animals.
7. One of the common features of Malawian folktales is that small characters play important roles. What great role did the mouse play in the conflict that arose between the lion and Ndavutika?
8. Similary, small animals fool big ones. How does the mouse fool the lion?
9. What moral lessons can be drawn from this folktale?

VENTURE INTO THE NAMELESS VILLAGE

Marvin Kambuwa

SALIYA CHUCKLED to himself nervously and wondered what madness had compelled him to venture into the nameless village. He was an enlightened member of the board of town planning and human rehabilitation. Maybe it was because he had vigorously campaigned for the eradication of the nameless village and his efforts were soon to be rewarded by the confirmed relocation of the inhabitants of the village elsewhere, and the final demolition of what constituted this thorn in the board's flesh. He therefore felt a strange compulsion to see the village for himself - for the first time admittedly - before the bulldozers rolled in to roll everything down. It was a compulsion akin to that which drives the boxer to spend a quiet moment alone in or near a ring on the eve of a tough tournament.

He boarded the bus and sat comfortably to savour the moment that was slowly approaching.

"Your fare, Sir," the bus conductor said. He received some loose change from Saliya. "Where to?" he asked, curiously observing that he had not seen this man on this route before.

"The nameless village," said Saliya, a nervous twitch of his upper lip widening into an unsure smile.

"I wouldn't smile if I were you, sir," the bus conductor said. "We don't go there anyway. You will do well to get off at Mathero bus stop and walk the rest of the way."

Saliya received his ticket and put it in his jacket pocket. He looked around him and noticed that the other passengers were regarding him with a mixture of curiosity and doubtful concern.

"I don't live there, you know." He said to no one in particular. The other passengers continued to stare at him. A woman who was sitting on his left hand side stood up and moved to another seat. Saliya felt like a leper.

In an hour the bus stopped at Mathero bus stop. Saliya stood up and walked towards the exit. As he stepped out he heard laughter break out behind him. He did not turn back to see what was going on. This was it, either he or the village would have to go. He resolved.

The nameless village rested enigmatically at the foot of a mountain. Saliya approached it by way of the only footpath challenged by two hungry and absent-minded girls who were manning the barrier to the village. A poster in faint white paint hang partly off its peg and pointed upwards. He read NAME-LESS VILLAGE - NO PROBLEM.

"Stop!" One of the girls shouted to Saliya. Her colleague stood a yard or so away, frantically waving a thin long pole at the end of which was the gaudy remnant of what must once have been a full size flag. Its original colour scheme had since been replaced by numerous patches, some of which were struggling for places of honour on top of the others.

Saliya did not know how to react. The barrier, manned by these two girls seemed nothing more than a farce. But something warned him that they were to be taken seriously. He placed his briefcase on the ground.

"Submit to a search!" Ordered the girl who was waving the flag, seemingly looking beyond Saliya. Saliya emptied the contents of his pockets, placing them on the ground.

"What are you doing?" asked the girl near him.

"Submitting to a search," answered Saliya.

"Your mouth, you silly man. Open your mouth - wide!" Commanded the girl who was waving the flag.

Saliya jerked himself upright and opened his mouth wide.

The girl with the flag continued to wave it frantically, a couple of tears now flowing gently down her cheeks. Her colleague searched Saliya's mouth, probing the corners of his mouth with dirty thin fingers. Then she started humming to herself - 'hear no evil, see no evil, speak no evil.'

"Perfectly in order." She called out to her friend, who was now waving the flag slowly. "A bit of foul breath, but I suppose that's because of the chibuku he drank for lunch." Pronounced the girl who had examined Saliya's ears, eyes and mouth. Saliya stood flabbergasted at both the method of searching as well as the choice of objects to be searched.

"You may now proceed," said the girl with the flag.

"Sambo will be your guide - O, I am so hungry."

"What are we doing here?" asked the other girl.

"Submit to a search!" barked the two girls at Saliya simultaneously.

"But you just searched me." Saliya complained, both anxious to go through the whole process again.

"What did we find?" Asked the flag waving girl.

"Chibuku, what does it matter? Let him go," said the other.

"Sambo will be your acolyte."

For the first time Saliya noticed the young man, probably in his twenties, who was sitting up a mango tree, chipping off bits of the tree's bark with a blunt knife. The young man climbed down and started jogging towards the village without so much a glance at Saliya.

"Quick," said the girl with the flag to Saliya. "You have to catch him. He is your other self. If you lose him you have lost yourself; and you have been waiting for this moment for a long long time.

The old man came towards Saliya walking backwards. All that Saliya could see was a hunchback, above which peeked bristles of uncombed grey hair, and below which a pair of unproportionally long legs propelled the trunk. The old man descended the three steps leading from his hut and stopped a few feet away from Saliya.

"Welcome to our village." The old man said in a surprisingly clear and resonant voice.

"Thank you - Sir." Saliya heard himself saying, at the same time walking round the man in order to face him.

"Stay where you are!" ordered Sambo, speaking in an unnecessarily loud voice. He was tugging Saliya's jacket, bringing him to an abrupt stop.

"Is it not bad manners to speak at an elderly person's back?" Saliya asked in surprise.

"You do not look at his face unless you have been initiated into the secrets of truth," Sambo said. "Greet him."

"How do I do that if I am not allowed to face him and shake his hand?"

"Pull his leg!"

"Yes, pull my right leg. But be gentle. At two hundred years of age my back is becoming very very weak." The old man raised his right leg and extended it backwards to Saliya, who was not sure about how much pressure to apply in pulling it.

"Pull," urged Sambo.

As he pulled, Saliya observed that the old man's hunchback was gradually distending, making small noises like bones cracking. It sounded and looked weird.

"That's enough," sighed the old man. "You may stay with us for a year. Sambo will show you around." The old man was about to walk away when Saliya realized that he had to say something. His mind seemed to be clouded with uncertainty. First, he was not sure that he had heard right about the man's age. Then about spending a year in the village - how could he....

"I am here only for a night, thank you," Saliya said.

"I must present my findings to the board of housing and human rehabilitation tomorrow."

"You will be here for a short time," Sambo interrupted. He was piercing a sharp stick through his noise. Tiny beads of blood dotted the area round where the stick had entered the nose. He appeared restless and agitated.

"How old are you, young man?" the old man asked Saliya, at the same time falling on his belly and thrusting his hunchback up and down in fast push ups. Saliya was puzzled.

"I am forty three. Why?"

"Forty three, eh. Then what is a year or so spent with us?" asked the old man rhetorically.

"I do not understand," submitted Saliya.

"The quest for the self, the pursuit of truth, and the endeavour for the unification of the apparent and the essential self, is that not worth a year of your life?" asked the old man.

"You came here not because you were lost. You came on a quest, n'est cest pas? How, then, would you return without the fulfilment of your mission? You stay." And with that the old man walked back into the house, this time he was walking forwards.

Sambo beckoned to Saliya to follow him.

122

"You are to come to the kitchen. Come."

And that is how Saliya came to meet the young old man and the randy sad rabbit who always almost mounted the eagerly patient bunny.

Saliya was ushered into the kitchen which was a few yards away from the house. It was a small grass-thatched affair without any windows.

"Step on the stone before you cross the threshold," said Sambo to Saliya.

Saliya looked at his feet and saw a small rock which was embedded in the ground just outside the kitchen door.

"Do I really have to do that?" Saliya asked, observing that there was no clear reason why he could not just walk into the kitchen.

"Ritual," Sambo said. "There is a price to pay for everything. You must realize that the attainment of the ultimate is not easy to accomplish."

Saliya was too tired to argue. All he wanted was to go inside the kitchen and sit down. He had even lost track of time!

"Clap your hands to indicate that you are here," said Sambo.

"Why are you piercing your nose with that stick?" asked Saliya.

"Clap your hands or else she won't know that you are here," Sambo said, shoving Saliya in the backside with an elbow. Saliya clapped his hands once, twice, then three times.

"This is not a football match," admonished Sambo. "Clap your hands like this," he said, cupping the palms of his hands, and clapping them at three uniform intervals in a regular pattern.

"I wish you would tell me what is happening," said Saliya just as the grass door of the kitchen was opening to reveal a young old woman with a girl's body and an old woman's face. She was beckoning to Saliya with some urgency. Saliya ran across the threshold into the kitchen.

"You see, sometimes it is wiser to take the plunge without too much reflection," said the young old woman. "You did not remember to set foot on the stone because you were possessed by my appearance. You made a leap into the unknown - that is faith. Come, sit down."

"I will wait for you out here," Saliya heard Sambo say outside the kitchen. His voice sounded very distant. Saliya peeped outside and saw Sambo, left leg perched on a tree trunk while his right leg was on the ground, bent forward with both arms outstretched. With his hands he firmly gripped his left foot which was stretched out at eye level on top of the tree trunk. He sighed with relaxation as he bent his body forward.

"What is he doing?" asked Saliya.

"Never mind him." The young old woman said as she ushered Saliya back into the kitchen. "He is only suffering for your pleasure. You see, just like you need darkness to highlight the intensity of light, so too do you require pain to give meaning to pleasure."

"But he cannot possibly sleep like that, with one leg up a tree trunk and the other on the ground," pleaded Saliya.

"How else do you suppose he can sleep when one half of him is here and the other half out there?" asked the young old woman, indicating that Saliya was that one half "in here." Saliya was baffled.

"I thought you would never come," the young old woman said, sighing with relief. She put chips of marble stone in a hole in the centre of the kitchen, and went through the motions of kindling a fire. "We must keep warm," she said, fanning the chips of marble stone with an old tin-plate.

"But those stones... don't you think that it might be a better idea to get firewood and make a proper fire?" suggested Saliya. "I really am cold, you know."

"Tut, tut, tut. I thought you had come here to save me?" The young old woman asked Saliya reproachfully. "I see you are not yet ready to take the plunge. Did they search you at the barrier?" The young old woman was now crossing her legs in a yoga position. She looked almost obscene.

"Search me? All they did was ask me to open my mouth and they unceremoniously proceeded to probe into my open mouth with their dirty fingers. What kind of weapon or offensive article might one conceal in one's mouth?"

"Words, words, words."

"These are not mere words. I am serious. That's all they did, probe, probe, probe."

"The frog," commenced the young old woman. "The frog was sent on a spying mission into enemy camp. He infiltrated the camp and camouflaged himself successfully. As it was cold, the frog joined the enemy around a camp fire. The

124

warmth of the fire stole upon him and, being tired, he soon fell asleep. But sleep stole upon him like a thief. He dreamt that he had completed his mission successfully and that he had returned home to a hero's welcome. Pretty girls were putting garlands of flowers round his neck, orchids, chrysanthemum, daffodils, geraniums - all sorts of sweet smelling flowers. "Tell us about your mission," they were all shouting to him. With a smile on his face, the frog started to recount how he had crept upon the enemy, disguised as one of them; and how he had joined them round a fire to listen to all their strategies without anyone discovering his true identity. That is how the enemy knew that the frog was an impostor.

"They apprehended him and tied his legs to a post. Then they boiled some water and slowly poured it on his back until his skin was totally scalded. The frog confessed. Then the enemy told him that they would release him and make him a warning to others. They put an egg on fire. The shell cracked with the heat. Just when the shell was getting charred, they opened the frog's mouth and forced the egg in. That killed all words inside the frog's mouth. Till this day the frog tries hard not to speak about his exploits as a spy. Sometimes the urge to speak so overwhelms him that he ends up panting and perspiring with the strain of keeping words to himself - lest he be dreaming in enemy camp again."

"That is something!" exclaimed Saliya.

"But quickly, you must eat and then you go to the ceremony of absolution of the thieves," said the woman. She proffered a gourd containing a juice of papaya mixed with guava and mango. Saliya took a cautious sip. The juice was exceedingly refreshing. He gulped it all down and asked for some more.

"Do not wet your lips," cautioned the young old woman.

"And how does one do that?" he asked quizzically.

"You will learn, by and by." The young old woman was preparing what was to be their dinner. Saliya, meanwhile, occupied himself examining kitchen utensils. There were marble stones in one corner. An empty basket lay on its side close to where the young old woman was sitting. Then there were a couple of wooden ladles. Also an empty packet of Players Gold Leaf cigarettes stood carefully preserved on top of an empty tin of Covo Cooking oil.

"Do you smoke?" ventured Saliya.

"Why, no."

"Then why do you keep that packet of Players Gold Leaf?"

"To remind me of my redeemer."

"And who might that be?"

"I am she," answered the young old woman, regarding Saliya sternly. She was just about to say something when a movement in one corner of the kitchen caught her attention. She immediately lit a match and illuminated an aging rabbit which stood sadly beside a larger rabbit crouched on the floor. Then it seemed to change its mind. Saliya watched the rabbit raise its front leg instead, placing it on the female rabbits neck. As soon as it touched the female's neck, the sad rabbit jerked its bottom as if it had received an electric shock. Saliya looked closely and noticed that watery droplets were showering on the sides of the female, and that she too seemed to be experiencing an electric shock.

"What the hell is going on here?" he asked the young old woman in shocked disbelief.

"Rabbit injection," laughed the young old woman, then she added seriously. "He is randy, this old rabbit. My redeemer tamed him."

"What do you mean?"

"What do you see?"

"This is crazy!" Saliya exclaimed, trying to look away from the rabbits but finding his attention arrested by the strange spectacle.

"No. You are the one refusing to conmerge with reality," said the young old woman. "You see, this rabbit did not choose to be horny. However, every time he mounted the female, a whole bunch of offspring were born. Not his fault, you understand? Nor hers either. So my redeemer decided to do something without physically interfering with..." She made a gesture of castration to which Saliya grimaced.

"I see."

"You do not," continued the young old woman. "Every time my redeemer saw him about to mount the female, he would strike a match close to the rabbit's you-know what. The flame and little heat would scare the randy rabbit into quick withdrawal. This had a would be equally eager female quickly withdraw. This had a dual effect. Firstly, the randy rabbit began to time his ejaculation to occur as soon as he touched the female, but before the match was lit - sort of beating the match to the draw, you know. And so too did the female learn to synchronise her response so that the mere touch of the male is enough to trigger her response. Secondly, a sexual reaction can be induced in both rabbits by the mere strike of a match. Since both rabbits are too old for the arduous task of mating, they are grateful for the less taxing method which they were taught. At least that way the risks of a heart attack through over-excitement are minimised," she said.

"Whew!" sighed Saliya. That was more than he had bargained for.

"Remember, pleasure is sweeter when you steal it," concluded the young old woman.

That morning Sambo was in jovial mood, while Saliya seemed to be less sure of himself. In fact he was feeling rather funny.

"I feel funny today." Saliya said to Sambo as the latter came to take him to the ceremony of absolution.

"Funny ha-ha or funny peculiar?" Sambo asked.

"Funny peculiar. You are in a jovial mood yourself - why?" Saliya asked.

He observed that Sambo was hopping on one leg, the other leg being hooked by the knee round the back of his neck in an acrobatic manner.

'All those who matter in our village are attending the absolution of the thieves. That is why I am in a jovial mood today, Saliya," explained Sambo.

'But what has that got to do with you?" Saliya asked with genuine surprise. "I am genuinely surprised at your high spirits."

"You don't have to echo me," responded Sambo.

"How do you mean?"

"Well, no sooner do I pass a thought into your mind than you repeat it to me. That can be monotonous, you know. Or do you forget who we are?"

While Saliya puzzled this out, Sambo hopped ever so fast on his one leg that Saliya needed to jog to keep up with him.

"That is called being one step ahead of yourself," Sambo laughed over his shoulder at Saliya. Soon they were at the place where the absolution of the thieves was to take place.

"Over this side," said Sambo, guiding Saliya through a throng of people who were dressed in their best clothing.

"The cream of our society," said Sambo with a smile of satisfaction. "That over there is the hang-man," said Sambo, pointing at a miserable looking man of about sixty.

"He sure has the mean and hungry look of someone who has hanged a few in his life," observed Saliya.

"On the contrary," replied Sambo. "He has never hanged anyone in his life."

"Then what for is he a hangman?"

"He hangs around waiting for the chance not to hang anyone. You see, there is no cause for anyone to be hanged in our village. However, we need a hangman to give us the semblance of a truly democratic village. It gives us a sense of pride and satisfaction to know that if we wish to hang anyone, there is always someone to do it for us," Sambo explained, easing Saliya to one end of the arena. "Anyway, the hangman doesn't even know what the gallows look like. In fact he has persistent nightmares that he is hanging someone, and we all pity him."

"And who is that pompous man dancing with the drunken woman," Saliya asked.

"O, that is the maestro. And she is the hospital nurse," answered Sambo.

"But if he is the song composer how come the two of them are dancing without the accompaniment of music?" Saliya puzzled.

"Precisely. He dances all the time and at every occasion so that perchance his steps might conjure up some music. So far he has never composed any song. But because he has an open ambition to compose sweet songs, we rejoice with him in his hope to realise his potential ability some day. Deep in his heart, we know, he must be a Mozart. Such geniuses are hard to come by. That is why we rejoice in our faith in him. We all need to take that leap, don't we? Are you a believer?" Sambo asked.

"What has that got to... ah, I see your point." Saliya was not sure whether he found this fascinating or merely intriguing. "I take it that the hospital nurse is really not a nurse then," he said.

"You are wrong." Sambo corrected. "She nurses our hangovers. She tends to the darkest of everyone's fantasies."

It was at precisely this point that the soldier who never fought any war marched into the arena at the head of an invisible brigade of thieves. They were invisible thieves because in reality they were not thieves at all. They were law abiding citizens who had obeyed the call of the full moon.

The soldier who never fought any war led the procession to a huge rock on top of which were a hundred and one sharp knives each wrapped in a piece of white Kleenex tissue.

"Somersault!" barked the soldier who never fought any war coming to a halt. The whole procession somersaulted like a wave, everyone landing upright on their feet.

"Diffusion!" commanded the soldier who never fought any war.

"Hooray!" cheered the procession as everyone sadly reached for the knives on the rock. With these they each proceeded to cut off the tips of their fingers, one at a time. Those who couldn't sever their fingertips begged their colleagues to assist them.

The spectators started to throw light bird-feathers vengefully at the procession in abuse. A thirty year old child ran to his one hundred year old father and cursed and swore at him while torturing him by pouring cow milk on his head. He was punishing him for being responsible for a theft and aggravated burglary which he had not committed.

"What's the point of all this? Could you tell me, please?" asked Saliya who soon discovered that Sambo was no longer at his side. In his place was an old man with a little hair on his head. He smiled at Saliya and nodded with understanding.

"You desire to know the meaning of all this?" the old old man asked, linking hands with Saliya.

"For God's sake, if only someone could explain this to me!" nodded Saliya.

"I can only explain this to you very simply," said the old old man, steering Saliya to a vantage point of view, up a leafless tree, where the two of them perched on a rotting branch.

"Bite a few leaves," the old old man advised Saliya.

"What for? There are no leaves on this tree anyway."

"Then pretend that you are biting some. That will save you from your fear of heights."

"How did you know that I am afraid of heights?" Saliya asked, surprised. The old old man evaded the question and reached for Saliya's hand.

"About the absolution of the thieves."

"I thought we would never come to that."

"It's like this. Every full moon, men and women of the village who have never committed theft in their lives come here to pledge themselves to a life of no theft. Every full moon the whole village gathers here to abuse and punish these people for the theft they never committed, and the aggravated burglaries they never perpetrated," the old old man said, waiting for Saliya's reaction.

"But if they neither stole nor committed any burglary, why do they need to be tortured and to torture themselves in this way?" Saliya asked.

"Lemmings," the old old man said.

"Sorry?" Saliya was puzzled.

"Forget it," the old old man dismissed the question with a flourish of the left hand.

"But..."

"Because in subjecting themselves to this degradation they learn to experience and appreciate the unpleasant treatment which they would receive if they did commit the crime. Can't you see?" The old old man said to Saliya confidentially. "All the so-called respectable men and women you see are thieves and cut-throats at heart and mind. But if they are caught sooner or later then...." The old old man ran his index finger across his throat in a gesture of decapitation.

"The hang man?" Saliya asked.

"For once you've got it. That is what makes hangman sad. All the thieves and cut-throats whom he will not have to hang. He hopes to retire before that dark day comes."

"Do they really need to cut off their fingertips?"

"Of course yes," the old old man retorted. "If they cut their fingertips off they

130

ensure that they do not pick what is not rightfully theirs. The pain is a constant reminder. Imagine what this world would be if we all introduced a permanent element of pain into our lives, to be activated whenever dark thoughts enter our minds."

"And how long does the ceremony last?" Saliya asked. He was surprised to observe that more and more people were filing into the arena. Others were bringing their domestic animals with them. Cows, pet monkeys, chickens, ducks, and few puzzled tortoises were in the procession.

"Do they have to punish the animals as well?" Saliya asked.

"Who said that the animals were being punished?" The old old man asked, perplexed.

"Well, but surely, those animals haven't done anything wrong to deserve this. Besides, they don't even know what's going on," Saliya asked.

"But precisely," responded the old man. "The animals have committed no crime at all, just as their masters have committed none. Listen young man, this is a democratic society. There is no discrimination here. Human beings and animals have equal rights. So whatever goes for human beings goes for animals as well, and nobody asks questions." The old old man was now obviously annoyed and vexed with Saliya's doubtfulness. He shoved him with his elbow, knocking him off the branch. As Saliya was falling to the ground, he picked the old old man's parting words. "Quite frankly people and animals do not always only get punished for the crimes which they commit. Perhaps you should go and see the Guru."

And that is how Saliya ended up at the invisible court of the Guru.

The path to the court of the Guru was long and winded. But in reality the court was not further than a quarter of a kilometer away.

"Tell me Sambo, why do we have to go up to the hill and then down again just to reach the court of the Guru when we could reach it in less than an hour if we walked by a direct route?" Saliya asked.

"I don't know," Sambo answered, piercing more pieces of sharpened sticks through his nose.

"But surely you know where we are going?"

"The court of the Guru?"

"Yes."

"But the Guru has no court at all!" exclaimed Sambo as if he had just made a brilliant discovery.

"What? Are you telling me that this whole trip is a waste?" Saliya asked.

"Are you married?" Sambo asked out of the blue.

"Yes. What relevance has that question to our present predicament?"

"Marriage is an institution, and not everyone likes to belong to an institution." Sambo said, laughing heartily.

"This trip." Saliya prompted.

"No trip is ever wasted."

Saliya regarded Sambo with sudden interest. He was observing for the first time that for some unexplained reason, Sambo was metamorphosing into a mature significant adult from the dirty insignificant lad whom he saw at the entrance to the village.

"Sambo," Saliya called. "What are you up to?" He asked, also noticing for the first time and with alarm, that as Sambo gained in stature, Saliya himself was beginning to look small, confused and exhausted.

"The Guru's court does not exit," said Sambo, evading both Saliya's eyes and his question. "In fact, the distance to the Guru's non-existent court is less than twenty yards from where we are standing now."

Saliya looked around him for signs of the Guru's non-existence court. He could not see any.

"I cannot see any signs of the Guru's non-existent court." He pronounced with resignation.

"Of course you cannot see it. But when we have travelled through the torturous route almost to the top of the mountain, and when we have retraced our steps back to this place, then the court will be less than invisible," Sambo said. "In fact at this point in time the Guru is walking in the opposite direction to the route which we will take before we converge. That way, by the time we converge we will all be tired. We will then be able to exchange words from a position of fatigue. You see, that is the only way to ensure fair play."

Sambo and Saliya crossed creeks and climbed rocks, they narrowly escaped from imaginary enemies wielding invisible ferocious pangas, and drank brackish water from shallow wells before they almost reached the summit of the mountain.

"We have almost reached the summit of the mountain!" exclaimed Saliya with joy, feeling a renewed surge of energy passing through his body.

"And I can feel a renewed surge of energy go through my body."

"There you go echoing me again," Sambo complained.

"Let us reach the summit."

"Stop it!"

"But why?" he asked Sambo.

"Commence descent!" Shouted Sambo as if barking an order to an invisible army. They descended until they were at the foot of the mountain. Throughout the remainder of the journey, Saliya was examining closely the faces of all the people they met in the hope that he might come across the Guru, who was at this time supposedly walking in the opposite direction. At one point he was sure that he had finally unravelled the secret. This was when he and Sambo stumbled upon two girls aged forty years old and a young boy of thirty-eight who were moulding clay models.

"Let us go piss," suggested one of the girls.

"Yes, let us go piss," agreed the young boy.

The girls squatted to piss. The boy casually strolled to a tall grass, and proceeded to aim his urine up a blade at two mating flies. One of the girls happened to turn towards the boy at that time and she saw something that had never appeared unusual to her before.

"Look," she shouted to her friend. "This one is a boy!" she said.

"Yes, look. He is a boy!" the other girl exclaimed.

The girls gathered round the boy, who stood confused. He examined himself with puzzled curiosity. Satisfied that he was indeed a boy, he took to his heels and ran like mad. Without any enquiry, Saliya joined in the chase, believing that this was the Guru in flight. Sambo came close at foot. But the thirty eight year old boy started to run on both fours and Sambo and Saliya could not cope with his stupendous speed.

"Why are we running after him?" Sambo asked Saliya, puzzled.

"Because he is different from the others," the latter replied.

"But of course, any fool can see that."

"Yes, but I am not any fool. He must be the Guru," said Saliya who, in his exhaustion, fell to the ground. It was at that moment and in that position that Saliya came face to face with the Guru.

"You have come face to face with the Guru," said the Guru, gathering herself up. Her face was so ordinary that Saliya could not have believed her if Sambo hadn't confirmed her claim. In any event, Saliya had not expected the Guru to be a woman.

"I did not expect the Guru to be a woman," said Saliya, to no one in particular.

"That is right," said the Guru.

"But that is not right," contradicted Saliya. "There must be some misunderstanding somewhere." Saliya paused and looked around. Then he shot his fingers at the Guru and exclaimed: "Ah! The evidence. Where is your non existent court then?" he asked.

"Right here where we are," said the Guru. "Listen here my son. I am here to make known to you the obvious facts of life which you so much take for granted that you fail to perceive them. Listen very carefully to every word I say."

"No. First I have a few questions to ask you," insisted Saliya.

"He was searched at the barrier," Sambo said to the Guru reverently.

"A most peculiar barrier, what exactly is going on here?" he asked, turning to face the Guru squarely in the face. "I am facing you squarely in the face!" he declared.

"That, I can see," responded the Guru. "What brought you to our village?"

Saliya thought for a moment. He did not seem to remember what the purpose of his mission was. But he would not allow himself to be intimidated by this woman, Guru or not.

"I won't allow myself to be intimidated by this woman, Guru or not," he declared to no one in particular.

"Who are you talking to?" The Guru asked in a patronising tone as if she was speaking to a child. "There are just two people here. You and I."

Saliya looked round. Indeed there were just the two of them. What had made him think that there were more than the two of them?

"I am sorry."

"That's perfectly in order. A slight confusion is bound to occur when we converge with our other half," comforted the Guru.

"Why girls, and why an old nondescript flag? Why all this?" asked Saliya in exasperation.

"Sit here and you will learn," said the Guru, making Saliya comfortable on a rugged rock. She reached out with an open palm and somehow conjured two mugs of mixed fruit drink garnished with chopped parsley.

"Drink," she said.

Saliya took a sip. The drink was exceedingly invigorating. He asked for more. She gave it to him. Then Saliya saw for the first time.

"My, you are so beautiful. How come I hadn't noticed before?" He asked, regarding the Guru with active interest. She, in turn proffered her mug to him and he bent over to drink from it, but instead found that he was filling the Guru's proffered mug with a cocktail he did not know he had. It was an unearthly, pleasant and potent cocktail which put both of them in a semi trance.

"You see, it is a matter of what you choose to perceive. A matter of frame of reference," cooed the Guru. "Right now you are in the process of convergence. That puts you in our frame of reference, and that is how you perceive us. But so much for that, first things first." The Guru touched Saliya lightly on the forehead. This set him deeper in the trance. And that is how Saliya heard the lessons of the Guru.

"Symbols," she said. "Anthems, boundaries, flags, heroes. What world would it be if we did not have symbols to give us hope? You wondered about the girls at the entrance to the village and the ancient flag they tote? That gives hope. The barrier is the beginning of their frame of reference. Everything inside they identify with and relate to. The identity of the village hinges upon the flag, whose age symbolises the ancient traditions of the nameless village. It used to be a new flag once. O, yes it was. Now it is a gaudy remnant. But you see, as time passes, we do not lose our identity or history, but like the original flag, the colours and fabric of that youthful past wear off, to be held together by patches of the passage of time. True, the flag gets heavier - but is that not an enrichment and convergence of what was, is, and shall be?"

"Your Sambo was a bearer of the flag before the girls. That gave him hope of your coming. Now you are here, and Sambo and you are completing the process of convergence. Come now to the archives of the village."

Still in a trance, Saliya followed the Guru to what was by all standards a modern archive. In it were rows and rows of neatly bound manuscripts. Saliya picked up one of the volumes and took it to a table. He placed the manuscript under a reading lamp. He turned a page. What he saw amazed him exceedingly.

A passport size photograph was neatly printed on a front page. Saliya took a good look at the face in the photograph. Underneath the photograph was a caption which read: Venture into the village without a name by Maliki Guluka. Saliya knew Maliki Guluka very well. He had been Chairman of the Manpower Resources Planning Committee a couple of years before. A very distinguished young man in his mid-forties, Maliki Guluka had disappeared without leaving any trace. Saliya sat puzzled, head in his hands.

"I am sitting puzzled," he said. "Head in my hands." He was still in a trance.

"You can say that again," said the Guru as she gave Saliya another neatly bound volume. Saliya read the print on the cover. It read: The nameless village - a leap of faith by Gondola Mkonzi. Saliya could not believe this either. Gondola Mkonzi was his own step-brother who had disappeared only a couple of months before. Gondola was a religious man in his fifties, he never had any literary or academic pretensions. And he had written this manuscript? Saliya opened the book and, true enough, there was Gondola's most recent passport size photograph neatly printed inside. He seemed to be peacefully pleased with something. Saliya sat bolt upright, slightly dazed with confusion. He dropped both his hands from his head and said:

"I can't believe what I am seeing. I am sitting bolt upright, slightly dazed with confusion. I am dropping my hands from my head or is it both my head from my hands?" He was puzzled. At that moment Sambo appeared.

"Ah, my saviour. You have come to save me from myself at last!" exclaimed Saliya.

"Redemption at last," he said, hugging Sambo.

"Stop stealing words from my mouth," Sambo said to Saliya patronisingly.

"You have stolen my thunder! He says," Saliya said to Sambo, observing at the same time that heads were turning in his direction all around the archive. Some of the heads were falling off modern shelves and rolling towards him on the plush golden carpet. Others were jammed between obstacles, caught by swollen lips and protruding remnants of their necks yet there were some which merely popped their eyes resignedly at Saliya, preferring to remain in position, whistling audible tunes, while their eyes joined the throng of heads which were proceeding in the direction of Saliya's table.

"Quick, here is a dictaphone - your version of the village without a name!" said Sambo, handing over a dictaphone to Saliya.

"But I have nothing to say. There are questions I still want answers to."

"More questions?" Sambo asked. "The quest for knowledge and answers is a never ending pursuit."

"Indeed it is," responded the Guru, who materialised from somewhere. She was now resplendidly clad in a beautifully flowing velvet costume.

"Knowledge," said Saliya.

"The shroud of Turin," said the Guru. "Have you heard of it?" she asked, resting one foot on a head which had rolled too close to her, its eyes were lustily gazing up the Guru's costume, a mischievous grin written all over its face - until the Guru put her foot down firmly on it.

"Okay, if you insist. But do not blame me if I have very little to compliment you on. Wait a minute," said Saliya scratching his head in thought, only to discover that he was scratching Sambo's head. "Now I can see truth!" He said, gazing at the Guru. "I have discovered the secret of life!"

"Now I can be free again," said Sambo joyfully, linking hands with Saliya while both of them hopped and skipped with excitement like little children.

"Let's go," said Sambo leading Saliya away.

"Is this it then? Free at last! I can't wait to see the last of this."

"Me, neither. But end it must, like all things," Sambo said.

"To end, to begin, to end - the ending being the beginning of another end," he enthused. "DNA, RNA, ectoplasm, amphioxus - hoora!"

"What was that?" Saliya asked, puzzled.

"What was what?" Sambo asked, puzzled.

"DNA, RNA and the others."

"Deoxy... Rebonuc... but you already know this - damn it!"

"I can't wait to tell the outside world about this," Saliya said. He was exceedingly excited. They were now approaching the barrier to the village. Two more old girls were now manning the barrier.

"This is it then. Free at last. Bye-bye." He proffered a hand in farewell but noticed that Sambo was no where to be seen. Then he sensed a movement behind him. He turned round, too late to evade the blow which struck him on the head. But in that instant between the twilight and dawn, Saliya knew the secret of the nameless village.

The End

Questions

1. Of what board was Saliya a member?
2. What reasons does he have for undertaking this trip? Does he fulfill his mission?
3. Explain the meaning of the word 'acolyte' as used in this story.
4. What reason is given for not allowing Saliya to see the face of the old man?
5. At the gate to the village, Saliya's mouth was searched. What weapon were the girls looking for?
6. Describe, in your own words, the ceremony of absolution of the thieves.
7. The hangman of this nameless village does not hang anyone. Why then do they have him?
8. In what way is the ending of this story a particularly sad one?
9. Choose one of the characters that Saliya met in the nameless village and say why you like him/her.
10. Do you think it is an appropriate title? Explain
11. Discuss the following themes from this story:
    (a) Quest for knowledge and answers
    (b) Faith
12. The story explores some traditional religious beliefs. What are these? Discuss.
13. From what point of view is the story told?

14. In the nameless village, there are things happening which are contrary to real life. Make a list of such situations and hold a discussion.
15. What things in the story resemble what happens in a democratic society?
16. In the story there is one statement which suggests to the reader that the characters are of two different natures; human beings and spirits. Find the statement and analyse it.
17. It is generally believed that secret societies of the world like Nyau are inhabited by spirits and if you want to know about them you should be initiated first. In your opinion, is Saliya initiated into this society by the time the story ends? Discuss.
18. Examine the dialogue and say whether the dialogue of the spiritual beings resembles or differs from that of Saliya.
19. In your opinion does Saliya's way of speaking and thinking change or remain the same from the beginning of the story till the end? Explain.
20. Examine the use of suspense in the story.

ACHITIYENI, THE NANNY BIRD

Dickson Vuwa-Phiri

EVERY MORNING she woke up before anybody else in the village. She would make the fire, boil water for her husband and leave breakfast ready for him before she proceeded to the garden. She had to walk about ten kilometres to the garden. They had one little child - a baby which often cried a lot. The mother had a lot of difficulties attending to it and work in the garden at the same time.

One day when the baby was quiet for some time as it lay on a mat in the shade she tried to take advantage of this to hoe as much as she could. She had been hoeing for some time when she heard the baby giggle as if it was playing with someone. She wondered what could be tickling it. She stopped hoeing and tip-toed to where the baby lay to see what was making it happy. The baby had a nanny. It was a big bird. It sang to the baby while fanning it with its big wings. The song it sang went:

Achitiyeni kulakwa, alakwi weneku!

Achitiyeni kulakwa, alakwi weneku!

The song said "do good to them, and let it be them to make the mistake". The baby seemed to enjoy the company. She decided not to disturb them and went back to work. The baby never cried again. In the evening when she returned to leave, the bird flew away into the bush and she left for her home.

The following day the bird came again almost as soon as she laid down the baby. It came everyday thereafter. She called the bird, Achitiyeni. With a nanny bird, she was able to cultivate a larger part each day than she would have cultivated with a crying baby. She was soon nearing the end of her garden.

One evening she decided to tell her husband about this wonderful companion for their baby and what a help it had been. The husband, however, got very angry with her. He accused her of being so careless and stupid as to allow a grizzly bird take care of the child. He said the bird would one day steal the baby or harm it and sternly warned her of serious consequences if she continued with her nanny bird. She tried to explain that this bird was different, so kind and friendly that without it she would not have done even half of the work she had done. But he could not have any of it.

The following morning, after she had gone to the garden as usual, the husband decided to follow her, armed with a bow and arrow. As usual, she laid down the baby on the mat under the tree and proceeded to the part of the garden she was to work on that day. The bird immediately descended and landed where the baby lay. Soon it was playing with the child. The child bubbled with joy and was trying to sit up. The husband hid in a bush nearby and saw all this. His anger welled up in him. He was sure his wife would not chase away the bird. He aimed his arrow at the bird to kill it. He pulled the string but as soon as he released the arrow, the bird flew away. He saw the arrow as it hit the baby in the head. The baby gave one loud cry and went quiet. The mother heard the cry and immediately rushed to where she laid the baby. She was sure something serious had happened to it. The father also dashed to where the baby was and almost bumped onto his wife. The baby lay in a pool of blood with the arrow stuck into its head. It was dead. The mother collapsed onto the ground. The father looked at the child, then the mother. He was mute. From a tree nearby the nanny bird sang:

Achitiyeni kulakwa, alakwi weneku!

Achitiyeni kulakwa, alakwi weneku!

The End

Questions

1. Who is Achitiyeni?
2. Why was it possible for the woman in the story to cultivate a larger portion of her field than usual?
3. What do you think about the husband's action in the story? Give reasons.
4. This story portrays some of the gender imbalances which women face in some cultures in the world including Malawi. Hold a debate on the motion: "Shared responsibilities between men and women in a new gender sensitive world".
5. Discuss the portrayal of men and women in this story.

THE MZUNGU OF MKANDANDA VILLAGE

Cecilia Hasha

THOUGH IT was harvest time, the village had nothing to harvest. They had not planted that year. Why should they bother? It had been obvious that there would be a drought. The village elders had also foretold it. Six years of plenty were to be followed by three of famine. The previous year had been the last of the years of plenty.

And when the rain came, it was too little, too late. The villagers had therefore to buy maize from Chembiya. He was the only one who had food to sell. He had everything; maize, groundnuts, rice. He had been clever. Despite the threat of a drought, he had hired men to prepare his fields. Three maize fields, two groundnut fields and a large rice field. People had thought he was crazy then but during this time they all admired him.

It was during this harvest time that Chembiya's wife had another miscarriage. The third time. The first time, a baby boy died during delivery. Midwives had spread the rumour that the young woman was in unusually great pains during delivery.

"The man is unfaithful," accused relations of the wife. "You don't count chickens before the eggs are hatched," others commented.

Chembiya had indeed counted chickens before the eggs had hatched. A month after marrying his wife, he had gone to the city to prepare for the coming baby. He bought shawls. He bought a basin, clothes and milk. His child should be the first in the village to drink milk from a bottle. Why not? He was a rich man. His children should also be treated as such.

And then, there was a second miscarriage. A baby girl. Big. Healthy. It was born on a Saturday at dawn. By morning, before the dew was gone, it was dead. It was then that Chembiya went into serious farming. What else could he do? He had been disillusioned.

And when it happened this third time, he was furious. Yes, he was angry. Not sad. Angry. He was not angry with his wife as most men would have been. He loved her. He knew that she too was in pain. He was angry with fate. Why should it be him? Every family in the village had children except his.

"Chembiya!" called his younger brother, Che Saidi. His heart beating fast. So heavily.

"The spirits are speaking through our sister. They say they have a message for you."

Chembiya woke up from his day dreams. He rushed to his sister's hut. He found her lying on a mat. She was still calling out Chembiya. "He is here, he is here," said Che Ali, Chembiya's uncle.

"I am the spirit of your mother. Your father and I, are angry with you. We are the one visiting your house and we will do so if you do not change." The spirit was now shouting. "Your father and I need a decent lodging. We are hungry and thirsty. If you do not give us these, you too shall never rest."

Chembiya was frightened. He now saw what was behind the miscarriages. He believed it was his dead parents. How had he not seen that? How could he be so ignorant? He should have known from the start.

His parents had died six years ago when he was away to TEBA in South Africa. He was away for three years. When he came back, rich, he never spared anything for them, not even a prayer. They must really be angry with him.

So the next day he went to the graveyard. He went there with other men and his relations. He cleared the place himself and together with his relations, they built a tombstone on each of the graves. He planted flowers before they left for home. Back home he prepared a big feast, sadaka. He slaughtered the fattest cow. Five goats. Ten chickens for chiefs. There was nsima, rice, and tradition-al brew, thobwa. There was food of every kind. His sister was the over all in-charge for the kitchen. After all it was through her that the spirits demanded this feast.

It was the biggest and the best sadaka people in the village had ever had. There were many people. Chiefs from surrounding villages, men, women and chil-dren all ate and took back to their homes whatever was left over.

In the late summer of that year, Chembiya's wife conceived again. This time, there was great expectation. Why not? The family had made peace with the dead. The spirits which had been taking the children in the past now lay asleep, satisfied. Chembiya wanted to choose a name but he didn't. Why should he make another mistake?

On the ninth month, midwives gathered in Chembiya's house. Six of them. Not out of necessity. They each wanted a price for their part in the delivery. Soon the baby was born. It was a boy. A dead baby boy. There were no questions and no crying. They immediately buried the 'thing' quietly and quickly.

"What is it?" "What must we do?" asked Abiti Joni, his wife, after some days.

"I know there is someone behind all this. Some one is playing tricks with me," Chembiya said.

"I have been thinking about that too," added Abiti Joni. "But what can we do?" she asked.

"Well, we will have to go to Chilindi and consult Cheng'ambi, the *sing'anga*. He may tell us the truth."

"I have been thinking about that too," she said feeling relieved.

The *sing'anga*'s hut was a small place with a heap of herbs on one corner. The other side was laid with a goat's skin serving as a seat for patients and enquir-ers. On the walls there hung beadstrings, strange horns and bird feathers. there were also goats and cow tails hanging there.

Cheng'ambi himself looked as strange as the paraphernalia. Short, small with a deep voice bigger than his size, he was wearing a white robe that dwarfed him further. He wore a black collar and a hat with horns on each side.

He did not ask questions or give greetings to the patients or enquirers as they took their turns in front of him. Such formalities are not for the spirits. When

Chembiya and his wife's turn came, he told them that he knew why they had come. The spirits had told him everything. He went to the mirror and rubbing some concoctions on it he showed to Chembiya and his wife to see for themselves the source of their misery.

It was an unbelievable sight. His three brothers, the uncle and his sister all appeared sitting in a circle. Each held a club in their hands. A baby appeared in the middle and was quickly hit on the head by his sister. Then another came in and was hit by his uncle. The third and fourth were hit by two of his brothers. After this they all sat back apparently waiting for the next, ready to attack.

"Why do this to me?" he asked no one in particular. He remembered all the money he had given each of these relations when he came back from South Africa. He gave them blankets and clothes. He has always shared maize to them when they were hit by hunger. He could not believe this cruelty. What wrong had he done them? What wrong had his children done? What about his wife?

It was obvious that he was rich and if he were to die leaving children behind, they would be the ones to inherit the wealth. This was definitely the reason for all these killings.

"They will stop at nothing," said the doctor. Chembiya pleaded for assistance.

"No," the doctor said. "They are too advanced for my medicine. Their skills are not of ordinary witchcraft that I deal with."

As the two walked back home, Chembiya felt a sense of helplessness. His hopes of a family were gone. Miserable. Chembiya now understood why his only sister was always quarreling with his wife. He saw why his brothers only visited him in the night and why they hung clubs in the houses. He decided not to talk to them anymore.

Then suddenly Chembiya fell sick. Very sick. He believed it was now his turn to be bewitched. When he went back to Cheng'ambi, it was only confirmed that his siblings were responsible. But as before, he could not help.

Chembiya grew wild. He started selling his possessions. Bicycles, cattle, goats and clothes. Even his wife's clothes were sold. His brothers tried to stop him but he refused their advice. Actually he didn't even talk to them. He had stopped speaking to them after the first visit to Chilindi. He then sold his house and moved to the lake where he built himself a small hut on the sandy shore. His wife simply followed him. She could not stop him. She was told that she would be the next to die.

When his condition became worse, as he gasped for breath, he saw death so near. Every heart beat was like the last. He stopped eating. He couldn't open his eyes. He could not sleep either. He seemed to hear the sound of owls on top of his hut heralding his death. In his mind, he could see the beautiful wife he was to leave behind. He recalled the day he first met his wife. He had just returned from South Africa. He had come back with two bicycles, one for himself and the other for the would-be wife. He was the first man to own a bicycle in Mkandanda village including the surrounding lake shore area. People called him the Mzungu of Mkandanda village. Abiti Joni was the first woman who came his way and said yes to him. She was a cousin of his and actually prepared food for him and a bath immediately upon his arrival from South Africa. She was dutiful, polite and beautiful.

As he lay seeing death come, somehow he felt a sense of energy come back to him. He opened his eyes and moved his head. He looked around and saw his sister, uncle and brothers sitting around him. But his pregnant wife wasn't there. He was sure she had deserted him. What else was left of him. A living skeleton. When he moved his lips he uttered one sentence. He told those sitting around him to go away. He was so firm though weak. No one questioned or insisted. They dispersed.

Left alone, he moved his feet and rose from the bamboo bed. He pulled himself up and reached for the bag of money under his bed. It had all the money from the sale of his property and what remained of South African earnings. It was heavy but he managed to lift it. He staggered out of the hut and the little fence and headed for the lake fifty metres away. As the tidal wave hit the shore, he raised the bag with his last might and sent it with the wave as it returned. After all, who had any use with the money when he is dead. He felt light. Even his heavy heart felt light too. He was relieved. His greedy siblings will have nothing to inherit. He was going to die a happy man. When he tried to walk back, he fell down and collapsed. He was picked up by fishermen to his hut. People thought he was trying to throw himself into the lake.

A year later, the Mzungu of Mkandanda village was sitting by his hut leaning on the wall watching his half naked pot-bellied son eat yesterday's leftovers. His wife sitting beside him mending patches onto remnants of their lost glory. His younger brother brought him roasted maize as his sister shouted to her sister-in-law that they can join them for lunch.

The End

Questions

1. Why did people think that Chembiya was crazy in the sixth year of drought?
2. Although Chembiya was well-to-do, he was not a happy man. Why?
3. What do you think was the motive behind Chembiya's relatives when they persuaded him to organise the *sadaka?*
4. What did the medicine man tell Chembiya on his request? Do you think the medicine man told him the truth? Give reasons.
5. What evidence in the story shows that Chembiya may not have been told the truth by the relatives and Cheng'ambi?
6. Why was Chembiya still unhappy although he gained what he had always wanted?
7. Look at the sentences in the story and explain how the author uses them to emphasize important points.
8. The author is criticising some of Malawi's traditional and cultural beliefs. Explain this with examples from the story.
9. Although the Mzungu of Mkandanda wanted to die he did not. In your opinion do you think this makes the story comic or tragic?
10. Comment on the plot of this story.
11. "Chembiya had indeed counted the chickens before the eggs had hatched." What other proverbs would you use to describe Chembiya and his family matters?

WALLS OF SHAME

Steve Sharra

A KEY was violently inserted into the keyhole, and equally roughly, turned. The sound made her start up. It's my nerves again, she thought. She heard the noise made as the lock gave way and the metal rod was pulled to one side. The cell door opened and a face peeped through the doorway. The woman inside made no move. She just lay huddled on her narrow bed along the thin mattress, her head resting on the side of her straightened hands clamped together as in prayer.

The face in the doorway lingered on for a moment, and then moved one step forward. It was a woman sergeant. Such was the smallness of the room that the

146

one step took her just a foot away from the edge of the bed where the prisoner lay. The light had been on all night, and the sergeant could see the dried tears on the woman's face.

"The Life President of the Republic, the Head of State, has permitted that you be allowed to go and pay your last respects to the body of your late husband. A vehicle is waiting outside," the sergeant regurgitated a memorised statement.

She rose from the bed feebly and stood up. She did not look up at the Sergeant, who felt obliged to go on.

"I'll be back shortly with fresh clothes for you to put on, and shoes."

"Don't bother," said the prisoner, without raising her voice. "I don't need to change. It serves no purpose. I will go as I am."

"I am under orders," the sergeant said and disappeared almost immediately. She returned soon with a crumpled parcel in her hands, which she hurriedly gave to the prisoner.

"You must dress, now!"

She hesitated for a moment, then looked up at the sergeant. Their eyes met briefly before the sergeant averted hers. Her eyes were barely visible just below the shade of her cap. She wore a skirt of pure cotton khaki and a khakish woolen blouse neatly tucked in. A whistle lay slotted in her right breast pocket, its lace stretching from the left. She had a thick short baton stick in her right hand, which she often used for gesturing and pointing at things as she spoke. More than once before, she had worked herself into a temper enough to propel her to cruelly use the baton on the woman. It had been more frequent in the first two years of the detention.

She and her husband had never seen each other since they got detained here. They were both convicted of trying to overthrow the legitimate government. They had been tried in silence since they could not argue against the evidence presented. It was now almost ten years in this camp without seeing each other. They would have long hanged if it were not for the international pleas against their death sentence. Thus the Almighty Head of State condemned them to life imprisonment instead. The warders were under strict orders never to allow the two to meet until their deaths.

She changed slowly and reluctantly into the dress brought her by the warder who did not go away. She watched the prisoner's deliberate movements as she changed. In normal circumstances she should not have been watching an elderly woman, old enough to be her grandmother, change clothes. But this was detention. A Maximum Security Prison. And the prisoner was not her grandmother.

"Let's go," the warder said. She drew back out of the three-metre by two-metre cell, waiting for the elderly woman to come out first. The woman looked down at the length of her dress, one of the few clothes she had been allowed to bring with her tó detention. It was a long maroon dress reaching down to just before her ankles. Her black, heelless canvass shoes were a pale yellow and now felt tight after more than eight years of disuse. The dress too felt strange on her.

They got to the Officer-in-Charge. She was immediately ushered out to a waiting car after very brief statements than explanations of why the about turn in the decision to allow her to see the dead body of her husband. She had been told that there would be no chance to see the dead body. But then, "The Life President, in his mercy, has sympathetically considered your request to see the body of your dead husband before it is taken for burial. You are only permitted to view the body, not to attend the burial. The Life President has felt that it is not in the interest of national security to do that." The Officer In-Charge read the statement.

The woman felt a stony lump block her throat and she so much wanted to cry. She resisted the urge. She looked down at the floor and two tear drops fell from her eyes.

"Sergeant, take her to the Landrover!" ordered the officer-in-charge. With tears in her eyes, the woman lifted her head and looked up at the officer. Very quickly the officer withdrew his and instead looked at the shelf on his right and started fiddling with files. A middle-aged man quite light in complexion. He wore his cap firmly on his head, its peak half shielding his eyes. The peak was a shiny creamy white and together with the lion's head and miniature star on his epaulette, they indicated his seniority as chief of the country's most significant prison. This was one detention camp, where the resolve of even the strongest of human beings was broken. This was where you rotted and rotted, your memory entirely erased out of the minds of even your closest of kin. The authorities had a way of sniffing out even mere thoughts playing on the edge of your mind. You were betrayed even by the subversive wrinkle on your forehead.

The police Landrover pulled to a stop just outside the main entrance to the

Police Infirmary. First to jump out of the tarpaulin-covered van was the woman sergeant, then a male prison officer. Two policemen followed. They helped her to come out. The four made a circle round her as she was led through the entrance into the hospital. Another police officer, clad in medical uniform, led the way and showed them to a theatre room.

On the doorway into the room the woman froze. She lifted her hands above her head and was about to let out a loud wail when the four body guards quickly grabbed her hands and hushed her up. Across the room, on a carelessly laid out blanket on a hospital bed and half-covered by one woolen sheet, lay her dead husband. The four bodyguards led the woman closer. She shut her eyes and violently shook as if in an epileptic fit. She made a great effort not to scream. Her body went limp in their hands and they spontaneously tightened their grip on her, steadying themselves in the process.

The medical police officer was moved and he attempted some reassuring words. "Sorry, Madam, but he was brought here too late. Cancer of the throat. He was not able to..."

"Those details will be handled by more competent authorities." Another officer who was also in the room, the most senior officer of them all, interrupted.

The woman prisoner turned to the woman sergeant and softly whispered into her face. The sergeant then stood at attention and saluted the most senior officer, before announcing or begging: "She wants to be left alone for a moment, Sir."

"You shall remain with her," the senior officer answered without bothering to see the reaction of the prisoner.

The senior officer was the last to come out, carefully closing the door behind him. The woman suddenly lunged forward and wrapped her flailing hands around the inert body of her dead husband.

"My loved one, what have they done to you? What wrong did we do to deserve this?" She broke into soft sobs and tears freely flowed out of her eyes, wetting the shroud. She stared into his closed eyes, touched his parted lips with her index finger, and tried forcing them together. They felt stiff. He had been dead some time, she thought.

Still bending over his still body, she closed her eyes and made the sign of the cross.

"Go in peace, my loved one. Until we meet again. Good-bye," she said more to herself. "Lord, have mercy on your son. You alone know what sin we have committed...." She broke into more sobs and wiped her tears onto the shroud. All this while, the woman warder just looked on. She was for the first time moved to the point of tears. She wiped her tears with a handkerchief which she quickly returned into her bag as if afraid of being seen crying. They heard a soft knock on the door from outside and immediately the warder stepped forward while trying very hard to steady her voice. She told the prisoner that it was alright, now. "The others are coming in," she said almost in whisper.

But the woman just lay by the bed side where the lifeless body of her husband lay. The door opened and the officers came in.

"It is time, let's go!" the senior officer ordered. He had his cap in one hand, his baton stick firmly tucked in his armpit.

Later she lay staring at the blank ceiling. She tried to figure out what time it could be, but could not. Faint rays of sunlight were still filtering in through an opening high on the wall. Was it late afternoon now or late morning? It could also be early morning. You lost count of the hours in an enclosure like this one. You lost the sense of time. All you did was sleep, open your eyes, yawn, sleep again. And bathe, whenever allowed, and attend to nature calling. And wait for the warder to bring you your next meal, two for the day. Sugarless, saltless porridge, very watery, for breakfast in the morning, and nsima and beans, sometimes with cabbages, at two every afternoon. This served as both lunch and supper. And wait for the day you would develop a serious sickness and then die, or some divine force would intervene and you would be told you were now free.

If this was now afternoon, then they were lowering his body into the grave, she imagined. So he has gone, leaving her to face the cold, cruel world single-handed. What did he die of? Maybe they poisoned his food? Would they...? she tried to reason with herself. Fresh tears welled up in her eyes.

That man in a white dust coat wanted to say something, she remembered. But was not allowed to. Could he have mentioned why he died... or at least how. Why didn't they inform her soon when he died? No one told her he had been sick. She could not find answers to all this cruelty. Someone should certainly have said something even just to say that he was not feeling well. She now freely cried.

She tried closing her eyes to salvage some sleep, but the glaring light still burned inside her eyes. It was always on. Even when you closed your eyes, you still felt it. She felt her head ache.

This particular morning the woman warder was strangely pleasant. For the first time since, she entered the cell and sat on her bed. She found the prisoner seated, reading her Bible. To get a Bible was not an easy struggle.

"It's the system that is bad... and we are only supposed to follow... It ...."

The prisoner felt disturbed. What was she trying to say or who has now sent her to say this. She had been reading Isaiah chapter 43, on first verse, fourth line, when the sergeant walked in. She thought it was routine check.

"Please, remember me in...," she hesitated thinking the prisoner would interrupt her. "Whatever becomes of you... whatever.... please forgive me... all that I did..." she was now stammering.

"I hope you ..., Please mother, you will remember when I tried to be... when I, I..."

"Let me tell you what I'll always remember," the prisoner now spoke. "These walls, this bulb, that baton stick. The stench of my own waste..."

They heard footsteps approaching from outside, and the warder quickly changed the subject.

"If you could now change into the clothes I've brought you. I'll lead you to the officer-in-charge,' she said smiling for the first time.

"I'll wait out here while you change," as she closed the door behind her gently.

The End

Questions

1. From the story, what evidence is there that the woman and her husband may have been unfairly detained?
2. What tells us that the woman's husband died without anyone attending to him?
3. Find in this story parts that record extreme sadness experienced by an individual.
4. Would you sympathize with the woman sergeant on her change of attitude

towards the female prisoner? Why?

5. "The Life president, in his mercy, has sympathetically considered....." Discuss the irony in this statement.
6. A cruel government may employ the police and other forces to enforce its regulations. However, this does not mean that these forces support the regulations. With reference to the story, discuss whether this is true or false.
7. Part of the torture in this story is psychological. Explain with examples.
8. Towards the last section of the story there seems to be hope for the prisoner. Explain.

FRAGMENTS

Felix Mnthali

THEY ...

SCAMPERED on Songani Lookout like goats in search of fodder. They plucked leaves from ferns and engraved each other's heart on the wet slippery ground at their feet and on the banks of the pines under whose shade their little car rested like a chariot of fire whose mission had now been accomplished. The saints were now in heaven and were running like demented paupers through the footpaths of that artificial forest. At Chagwa Dam they dipped their weary feet into the purring waters below the bridge and waited for sunset as well as for the dawn within them on the smooth grass at the edge of the Dam. The ritual over that mountain remained unchanged. It balanced its wings below the golden rays of the setting sun, above the murmur of brooks and the chirrup of lonely birds and in the fear and trembling of tender hearts.

HE ...

the man of the hour, Didier St. John Sazamuleke saw himself sinking below the accumulated scorn and shame of his invited guests while like a defiant angel of vengeance she, Sizeline the girl he had chosen to honour with his name and prestige floated into the lightning and thunder of the approaching storm - and the master of ceremonies moved and sneezed his jokes like Lucifer presiding over the darkest cloud at the centre of hell. The earth cracked and gave birth to rift valleys and inland lakes. Heat had usurped the long and undisputed reign of the ice-age and the soul of man saw that it was good ... and the soul of man sang and danced and ululated at the weddings of the celebrated without forgetting the poetry of humbler folks. Perched on the crest of his storm-centre the master of ceremonies belched fire and recited some of Kizito Wavisanga Kanonono's verse:

"In these waters and on these sands
we are no longer cockroaches
trapped in the glare of artificial light
but glistering black submarines
who enter the lake from one end
and come out at the other.
You are WOMAN and I am MAN."

SHE ...

allowed tears to disfigure her make-up. This was one of the lyrics she had pasted on her wardrobe at the College of Arts and Sciences. She nodded proudly to the massive congregation of invited guests and before her bridesmaids could hold her back she was on her feet with hands outstretched in the manner of an actress declaiming Shakespeare:
"Let Rome in Tiber melt ... Here is my space'
while we joke with the clear skies above us
and the blue mountains across the lake;
while we leap above the waters like demented dolphins
adding a sound-track to the movie of your smile
and the glow of your birth-mark."

The woman dressed in the colours of the wedding rushed to surround the bride and to drown the "Bravo!" of invited guests in a throaty rendition of
perekani, perekani
perekanitu!
mukapanda kupereka
mkazi salowa!

and the Ndirande Sunset Quintet hit their drums and strummed their guitars in accompaniment. What a joyful noise! Kwathu Community Centre had never seen anything quite like this before but

SHE ...

with her arms outstretched and her eyes glaring at the ceiling was no longer at
the centre of her wedding but out there on the road to Mangochi where Kizito's
tough little car which had cruised the entire length and breadth of our land was
bouncing away on its threadbare tyres. Somewhere in the haze and glow of
happy days recollected in the hour of stress floated the wide-brimmed palm-hat
she used to wear. Her eyes were fixed on his face and her heart was dancing
with the incessant flow of words, jokes and music. A new kind of demon was
in possession of his soul and there was no telling how long he might go on in
this vein. It was enough for her that he worked hard at bringing her into the
rhythm of his ecstasy and that although she flew only an earthly pitch while he
wandered in space with his "chain of being" and his "hierarchy of values,"
there was an exhilarating classical music and traditional dances. He told her
playboy jokes and recited speeches from Julius Caesar. He kissed the air in her
direction and asked her in a mocking sing-song voice,

"Sizeline Mwaiwamphepo, my friend,
how fresh are the breezes at the apex of being?
What colours are the rungs on the hierarchy of values?"

"Do you mean, Sapitwa?
We have only been as far as Nalipiri Rest House.
Yet you swore and promised to take
me to all those treasures of our land
which have been here since time
began but which until now have
been patronised only by foreigners ..."

"Yes, of course, I mean Sapitwa.
Is it true then
What they say about this peak
that aimed at infinity
like a Gothic spire in the age of faith
and like infinite joy in our faithless age
it is the invincible peak
to which man aspires?

"Do you mean, 'tourist man'?"

154

The little car bounced and rolled its way to the lake through centres of exquisite palm-baskets, fancy hats and multi-coloured mats. There were here and there stacks of fresh fish from both the great lake and the Shire River. Smoked fish vied with freshly grilled fish and the aroma mingled with the aroma from Sizeline's perfume. From the nearly dense forests of Machinga the little car bounced its way to the baobabs and palms and dark-gray loams of Mangochi. They stopped now and again to look at the handiwork more closely and sample the grilled fish. They also stopped to admire some birds and butterflies and Kizito remembered a poem by one of his childhood friends:

I returned to the desert
to embrace the miracle
dancing in the whirlwind
and perhaps to stumble
on the memento of millennium that was
when I discovered to my joy
a butterfly conversing with the sun
I am doomed oh I am doomed
to look for the miracle dancing in the whirlwind
and perhaps to stumble on the
memento of a vanished millennium.

They entered along the sandy beach at Nkopola Lodge and giggled and kicked the waters of the lake like toddlers in a bathtub. They decamped to Muona Inn when word reached them that the Ndirande Midnight Revelers would be playing there for the weekend. They danced until the early hours of the morning though during one of the breaks their table had been surrounded by tourists intrigued by the flow of words from a man who seemed to be hypnotising his partner:

"We writhe and yawn and
    backslide
    to the tango of our illusions and
    the foxtrot of infinite desire
    We dance with the wind
    and breathe the dust of the earth
    to bury the self now shattered in that blinking
    orgy of neon lights."

155

The earth and the seasons changed. Early May found them standing above Chingwe's Hole and surveying the course of the Shire sniffing its way from the great lake to the Zambezi. When they returned to Chagwa Peak, Chagwa Dam, Queen's View and Emperor's View he could no longer contain himself. He turned her face first towards him and then to Zomba Town and the wider valley below, then back to poetry:

"For us also the sun will rise
trailed by the iambic pentameter
of children marching to school
of hens cackling beneath the nkhokwe
and marbles crackling on the bawo

We shall chant lyrics
not to the semblance of a dream
that might have been
but to the labours of man
who dresses mountain-slopes
with man-made forests and gardens of maize
who tattoos valleys and plains
with acres and hectares of tilled land
and triumphs over leopards and hyenas
cruising the heart of darkness."

When summer turned into autumn Kizito's little car had already been driven "round the clock." It had been to the hot springs of Machinga, the Game Reserve at Kasungu, to the gigantic forests on Vipya Plateau, to Ndirande Mountain, to Lake Chirwa. Kizito recited his poetry and was in turn inspired to write more. It sometimes came back to the office we shared at Smart Higginson (Malawi) Ltd. on the menus of Hong Kong Restaurant, Rahiti Restaurant and at times on the statements of such interesting places as Sunrise Night Club, Fig-Tree Bar, Tiyanjane Rendezvous - and

SHE ...
was with him all the time, buried in his life-style, breathing his system of likes and dislikes. Little wonder I would often find carelessly lying on his desk letters written in a childlike hand reading like our own attempts at creative writ-

ing when we chose this course at Chancellor College:

"Kizsy, Navy, keep it up!
I mean the way you love
me. I am floating on the
crest of a mountain-like
wave and unless you remain
firm like a plank from a
sinking ship, I will drown.
Cover me; keep me afloat
etc etc."

Even now it is hard for me to bring together the marathon confession which both of them poured on me after that pandemonium of a wedding, when I had to snatch the keys from Kizito and drive his little car to the house of Didier St. John Sazamuleke. Sizeline had broken off from the solemn procession entering Didier's company jaguar to run to that little beetle of Kizito's. And the soft-spoken Didier had also said his thing and I had come to like the guy. It was not for nothing that Systems Analysis Corporation had elevated him within two years from being a management trainee to Company Secretary. The times were grand and the man rose to the occasion. How he changed Sizeline's mind is something that will take time to follow especially as I am not good at understanding young girls from College even if they are closely related to me as Sizeline Mwaiwamphepo is. You see, she is my sister, that is, the daughter of my mother's sister. I still remember the gloomy scene in our little office at Smart Higginson (Malawi) Ltd. For hours on end Kizito stared at the ceiling without really seeing anything. He who had never even at the funerals of his closest relatives shed tears, was now allowing tears to roll down freely over his sideburns down to that immaculately preserved suit he wore to the office when he was in a happy mood. We work for a firm of Chartered Accountants and have to look smart all the time. Tears were out of place, unseemly, unmanly, even in a man who had been known to write poetry and to weep at good music since leaving Chancellor College. I took the liberty to snatch and read the letter lying under limp hands on his desk. It was short and "to the point":

"Dear Kizsy,
A man we chatted with briefly that weekend we were at the lake has asked me

to marry him. *I am sorry to let you know that I have accepted his offer. In time you will understand my decision and perhaps forgive me. Meanwhile I thank you for every bit of love you gave me. It was 'super.' Please come to our wedding. Both Didier and I would be happy to see you among our guests of honour. Invitations are going out in May. Be sure to come.*

Size.

Only a saint or a clown or perhaps a cloud would have accepted this invitation and I told Kizito to be a man and forget all this bacchanal.

"Take a holiday and disappear with one of our curvy secretaries. Considering the things you can do with language such a secretary will thank Sizeline for vacating her position and perhaps curse her secretly for having taken this long in coming to her decision. May is the time for such a holiday. Who knows, you may come back determined to send your own invitations in June." Nothing doing, he would attend the wedding and no, he had no interest in anyone else at that time.

This was to be the beginning of many a frank and useful exchange of views (as diplomats say) between Kizsy and myself. His emotional life was none of my business but he was such a good colleague, so good at accounts, darts and beer that he became a substitute for my brothers, all of whom are far away and when I discovered his love for my sister Size - I made him a blood-brother even before Size - found the time to ask me. His poetry moved me and I envied him for that but I had no time to delve into his hidden meanings - not with all these accounts and audits hanging on my desk. I believe in the sweat from a man's brow not in his anguish. That is why Didier fascinated me and had all my sympathy.

The End

Questions

1. Read through paragraph 1 and identify words or phrases that indicate that the 'They' were in love with each other.
2. Whose wedding do we read about in paragraph 2?
3. During the celebrations, the woman getting married remembers the experiences she had with someone else. Who is this person? In what way did the

woman disappoint this person?

4. In groups, discuss whether the title of this story is suitable considering the events in it.
5. The author of this story uses flashback to tell the story. Arrange the events in chronological order starting with the first one to the most recent event.
6. Suggest reasons why Sizeline changed her mind.
7. This story does not just contain pieces of poetry but it is also poetic. Do you agree? Explain.
8. Look at the sections that are in stanza form and discuss how they comment on the themes of the story or the story as a whole.
9. The story is divided into several sections each starting with a pronoun. How does this technique assist you to understand the story?
10. Discuss characterisation in this story.
11. It is typical of Felix Munthali's writings to use Biblical or religious symbols. Read through the story again and explain how biblical or religious symbols are used.
12. Discuss the theme of materialism in this story.
13. Explain how the plot develops in terms of conflict, climax, and resolution.

OLD NSIMBI'S SHADOW

Peter Kalitera

TALL, THIN and willowing, the old man edged his way slowly but steadily through the crowd of his fellow job seekers, feeling the way with his walking stick in a blind man's fashion. He finally placed himself in front of the crowd that was standing before the closed company gate.

The crowd looked hopeful and anxious. In the small shed by the gate, the gate attendant studied the crowd with a tired eye. He rose to his full height; a beefy man with square shoulders and a pumpkin shaped head. Flexing his muscles, he reached for a stout baton stick and walked slowly in deliberate steps to the gate. The job seekers jostled and pushed one another at seeing the gate attendant.

"What do you want?" asked the gate attendant in his booming voice, while clinging to the gate.

"Employment!" the job seekers responded in unison. Hundreds of them.

"What does it say there?" he asked, indicating to them a sign that read: "**NO VACANCY**".

"But it was on the radio!" again they chorused. The gate attendant looked at them quizzically. He never listened to the radio and in any case, his own radio was all but a box with no speakers and wires. He had taken it to a radio repairer who removed things from it instead of repairing.

"What did the radio say?" he inquired.

"There is employment here!" the crowd shouted at him.

The gate attendant could not understand. Vacancies here? When did they say that? The gate attendant thought to himself.

The three-week long strike at the factory had just ended. Workers had reported for their duties that very morning. Except for the two ring leaders who were fired in the process, all had come back.

The gate attendant hesitated a little and then turned and sauntered to the offices. The factory chimneys sent thick black smoke into all directions as the machinery made deafening noise. Workers moved up and down in a busy mood in their orange overcoats. The job seekers outside the gate waited patiently. The gate attendant returned, walking humbly beside a young man in an expensive cream suit. One could tell from his face that he was an adolescent. He looked hesitant.

There was a tremor in his voice as he addressed the crowd. "The company wanted to employ people because of the strike. But now that it is over, we are employing no one for we have just retained the same staff. So there is no employment here. I am really very sorry ladies and gentlemen!" he concluded his brief speech.

The crowd protested. They looked more like agitated animals. Everyone was now talking at the same time. Tempers frayed. In his heavy woolen overcoat, the old man who had been squeezed away from the front pushed his way forward again until he faced the young man. He spoke slowly but deliberately. "My son, can't you take pity on us? I, for one, haven't eaten for three days now and ..."

"Keep quiet old man or ...!" the gate attendant threatened. The old man did not back away. He fixed both the young man and his gate attendant with his eyes and without saying another word, retreated to go and seat on the ground across the road.

"You have heard for yourself from the Personnel Manager. There is no vacancy here!" the gate attendant said with emphasis.

A woman rose to challenge him. "We are here because of the advertisement over the radio. It says that as a result of a strike at this company, all workers have been dismissed and new people of all skills are required. We could not have come here if it were not for your advert?"

"No!" came the chorus. The gate attendant looked at his boss who passed a thin pink tongue over his dry lips.

"Just as I have already said, that is true. We had at first decided to sack our striking staff. But we have since settled our differences, and all are back to work. We don't need any one else!" the personnel manager said trying to raise his trembling voice.

The crowd raved. They pushed and shook the factory gate. Several suggestions were put forward: burn up the factory; beat up everyone at the factory; go to the labour office; or take the company's management to court for cheating them. They finally agreed on a demonstration to the Labour Office to present a petition.

As they turned round to start the march, a group of heavily armed policemen stormed at them and spread tear gas.

The crowd dispersed instantly. They had not seen the police come and camp just behind them.

After the encounter with the police that morning, old Nsimbi took refuge at the Blantyre City Golf Course along the polluted Mudi stream. He had fallen asleep when he was suddenly awakened by some noises. He looked up and saw a group of white men with golf clubs walking with a set purpose, it seemed, across the whole length of the golf course. Young black boys followed pulling gold handicaps behind them. He gasped. He had been sleeping the whole afternoon. He decided to go back to his squalid home at Manyowe beyond the suburb of Sunnyside. He walked slowly along the road passing through the suburb which then joins the pathway to Manyowe. He didn't walk a long distance before he heard a glittering touring car screech to a halt just metres from him and hooted. The old man wondered what was happening. He was so sure he had not committed any offence.

"Come in madala," the driver called out. The old man realised that the man in the car was the young personnel manager he had seen that morning. He felt relieved. The old man squeezed himself in at the back seat.

"Have you found employment madala?" said the young man as they drove away.

"No bwana," the old man answered looking hopefully at the young man.

"I am looking for a garden boy. Would you manage at your age?" he asked, looking at the old man who was already reaching for the inner pocket of his heavy overcoat. He quickly produced some crumpled papers which served as testimonials. The car pulled up at a lavish house within Sunnyside. The young man quickly dictated terms which the old man readily and unreservedly accepted. Thus, though not a boy in anyway, the old man became employed as a garden boy. Old Nsimbi soon settled in his job. He worked on the flowers very carefully and maintained the huge yard neat. Sometimes during the day, he helped open and close the gate whenever a vehicle came. The watchman only worked during the night.

One day, as old Nsimbi sat near the gate, smoking his chingambwe cigarette, he heard his boss's car come and he quickly dashed to open the gate. He stood at attention as the boss drove through. He immediately shut the gate and picked up the wheelbarrow, the long handled broom and shovel to go and finish the day's work. However, as the boss drove through the gate, Nsimbi had noticed that the woman seated on the passenger's seat was not unfamiliar. When he asked the houseboy, Moffat, he was told it was their boss's mother. Moffat said that she was a prosperous woman possessing fishing boats at the lake. Since, he knew no businesswoman, he felt he must have made a mistake to think the face was familiar.

Three days later, Old Nsimbi had cause to see his boss in the evening. He wanted to brief the boss about the need for fertilizer for the flowers and vegetables in the garden. He timidly knocked at the door to the sitting-room and then squatted by the door. His boss was sitting in a big sofa reading a copy of the Daily News, a glass of orange squash by his side, his feet on the glass topped coffee table. The mother was watching a movie on the video. She too had a glass of orange squash.

"What can I do for you madala?" asked the boss, putting the newspaper away. The old man blinked and then licked his dry lips.

"I have come to inform you that flowers in the garden need ...," he was saying, looking at the boss's mother for the first time. He had also noticed that the woman kept looking searchingly at him. And before he had finished, the woman asked, "Forgive me for being inquisitive, father. Is your name Ndileya?"

The old man brushed his eyes with the back of his hand and said with a trembling voice.

"I am eee Ndi...Ndileya, mother."

"Do you recognize me?" she said in a rather low tone.

Ndileya's gulled face contorted with the effort of remembering and suddenly smoothed out.

"Is it Na-na-Nachanza?" he stuttered.

"Absalom, this is your father, Mr. Ndileya Nsimbi."

She looked at the old man. Tears rolled down her eyes. "You remember that at the time you chased me from your house I was pregnant?" she said to Old Nsimbi. "This is the child." she explained. There was silence.

"My father!" Absalom sobbed.

The End

Questions

1. In paragraph 1, we read about an old man. Describe his appearance in your own words.
2. Why did the crowd at the gate look hopeful?
3. Are the hopes of the crowd fulfilled? Why?
4. The old man finally finds a job. Where? What type of job?
5. The personnel manager discovered something that shocked him. What is it? Why is he shocked?

6. In groups, work out another possible title for this story.
7. This story moves very fast but it has rich lessons that the reader must know. What are these lessons?
8. Does this story have a climax? Explain.
9. Are there any events which foreshadow what will happen next in this story?

RAZIA, MUM'S GOOD GIRL

Greyson Bongwe

THE PERSISTENT knock on the main door disturbed my reading. Who could it be? I wondered. It was 3 o'clock in the afternoon and mum was obviously at work. She had never come back at odd hours. Even when she was struck by asthma, she would still wait till knock off time – 5 o'clock. Razia, my younger sister, had just left for Ndola Township to collect notes on Scarlet Song from a friend and she certainly could not be the one knocking. The knock was heard again, this time a little deafening.

"Who is it?" I asked wondering.

"The owner of the house." It was my mother.

Knowing her volatile temper, I jumped from the chair, rushed to the door, kicking stools on the way, and opened the door for her. Already mum was trembling with fury like a leaf in a windstorm.

"How dare you hold me out like this as if it's your house!" her aging face was all wrinkles.

"I am sorry ... I was studying ... besides I was not expecting you now," I said, keeping a safe distance from her for fear of being smacked. It was a long time ago since she last slapped me but her fury made me be on my guard.

She looked around then at the table where my books were as she rushed to her bedroom. I packed my books to prepare her some tea. She came back from her bedroom wearing her flat shoes. I always wondered why she never wore them when going to her place of work, a bookshop owned by an Indian in town. As she took a seat she noticed Razia was not around and I told her where she had gone.

"You mean your Masongola and her Likuni Girls notes are not enough."

"No mum ... it's just that she wants to read a variety of notes since she didn't understand the book when her teacher ..." I had not finished my explanation when I noted that she had already switched off her attention.

She looked worried. She loved Razia more than she loved me. That I knew. Often the two would sit and chat while I was busy preparing meals or working around, not necessarily because I liked doing that, but because mum didn't seem to like sitting with me. Often times she would ask Razia to plait her hair. As Razia's flimsy fingers moved about in mum's scalp removing dandruff while doing her hair into a smooth and orderly frizzy, I stole glances at her with envy. Why can't she ask me to plait her hair, I wondered. I wished to sit with her, talk to her and laugh with her.

"Do you want some tea, mum?" I asked.

"No, it's alright ... Razia will do it ... go back to your studies."

I felt ashamed but quickly resumed my work on the table. At one point our eyes met. I felt something was really troubling her in particular. She looked at me rather suspiciously.

She came to the table, picked up one book, Senior Biology, and browsed through it. She got to a page on human sexual organs and after sometime she asked me a question that sent a cold chill down my spine.

"How much of reproduction do you cover at school?"

"Not much .... Why mum?" She felt embarrassed and shied away from further discussion on the topic. She dropped the book and went to the kitchen. I heard her talk to someone. It was Razia, with an exercise book in her left hand.

Mum told her to prepare supper and asked me to accompany her to hospital. From Chikanda to Zomba General Hospital was quite a distance. Reluctantly but not showing it, I accepted. I surmised she was under her asthmatic attack and needed some drugs.

At the hospital were a lot of people. Mum kept bumping into them as she ploughed her way to offices that belonged to senior nurses and clinical officers. I simply followed. The stench from drugs and dust bins was nauseating. We stopped at the door labelled Chief Nursing Sister and she stood there waiting for the door to open. Three women who sat on the bench near the door awaiting their turns to get in could not hold their fury. They openly murmured in protest that mum had not observed first come first served rule. One of them actually swore at mum provoking me to anger which I quickly suppressed. All I cared about was that mum should be treated fast.

After sometime, the door opened and the woman who had sworn quickly squeezed in, only to be shamefully sent out. Mum beckoned to me from inside the room. I entered as women outside mouthed condemning words at me and the nurse. The room was furnished with a big table, three chairs, a stool and a bookshelf with dusty books and files on it. At one corner of the room was a bed with a green mattress and movable curtains. The smell of drugs was thick.

"So this is the girl? The nurse asked mum. She was fat, round faced and in her late forties.

"Yes ... just imagine ..." Mum looked worried. I was confused because I could not understand what they meant. As the nurse stood up, her body danced about in her baggy nursing uniform that exaggerated her obesity. She motioned me to follow her to the corner where the bed was. As I followed I looked at mum. I was bewildered.

"Mum I thought I was accompanying you? ... You know I am not sick."

"No monkey tricks here ... just follow her!" She retorted.

Like a sheep led to the slaughter, I followed the nurse who jostled her behind mercilessly. She drew the curtains halfway around the bed leaving enough space for mum, who had turned and was watching us. The nurse carefully palpated and prodded the lower part of my abdomen. I could see her send speechless messages to mum using her eyes and facial expressions. My nipples and my navel were carefully studied. We then retired to the chairs where my mother sat expecting to hear a confirmation of what was in her mind. I was now sure what they were looking for. I sat expressionless, yet anger was welling up in my heart. How could she do this to me when she could have just asked me? I wondered. When the nurse asked me when I had my last menses, I told her I was actually mensing. My mother's eyes opened wide in disbelief. I looked at her while laughing inside me. I was asked to go out as the nurse reported her findings. Outside the room, two pregnant women lay on the floor impatiently awaiting their turn. The one on the bench was justifiably angry. She cast an insulting glance at me. My eyes avoided hers as I waited for mum to come out. I was getting tempted to leave her behind so that I get home as quickly as I could to go through the humiliation I now felt.

We walked back home without talking to each other, mum looking more confused. We were at home at 5.45 p.m. and Razia shouted, "Welcome back," from the kitchen as we entered. We thanked her in unison.

"Don't worry daughter … That's what we mothers ought to do sometimes just in case …." Mum said casually and in a soothing manner after we sat down in the sitting room.

"That's not true. You thought I was pregnant or you wish I were. I know you don't like me mum. Why did you take me only?" I fumed as I sobbed.

"Tomorrow it will be Razia's turn." She whispered for obvious reason, unmoved by my fury.

My anger simmered down and I joined Razia in the kitchen. She was four months pregnant at seventeen years of age. Every day of the vacation that ticked by invigorated her determination to abort. Her fears of mother's reaction if she heard of her condition coupled by her desire to sit for the Malawi School Certificate of Education examination swallowed her fears of death from abortion complications. I loved Razia despite her closeness to mum that put a wedge between me and mum. I did not want her to lose the baby she was carrying even her own life. But every evening she tried on a new drug. It seemed the pregnancy had stuck to her. It could not budge an inch. Fear gripped me one day when we struggled over a black staff she was about to take. I managed to grab it and flush it in the toilet raising mum's suspicion. She saw the dissolved stuff in the toilet but Razia, in a subtle way, explained it away. I could not gather courage to tell her the truth. We never discussed Razia, her good girl.

Supper was ready and silence took full control as we ate. Despite Razia's craft in preparing the fish, mum did not give in any compliments, as would have been the case. Once in a while she would cast inquisitive glances at Razia as I stole gazes at her. She was confused. After supper we silently retired, each to her favourite seat. Mum poured some tea from the flask. Her violent cough that made her sprinkle some tea on the floor broke the monotony of the silence.

"Why not sit a little closer?" Her lips shook visibly as she painstakingly searched for what to say next. She looked as though bereaved and it did tell us the demented state she was in. I moved closer to her. Razia did not move.

"My daughters," she started, "you are now grown ups. Much as you have the freedom to behave the way you want with children's rights around us, you are girls in school who must be responsible and concentrating on your studies."

"That's exactly what we try to do much of the time." I said in response though she had not invited answers. There was an expression of doubt on her face. Razia swallowed hard as she positioned herself on the seat.

"You are aware that since your father died five years ago in that tragic plane crash, I have struggled single-handed to provide for all your needs. I provide for you all that you need. Why is it that of late you have decided ..."

"We always tell you when we have a problem mama," Razia quickly answered.

"No ... there is something you two are hiding from me." It was as if Razia's statement had touched the most sensitive code of mum's heart. Her eyes danced about with fury as she took deep breaths. She raised her legs, pulled out a khaki envelope from under the cushion and put it on the stool. One of you, read this!" she commanded.

I recognised the envelope and the handwriting. Razia was panic stricken as she pointed at me to read the letter. So she had received it, I thought, as my fingers pulled out the note from the envelope. It read:

Dear Mrs. Fulika
One of your daughters is pregnant and she is contemplating an abortion. She is busy looking around for herbs and drugs. Since "kubala nkumodzi", I thought I should tell you.

    Nakubala

Razia, guilt-possessed, was trembling. She was standing up when a gush of urine run down her legs. Fear and not blood must have been flowing in her vessels.

"I am sorry mum ... I ..." Razia sobbed

"So it's you ..." mum retorted. "Why Razia ... why?" She craned her neck towards Razia in fury, her eyes wide open and threatening to fall off their sockets. She clenched her hands into fists and I knew what that meant.

"Mum," I begged

"Shut up!" She said, her eyes fixed on Razia. "How many months ...? Who is responsible...? Why didn't ... didn't ...?" she asked.

Four ..... Bob Dekhani ...." Razia stammered while trying to maintain her usual girlish innocence.

"A teacher at Likuni Boys Primary School," I said, rising to stand by her side. Mum shook her head.

"And you ... big for nothing girl, why didn't you tell me Razia is pregnant?" She asked me.

"How could I... how. Razia is your good girl. I didn't want to stain your relationship. ... You hate me ... you wanted me to be pregnant ... mother why?" I was crying.

"What I hate is that it had to take someone to write me ..." She now sobbed.

"Who ... I am the one who wrote that letter! ... and you are to blame."

"You stupid rat .... Was I the one who ...." She shook visibly in her chair, angry.

"Look here mum," I gathered courage to explain. "How many times have you warned us against men and sex? As if we were kids, how many men have you introduced to us as uncles since dad passed away ... you expected us to ..."

"If I am to blame ... why didn't you fall pregnant ...why?" She stood up.

"I kept away from men. But Razia ...!" Mum disappeared into her bedroom banging the door closed behind her. She was inconsolably angry.

"Sister, what should I do? ...My future is doomed!" Razia said amidst sobs. I walked Razia to our bedroom, comforting her that life was full of fluctuating fortunes. I told her to accept her situation and take care of herself. She could go back to school after delivery, I said.

She muttered a thank you and she flopped into her bed. I rushed back to the sitting room to switch off the lights and check if the doors were locked. A knock on the main door startled me.

"Who are you?" I asked.

"Uncle Gregory ... open." I had met him once. He was the new uncle mum had introduced to us. I opened the door. His beefy belly entered followed by his bald head and the entire body. Here was evidence of mum's idiocy and moral philistinism, I thought.

"Is she asleep?" He asked beaming a smile that disarmed me of my anger.

"Yes ... let me wake her up." Before I could knock on her bedroom door, she opened and without greeting the heap of a man on the chair, she told him to come next time when she tells him to do so. She sounded so serious that he left without saying a word and was visibly surprised. Mum disappeared into her bedroom.

I locked the main door, switched off the lights and went to our bedroom where I found Razia sleeping but still sobbing.

The End

Questions

1. Why does the mother in the story come back from work earlier than usual?
2. Where has Razia gone?
3. What evidence is there in the story that the mother loves Razia more than her sister?
4. What was the medical check-up that the nurse did on Razia's sister aimed at? What do you think were the results?
5. Why do you think the medical check-up was not fair?
6. Why does Razia's sister blame her mother for Razia's pregnancy? Do you think she is justified?
7. Write a short paragraph advising the mother of these two girls.
8. The story uses the "I narrator point of view". How does this affect the unfolding of its events?
9. One of the major techniques that makes this story amusing is its use of irony. Explain how this has been done.
10. The story is set in an urban area but there is not much detail given about this area. What do you think should have been said about this area for you the reader to appreciate it more than you have done now?
11. As mothers and fathers of the future how do you want to treat your children?

TIGER

Ken Lipenga

What immortal hand or eye
Could frame thy fearful symmetry?

A TIGER came into our village. At first no one believed the rumour. Makoto's wife said she had seen the tiger plunge into a bush on her way from the river. But then we all knew Makoto's wife, so no one took her seriously. Later, however, when goats and chickens began to disappear mysteriously, the population of unbelievers dropped abruptly. Tiger footprints became more common, and soon everybody said they had seen the tiger too, either as they returned from the river or in the hills. From the nature of the numerous descriptions (no two were identical), it was not clear whether there was one tiger or a whole pack of them. But that there was a tiger in the village, there was no doubt.

As well as goat-owners and chicken-keepers, we all had our reasons for not liking the presence of the tiger. There were, for instance, those who had children and feared that the tiger might eat up these children. Generally, the majority of us just could not stomach the idea of sharing our humble village with a tiger; we thought Providence was really demanding too much from us.

Our fears were soon proved right. Late one evening our uninvited guest launched a surprise attack on the witchdoctor's hut. Curiously, the tiger left the witchdoctor alone, but caused the most abominable destruction, breaking, among other items, the very sacred pots and gourds in which he kept the ancient medicines and charms. The attacker had apparently meant no harm to the witchdoctor himself, but the poor fellow was so shocked that he died the next morning anyway. He was the last of the ancient herbsmen, and he had passed away without handing over his precious knowledge to the new generation. His death was therefore a great loss to us. The future looked gloomy.

Even as we mourned the witchdoctor the tiger struck again. His latest target was even more bizarre. The tiger invaded the ancient place of circumcision situated by the river, scattering the young men who were there with the nankungwi; I hear the nankungwi himself lost his holy stick as he ran. Some of the young men had just undergone the physical test of circumcision, and under-

171

standably had quite a terrible time running away from the tiger. Most of them ran straight to their homes, and the elders had a rather difficult time trying to persuade them to go back. There was an obstacle: after the invasion the tiger had sought a hiding place very close to the shrine of circumcision, as if to make sure that no one went back. And of course no one dared.

The elders were extremely embarrassed. This latest attack amounted to no less than a direct assault upon the spirits of the ancestors, and many of our elders began to think of the tiger with anger and hate in their hearts. The council of elders met, and it was decided something had to be done.

At first no one had been in a hurry to preach action against the tiger, mainly because most of us thought that this tiger was in fact one of our dead come back. True, there had been individuals who, by way of private enterprise, made several attempts to fight the tiger. Two of these gentlemen were now known to be hiding in their houses, secretly nursing severe scratch-wounds. As time went by, however, the man-tiger theory began to lose credibility. For one thing, there had not been any funeral in the village of late. Besides, this tiger left real tiger-footprints, and not human footprints as would have been the case with a man-tiger. So, although Makoto's wife strongly insisted that the one she had seen had human footprints, we no longer regarded the tiger as a messenger from the grave. Which is why everybody now supported the idea of action. The tiger must be killed. Or chased out of the village.

But first we had to consult old Mtemanyama. Mtemanyama was the village seer, whose opinion had to be heard before all major decisions. He was the oldest person in the village, and had been blind all his life. But he enjoyed a status higher than that of the Chief, for he was the one through whom the people spoke to the great spirits, and spirits spoke to men.

"Yes," said Mtemanyama, when the Chief and his elders went to see him one morning. "The beast must be hunted down and put to death; but the ancestors have spoken to me about the manner in which this shall be done. You shall not send all your warriors after the tiger. You are to send only your best warrior. He alone shall kill the beast and save the village."

Everybody agreed with the wise old man's words, for although we had all been quite loud about "action", few of us were ready to take part personally, not with two of our neighbours nursing ugly wounds.

172

This was so, although more goats and chickens continued to disappear in the middle of the night. There were even more weird stories as the tiger continued to appear in various parts of the village. According to one report, the tiger was seen playing with some children late one afternoon, and disappeared when adults came on the scene. And one morning we heard a story from Makoto's wife: she swore that she heard the tiger walking on top of her roof the night before. Since it was her own roof and her own ears, it was hard to dispute her story. In any case, we were now all used to the tiger appearing in all sorts of places. By now we were resigned to our fate until the tiger was hunted down and killed.

By unanimous vote, the elders decided that the man for this task was Phomu Diga. They were right. Who in the village could outrun Phomu Diga? Who could outwrestle him? Who in all the villages around was braver in war and peace than Phomu Diga? Who always insisted on leading every hunting expedition, and excelled in each one of them? Who other than Phomu Diga? Yes, even those who had lost their wives knew it. Now Mtemanyama's oracle pointed at Phomu Diga as the man chosen by the spirits of our ancestors to confront the tiger. We all cheered the decision, and prayed that Phomu Diga should do well.
Armed with three spears, a club, and the very best of our wishes and prayers, Phomu Diga marched into the bush to meet the enemy. And we all went on applauding till the great warrior disappeared into the thick bush. We were all full of hope. Our tense hearts were relaxing, our blood was again flowing, of Phomu Diga's triumph and eternal peace and bliss that would follow. We could already see ourselves living normal lives again, without uninvited tigers to disrupt our peace. The women, imaginative creatures that they always are, came up with the idea of preparing a feast with which to welcome the triumphant hunter; I hear they were acting on the advice of one of the elders. Anyway we all thought it was a jolly good idea, and were not slow in catching up with the beat of the moment. Some of us men started huts for the grand feast, others fetched firewood, while yet others prepared the old drums for dances. Many goats and chickens were slaughtered, and the good Chief sacrificed two of his fat cows for the occasion. It was clearly going to be a grand show, and not a small number of us secretly envied Phomu Diga for the grand welcome.

All this was two or three months ago, I remember. And Phomu Diga has not yet returned. No one knows what happened. The scene of that two-legged mortal confronting the elusive four-legged monster is not easy to imagine. If indeed Phomu Diga did face it, there would appear to be no doubt as to who won the battle. But no thin mortal even took the risk of going after him; in fact as it appears to me no one seems to consider it necessary. Besides, old Mtemanyama has said it would be an offence to the spirits to follow the chosen warrior. I am not sure about that taboo myself, but then I don't quite care. I was more worried about all that meat. I suggested to the Chief that we share at least some of it before it went bad. But our Chief is the optimistic type; he instead insisted on smoking it. And to date the meat, now smoked to blue-blackness, is still there.

So is the tiger, I am afraid. We see fresh footprints everyday. And the goats continue to disappear, and the tiger continues to roam our village. Phomu Diga has not yet returned. No one knows what happened. To the mystery of the omnipresent tiger has been added that of the great warrior, Phomu Diga. I hear there has been a search recently, and that not a trace has been found. There is not even evidence to suggest that the great hunter is dead. There has been a story very recently, that Phomu Diga was seen on three occasions, riding on the back of the tiger. The eye-witnesses to this are persons, and that would seem to make credibility. But I rather suspect that this story also may be traced to Makoto's wife; and we all know Makoto's wife.

The End

Questions

1. Who was the first person to see the tiger?
2. What was the people's greatest fear when their animals started disappearing?
3. Why was the death of the witchdoctor a major loss to the village?
4. In the end, the village decided that the tiger should be killed. Why did they decide to kill it?
5. Explain in your own words how they were going to kill the tiger.
6. Conduct a debate on whether Mtemanyama's advice was wise or not.
7. Imagine you were Phomu Diga. Write a short story on your experiences in the bush as you went about hunting the tiger.
8. Do you think the tiger really existed in the village? Give reasons for your answer.

9. The author implies the destruction of a people's tradition and culture due to foreign influence. Explain how he has done this.
10. The story is a commentary about the political system of Malawi during the reign of Dr Kamuzu Banda. Draw analogies from the story to justify this claim.

GO BACK TO YOUR ROOM

Steve Chimombo

NDAZIONA'S ELBOWS ached from the prolonged contact with the wooden table top. The first joints of the middle finger, forefinger and thumb were cramped from the extended gripping of the multi-cornered plastic ball pen. He felt as if the outerside of the little finger had been rubbed thin from moving too closely and too often on the smooth pages of the exercise books. Ndaziona had been on his homework - history, biology, English with more to do - for almost three hours now. He felt the strain on the other parts of the body too: neck, back, buttocks and back thigh muscles. It had taken him longer to work on some parts due to the periodic bursts of conversation between his grandfather and mother in the next room.

Akunjila, his grandfather, had landed on them from the village that afternoon. His mother knew what his father, who was away then, would have done had he been around to do the entertaining: bring him a litre of kachasu, the home distilled gin. Akunjila approved of this gesture as soon as he saw his grandson plonk the tall bottle on the table in the sitting room. A short squat glass accompanied it. Ndaziona poured some of the pale faint yellow fluid into the glass. The fumes wafted up to his bent face, stinging his mouth, nose and eyes. They swirled into his lungs and he almost choked as he turned away to offer his grandfather the first drink for that day.

"May our forefathers be blessed," Akunjila intoned. "This is hospitality at its best."

Kachasu, Ndaziona had been told, was the only effective drink for the octogenarian. He regarded any other alcohol - bottled beer, maize beer or the packeted stuff - as women's or children's drink. When he resorted to them - which was rare and under extreme pressure - he still mixed them with the hard stuff.

"This is entirely unacceptable," Akunjila complained in the next room when his daughter-in-law came to collect something. He seemed to have reached the

175

early stages of inebriation. "I can't drink alone like this."

"I'm preparing supper in the kitchen," his daughter-in-law said, "so I can't sit and chat with you all the time."

"I don't mean you," Akunjila almost snorted. "You don't drink."

"Your son comes home late especially at the weekends," was the apologetic reply.

"I can't wait for him all night, besides the bottle is almost gone. Is there another one?"

"We bought only one."

"Are you sending the boy for another one?"

This was what Ndaziona dreaded: having to be sent for refills or replacements. His mother saved him.

"It's rather late and not safe for him to go back to the township for more. Besides, you know what happened to him the last time you were here."

"I could go with him."

"There are a lot of drunks and thugs out there. They go about molesting kids, old women, and men."

"It's alright, my daughter. You're doing enough to look after me. It's just that I came to visit my son, and what do I find?"

"He didn't know you were coming and he had no reason to stay at home. You know your son ... ."

"Of course, I know my son," Akunjila chuckled. "Who else knows him better than I do?"

Ndaziona could not concentrate on the maths he was working on. He dreaded to think what it would be like to eat supper alone with his grandfather in such a state. He looked at the textbook and the hieroglyphs he had made on the page of his exercise book. His gaze wandered over the table to the other textbooks and exercise books in two separate piles. The maths set box, ruler, rubber and pencil were in the middle.

Ndaziona's room was a converted store of the two-roomed house. There were cartons, baskets and mats shoved to one side of the room. A concrete slab shoulder-high was midway between the floor and the roof on one side of the wall. He used the slab as a shelf for his other books, suitcase of clothes he was not currently using and more cartons of knickknacks he had accumulated over the years: torches, batteries, pieces of wire, catapults, pebbles, shells and the like. The other length of the wall was occupied by a single bed above which he had pasted posters of pop singers, soccer stars and athletes. There were also pictures of pen pals he corresponded with from England, Europe, USA and even Japan and China. It was more fun writing to them than doing his homework or entertaining a drunken grandfather.

The table Ndaziona was working on was pushed against the width of the wall between the bed and the concrete slab. During the day, the gloom of the room was alleviated by the light coming from the small three-paned window. The window overlooked the garden and the grass and trees outside. Ndaziona had been working in his room after cleaning, washing and ironing. He had looked up to see his grandfather approaching from the road connecting the staff quarters to the main road. His look held dismay if not dread and resentment at the visitor advancing towards the house. He harboured all these emotions because something always happened when his grandfather came visiting. Akunjila's last visit to town had almost been fatal.

During that visit, his mother had sent him to buy, as usual, a bottle of kachasu from his father's favourite distiller. The township was about three kilometres away and he used his father's bicycle. Since Ndaziona was small and short he could not ride the bicycle on the crossbar and use the saddle on top. He peddled the adult bicycle by pushing his legs between the three bars instead. On the return trip he coasted down a slope at greater speed than usual. He lost control of the bicycle. The handle bars moved to and fro on the steep slope and the next moment he found himself on the embankment amidst broken grass, twigs and churned earth. He must have passed out because he suddenly found several hands of women on him and the bicycle. They lifted both of them, boy and machine uttering sympathetic noises.

"He's too young to ride that bike," one of them said.

"You shouldn't ride it again," another admonished, "or else you'll fall off again."

"Just walk it home," a third concluded.

Ndaziona had righted himself, walked the bicycle for a few meters and then ignored the women's advice.

On reaching home he parked the bicycle against the wall dividing the main house from the outhouses. He went into the kitchen and emerged with a cup of water. He sat against the outside wall to clean his wound. There was a three - inch gash on the inside of his right thigh where the bottom bicycle pump hook had torn at him when he had fallen down. Fortunately there was not much blood coming out.

"Mwana wanga!" his mother wailed as she came out to investigate what had happened to the errand boy.

"Look!" Akunjila had come out, too. "The boy is hurt!"

It was the first time he had cried since he turned into a teenager. They took him to the clinic. He came back with several stitches on his thigh.

It was also with curiosity that Ndaziona watched the progress of the bent frail frame of his grandfather. He looked so out of place in his floppy frayed black trousers and long khaki shirt hanging out. He tapped his way past the row of four houses to theirs, the last one. It was only then that Ndaziona galvanised into action.

"Mother!" he shouted. "Grandfather is here!"

He ran out of his room past the sitting-cum-dining room to the front door. He found Akunjila's bent form at the bottom of the steps. He had a small bundle in the other hand.

"Grandfather!" he went down the steps. "Let me carry that!"

He reached out for the bundle and proffered the other hand to help the visitor up the steps.

"May the spirits of the forefathers be blessed," Akunjila breathed. "How you have grown. Is your father home?"

"Not yet. It's Saturday, so he won't come home till late."

"Still drinking heavily, is he? I thought he nearly died when he fell off the bicycle on one of his binges?"

Ndaziona only knew about the accident the following morning when he saw his mother helping her husband go painfully to the bathroom and staying there to bathe his wounds. His father could hardly wash himself or walk about. He could not hold a pen between the swollen fingers. He was given sick leave for a fortnight or so. Ndaziona got only fragments of what had really happened: A bicycle accident could not have caused the kinds of bruises, cuts and wounds his father brought home that night. There had been a woman involved and it was a rival that had got together a gang to dissuade his father from continuing with the affair.

"At least your mother is here." It was a statement.

Ndaziona assented as they finished climbing the steps, got onto the khonde and went into the house.

"Mother!" he announced again unnecessarily. "Grandfather is here."

"I'm coming!" came from the outhouses at the back.

Grandfather tapped his way to a seat and fell in rather than sat down onto it.

If a equals ten, b equals fifteen and c ... . It was not as if Akunjila was always associated with misfortunes. Some of his visits were uneventful. In actual fact, there was a good side to them: he always brought something from the garden: bananas, groundnuts, pears, sugarcane - things Ndaziona could boast about to his school mates especially to Nkhutukumve, the bully and his gang, things other people had to buy in town. They were home grown and freely given. Yet much as he itched to, Ndaziona could not open the bundle to find out what grandfather Akunjila had brought this time. It was the privilege of the adults to do that. There would be a special ritual for the gift presentation. It would be considered an impertinence if he did. Find the value of y...

"Ndaziona!" his mother called out to him.

"Ndazi-!" his grandfather echoed impatiently. "Your mother is calling you. Why don't you answer?"

He had heard his mother, first time. His mother knew it, too. She had thus several times a day ever since he could remember. Akunjila's previous visits had also witnessed similar calls. His grandfather knew it, too. The dividing door was too thin to keep out even normal conversation at any time. That's how he knew of his parents' numerous quarrels and fights, yes, even fights. He knew quite a lot from his room.

"I'm coming!" He left the books open on the table.

"Why are you hiding?" Akunjila confronted him between sips of kachasu as the boy passed him. "What is it you do in there?"

"Home work. I told you that before."

"You're just avoiding your grandfather, that's that. Like your father. I wrote to him that I was coming today. I don't come here often enough, yet everyone is running away from me."

"You know I enjoy having you around, grandfather," he said before opening the backdoor, "all those stories you tell me when you come..."

He opened the door and descended the back steps. The outhouses consisted of kitchen, bathroom, toilet and pantry.

He joined his mother in the kitchen. The only illumination was the open wood fire in between the three firestones in one corner. His mother was sitting on a low stool. Beside her were plates of nsima and ndiwo: hers to eat in the kitchen and the visitor's to share with Ndaziona.

"Take these to your grandfather."

He reached down for the covered plates and placed them, one pair on top of the other for a single trip. He had left the back door open to ease his re-entry.

"Here's the food at last."

Ndaziona did not answer. He went back to the kitchen for the wash basin. He found his grandfather already at the table. He had uncovered the plates.

"I love dried mlamba," Akunjila commented. Ndaziona did not answer. He pulled out his own chair and held out the water for the old man to wash his hands first.

"Dried fish goes well with kachasu." Akunjila looked at the peppered open mlamba on the plate. For a moment Ndaziona thought the old man would start drooling. He sat down and they attacked the food without any preambles.

"This is why I enjoy coming to town," Akunjila cut off a chunk of fish from the tail end. He champed on it. Ndaziona wondered how many teeth the octogenarian had left. "In the village there is only pumpkin leaves today, cassava leaves yesterday and potato leaves tomorrow. Leaves, leaves, leaves everyday."

"I thought there's fish in Mzimundilinde River."

"Gone, all gone, not even matemba left." He shook his head and then a sparkle came to his eyes. "Do you know it was your father who dug the channel from

180

Mzimundilinde right into and past the village to irrigate the dimba?"

"Did he?" Ndaziona remembered the channel. It was almost half a kilometer long from and back to the big river making a big curve to encompass the village and water its gardens right to their doorsteps, so it seemed. What a feat!

"He didn't tell you that? That was all his doing. Single handed. Not his useless elder brother. All Ndilekeni did was brag about this or that but with nothing to show for it."

"Where's uncle Ndilekeni now?"

"Back to his wife's village. That's where he built his house. He left no mark in his own village. At least your father had the stream, its more than just a channel: it never goes dry. Even at the height of summer it trickles on heroically. That's it, heroically, like your father. You know, your uncle and father actually fought by that stream one time."

"Did they? Why?"

"Just childish quarrels. It must have been over a girl, that's what Ndilekeni was always boasting about. It was quite a bloody fight, I tell you, with almost anything that came by: sticks, stones, legs and all."

"Who won?"

"Your father, of course, although the younger of the two. Do you think any one can beat your father?"

Ndaziona nearly choked on his food. He looked around the table and realised that he had forgotten to bring the drinking water. He excused himself and went out hastily.

The first and last time he saw his father in a fight had not demonstrated any heroism in him at all. On one of those rare occasions he had stayed at home to drink with his friends he had invited. They were at it from afternoon through supper to mid-evening. Since Ndaziona's room was just beyond the sitting-cum-dining room it meant that he went past the revelries periodically. It was bearable in the afternoon: he could play or work outside on the khonde. He went away to the shops and returned before dark. It was different in the evening. After supper he could not work or sleep in his room as the festivities grew louder and even angrier. They were brought to a rude halt by a clatter of chairs and bottles. There was the sound of a scuffle and a falling body. Ndaziona had darted out of his room to find his father sitting dazed on the floor.

The two other men were holding Mr. Ndakulapa, their neighbour, restraining him from continuing the fight.

"Go back to your room!" his father snarled when he saw Ndaziona.

Ndaziona shut the door quickly behind him. He was angry and embarrassed as he sat back at the writing table. His father had looked so stupefied, even so childish as he sat there on the floor trying to get up. It was like the time Nkhutukumve had knocked Ndaziona down on the school playground, with the gang holding the bully back.

"Here's some drinking water, grandfather." Ndaziona came back with the glasses and placed one in front of him.

"Drink water? Who? How can I drink water when I have that?"

The kachasu bottle was still on the little table by the settee where the old man had sat the whole afternoon. It was now just below half. There was some in the glass too. The old man must have been taking it easy. Perhaps he hoped his son would come back soon to join him. Ndaziona wondered at what stage in the bottle's drainage the drinker would be too drunk to continue. Like Akunjila, his father never knew when to stop if he was angry at something or with someone.

The night of the fight Ndaziona's father was not only angry at somebody, he was jealous. He had always suspected Ndakulapa of having an affair with his wife. Ndaziona had caught fragments of exchanges between his parents at different times. The angry words between the men on the night of the fight only confirmed this. Even when the visitors had left his father continued drinking. Ndaziona must have slept for some time when he heard a crash that seemed to shake the whole building.

"Amayo!" a cry from his mother. Ndaziona jumped out of bed and opened his door just as his mother rushed out of the bedroom. She collapsed in one of the chairs holding her forehead tightly with both hands. There was blood spurting out between the fingers, reddening the knuckles, wrists, arms and dripping on her clothes. Ndaziona ran to her and stopped. He looked down at his mother waving her head back and forth, her eyes closed tight, her face proclaiming silent agony. There was a two-inch gash on her forehead. Ndaziona did not know what to do. He felt faint.

"Go back to your room!" His father stormed out of the door.

Ndaziona whimpered, backed out of the room looking at his father, then mother, father, mother. The last vision he had was his father towering over the cowering mother. Ndaziona's head swam. He nearly threw up. He did not sleep that night.

The following morning his mother's head was in bandages.

"He pushed me against the cupboard. The corner __" That was all the explanation he was given. At least the father had taken her to the clinic in the night. Yet the following morning he was not there to face her. It was Ndaziona who saw and felt the great pain she was in. She could hardly see. Squinting pulled at the stitches causing fresh blood flow. Ndaziona helped her in the kitchen and in the house.

"Your father was really a man." Akunjila was washing his hands. The fish and nearly all the bones were gone from the plate. "At your age he was already fighting for his women. He wouldn't let anyone, even his brother, touch his women."

Ndaziona was confused: he piled the plates on top of each other, regardless of which could not fit into the other. He washed his hands as his grandfather groped his way back to the easy chair. He reached for the bottle and poured himself some more.

"This is good." He took a sip. "Do you know when your father started drinking?"

Ndaziona felt like bolting out of the room. He picked up the plates instead, shakily.

"At your age, actually." Akunjila answered his own question. "That's it. It made a man out of him."

Ndaziona dashed out of the room.

"What's the matter?" His mother peered at him from the gloom of the kitchen fire. She, too, had finished eating.

"Nothing," he almost sobbed. "I-I- think grandfather is drunk."

"Don't mind him. The Mwaonekera's are all alike. Him and his son."

"I don't want to be like them." Ndaziona almost screamed into the night.

"Of course not. You're different. People say you take after me. Why, you're both son and daughter to me."

That was it: daughter. Ndaziona, like his mother, had always wanted a sister to care for, watch growing up. To play with at home or take to school, but no one came after him.

His mother never talked about it afterwards but she had been pregnant at least once as far as Ndaziona could remember. During her pregnancy she joked about the little sister who was coming to join them soon. She did not mention a little brother. She grew bigger. Then it happened. A cry in the night. A night trip to the hospital. Several weeks in hospital. She had lost the little sister. Ndaziona knew why: his father had hit her in the stomach in one of his drunken moods.

"It's not mine," he had heard him growl on the night of the hospital. Then the piercing scream.

"Go back to your room!" His father snarled at him when Ndaziona peeked out. He cowered back and bolted the door trembling and sobbing uncontrollably.

Ndaziona was told the following day he could not see his mother for several days. When he did he joined his mother in weeping. Back in his room he could not hold back the tears the whole day and night.

He cooked, cleaned and looked after his father while his mother was in hospital. His father was as uncommunicative and sullen as ever. He growled and snarled his wishes at Ndaziona. Ndaziona had kept to his room in between chores. Mute. Terrified of his father's fury now that the other victim was out of the house. One wrong step or word and he would break just about every one of his bones.

"Your father took after me." Akunjila chuckled in his seat. "I, too, was drinking at your age."

Ndaziona had finished clearing the table of the wash basin and the drinking glasses. He was going back to his room.

"Now, be sociable." Akunjila's voice was slurred. "Don't leave me alone again. Come and sit here. I will tell you the other adventures your father had growing up."

"I haven't finished my homework."

"There's tomorrow."

"I go to church in the morning. And I have soccer at school in the afternoon."

"I want to make a man out of you," Akunjila quavered and gestured to the bottle. "Come, finish that. There's only one shot left. That's good enough for a start."

"No, grandfather." Ndaziona was shaking again. "I'm too young to drink."

Ndaziona could hear Nkhutukumve, the class bully and his gang boasting how drunk they were at the disco last Saturday afternoon. If Ndaziona complied with Akunjila's invitation he could join his classmates boasting about their weekend sprees. He would be a hero, too. The gang would begin to respect him, then. Perhaps they would let him play with them, too, smoking even. Nkhutukumve and his mates smoked other things, too, not just tobacco. If he joined them... . Perhaps he should accept Akunjila's invitation and let his father find him stupidly drunk. Ndaziona would beat him at his own game. He would turn the tables round. His father would mend his ways and would stay at home and care for his family. Perhaps his father would then stop beating his mother, and she would have a baby girl for him to play with. Perhaps they would then be a loving family together.

His father was not entirely cruel: he took his wife to the hospital after beating her up. His mother might not have been entirely demonstrative either but she had not run away from her wife-beating husband. On the contrary she stuck it out, she had even nursed her husband after his bicycle accident. Sometimes his father brought Ndaziona some magazines and books from his work place for his son to read. Ndaziona had put them on the slab of concrete in his room as part of his growing library. His father's additions made more delightful reading than the dreadfully boring textbooks surrounding him, threatening to drown him in his own room.

Perhaps, given a chance they could renew their loving ways. His father had once started teaching his wife how to ride the bicycle. Ndaziona had always trailed behind them during the rides. They had stopped the lessons because his mother had developed swellings between her legs after a few days. It was not his father's fault that they stopped the riding lessons. Then again his father allowed him to ride the bicycle on his own. It was not his father's fault Ndaziona fell off it once. There must be something they could go back to and start all over again as a loving and caring family.

No, his father would not beat him. Why should he? It was Akunjila, his own father, who said that he wanted to initiate him into the ways of the adults.

Akunjila could even take his side: you, too, started drinking at Ndaziona's age, he could reiterate. I, too, started drinking at your son's age. So what's new? What's wrong with the boy taking after us?

No, no, his father was too much of a bully to see the logic in that. He would beat Ndaziona from room to room into the garden and beyond till he could not stand up straight anymore. Ndaziona would end up like his mother: several weeks in hospital. Ndaziona could feel the sweat wetting his arm pits although his teeth chattered as if chilled. A sob he wanted to stifle started building up under his chest. He ran to his room before it exploded in front of his grandfather.

"Coward! You're no better than a girl, really."

The words were flung at him from the octogenarian. They ricochetted on the closing door as Ndaziona bolted it behind him. He trembled in front of the writing table. That's what Nkhutukumve and his gang called him at school. His knees melted under him. He supported himself with the back of the chair as he sat down. He had planned to do Bible Knowledge before going to bed and to prepare himself for church the following day. He looked at the piles of textbooks, notebooks and other school materials. No more than a sissy, really, they seemed to jeer at him. He groped for the Bible under one pile of books. As he opened it randomly tears blurred his vision. His mind did a kaleidoscopic swirl: for God so loved the world he sent his only grandfather... birimankhwe maso adatupa ninji... change the following sentences into the passive ... when angle C is produced to D. *Ababa apha bakha bakha wapha ababa...*

The End

Questions

1. What do we learn about the character of Ndaziona in paragraph 1?
2. In paragraph 2, we learn about an elderly person, Akunjila. What is his main habit?
3. What was it that Ndaziona feared most about Akunjila's visit? Describe what happened on one such visit.
4. Did Ndaziona's father really fall off a bicycle? Explain your answer.
5. Why did Ndaziona not really enjoy the dinner with his grandfather? Explain in a short paragraph.

6. Is Ndaziona a coward or just a good boy? Explain your answer.
7. Parents and guardians can be good or bad models for their children. In your opinion are the parents in this story bad or good models? Explain your answer.
8. Ndaziona is a traumatised child. Explain.
9. Chimombo in this story has shown that he is interested in details. Give examples of instances in which he has devoted effort to give details of objects and activities? How does this affect your understanding of the story?
10. "Your father took after me," Akunjila chuckled in his seat. Explain the irony in this statement.
11. One of the techniques for developing the title of a short story is to quote or paraphrase a very important and/or moving statement in it. In this case, the author has used " go back to your room". Are you satisfied that this is the right title to this story? Explain why.
12. Find the meanings of the names of the characters in this story and explain how they match with their character traits and their experiences.
13. The author seems to give us an impression that wives are abused by husbands just because they are women and not because the husbands are powerful. Discuss the theme of violence against women in this story.

SUITS AND JEWELS

Amos Chauma

VICTORIA DECIDED to spend a few days of her holiday in Zude where she was born and grew up. She had never been there for quite sometime. Felix, Victoria's brother, escorted her to Phodo bus station. "While in Zude behave yourself," he advised. "Avoid staying late in the township. You have just been employed and you are not yet married. The world out there is now dangerous, full of Aids. And another thing, keep your mouth shut. You know the political environment. It is not safe to speak."

"About the Aids, don't worry," Victoria laughed. "I'll behave myself. I'll be safe. I've seen girls like us die a painful death. I'll take care ... I know..... Even the environment you are talking about is not as ... I am not that careless."

The journey on the Phodo - Zude bus was uneventful. She hired a tax to Zude Inn immediately she dropped off the bus. She had decided to stay in the Inn and visit her folks in the village from there. She knew some of the folks would misunderstand this as pride but most of them would appreciate that there was no place to stay in at the village. In any case she valued her comfort as well.

Guests came to Zude Inn because it was quieter than other places in the locality. This time there weren't many people. Zude was the home of the country's leader, whom though many said was cruel but not the people here. He was a hero. Victoria had never really made up her mind about him. Of course she felt a sense of pride that the leader of her country came from her district, village to be more specific.

Victoria felt the place was clean and found the food to be good. Zude was one of the districts that produced a lot of tobacco and during the market season, it was so difficult to find a place at the Inn. Farmers would be crazy with their money and would book themselves for weeks in the Inn, drinking with women. However, this being off season, she and the five other guests had the Inn to themselves. The others were an elderly couple, one elderly man, a woman in her forties and a young man. Victoria guessed that the young man was in his twenties.

Victoria soon learnt that the woman in the forties was Agness while the young man was Raphael. Agness told Victoria that she was in Zude escaping the pressures of the city. Just to relax alone for a week. She looked rich and wore jewels with her suits which also looked expensive. She did not hide that fact herself. She talked about how expensive her jewels are and where she buys her suits. Though she was not driving, she claimed she owned a Camry back in town. Victoria was convinced. Agness looked happy and enjoying herself. The only thing she said bothered her was Raphael whom she felt was at the Inn for sinister motives. Though Raphael spent most of the time reading or writing, Agness claimed that he was probing into her affairs too much. Victoria found it hard to understand or believe. However, she thought it was none of her business.

For the next three days, Victoria visited her village during the day and only returned to the Inn in the evening. But each time she came in, Agness would be there bitterly complaining of Raphael. She felt puzzled because she found him reserved and talked little each time she tried to engage him in a conversation. "What do you mean?" Victoria asked Agness when she insisted that Raphael cannot be trusted.

"What's a young man doing in a place like this?" Agness queried. "A young man of his age should be out to discos and be visiting such other exciting places of entertainment than hang around an empty Inn."

"He told me that he is a playwright," Victoria defended him. "May be he finds it quieter here for his work."

"What work. Peeping at old women and pretending to be an innocent man?" Victoria felt she needed not interfere. She didn't know either of them enough to be of assistance.

Everyday, Agness wore a pearl necklace and diamond ear rings. She would have bracelets on both wrists that appeared to be gold and she wore four gold rings. They must have been worth a lot of money. She had three different collections; one for the morning, one for the afternoon, and one for evenings to much with the suits.

"He's been always asking me about what I am wearing," she once told Victoria during her daily briefing that Victoria was getting wary of.

It was in the evening of her fourth day at the Inn when Agness came into her room crying that she had been robbed. Victoria was still thinking of how to react when Agness began to explain. "I was having a bath," Agness said, "when I thought I heard someone in my room but then there were no more sounds. When I had finished my bath and went back to the bedroom I found the wardrobe open. I kept all jewelry and suits in there. And they are all gone."

"Dear me," Victoria said. "This is terrible." She suggested calling the Manager and the police.

While Agness was busy repeating the story to the manager, Victoria examined the room. She noticed that the wardrobe was open and also the window which led into the balcony. From there she knew that a fire escape led down to the yard at the rear of the Inn. Had the thief entered and made his gateway that way? She imagined. She walked across to the bathroom. The bath tub was wet but only at the bottom. The window was closed. It was a chilly day with a cold wind blowing and obviously Agness wouldn't have the window open. Victoria checked her appearance in the mirror. The mirror was also dry. As she turned away a thought struck her and she stopped short. The manager called for the police.

"It is Raphael who did it," Agness was saying. "I don't care what you say. He was always asking me about my suits and jewelry. One day he even asked me where I kept them. Why would he ask me that? He climbed up the fire escape and in through the window. He knew where the suits and jewelry were kept. He did it or told one of his friends to do it. That's what happened, I'm sure."

It was a matter for the police, Victoria thought.

A Criminal Investigation Officer, Sergeant Edwards, came to interview Victoria after speaking to Agness. It turned out that he knew her. She had helped him at an earlier time tracing a missing mad woman. After their pleasantries, Sergeant Edwards got on with his investigation. Victoria expressed her reservations about the woman's story because Raphael seemed not the kind to get involved in such kind of work. She explained that she had seen some of the unfinished plays that he worked on. He looked sincere. The other guests expressed similar sentiments. Sergeant Edwards spoke to Agness again before leaving.

Two days later, Victoria was surprised to hear that the Manager and the Security Guard were picked up and that their whereabouts were not known. It was years later that she pieced together the story of Agness and Raphael. The two knew each other sometime when in college. They both got employed as Special Branch officers in the police. However, they were also playing tricks in order to get money through dubious means. At the Inn they pretended to be strangers to one another. Then Raphael disappeared just before Agness cried that she had been robbed. They had done that in several places.

The End

Questions

1. Felix warns his sister about two things in Zude. Write them down.
2. Who was Agness and what had she come to do in Zude?
3. What was it that Agness said bothered her at the Inn?
4. Did Victoria believe Agness about what bothered her? Explain.
5. Who was Agness's main suspect in the alleged theft?
6. Why do you think the manager of the Inn and the security guard were arrested? Do you think they really committed a crime? Explain your answer.
7. Give evidence from the story that Agness and Raphael were working together.
8. The story has a neatly tied conclusion. How does this characteristic affect the structure of the plot and the way you enjoy it as a reader?
9. What moral lessons can one learn from this story?

PRISCILLA'S BIRTHDAY PARTY

Ken Lipenga

NOTHER BIRTHDAY-PARTY! And this one smack in the middle of the
illage! How marvelous, thought Mrs. Magalasi. As her daughter Priscilla had
aid, it would be a great change from the city atmosphere, where the family
ved, and held all their parties.

hrowing parties was a great favourite of the Magalasis. Mrs. Magalasi simply
oved them. It was her earnest conviction that all who could afford it should
arow some party once in a while. There was no shortage of excuses for parties
a the Magalasi family: there were six children, with their birthdays spread con-
eniently throughout the year, not without some clever modification on the part
f Mrs. Magalasi, so that there was equal time space between parties. The
nother herself, who was now in her late thirties, did not quite know her own
ate of birth, (for which she privately cursed her long-dead parents); but she
nade do with a date arbitrarily set in one of the 'vacant' months.

o-night's was Priscilla's birthday party. Priscilla, the third born daughter was
n Form III at the Convent in town. She was on holiday, and it had been her idea
nat the party be held at their village home, which she preferred to the city but
vhich she seldom had a chance to visit. She too was of course very excited
bout the party. All her friends - Judith, Kate, Lucy, and Barbra - classmates at
he Convent had arrived during the day. There were other guests too, girls from
he families of mum's and dad's friends. Almost all these guests lived in town
nd had been brought in cars by their parents. That the party should be so heav-
ly dominated by town folks did trouble Priscilla a bit; but then inviting too
nany 'villagers' was not exactly in mum's line. Which was awkward, because
he Magalasi's were the only well-to-do family, owning a car and a modern
nouse which looked out of place in the village, red brick, iron roof and all.

Priscilla was sitting with the other girls in the spacious carpeted living room.
Also there was her brother George. It was getting dark as they impatiently waited for the servant mumy had sent to buy a battery for the radiogram at the near-
ry shops. Presently the little girl arrived, and Priscilla rushed excitedly to
eceive the battery. The girl, however, held the battery tighter, seeming to
efuse to give up, and for a moment Priscilla wondered what was happening.
Then the girl skillfully knelt on the floor and respectfully presented the battery
and the change.

"Sor... sorry," Priscilla faltered, feeling cheated and humiliated. For a while she stood rooted at the spot, deeply astonished, and even jealous. The village girl had actually knelt! They still knelt out there!

As she went to fit the battery into the radiogram, Priscilla's mind became deeply immersed in disturbing thoughts. Why was it that she, with her city-convent education and all, felt inferior when the little girl knelt? Why, she wondered, why did they not teach kneeling at school? Kneeling was so much more graceful and meaningful than the hurried courtesy!

The other girls had broken into suppressed chuckles, and Priscilla wondered if they were laughing at her or the little girl.

"Hey, what's your name little girl?" She heard George asking teasingly.

"Nazimbiri," said the girl, smiling shyly. Lord, thought Priscilla feeling even more humiliated. Nazimbiri, simply Nazimbiri. As easy as that. Na-zi-mbi-ri, it was like a song when you pronounced this name, and Priscilla found herself mumbling it to herself over and over again; she compared it with her own name and felt even sadder.

"Hey! Beautiful." George was saying. "I'll marry a village girl who'll kneel to me every time, make me feel like a king!" All the girls laughed heartily.

"And I am going to choose one who doesn't know her birthday. National economy. Just think of the money that would be saved if all of us did not know our birthdays!"

"Just think of the hundreds of free gifts you would be deprived of!" retorted one of the girls, and the others chorused their agreement. George just laughed and laughed and said he was going to marry a villager anyway.

Meanwhile Priscilla overheard the girl bidding Mumy farewell. Priscilla rushed out of the house and caught up with the girl as she walked towards her home. She admired the girl very much, and she had decided to invite her to the party tonight.

"I can't come," said the girl.

"But why?" Priscilla was disappointed.

"There is a funeral near our house - that house over there," she said pointing at a cluster of huts about a hundred yards away. "A child who has been ill has just past away."

Listening, Priscilla could hear the wailing of women from the neighbourhood. She was struck dumb with horror. A funeral not even half a mile away, and she, holding a birthday party! To the girl she said, "Thank you for telling me," and rushed to the house. At the door she bumped into her mother, who said, "Oh God, what's happening to you, child? What are you running mad for?"

"Mother," said Priscilla hardly able to speak. "Mother, you haven't heard, have you? That there is a funeral in the neighbourhood?"

"Of course I've heard - now who told you?"

"Mumy, of course we'll have to call off the party, shan't we?"

"Why, child?" said Mrs. Magalasi seriously.

"I mean, with the funeral so near, we can't possibly ..."

"Of course we are NOT putting off the party Priscilla; no one expects us to. However, who put those ideas into your head?"

"But Mumy!" Priscilla was bitter now. "They'd hear us, wouldn't they? The radiogram, the songs and all that?"

To Priscilla's great astonishment, her mother behaved as though nothing had happened at all. She even seemed amused and refused to take her seriously.

"Now, now, my dear child, use your common sense, won't you? Sentiment won't bring that dead child back to life, never!"

"But, Mumy ... is it not very heartless and unchristian of us ... just think of how the radiogram will sound to the mother out there ..."

"How absurd you sound!" Cut in Mrs. Magalasi, now losing patience. "Look here, we only accidentally heard of that funeral. I'm myself no less sorry and sympathetic than you. Now, what if we heard of funerals everyday, we would still go on living normally, wouldn't we dear?"

Priscilla, bewildered, found herself having to say "Yes" to that one; but she still felt it was all wrong.

The party took place as planned. Everyone enjoyed themselves; everyone that is except Priscilla herself, although she did not show it so much as to affect the others. Apart from the music from the radiogram, the girls also sang various versions of "Happy Birthday Many Returns" in chorus; but Priscilla was absent to it all. The worst moments were in the pauses between one disque and another, when in the interposing silence the wailing and hymn-singing from the funeral place drifted into the party room, causing Priscilla to shed tears on a cake or piece of meat. In the end she could bear it no longer and feigning stomachache, she escaped into her bedroom and sobbed till she fell asleep.

In the morning, when all but few of the guests had left, a sullen Mrs. Magalasi called her daughter into a room. "So you cleverly managed to ruin last night!" She exploded into a series of over-lapping accusations and resolutions ... that Priscilla had no manners, that the learning she got at the Convent was worthless and she was big for nothing although she was now seventeen, and that that was the last party they would ever hold at their village ... all subsequent parties would be held in town.

Priscilla said nothing. You didn't say anything when Mumy was in this mood. Not that Priscilla really felt like saying anything. Her mind was too confused trying to make sense out of village girls that knelt for politeness and made you feel uneducated, birthdays and funerals and sentiments ... Why was she called Priscilla, a name she herself found difficult to spell or even pronounce! Why!? Perhaps Mumy was right after all, she was really big for nothing ... Yesterday might as well have been her first birthday.

Yes, yesterday might as well have been her first birthday.

The End

Questions

1. What one special thing about Mrs Magalasi do we learn in the first two paragraphs of this story?
2. Where does Priscilla go to school?
3. Priscilla meets a girl in the village whom she admires greatly. What two things does she like most about the girl?
4. Priscilla does not really enjoy the party in the village. Explain in your own words why this is so.
5. George says he would like to marry a village girl. What reasons does he give for this? Do you agree with his reasons?
5. Do you agree with Mrs Magalasi's reasons for not calling off the party? Why?

6. Hold a debate on whether or not it is alright to have a party while your neighbours are in mourning.
7. Describe the conflict in this story.
8. "You didn't say anything when mummy was in this mood". What does "You" refer to?

THE UNSUNG SONG

Zeleza Manda

Friday: 7.30 a.m

Vladimir: After having sucked all the good
Out of him (Lucky) you (Pozzo) chuck
Him away like... like a banana skin.
Really?

"You look strange brother. Problems?"
"No. Nothing. I am fine."
"You look sad, brother."
"Just bad dreams."
"Bad dreams?"

"Yes. A man harvests his bananas. He cuts down a big bunch with yellowing green fruits. Two of the bananas are ripe. He peels one and eats it. He lifts the bunch to carry it home. He can't. It's too heavy for him. Then he has a brain wave. He cuts green banana leaves and shrouds the bunch with them. Satisfied, he says to himself: In three days, money in my pockets. Three days later, he comes back. He removes the leaves from the bunch. Bats and ants are busy eating the bananas. So he returns home empty handed, complaining. All my efforts in vain."

"That's all? And the whole world reels before you because of that simple dream?"

"Well, I don't understand it."

"Listen. The banana tree bears fruit and man personalizes it: 'my fruit', Leaves manufacture food for the tree, hey, but the farmer eats the fruit. After harvest, the leaves, the real food makers, cover the bunch of your dream, bananas, to hasten ripening. After that the leaves are nothing, only history. They have to decay. As for the fruit, simple. The eaten are eaten whoever the eater is. It can be man, ant, bat, dog, even a fellow banana, hey?"

"You mean, leaves are the makers of fruit?"

"Eh, at least scientifically."

"Sure?"

"As I was saying, Buwani, things eat each other. The eater chooses what to eat but the eaten are eaten whether they like it or not..."

"I'm getting confused."

"When I was a teacher I used to tell my pupils, boys and girls, plants eat this soil. Plants are eaten by men. Men by lions. It's the Eating Law. You can't avoid it. They usually asked, 'But sir, who eats lions?'"

"I was about to ask as well."

"Lions are not eaten. That's why you hear people calling themselves lions. All they mean is that they are the invincible final eaters. They are parasites. They wait for others to work and they just sit on top to eat."

"Ah. Tafu, I know now why you retired early. How many can understand your interpretation of a simple banana dream?"

"Hum?" Tafu asked standing to go to the toilet.

In his bed, Buwani turned and looked at the roof of the hospital ward. Spiders had crocheted beautifully replacing the disintegrating ceiling. The walls appeared to have been painted once upon a time as revealed by remnants of green paint. Here and there finger size holes had been drilled into the walls. Incidentally, Buwani saw two cockroaches emerge and start chasing each other until they made love.

Tafu had left the toilet door ajar and a pungent smell invaded the ward. The bitter smell came from the urinals. As instructed, after using the urinals at night, patients or their relatives placed them in one corner of the ward toilet from where they were supposed to be collected every morning. But Buwani could not remember a day when the hospital cleaners willingly came to wash the toilet.

Sometimes, the floor was a mess. There was dust on the floor, unwashed plates, blanket hairs. Flies buzzed, hopping from one patient to another.

Just above the door, a slogan, as old and dirty as the building itself, cried: CLEANLINESS IS NEXT TO GODLINESS.

Friday 1.15 am
Men are so simple, and so much
Creatures of circumstances that
The deceiver will always find
Someone ready to be deceived.
(Niccolo Machievelli, The Prince)

The odour of overcooked beans wafted through the hospital. Conditioned to regular meals, the smell of beans whetted Buwani's appetite. They were served by very efficient and fat cooks. Patients had discovered why the cooks were so fat. When the Health Ministry sent tins of milk, bags of flour, meat and beans for patients every fortnight, hospital officials packed them in a room for STAFF ONLY. And every evening, tins, half-bags grew legs and walked out of the storeroom. Then at meal times, patients had weeviled beans with undercooked mgaiwa, tea without milk and sugar. No meat. Rumour had it that meat could not be preserved because someone at the Ministry of Health Headquarters had personalised deep freezers a foreign donor offered to the hospital.

A silver trolley carrying steaming food drove into the male surgical ward.

"Quickly! Quickly!" The man driving the trolley announced. He was dark and tall. When he smiled his white teeth stood out like a white spot on a black cloth. He pushed the trolley not without pride. He was a practitioner of the President's creed that one must be proud of one's job.

As if they hadn't heard anything, not even one patient moved.

"I said," the trolley driver repeated, "you must make a straight line to facilitate my work or I go into the next ward."

"It's this one!" Buwani complained pointing a finger at his fellow patient as he saw the trolley-man's gaze squared on him. He had been organising his energy to stand up and queue. He was late.

"Why? Are you really ill? You must be a refugee running away from starvation in your home."

"Forgive me son."

"This is your food old man. I don't understand why a big man like you should rush for food like a puppy."

Rushing? Buwani said to himself, feeling anger rise inside him. This boy must have worms in his brain. He says "Queue", you queue. Then you are rushing puppies.

When Buwani regained his senses, he saw his fellow patients eating. They had maintained an uneasy silence. The trolley-man still serving from the pots. Buwani lay on his bed. He sighed and yawned. He remembered the ways of the German War in Nyasaland, Tanganyika, and Burma. Boys, or African aides de camp as were called, carried ammunition for British soldiers to kill their fellow whites. When they camped for meals, the boys opened the tins and served their masters and waited for crumbs amidst shouts and deja-fait eulogies; Long live the King; long live the Empire.

Seeing that they were dying, the Masters took the boys to the battle front. Buwani and others joined in the fight after two days of training. Bullets would whiz past their bodies as they snaked through bushes, thorns and gullies. And death was everyone's daily bread. They were dying.

Why? The Germans were quarreling with their masters.

Why? A dog that does not defend his master in times of trouble does not get any food in times of serenity, plenty.

Why? A good dog does not ask when the master sends him to an enemy.

Why? The boys could not bear the infamy if their masters lost.

Why? The boys were promised good things and so they had to fight, fight their hearts out, day in day out.

Why? That the blacks would sit in the house of ruling on the slopes of Zomba plateau and control their own fate, everything, was next to Godliness. That was freedom. And once free, no forced taxation, no tribalism, no regionalism, free everything, freedom. Freedom.

Who love that? That freedom.

Who could not love that? That those who fought hard denying themselves and carrying Britain's cross to Calvary, ready to be sacrificial lambs to the Germans, were, after the war to be decorated with medals, MBE (Member of the British Empire), and given big houses, and their names were to be littered in every history book, sung by women in every song for generations to come, was a shark bait.

"Buwani!" the trolley-man called.

"Bwana."

"Give me your plate. Fast. I want to serve this next ward."

"I have no plate."

"What?"

Buwani did not answer. He saw his fellow patient looking at him with pity, or was it respect? But not that contemptuous look the Out Patient Department Bwana had given him before admission:

Bwana:	Name?
Buwani:	Ndema Buwani
Bwana:	Age?
Buwani:	Hunh?
Bwana:	What's your year of birth?
Buwani:	I don't know. But I was already a man during the German War. In this battle for our independence I fought...
Bwana:	Irrelevant. I'll write anything, say 80 years
Buwani:	Silence
Bwana:	Home address
Buwani:	Mphamba, Chief Silongwe
Bwana:	Occupation?
Buwani:	My son, look at me. You think if I were working I would look thus?
Bwana:	Disease?
Buwani:	A thing comes from this dying leg... this independence foot... up, up and when it enters this chest. Oh how it stabs my heart. I die and come back.

199

Bwana:	Okay. Take this card with you to the CO's office. You will find a nurse at the reception who'll take this card to the CO who'll see and give you further recommendation, if he deems it necessary. He will check if the bed you're supposed to occupy is vacant or not. If vacant, the attendant will assist you and show you your bed. Later you'll receive treatment. Keep this card or the hospital won't recognise you. You get me?
Buwani:	No, you're not clear. And who is CO?
Bwana:	Rise and walk
Buwani:	But what shall I say there?
Bwana:	Next!

"Where then do I put your food?" The trolley man asked, interrupting Buwani's reminiscence.

"I don't know Bwana."

"Here is your food," the trolley driver said as he placed hot food into Buwani's palms.

The food fell down, onto the dark man's bare foot. He jumped exaggeratedly. Angry, he showered Buwani with saliva and slapped him in the face. Buwani fell down, tears streaming down his face.

"You," said Tafu.

The trolley man looked at him.

"You lack the most basic civilities due your elders. You're a social worker and you must be disciplined," Tafu said.

"Old man, I'm doing government work. I'm not going to be pushed about by a dying patient," the trolley man said and drove out of the ward.

A minute or so later, a young man in white hospital uniform entered the ward. Pulled Buwani from the floor onto the bed. Buwani was still breathing angrily.

"Are you a patient?" the hospital attendant asked, rather playfully.

"I'm a fighter. I fought the white DC at Nkhata Bay, Mutchona's son."

"No Papa," the hospital official said toning down his voice, "My father was studying in England then. And he fought hard from there."

"The battle was not fought in London, Mutchona's son. We fought at the jetty," said Tafu.

"Mutchona's son, no battle is fought from a sofa seat while reading books. Your father is a liar, a usurper, and a parasite," Buwani said and angrily stretched himself on his bed. He took his torn bed sheets and a gray unkempt hospital blanket and covered himself from foot to head.

Friday 1.10 pm
> Greater love has no man than this
> That a man lay down his life for his friends
> (John 15:13)

His experience in the German War, as the Second World War was called, seemed to have baptised Buwani into the world of violence, agitation, and political protests and killings. In the late 1950s Africa knew a lot of bloodshed. Many people were killed in the name of freedom and independence. All over people wanted to stand on their own to rule themselves, to control their economies, to sit in the house of ruling, to chase away all colonialists.

Everywhere people heard their political leaders denounce the colonial regimes. "The white man came to this land and paralysed our ways of thinking with his religion. We don't want him any more. The whites are exploiting our resources and enslaving our people. Dear brothers and sisters, this is the time to show our solidarity; since united we stand and divided we fall. We have to be independent."

Women ululated. Men whistled. Children shouted. Buwani was among the many tertiary organizers. His mind was a screen of such events. The 1949 drought, the locusts, how they burned the sell outs or Capricorn in their own houses, the 1959 State of Emergency, how they defeated Operation Sunrise, all loomed large in his mind.

On Saturday, February 28, 1959, there was a political meeting at Nkhata Bay market. Most people did not know whether it was the banned party or the new one because the leaders were the same and rode in the same cars.

On Monday, March 2, there came twenty vans full of white soldiers. People saw the vans being ushered into the jetty one by one. Docked off the jetty was Mpasa, an old ship. It was rumoured that major political leaders, Kamuzu, Ching'oli, and Chisiza had been detained in there. In the meantime planes showered letters to warn people against protesting against the detention of their leaders. Fear was registered in everyone's heart. Was not this the end prophet Eliot Kamwana had preached way back? Were these not the signs?

On Tuesday, March 3, the sky was cloudy and threatening. However, pupils went to school. Before eleven o'clock that morning, a group of black men, Buwani included, came to organise pupils to start singing political protest songs against whites. Sing... songs... singing around the market, the police station, the prison, up and down the ridges.

Kwacha Africa
It's dawn, Africa wake up
Alongozgi widu kwacha
It's dawn, our leaders wake up
Longozgani nyengu yakwana
Lead, this is the time

Pupils marched, armed with stones. Soldiers marching as to war. Yes, steps. Left, right, left, right... Right turn, left, right... up, up the ridgy peninsula, towards the DC's office.

Ndamkambiya Buloko
I told DC John Brock
Lutanga kwako ku London
Go back to London
Ndawelezgapu kachiwi
I repeated
Lutanga kwako ku London
Go back to London

Wadandaula Buloko
Brock complained
Kwidu nkhutali ku London
Home, London, is far

Kulivi malu ghaku jaku
I don't own land there.

The old, the young, marched as to war, singing towards the jetty. At the main gate near the ticket office, they stopped but intensified their shouts. *"Wakenge! Kwawo! Sono!"* (Let him go now.)

Then two or three soldiers approached the gate from the warehouse. More armed soldiers come añd stop - about twenty feet from the DC who is desperately trying to calm the protesters' tempers. He finally gives up and asks:

"What do you want, death?"

"Do whatever you want. We want our leaders from that ship." (A few stones are showered)

"What? Get out of here you black demons," the Commandant shouts as he whisks the DC away.

"We want change, we want change!"

(Stones rain again)

Then one soldier opens the gate and people flock in. The Commandant shouts: "One, two, three, Fire!"

Guns clutter. Stones scatter. People fall, dead, maimed, mutilated, frozen by fear. And blood flows into the lake. Buwani feels pain on the left leg as he lies along the fallen. Something asked him: Buwani, why are you dying? Where are your leaders now? He snakes his way into the water and swims to the shore, near the trading centre. His foot is minus one toe, blood is gushing out. He is mad. He runs... home....falls... sees armed soldiers in an open landrover... rolls himself into long grass... holds his breath... people are wailing all over... the soldiers are laughing... picks a few words from their conversations.... "The niggers are fools. They are dying for someone who is safe in Gwero..."

Friday 2.00 pm
All right! it was a heroic act.
The heroes are those who die.
(Ralph Ellison, Invisible Man)

Tafu removed the gray blanket from Buwani's face. Buwani lay there, his eyes wide open, fresh tears were still running down his cheeks.

"Buwani! Buwani!" Tafu called as he shook him. Tafu pulled back the blanket over Buwani's face and went to call a hospital attendant.

The attendant came with a stretcher and Buwani's body was taken out. There was no singing, no talking. Silence.

The End

Questions

1. Describe in your own words, the dream you read about in the first part of this story.
2. Life can really be unfair. Support this statement using Tafu's interpretation of Buwani's dream.
3. What evidence is there in this story to show that the hospital is not properly looked after?
4. Identify two cases of corruption that have been described in this story.
5. The hospital trolley driver is not considerate. Explain why this statement is correct about the trolley driver.
6. The trolley driver and the OPD *bwana* should have been grateful to Buwani and Tafu. Why?
7. What were the main demands that the protesters presented to the DC's office?
8. In what ways is this a sad story?
9. The story seems to suggest that people who fought for the betterment of the country do not themselves benefit from their labour. How far true do you think this observation is correct?
10. In groups, prepare a sketch of the story which you should perform to the class.
11. Describe the ills of the World War and the fight for political independence on blacks.
12. Each section of the story starts with a quotation. How does this help the reader to understand and enjoy the story?
13. Why should this story be titled "The unsung song"? Explain.
14. The events of the story are presented in form of entries of a diary. What impact does this have on the story.

ZABETA

Zondiwe Mbano

THE BUS stopped. I leapt out. I wanted to have some cool fresh air because inside the bus there was so much dust and it was hot. The conductor was giving back change of 2 tambalas, 3 tambalas, 6 tambalas; this he did by digging his right hand into his brown leather bag, shaking it a bit, and bringing out such small amounts to give to people who patiently waited as he counted the small coins while dropping them one by one into each passenger's open hand. Outside the bus a group of children and women came running towards the bus: Baasi! Baasi! they shouted as they came to sell boiled eggs, milk scones and cakes - baked from unrefined maize flour mixed with milk, sugar, salt and soda; referred to locally as *chikondamoyo*, "that which satisfies life." A woman came trotting from the other direction. She wore a green flowery dress of light synthetic material, and a pair of cheap black plastic shoes; her hair was neatly pleated. As she approached the bus, she started chanting:

Eyes eyes
Eyes everywhere
Eyes on the tall grass
That whistles and sways
To the passing wind

Eyes on trees
That sigh and dance
Displaying flowers
That pour out the aroma
Of love to the sun

Eyes as the loerie
Sings his kok-kok song
While spreading his plumage
Of the colours of sunset
And gliding between trees

Eyes everywhere

Eyes in raindrops
Sparkling as they trace
Their windy paths
Down to the Kasito...

A few furtive glances at her landed on a face that seemed vaguely familiar, but I could not examine her for fear of inviting trouble should she notice it. The children and women did not pay attention to her; they scrambled under the small open windows high up on the bus, where long hands extended, calling for various items. The sellers, acting on trust, jumped to place the items into the receiving hands while shouting the prices for each, and soon they got the coins thrown into their baskets or on the ground near their feet, if they did not have to run a few steps because the bus had started off before someone had time to fish out the coins from an inner pocket, or tied on a handkerchief hidden inside a bra.

I jumped back into the bus. The conductor had finished issuing tickets to those struggling to go into the bus from that stage, Kafukule. After some minutes, the bus started off. On the seat behind mine were three men. The one in the centre, wearing a big, dark, viscose shirt, with flowers of pink, grey and white, was Habile. He must have been in his forties. The other, called Nkunika, sat on the left, next to the window. He was a bit older, and was such a gentleman that even the heat - most of which came directly from the engine because the cover left big gaps, could not make him think of removing his tweed jacket and a dotted tie. Since Habile moved from his seat at the back to the present seat, next to Nkunika, the two never stopped arguing on topics relating to politics and the church.

"Independence cannot bring freedom to all parts of the country," said Habile. "You can change governments many times, but those of you who are in the minority will remain oppressed by those who are in the majority; oppressed until you are forced to take guns and shoot at the uniforms of oppression. Voting only gives power to the same people even if everyone knows they are dull and stink with corruption."

"Do not forget that leaders are chosen by God through this same process of voting, which you despise."

"No, no!" retorted Habile, frantically shaking his head, and bending forward his short torso. "Go and read Romans 13 again. The Bible does not say every ruler is chosen by God. When the Bible talks about authority coming from God, you must understand authority to refer to a number of things, among them: the chair, and the person sitting on the chair. God established the chair. But it cannot be that every person who manages to sit on the chair by whatever means, including Machiavellian means and getting the vote through bribery and regionalism, is chosen by God."

"But God allows these people to rule. It remains the responsibility of the citizens to see that they exercise authority accordingly. But your guns, nowhere have they brought a fairer system; they only bring fear, poverty, and death to innocent citizens."

"There is already too much fear, poverty, and death caused by people who campaign for leadership just to enrich themselves. Now the majority of the people cannot afford even the basic things which they used to buy; they cannot afford to send their children to a good private school, when the public schools have become hopeless."

"And guns will not solve these problems. Peace and freedom comes when people are ready to control their anger and come together to discuss their problems," said Nkunika, emphasizing the word, discuss.

"You talk like someone schooled by some of these international organizations run from the West. For them, as long as it is only in Africa where minorities are oppressed and quietly exterminated, there is peace; so they meet at their headquarters and celebrate with wine."

"You do not expect international organizations to bring peace and freedom to you when you are not ready to tackle your national problems with calm and maturity."

"Under what forum can you discuss them. Where did you hear of an oppressor coming to a negotiation table before you have blown his arrogance out?" said Habile, with saliva spurting out, as if he had already started blowing out the arrogance of those who kept the country desperately poor and underdeveloped while building palaces for themselves and their concubines.

"If you are courageous enough and concerned enough, why don't you initiate changes that will transform the whole society, so that anyone from anywhere can be judged on the merit of what he or she is, and is able to do? Our politicians are the product of a corrupt society; transform the society, and it will produce politicians with foresight and integrity. This thinking that you must be a politician in order to contribute to the improvement of your country is what keeps us backward and unnecessarily bitter," said Nkunika, preaching.

The argument raged on, winding like the road on which the bus was roaring and rattling, sometimes seemingly coming to a stop, and then suddenly gathering momentum again. The over-all speed of the bus, however, was very slow because the road was only fit for use by tractors and oxcarts. The journey was proving too long, especially now after seeing that woman. Several times I had tried to participate in the discussion - perhaps to bring in another facet of authority, perhaps to question the very concept of Malawi, whether it is a viable one, embracing all the peoples, - but failed because my thoughts were dissipated by the inscrutable face that kept on coming:

Eyes eyes
Eyes languid eyes
Staring from sunken sockets
Dark with pain and despair
But dry of any tear.

Eyes everywhere
And breaking the five loaves
And fish He said to the crowd
Take eat everyone of you
My love flowing to all.

Eyes everywhere
And changing water at Cana
He said be filled not with wine
Bubbling with lust and murder
But with the Spirit and fire.

I had decided to travel by this road between Mzimba and Ekwendeni in order to re-live the exhilarating experiences of days when I used to travel to secondary school and college in the South. It used to be the main road, passing along agriculturally rich plains where most of the people - the Ngoni who have turned their spears into reaping knives, and now have to stomach the arrogance of cowards who, in the past, at the sight of a Ngoni, developed rumblings in their belly - had settled. It used to be a well maintained road, such that by a fast express bus it took slightly over two hours to cover the distance. Now people going to Mzuzu and Ekwendeni take the new road, which is tarmac, and goes along the Vipya Plateau, where they have destroyed the beautiful forests and grassland, and chased away game to the Mzimba, Kasito, and Kabiya valleys where people welcomed the escaping animals with poised spears and drawn bows. Now, if you told young people that there was a time not long ago when roan antelopes, elands, and zebras graced these plateaus, they would not listen to you. They would think you are an indigenous artist trying to add a story or two to the repertoire of folk stories, which they find boring because they love watching Western films: a celebration of selfishness in which men and women pursue sex and money in their quest for happiness.

We were now travelling towards Mpherembe, having branched from the main road to which we were to come back to. The long argument had taken another turn.

"I tell you, the church is just a way of stealing peoples' money and goods," declared Habile.

"A year from now, come to Mzuzu, and you will see. I will start my own church, link it to some church in America; and soon you will see me driving a brand new twin cab vehicle and my house will be flooded with second-hand clothes."

"You will form the church only for material gains for yourself?" queried Nkunika.

"Oh, yes! The gospel reached this land almost a century ago, and churches were then established. Why else do you think people start new churches, meeting under tree shades, now? Or why do you think people join such churches, now?"

"Why not simply form a political party, a one-man party, and close to general elections, keep defecting to the big parties, one after the other, and back; then after getting the money start business," the other man, called Nyirenda, from Kafukule, who had sat on the left of Habile, decided to join in the discussion. He wore a rather faded brown suit and a paisley tie. Nkunika and Habile laughed.

"Anyway, what name will you give your church?" inquired Chibwatiko Mkandawire, who was sitting behind them, and seemed keen to steer the discussion back to its course.

"Names are not difficult to find," said Habile. "Gethsemane Church, Deep Waters Church, Fire of Pentecost, House upon the Rock, any name like this will do. The important thing is to make good rules that will draw back many to God, such as those who find spurious the claim of the church that it is the only institution that should officiate holy weddings to ensure happy and lasting marriages; the educated who resent the leadership of semi-literate pastors and church elders; educated women who do not want to hear, obey, obey, obey ... every time they go to church; the career women who do not want to be frequently reminded of the mistake in creation of putting breasts to suckle and cuddle babies to sleep on only one type of biped, while the other was given black beards that frighten babies; men thrown out of the church because they celebrate over much the first water miracle at Cana; and those with such a stoop that the head is controlled from the underpants."

"Will these rules be made to please people or to guide them according to the word of God?" asked Nyirenda.

"To do both," Habile said quickly, scratching his small head on which he kept long hair that did not seem to be subjected to much combing. "But especially to free and inspire them so that they perform according to their best instinct, not to paralyze them into passivity."

"You will form that church for selfish reasons."

"Selfish reasons? Well, that is why churches are there. Even those who you think are the most pious, are they not first and foremost selfish?"

"The word of God says..." started Nyirenda, but hesitated, not very sure which verses he really wanted to quote. He adjusted his tie as if this would remind him of what the word of God said in this matter. In such heat one would have thought the jacket and the tie were quite inappropriate. But Nyirenda and Nkunika must have retired as senior civil servants - Secondary School Headmaster, District Commissioner, or Senior Magistrate perhaps.

"Whatever the word of God says," answered Habile, "I have never heard of one so kind as to pray for another person to be saved even at the expense of his own salvation. It is always a question of me-first."

"My brother, to distort the word of God to justify one's own purpose is sin. And sin brings punishment." Preached Nkunika.

"This idea of punishment," queried Habile, "is it there to frighten people? Can't people be drawn to good because it is the most rewarding thing to do? Surely you do not have to bring in the idea of God, the ruler of the whole universe, spending all His time to follow minute details of what happens on earth. He created everything beautiful, in His infinite wisdom balanced everything in a self-sustaining system; and placed man with a corruptible will - man in whom irrational hormones easily boil over and blur reason - to run the affairs of the earth."

"Left!" retorted Nkunika and Nyirenda at the same time.

"Yes. Or perhaps let's say, delegated. He has delegated the affairs of this earth to man. Don't you wonder sometimes why our life seems like a joke? Someone can decide to kill you, and indeed you will die; a politician can decide to send soldiers to wipe out whole villages, and indeed a whole clan of innocent people will be massacred. Think of that mad woman we saw, looking so innocent, and, I would dare say, good-looking, but there she is, mad. You cannot explain such things."

The bus jolted as it went over a small concrete bridge, tossing the people high. A woman at the back-seat cried, *Adada-wee!* calling on her father to save her; and as they landed on the hard seats a man called, *Nyasoko-wanee!* the name of his wife, as he revealed later to people who inquired of him who this Nyasoko was. The whole bus roared with laughter.

"As I was saying," began Habile after the laughter had died down, "our life is a mere joke. If the driver had decided to leave the steering wheel and let the bus run out of this narrow road, down the hill, we would ..."

"Stop that!" fumed a woman who sat on the seat behind that of the debaters. "Do you have any sense in your head? These people listening to you have wives, husbands, children, and other close relations where they are going to or coming from. Do you think we like travelling to and fro in buses, just for the sake of it? And there you are talking about death as if it were a mosquito bite?"

Habile, apparently intimidated by this stout-looking business woman, who earlier on at the previous stage had been ordering boys to carry her bags of beans onto the bus carrier, kept quiet as she spoke with words flowing like water from a tap, while glaring at him. One of the two men who sat on a seat a far off, separated from the centre of debate by people who were standing in the aisle, whis-

211

pered to the other his support for the woman who was lambasting the debaters. "You know these people from here, they always want to show off that they are learned. Imagine arguing all the way, in English: can't they speak their language? She has really blown June on them, and at the right time."

"Yes, these people are pompous," whispered the other. "That's why the Ngwazi did not put many development projects in this part. He knew these people. And about their language, it is good that even they themselves do not like it: such a heavy, backward, and incomprehensible language - *mbwenu hinya badada, mbwenu murye dankha badada, mbwenu mazgu ghafika badada, mbwenu hambani makora badada!*" They both laughed heartily.

The bus rattled on. It was very hot and many people were now drowsing, except for a few who were anxiously waiting for the argument to resume. Such roads clearly demonstrated the disparities between this region and the other two which had a network of tarmac roads. So it had been, for a long time since the country became independent until recently, that even if you were half asleep, you would know you have entered the region, for where the tarmac road ended you usually saw a signpost, written: Northern Region Road Works; and similarly, if you were going to the Central Region, where the dusty road ended, there was a signpost for Central Region; and yet this did not stop the women composing songs to eulogize the Ngwazi as they locked him into ecstatic dancing of ngoma, ndolo, and visekese. As if keen to continue with this mentality, the new government left the major tarmac roads in the region, in such a condition of disrepair that it had become virtually impassable, and kept promising new tarmac roads to the people of the region while in the other region, some roads were silently being constructed to connect small trading centres and sub-bomas.

I must have dozed off too, despite the dust and bumps, for now the argument had stopped. Instead there was a narrative, about the mad woman of Kafukule.

"Listen, it was on a Sunday evening." It was Nyirenda talking, "Nyajuba, the pastor's wife, was preparing supper. The pastor had gone visiting his Christians. She was about to carry the food into the house when she heard, "*Odii!*" It was a man announcing his coming.

"*Odini!*" she replied. It was getting dark. The man came and sat on the verandah of the kitchen.

"*Monire!*" greeted Nyajuba, rather with impatience, for these people kept on coming and going for the whole day, without thinking about which is the best time to visit the pastor.

"*Yewo, Mama-muliska*," he said slowly, bringing his palms together, a demonstration of politeness due to the wife of the pastor, who was referred to as mother-shepherd.

"How are you?"

"A little bit of life we have, eeh - mama!" he replied, dragging the eeeh - mama so long as if it were meant to be music that would entertain to eternity. "Now being human, it is among fellow humans that one finds help. This is why I thought of coming here, eeh mama! And how are you?"

"Help!" retorted Nyajuba.

"Yes mama, help. I am very hungry. I have not eaten anything for a week," he said, imploringly. "You know the famine..."

"Very hungry? How many people shall I cook food for in a day? I also get tired."

"No, mama. You know there is famine..."

"We do not have enough food even here, especially when so many people come?"

"No, mama, forgive. There is famine in the villages.":

Nyajuba carried the plates of food and went into the house. She regretted having answered rather rudely, and was thinking about what she was going to give this man because the food she had prepared was for the pastor and, of course, with two or three shares more because he usually came with one or two other people, elders discussing church matters up to lunch or supper, which they seemed to understand as their due payment for the free work they were rendering. When she came back after some time the man was gone.

It was late in the evening. The pastor had taken the supper, as usual, with two elders, discussing church matters. There were no visitors spending the night at the manse, so he decided to put his Bible and other books in the spare bedroom, to be used for prayer and meditation at 4 a.m., as was his usual practice. He opened the door, and, "Oh, Lord!" he shouted as he jumped back and closed the door. What could it be? "Nyajuba!... Nyajuba!" he called. "Come and see!"

Now with his wife near him, and the two elders who did not wait to be invited, having noted that there was something dangerous, perhaps a snake, the pastor mustered enough courage to open the door again. The man was still lying on the bed. "Who are you, and what are you doing here?"

The man did not answer, nor did he stir.

The pastor stopped, turned his head, and fixing his wife with a scowl, asked: "How did he enter the room?" She noticed the voice was unusually abrasive.

"You are asking me...?" she hesitated. "I don't know. I did not have any visitor in the house." She replied politely. She had been well-trained in this. The elderly minister, the Rev. Kamanga, who had wedded them in the Presbyterian church, before they joined the present church, amongst other known scriptures, he surprisingly chose to read 2 Kings 9:20, and warned them that at crossroads if all motorists drove like Jehu, there would be terrible accidents daily. But if one is fast, the other must slow down and let the fast one go, and in time even the Jehus learn to slow down and wait for others. This, he had said is how it should be in marriage in order to enjoy the beauty of it. Nyajuba loved this teaching and repeated it to many women she counselled on marriage problems.

She wanted to explain about the man who had come asking for food, but there was no time for such explanation. Besides, that man was gone, long before the Pastor came, when it was not yet dark. He advanced towards the bed with his right hand stretched forward.

"Wake up! Who are you?" There was no answer. The man was in deep sleep.

"Perhaps, he is a madman, and came in through the window," one of the elders suggested. Nyajuba heard some sounds from the other room, and rushed to check that the children did not come out to this scene.

With the elders immediately after him, he stepped forward, touched the man on the leg, and quickly jumped back, "He seems dead!"

"Dead? No, it can't be!" the others exclaimed.

"Touch his feet, they are rigid,"

One of the elders touched, and gave the same pronouncement, "He is dead!" just as Nyajuba was coming in. The other elder, not wanting to be left behind, went the other side of the bed, followed by the first man, to look at the dead man's face, for he faced away towards the window, which was covered with a board. They examined the face and noted it was not the face of anyone they knew from the surrounding villages, not even from any village within the ten mile radius. They all stood silent, gaping at the dead man. Mama-muliska remembered the last words of the man who had come asking for food: "No, mama, forgive. There is famine in the villages."

Habile and Nkunika, having listened to the story for a long time, now punctuated their listening with dozing. The bus inspector, who had come in some where near Sokopo, was pushing his way amongst standing passengers while checking if everyone had been issued with a ticket, and the tickets had correct amounts written on.

The bus rumbled on, negotiating difficult bends of Sonjo, crossing small bridges right on the bends. It was great skill to drive a bus through these places, especially with the present condition of the road. In the past there were legendary drivers along these routes, amongst them were Lukhere, Chiboyi, and Yavi-yavi. People, especially women, walked long distances to the road just to see these and give them oranges, boiled maize, and fried groundnuts. They went home to demonstrate the vanity of drivers who - with their neatly combed hair, parted to form a line, called sheda, on the right or left side of the head, if they did not cover it with a cap, because of the dust - admired their own style by frequently looking at the bus mirrors and nodding. They wondered how the drivers managed to pull along the whole Jerusalem - the name given to the biggest church building in the area, which they likened to the bus.

I thought of my home, now three bus-stops away. I imagined my welcome on arrival at home, in our village with thatched houses built in a circle, outside of which, some hundred yards away, is a cattle kraal, from where they collect dung to smear the floor, which makes it look glossy and well patterned when dry, I saw how fast boys would chase a cock, if there would be no goat to slaughter, in order to relish my welcome after being away for a long time. It was at home that I was to hear about Zabeta, a girl who, because we could not easily produce the difficult sound, Elizabeth, which was the name her parents had given her, we simply called her Zabeta - which sounds more Tumbuka-Ngoni, like most of our names.

Zabeta was svelte, dark, with a pert smile, and bright eyes that seared an indelible mark in your heart. In Standard 8, among big boys and girls of over twenty years, who repeated so many times and not knowing what else to do kept on repeating the class, Zabeta found me repeating. We exchanged glances for several weeks until we realized we were in love: what a sweet feeling! But we were so shy we could not imagine talking to each other, face to face, or walking together, the two of us. The situation was made more complicated for us when her father, having taken a little beer from what had come from the people of Luhomero from where my brother was married, went home and brought me a big cock, saying it was a gift to me as his son-in-law; and my father responded by giving him a whole calabash of beer. Zabeta herself used to send me delicious banana and groundnut cakes through my sister with whom they were good friends. And whenever my father gave me money - six pence, nine pence, or a shilling - I made sure I sent to her half or more; and when there was a dance, for which we paid four pence for boys and two pence for girls, to dance the whole night to records of Shabalala and Mahotella Queens and rumba beats from Tanzania and Kenya, played on a radiogram hired from far away, I always paid for her whenever she came, although I never danced with her, for - how could we dance face to face, and perhaps holding hands also, while all the people were watching us?

But one day, when we had gone for football and netball matches at a far away school, and had a dance in the night, I did gather courage - after thinking about this for days, and doing press-ups to boost courage - and approached her. She refused. And despite my disappointment, I understood it was not wise to put ourselves into a romantically explosive situation, especially with her big brothers and uncles watching our every move like referees in a football match. At the end of the school year, Zabeta, being a brilliant girl who took number four or five, after a line of us boys, was selected to Mzuzu Government Secondary School. This was the trend for many years that girls got selected while none of the boys did; and later, for eight years, not even a girl was selected, and the first boy to be selected after that period had been repeating all these years, such that he went to secondary school when one of the girls they were together with in Standard 8 was completing her degree at the university. I lost touch with Zabeta. Later I heard that Zabeta had not completed her secondary school. She became pregnant and got married to one of the boys from her school.

In Lukonkobe - the area from Emteyeni through Engcongolweni, Entongeni, to Embombeni - story-telling is an art that has been greatly perfected. It is well understood that facts are malleable, and can be pummelled and stretched until they are made into a desired shape for building a structure of truth; otherwise, on their own, told without the skill of the Lukonkobe artists, and these are mostly female - some as young as six - facts would remain flat and insipid. It is therefore the case that reports about whatever sons and daughters of Lukonkobe do, far away, when narrated by the people at home are usually not without adornment; and misfortunes that befall them are explained in terms of witchcraft and malice. For it is believed there is a great deal of malice against sons and daughters of Lukonkobe, who are leaders wherever they go.

So the report at home was that Zabeta had an exemplary marriage to Pastor Benjamin Hlongo of the New Life Revival Church, at Mubanga, near Kafukule. At her house she kept a pot on the fire for the whole day, to feed any hungry person - a real Nyazuwulaninge, the bright star in the East, wife of Moon, who feeds Moon and any visitor so well, allowing them to eat any food even when it is just starting to boil. Zabeta was a great cook, who served people delicious meals, and because of her generosity the family got bales of clothes from America, which they distributed to their relations and members of the congregation. And so people left other congregations and joined theirs. This brought so much jealous that one evening a zombie was sent to spread evil magic around the house and die in one of the rooms. It was added that before the zombie came, Zabeta had seen a long black snake smoking a cigarette. Immediately after the encounter with the zombie, Zabeta became mad.

Unfortunately, they did not take her to Muyaluka, the herbalist of Lukonkobe, who was renowned for curing such disorders. People came from as far away as the lake, with mad people, some of them so violent. In few weeks the mad people would be calm and be orderly, and Muyaluka would send them to look after his cattle or do other challenging chores at the house. In less than a year, he would call the relatives to come and collect their people, now normal. There was nothing that Muyaluka did not have: cattle, goats, sheep, pigs, chickens, ducks, pigeons, oxcarts, blankets and so many other items given to him by people whose relatives he had cured. But Zabeta, they took her to Zomba Mental Hospital, far away in the South. After spending two months or so there, her condition got worse, and they had to take her back. After a day or two, she ran back to Mubanga, where she refused to be taken away because she said she had to feed many hungry people there. It was now being arranged to take her to Muyaluka, or his assistant for herbal treatment. Meanwhile, the husband went to Zambia, and the missionary overseeing the work never found anyone willing to go and continue the work in that congregation.

The inspector had completed checking the tickets and now stood near the door, talking to the conductor, perhaps inquiring about some anomalies he had observed in the tickets. Nyirenda continued with his narrative. But the house always frightened them. They had to ask for a transfer, but not too soon in case this raised suspicion. The missionary, Pastor Johnstone, lived in Mzuzu, and from there now and then he would pass by the church, in his big twin cab, going to Nyika Plateau to view beautiful sceneries and animals there. He was a tall, burly man: fit for American football. He spoke English with a heavy American accent - incomprehensible to any mortal, except his wife and children, perhaps - and never made effort to learn the local language, or at least to pronounce correctly the name of his pastor, Benjamin Hlongo. His wife, Marlene, was beautiful, with freckles and wavy hair. She made an effort to learn a few local expressions, such as those related to greetings. Whenever they came the man was always in a hurry: delivering whatever he brought, asking few questions about the work, giving a few orders, and, before he verified whether they were understood, he would leave for another congregation or directly for Nyika National Park. Their children were told never to leave the vehicle whenever they came to these remote places where pastors lived in thatch and mud houses. It was already a great sacrifice to come and work in underdeveloped countries infested with all sorts of deadly diseases. No parents would want to expose their children to high risk places. Eliza, as the missionaries called her, always made sure she gave the white lady something, a specially baked chikondamoyo, some eggs, green maize, groundnuts, or a chicken; although she felt that most of these were thrown away. For, how could one taste her chikondamoyo, into which she put all her cooking expertise - for she did study cookery for three years at secondary school - and never come asking for another later?

A week had passed. During this week, the Pastor became increasingly worried about his wife's health. Several times she would stop and look around her fearfully.

"What is it ?" he would ask.

"Nothing."

"Nothing really?"

"Nothing."

Yet it was not nothing, for the man would suddenly appear - his form indistinct, but his voice clear: "No mama, forgive. There is famine in the village." And there was also the word: "For I was hungry and you gave Me no food; thirsty and you gave Me no drink; a stranger and you took Me not into your house..." But the latter did not worry her very much for her Lord knew her heart, and: why would He choose to come as a hungry pauper, late in the evening, when the whole day she spent cooking for such people to the extent that she herself had nothing to eat sometimes? It was the man's voice that was rending her life. Although she had not accompanied the men that night, she imagined the grave they dug under the water, and the heavy stones they laid above it. Katope river can be rough. If the water swells to above your knees, you do not attempt to cross, for immediately you step in, the sand under your feet is eaten away and you collapse and get swept away. It was possible that the water had dug up the body, carried it down to the Kasito, or down still - carrying the body, with dark eye sockets staring in the water after the eyeballs had been gorged by fish.

One afternoon she reached the breaking point. The pastor was in his office when he heard people shouting. He rushed out, and saw them. They were dragging a woman towards the manse. He ran towards them, his oversized jacket and the tie - kind donations from the people of America - flying behind him. "What is it? What is it?" he shouted breathlessly. Two men ran towards him, and got hold of him, just before he collapsed. He did not get whatever they were saying, for he passed out. When he regained consciousness, he heard his wife chanting:

Eyes eyes
Eyes everywhere
Sinister eyes of a snake
Burning as it disappears
Slithering into a hole

Eyes everywhere
Eyes devouring the light
As a prickly weed
Spreads on the bed
In a dark room

Eyes eyes
Eyes in the waters
Flowing down the Katope
As it shifts the stones
Planted over the grave

Eyes everywhere
Those who die, depart
Leaving their eyes behind
Eyes bloodshot eyes
Writhing in pain

Eyes of the night
Piercing the placid heart
And drawing out red guilt
When you can only answer
By asking questions...

They managed to drag her into the house, held her onto the sofa, and started a long session of prayers after messages had been sent to the missionary in Mzuzu, and to the parents at Lukonkobe and Kajivi.

The End

Questions

1. (a) Why did the story teller get out of the bus when it stopped?
   (b) Why did women and children rush towards the bus?
2. Work out the meaning of the word "trotting" as it is used in paragraph 1 of the story.
3. A woman in a flowery dress approached the bus. Explain why you would say this woman is strange.
4. During the bus journey, Habile and Nkunika discuss politics. What is the difference between their political views?
5. Which of the views, Habile's and Nkunika's, would you agree with? Give reasons.
6. Write in your own words what Habile thinks about church issues. Would you sympathize with his opinions on church matters? Why?

7. Who narrates the story of Zabeta?
8. What have you learnt about Zabeta from this story?
9. Explain why you would support the view that the treatment which Zabeta was given was not fair but cruel.
10. Why does the story teller keep thinking about Zabeta throughout his journey?
11. This story is a combination of several stories but this does not make it several stories. Discuss how far this is true.
12. Discuss the linguistic style that the author uses to narrate the story.
13. Discuss the theme of civilization in this story.
14. Discuss the author's use of descriptions in this story and comment on how successful he is.
15. How does the author exploit the use of suspense?
16. We meet the poetic pieces concerning eyes several times. How does this assist you to understand the theme(s) which they highlight on?
17. In your opinion does this story deserve to be entitled 'Zabeta'? Explain your answer.

PART 5: POETRY

LOVE 1
by Jullia Mambo
Nothing is good without you
For you refresh like sleep
Full of sweet dreams;
You are a gentle wind
Sighing from fresh roses

You are my joy forever
For your tenderness
Keeps flowing like
An all season spring
Running down a rock

1. Mention 4 words from stanza 1 that show that love is a pleasant experience.
2. Have you ever experienced a sweet dream? How did you feel when you woke up?
3. What makes the tenderness described in stanza 2 pleasantly assuring?
4. The structure of each stanza is: declaration followed by justification or explanation. In stanza 1 the declaration is: *Nothing is good without you*. State the declaration in stanza 2. According to these declarations, do you think this love is from a human being or from God? Explain.
5. How is love related to goodness and joy

DEAR LORD 2
by Irene Chipeta-Zimba
My love
Like a cloud
Blowns away
Within minutes

But your love
Like the sun
Remains true
Ages and worlds

1. Compare the two types of love in this poem ?
2. How is the love in stanza 1 shown to be unreliable?
3. Explain what is meant by *ages* and *worlds*? How does the simile help in understanding this?.
4. How do clouds affect the sun?
5. Would you say that the persona has love or not? Why then does God love the persona?

MY LOVE 3
by Benjamin Chunda
Though you are far away
Where eyes cannot reach
My dreams are always there

If Paradise is made up
Of love and beauty;
You are my Paradise

Though the road be long;
If people can reach the moon
Why shouldn't I reach you

1. How do dreams reach the faraway places?
2. Three words in stanza 2 show that the person is very pleased with his or her love. Which are these?
3. If *Paradise...you are my Paradise.* What similarities are drawn between the loved one and Paradise?
4. According to the poem, which is more important: reaching the moon or reaching the loved person?
5. What makes the persona certain that he/she will reach where the loved one is?

LOVE   4
by Lydia Maideni

Sighs are sounds, they go into the air;
Cries are voices, they fade into nothing;
Tears are water, they go into the sea.
But I have always wondered:
When love is forgotten
Where does it go?

Gold is dug from mines,
Rivers descend from mountains,
Honey is extracted from beehives,
And milk is from udders;
But where can I find love?

Is love a mere feeling?
Can this feeling be resisted?
Is love a tangible power
That drives people mad?
Or is it an intangible power
That is stronger than death?

1. What three things mentioned in stanza 1 disappear and cannot be traced?

Is love like these things?
2. How can love be forgotten?
3. *Gold...Rivers... Honey... And milk...* These are four words at the beginning of lines in stanza 2. What characteristics of each of these make it a suitable image of love?
4. How is the structure of stanza 3 different from that of stanza 1 and 2? How does this suggest that the problem has not been resolved?
5. Which of these best describe what love is: a mere feeling; *tangible power... drives people mad; intangible power...stronger than death* ? Explain

THE LAST ACT   5
by Anthony Nazombe

After the curtain call
The actors go their separate ways
Never to meet again in this experience.

Only skeletons remain
To haunt the stage
And stir memories

Beloved, I desired you that moment
But you would not come; and
I sat on this rock, throat burning

Soon hounds were on the trail
And the hunted who must come to drink
Perished by the stream

1. What is referred to as *this experience*?
2. Was the experience real or made up?

3. Mention two words which show that the memories are unpleasant?
4. What complaint is registered in stanza 3?
5. Who do you think are referred to as hounds?
6. From stanza 3 can you identify the one who *perished by the stream*?

BRING SUNSHINE   6
by Matilda Luhanga

For long I have gazed
At your sullen cloud
To bring me sunshine

My thoughts hover about
Like an eagle in the sky
Not sure where to go

Remove the grey shroud
And come and wrap me
In your velvet embrace

1. How does a sullen cloud look?
2. Can a sullen cloud bring about sunshine? How?
3. Why are the persona's thoughts hovering about? Where will they settle? When will this be?
4. Look at the first line of each stanza. How is the last stanza different from the other stanzas?
5. What two words in stanza 1 does *grey shroud* refer back to ?
6. How would you feel if you were wrapped in *velvet embrace?*
7. The title is 'Bring Sunshine'. Do you think this has been used figuratively or literally?
8. Who or what is the *you(r)* being addressed in the poem?

MY BEAUTY   7
by Guyce H. Bvalani

Your voice is sweet music for my ear
Your presence perfumes my days
And your smile heals pain and sorrow

A painter gets tired of his masterpiece
And her only child can tire out a widow
But never will I tire of gazing at you

1. How is beauty described through the senses of hearing, smell and sight?
2. How does the presence of a beauty heal pain and sorrow?
3. How does the persona compare the attraction of the beauty to him/her to that of an only child to a widow?
4. Have you ever felt like this about a person close to your heart? Do you think such feelings come from love or from mere infatuation?
5. Write a poem, or sing a song you know that expresses similar feelings.

EXORCISM   8

by Anthony Nazombe

May I not see you again
Nor dance to your tune
Bound by your spell

I have met you before
In another form
Your claws betray you

I was a child then
Led by the hand in a sleepwalk
Blind to the wreckage at your feet

These platforms and
The luminous wood on your face
Make no difference

1. What emotion does the tone in stanza 1 reveal? What do you think it means to dance · to someone else's tune?
2. Do you think the spell that bound the person was from the power of beauty or witch- craft?
3. Although the subject (person) has come in another form, what has not changed? How does this reveal about his/her character?
4. *Make no difference* (final stanza) to what? What is the persona trying to say?
5. State three reasons given in stanza 3 that explain why the person made a mistake at first.
6. What in stanza 4 shows that the persona now sees clearly and is not likely to repeat the mistakes he made before? How is this strengthened by the dramatic start in stanza 1?
7. What does *exorcism* mean in this poem?

SONG OF NYAVITIMA   9

by Zondiwe Mbano

Once upon a time
There was love, and love
Whispered only sweetness

The sun rose bright
And cool rivers mirrored
White clouds sailing high

Love is like a tree growing
Which soon bears flowers
Pouring out aroma of beauty

Winds sigh in the trees
And birds trill in the branches
As day passes and night comes

In the night there are moths
That plant ravenous grubs
To gnaw away at the roots

Children, if you see love wilting
Do not ask questions; only
Remember once upon a time

Nya signifies that the name is of a woman, especially one who is grown-up and, in most cases, married.
Vitima means sorrows.

1. Which words in the first stanza show that this is a tale?
2. How are the following, sun, cool rivers, a tree imagery of love?
3. Which two things mentioned in stanza 4 show that love is calm and peaceful?
4. What two things bring about wilting?
5. What life experiences are moths in stanza 5 a metaphor of? How do these destroy a love relationship?
6. Would you trust love when it whispers only sweetness? How does this poem serve as a warning to young people?
7. How does the last line show that this poem has an endless structure, like a circle?

MARRIAGE   10

by Herbert B Kapota

It is like an oxcart
Where one ox is fast
While the other is slow
        Drover throw the whip

It is like a moving car
Sometimes slow uphill
Sometimes fast downhill
        Driver step on the brakes

Inside are the young
Innocent souls entrusted to us
To nurture and transport home
        Drover goad us, stop us

1. What will happen to the oxcart with oxen at different speeds?
2. How will the drover's whip help cor-

rect this situation?

3. In stanza 2, what will the brakes help to correct?
4. According to stanza 3, what responsibility do the parents have in marriage? Would they succeed in their responsibility if they get divorced?
5. A drover moves cattle or sheep from one place to another. Who or what is referred to as the drover or driver in this poem?
6. How is the oxcart and car, as used in the poem, appropriate metaphors for marriage?

PILLAR OF LOVE   11

by Jayne O Banda

Hazel was only nine months
When college called me
And I left with a heavy heart

Thank you, Lord, for my man
A pillar of love towering over
Jeers, taunts and sleepless nights

Now open your hearts, beloved
For before long I will flood you
With love in arrears of three rains

1. How did the persona feel as she left for college?
2. Who jeered and taunted the man? What do you think they said to him? Why?
3. How did the man respond to these people? If you were the man, what would you have said?
4. Mention two words in stanza 2 that show the man is strong and reliable.
5. For how long was the woman away? How will she compensate for this?

DEAR MOTHER   12

by Elizabeth Makhala-Nya
matcherenga

Dear mother, if only you had known
How I wish you were still alive
So we could be together on this day

Little did I know what you meant to me
If only you had waited for this day
To receive big parcels of my love

My dear mother you went so early
But I still send you flowers of love
On this special day, Mother's day

1. When is Mothers' Day in Malawi? What does the day commemorate?
2. What would the persona have done if the mother were alive?
3. *'But I still sent..'*.Is this possible? Explain.
4. What do you do for your mother, parents, or guardians on this day?
5. Do you think the day should be renamed Parents' Day? Explain?

MAMA 13
by Thomas Khumuwa

You walked the nine miles
Of pain and hope to Golgotha

And the next ardous twenty
You walked me to adulthood

For all the gruelling walk
I adore you sweet Mama

1. What pain and hope is there? What does Golgotha symbolise?
2. An arduous activity involves a great deal of effort and strength. Why do you think the next 20 miles are described as arduous?
3. Between the nine miles and the twenty, which do you think is the most difficult period for the mother? Why?
4. Which two words show that the persona greatly appreciates the role played by the mother?

WOMAN 14
by Chris Mwawa

On her back
She carries
A young baby.
On her head
A big calabash
Full of water.
In front of her
Is a burden
Of another one
Coming soon.
With long strides
The man ahead
Shouts at her:
'Quick woman!'

1. What three things has the woman carried?
2. What two things done by the man show that he is not considerate to the woman?
3. Mention things the woman should have done to solve her problems?
4. If you were the man, what would you have done to show a loving and caring attitude to your wife?
5. Describe your experiences of violence against women? What should men and women do to overcome these problems?

WHY THE OLD WOMAN LIMPS   15
By Lupenga Mphande

Do you know why the old woman sings?
She is sixty years old with six grandchildren to look after
While her sons and their wives are gone south to dig gold.
Each day she milks the goat, sells the milk to buy soap,
Feeds and washes the children, and tethers the goat.
In the evening she tells stories of old at the fireside:
I know why the old woman sings.

Do you know when the old woman sleeps?
She rests with the day, at night she thinks of
Tomorrow: she's to feed the children and graze the goat.
She's to weed the garden, water the seedlings beans,
The thatch has to be mended, the barnyard cleared,
Maize pounded, chaff winnowed, millet ground, fire lit...
I do not know when the old woman sleeps.

Do you know why the old woman limps?
She goes to fetch water in the morning
    and the well is five miles away,
Goes to fetch firewood with her axe'
    and the forest is five miles the other way,
Goes to the fields to look for pumpkin leaves
    leaving the goat tethered to the tree
And hurries home to the children to cook:
I know why the old woman limps.

1. What situation has led to the grandmother having to keep six grandchildren? What modern problems have led to many children having to be brought up by their grandparents, uncles or aunts?
2. What does the grandmother do in order to provide for the family?
3. What activity does she do which is usually done by grandparents? Why does she sing?
4. Out of the tasks in stanza 2, which ones will she do personally, and which ones is she likely to ask others to do for her?
5. Why do you think the old woman limps?

6. Examine the structure of the poem. How does each stanza begin and end?
7. If you met *her sons and their wives* what advice would you give them? Why?

FEEDING 16

by Steve Chimombo

Come, let us both eat
the freshly cooked *nsima*.
Come, let us both drink
the freshly brewed thobwa,
product of finger millet,
maize flour and water.
May their mingling slake
our thirsting spirits.
May the yeast sprout in us
new life and new hopes.

Come, let us take some
of this food and drink
and pour libations thrice
at the nearest rain shrine,
to fill the ancestral spirits,
to intoxicate them all with
the spirit of the new woman.

(From Part Three of *Breaking the Beadstrings*)

1. What is the other person being invited to eat and drink?
2. Why is the fact that the food and drink are produced from millet, maize and water important? Would it be the same if they were imported foods and drinks?
3. *...slake our thirsting spirits.* How does this show that the thirst that needs to be quenched is not very much physical? What do you think this thirst is? Explain.
4. How will partaking in this bring newness and real satisfaction?
5. Look at the first line in each stanza. How do these lines introduce aspects of love, sharing and worship?
6. Which other beings are involved in the sharing of food and drinks?
7. What will characterize the spirit of the new woman?

AUNT MAO 17

by Anthony Nazombe

The riddle that makes
The dutiful cock crow
Yields its knot to fingers
That knead the earth

You must wake up
With the dew
Face the morning wind
With childless hands at the back

This ear now hard of hearing
Has seen many tobacco rolls
Dry skins of maize cobs
From yester year's harvest

Yours are hard-bitten toes
Defying stumps and stonepricks
Hoes diminished by rust and age
Handles polished by sweat and sand

1. Mention two words from the first stanza which refer to something very difficult to solve.

2. What word used in the first stanza means the opposite of *lazy*?
3. What time for waking up is recommended in stanza 2? If there is no child, why are the hands at the back?
4. How does the woman carry her tobacco cigar? Use a pen to demonstrate this.
5. Mention three things from the last stanza which show that Aunt Mao lives a rather hard life.

TRAIN TO BALAKA   18

by Zondiwe Mbano

A train puffs round
And up the slopes

Its stubborn will, steel
Wheels that carry it along

So many wheels squeak
Under its millipede body!
******

A boy sits, sucking mango
After mango, while belching

And green flies swarm
The coach: so noisome!
******

A young woman scrambles in
Her beauty drowned in poverty

Only a worn out wrapper
From breasts to above knees.

In her hands, a smiling baby
Nude and round like a pumpkin:

A fruit thriving in the wild,
Lord, where is the sower

The roving sower who never
Deigns to come back and tend.
******

To love someone
What a commitment!

Christ on the ancient tree
Have patience with us

For days are so many
Fewer the hairs of a bull.

Some day we shall know;
Then love shall drive us

And love shall steer us
Like wheels of a train

1. Identify two verbs in stanza 1 and 3 which show that the train is moving slowly and with difficulty?

231

2. From stanza 2 and 3, pick out words that give a sound similar to squeaking when you read them.
3. A noisome thing is disgusting. Mention two things in stanza 4 and 5 which are disgusting.
4. *Scrambles in...* How did the woman enter the train?
5. Identify words from stanzas 6 to 9 which show that:
   (a) the woman is very poor
   (b) the baby is very healthy
6. Who is to blame for the woman's condition? Why?
7. Why is Christ mentioned in the poem? How does Christ compare with *the roving sower?*
8. *.Days are so many /Fewer the hairs of a bull.'* What argument or plea does this proverb support? Explain.
9 What characteristics of wheels of a train make them appropriate imagery for love?

LEADERS OF TOMORROW   19

by George Pungulani

You leaders of tomorrow
On what corner stones
Are you going to build?

Running away from school
Where true leaders are baked
You hide in dark corners

Can one find happiness
In sex, drink and smoke
The very horns of death?

1. Who are leaders of tomorrow?
2. Mention two things they do which will not help them to be leaders?
3. *...true leaders are baked...*Why is the verb 'baked' a good metaphor of the process of preparing leaders?
4. Mention the three things in which they seek happiness. Will they find it?
5. Why are sex, drink and smoke described as horns of death? What dangers does each of these pose to life?

THE SPEAR   20

by Christopher Matewere

My children, open your eyes and see
The spear is vanquishing the world

A woman seeking money in the dark
Does not see the spear poised to strike

A rich man wastes away in a poshy ward
Nourished only by drips and penicillins

The spear is inviting the whole world
To a banquet underneath the earth

1. What are the children told to do in order to see the spear? Is the spear visible?
2. Why does the woman not see the spear? What activities is she engaged in?
3. Did the rich man see the spear? Why is the man wasting away?
4. What do you think the spear symbolises. What is the banquet to which the whole world is invited?

LORD HEAR OUR CRY   21

by John E.B. Matope

Hoes wear out
Not because of farming
But digging graves

Hymns are learnt
Not in churches
But at graveyards

Hospitals are there
Not for healing people
But keeping them to die

At the end of the day
The coffin seller
Has a happy profit

Lord, we cry to You
Every day every night
Hear our prayers, Lord

1. Mention three things described in the poem that do not happen the way they normally should?
2. Why does the coffin seller have a happy profit? Would you say he is in good business? Explain.
3. Do you think these people have much time for farming and attending church servives? Why is it so?
4. To show that the Lord has heard the prayers, what is He being implored to do?

SONG OF TEARS   22

by Lackson J Chatha

Brother I warned you once
But you said life was great

I saw them in your house
Swimming into the rooms

Now I am left alone crying
How can they all disappear?

1. What did the brother mean when he
   said life is great? Have you ever felt
   that life is great? In what situation
   did you feel so?
2. *I saw them.../Swimming* ... Who are
   they? What were they actually doing
   in the rooms?
3. What has happened to the brother?
   Now where are those who were
   swimming into the rooms?
4. What message do you get from this
   poem?

SONGANI LOOKOUT   23

By Felix Mnthali

It looks daunting, doesn't it?
with its moss, slippery moss
with its crags, biting, sharp
blood-letting crags.

But if you were exposed
or marooned
on that perpendicular, mossy
greyness -

if you were pushed or pinned
to that perpendicular craggy
majesty
you would force yourself
and no doubt succeed
in reaching the top!

Men have swam
from the deep end
of Lake Malawi -
not only defying the lake
but achieving success

And so
if you were pushed
to scale the limits of nature
to reach Songani Lookout -
from the wrong end
bottom upwards, east and not west
you might as well
succeed!

1. Mention the things that make Songani
   Lookout daunting?
2. *But if you were exposed/ or marooned*
   How would this situation force you
   to reach the top? Describe an experience that motivated you to fight hard
   in order to succeed.
3. *Men have swam ...deep end of Lake
   Malawi...*What life experiences do
   you think are being referred to here?
   What examples of success are
   achieved?
4. To climb to Songani lookout from
   bottom upwards would involve scaling a cliff or precipice. How do the
   moss and crags make the climbing

almost impossible? What life obstacles are similar to moss and crags?

5. What life experiences can push people to scale the limits of nature? Mention men and women who succeeded in situations that looked impossible?

6. How can this poem encourage you as a scholar, or as an aspirant after a profession such as teaching, journalism or engineering?

CHASING PAGES 24
by Linda C. W. Saidi

I have walked a long way
During these few past rains

Those ahead are still walking
Those behind are still walking

Mothers leaving crying babies
Newly weds deserting spouses

This madness of chasing pages
Where can one find a cure for it

1. What do past rains refer to ?
2. Why are those ahead and those behind still walking? Where are they going?
3. Would you say the action by mothers and spouses in stanza 3 is good?
4. What is this thing that is referred to as the *...madness of chasing pages*? Why is it referred to as such?
5. What will happen if the cure is found? Would you be amongst those people lining up for the cure? Why?

DOMASI COLLEGE 25
by Ndekhane Kalumba

You have become a dream
Of fresh *chambo* from coals
Of chicken from the grill

Those straight as a pencil
Started talking about weight
After a week in the dining

Blow back our old days
Kind wind of the mountain
Remove the scourge of beans

1. What was the diet like before?
2. Is a person described *as straight as a pencil* thin, slim, fat, or plump?
3. *...talking about weight.* Were they talking about how to slim or how to put on weight?
4. What differences do you see in the way the last stanza is constructed and the first two?
5. What is it that is described as the *scourge of beans* ? What is the person praying for?
6. Sometimes pupils riot and destroy school property when there is a drastic change in their conditions. Is this a proper way to resolve a problem? Instead what should be done? Write a poem about the conditions in the your school.

HONEYBIRD 26

by Zondiwe Mbano

Honeybird you lure me
Away from the morning fire
To the cold wet forest.
On my shoulder, I carry an axe
In my hands, a spear and clubs;
Across the fields to the forest,
Honeybird you lure me on.
Through the forest, up the slopes
The desire for honey, like a fire
In the blood, drives me on.
My knees weak with fatigue, and
A smell of blood in my nostrils,
I look up the high mountain;
Honeybird you lure me on

1. What circumstances described in the first three lines make the call of the honeybird not pleasant?
2. What tools and weapons does the persona carry? Does he/she expect to find honey or something dangerous?
3. Why does the persona endure the hard and tiresome walk?
4. Have you ever felt a fire in your blood? How did it feel?
5. State two things which show that the persona is very tired.
6. Do the last two lines promise rest or a farther long and hard walk? Explain.
7. What do you think the honeybird stands for? Explain.

THE SERPENT 27

by Sophie Jobe

You came with smiles
And a sweet tongue
While showering gifts

Breaking hard hearts
And levelling deep valleys
You took me to your nest

Going to bed at midnight
And waking at cock-crow
Is the torture I now earn

Hot tears flood my cheeks
My bones fail to hold me
When I think of my home

1. What specific things did the serpent do to attract the persona?
2. What is this nest that the persona was taken to?
3. Mention problems the persona experienced when he/she went to the nest.
4. How did the persona react to these problems? Why does the persona think of his/her home?
5. Have you experienced a situation when you regretted taking someone's advice? Explain.
6. What does the serpent symbolise? Explain why you think so?

MY UNCLE E. P. MTUNGAMBERA HARAWA   28

By Felix Mnthali

Don't call it perfect timing
when my uncle emerges
from nowhere
leading a procession
of men, women and children
bearing groundnuts, potatoes
and fresh maize

With shoulders upright
and marching as to war
he has always been
the source of wonders among men
always emerging from nowhere
to stand where we needed him
at the moment we needed him

What would Malawians
round the mining towns
of Selukwe, Shabani, Guinea Fowl
have done without him?

I see him now
in his white coat
stethoscope slung on his shoulders
muttering 'Oh Yes'
through rows of patients
in the hospital at Camper Down

I see him again
Sundays this time
right in front of the congregation
and to this day up there in
Mbulunji, a tower of strength
in the Church of Central Africa Presbyterian

Will our children ever follow
the love that sends a man
at the break of day
to gather the choicest maize
the choicest fruit
and wait close to the roadside
to emerge quietly
as the van to Zomba
comes in view?

Don't call it perfect timing:
he has always been
where he was to be
at the minute he was to be
like his ancestor Kajimerere
who it is said
explained his origins by saying
'I grew out of this land.'

1. What did Uncle Harawa bring?
2. What specific things do you think he did for Malawians around the mining towns? What was Uncle Harawa before he came home?
3. What does he do in the church at Mbulunji in Rumphi?
4. *I see him now...I see him again...* Does the writer actually see him, or does he simply remember what he saw? Explain.
5. What specific things did he do in preparation for the journey to Zomba? How does this demonstrate love? How might children of today not understand this love? Would you agree with this? Why?
6. Read the line in the last stanza that

explains the meaning of Kajimerere.

7. Would you say Uncle Harawa is a seer who foresees where and when people need him? Or would you say he is a man who is always full of love and zeal to serve others?

8. Write a poem about someone who did something special for you, or someone who loves to serve others

THE NYAMWEZI   29
Andrew Bwenkha Thawe

Putting my head into the clouds,
True image of a young Nyamwezi;
Beautiful as a new moon

Robust legs, thick lips
And a tender dark skin:
Oh, true Nyamwezi!

Sweet soft language,
Full of song and wisdom:
Oh, my Nyamwezi!

Wetlands of a lake
Countryside; I see your beauty
My Nyamwezi homeland

1. Are the Nyamwezi tall or short people?
2. What makes the new moon look beautiful?
3. Mention characteristics of the Nyamwezi that make them beautiful?
4. Do you sometimes feel nostalgia for your home? Describe beautiful things you remember at your home.
5. Sing a song about the beauty of home, eg. *Kwathu ku Mlangeni...*

LAKE KAZUNI   30
by Zondiwe Mbano

Lap, lap ripples of Kazuni
Lap against your muddy shore

Lap and listen to the roaring storm
Tearing down the youthful boughs

Lap and listen to a dove's dirge
All her brood smashed by the storm

Lap and listen to a widow wailing
Her man capsized by the battering storm

Lap and listen to trumpeting elephants
Thunder and hail on Vwaza Marsh

Lap, lap you muddy water
Can't reflect my louring cloud

Lap, lap ripples of Kazuni
Lap against your shaking reeds

1. From stanza 2 and 3, state what the storm has done?
2. From stanza 3 and 4, pick out two words which mean the same as mourning.
3. Why can't the water reflect the lowering clouds?
4. What do these metaphors stand for: storm and lowering cloud?
5. Look at the marking (') of the beat in the stanzas.

   'Lap and 'listen to a 'widow 'wailing
   Her 'man cap'sized by the 'battering 'storm

   'Lap and 'listen to 'trumpeting 'elephants
   'Thunder and 'hail on 'Vwaza 'Marsh

Now read the lines while stamping the ground on each beat. Mark the remaing stanza
with four beats in each line.

239

THE LINGADZI   31
(At Kongwe Mission)

By Zondiwe Mbano

i

Indeed this river is lovely
So lovely and peaceful.

The water purls tunes
Salutary, and over stones

It leaps sportively like
A hare; then spreads out

Effervescently. Little waves
Ripple out, and out, and out

Then disappear. And slowly
With calm ardour, the water

Traces its windy course
Down to the hungry lake

ii

Up the valley and beyond
The wind is a madman

July wind charging at nothing
And craven grass and leaves

Rasp and rattle in terror.
A hill with horns rises high

Piercing the scowling sky.
Under the mellifluous water

Crabs skulk sideways
Around the mossy crags.

iii

I am listless today,
Feel cold and listless.

I must rest on this rock,
It's warm on this rock

That never stirs or shifts.
Come Nellie, my poetry,

It's broad and warm
Under the lambent sun.

And what have we
To fear on the rock!

There's nothing to fear
Under the lambent sun
Dowa, 1978

1. Describe the structure of the poem in terms of numbers of sections, stanzas in each section, and lines in each stanza
2. Generally what does each section deal with?
3. Describe the lovely and peaceful imagery contained in section 1.
4. Is the hungry lake part of the peaceful imagery? Explain.
5 Describe the metaphors of violence, fear and danger contained in section 2. How does the mellifluous water contrast with the crabs in it?
6. Pick out metaphors of power, love, warmth and security contained in section 3.
7. In spite of the dangers in the water and around, why does the persona declare that there is nothing to fear?

DOTOLO   32
(A Dotolo nawo mwe)
                    by Zondiwe Mbano
People of Ekwendeni
And of areas around
Forget not Dotolo

His hair cut and combed
Leaving a straight ridge
Like a crest of white

Dotolo in the market
Patrolling, and no thief
No litter-bug would dare

Dotolo down the street
Dancing classic malipenga
Like Soliyamu of Nkamanga

His shirt and short ironed
To razor-sharpness, his stick
Spinning like a fast wheel

Dotolololo-tolo, Dotolotolotolo
Dotolo rebuffs ticks
And ticks rebuff Dotolo

Then time for old English:
*One deck you see the man
Is he coming?* This means

When I called Nyaukandawire
She turned into an anthill,
Therefore Dotolo is a god

241

Children, we listened to him
The teacher from Nkamanga
Bewitched for his learning

He was our Ekwendeni
More than the Asian stores
Full of biscuits and sweets

But one day some men came
Saying he was their brother
And they were taking him

No one stopped our Dotolo going
And soon dusty winds blew word
That he turned into a red mound
Zomba 1993

*'A Dotolo nawo mwe.' a song children
sang for Dotolo, a madman at Ekwendeni, in the 60's*

1. In your own words, describe Dotolo's
   hair style.
2. From stanza 3 and 4, what two functions did Dotolo fulfil at Ekwendeni?
3. Have you ever watched a Malipenga
   dance? Can you demonstrate how to
   spin a stick the way they do it?
4. Find out from peers details of the Biblical story about what happened to
   the wife of Lot. Do you think Dotolo
   was simply retelling this story in
   stanza 7 and 8? Explain.
5. What brief background information
   about Dotolo is given in the poem?
6. Did children like Dotolo or not?
   Explain.

7. How did Dotolo die? How did the
   children feel when they heard about
   his death? Explain.

SHIRE RIVER _ 33
By Chris M Zenengeya
River Shire you flow majestically
Like a prince prancing into battle

Down the Mpatamanga your rapids
Challenge thoughts to harness you

You calmly meander the Lower Shire
While crocodiles patrol your banks

1. What means of transport is the prince
   using to go to war?
2. Pick out two words from stanza 1 that
   describe a person of royal birth.
3. Why would it be difficult to harness
   the river at Mpatamanga?
4. Despite the calmness, what dangers
   are there in the Lower Shire?
5. Compare the speed of the water as
   described in each of the three stanzas?

Dawn

in its full attire
emerging - is it that
our sights fall on
where darkness built
its dwells, coercing
sleep on eyes feeling
it least necessary ?

Dawn

in its majestic move
uncovering all that was
beyond sight is it that
every nose pack
all airs God created
for all days our
banking move ?

Dead

Does the moon that
faired poorly in its
part of making us
differentiate our right
from our left rightly?

Dream ?

I wonder if we 're
to see the sun rise
higher and our shadows
long enough be small.

How easy it is here
To be no longer at ease
among our own people
clutching their shadows!

The land reels
from the repeated blows
of what we did
and did not do

We wrestled with the devil
we snubbed temptations
oh how we fasted
for forty days and forty nights
while praying for the dawn -

When you come to see us
you will be haunted
by the incantations
around our bonfire

feathers shake our glory
in the noon day heat,
and spears and assegais
nod their assent
to the conquests that are sung

How easy it is here
among our own people
to clutch and hug the rags of yesterday
and sing and dance for the dawn.

1. One line in stanza 1 is a title of a
   novel by Chinua Achebe. Which
   one is it?
2. Which line in stanza 1 shows that

people live in fear?
3. In what state is the land? Why?
4. What 3 things did they do while praying? Were the prayers effective?
5. What type of dance is described in stanza 5? How do you know this?
6. What line warns against holding on to useless things from the past?
7. Has the beauty of dawn come? Explain.

WHY, OH WHY   36
by Zondiwe Mbano

Daughters of Lukonkobe
Dressed up in colours of flowers
To meet a blind suitor;
Daughters of Lukonkobe
Why, oh why?

Mothers of Lukonkobe
Elected an impotent slave
To marry the chief's daughter.
Mothers of Lukonkobe
Why, oh why?

Sons of Lukonkobe
Whistled and chanted praises
To embolden a craven bull.
Sons of Lukonkobe
Why, oh why?

Men of Lukonkobe
Danced the victorious *mgubo*
To welcome a famished runaway.
Men of Lukonkobe
Why, oh why?

Elders of Lukonkobe,
When a he-goat is mad,
Don't you knock off its horns?
Elders of Lukonkobe
Why, oh why?

Lukonkobe is a river. Mgubo is a dance performed when warriors return from a successful battle.

1. Read a line repeated within a stanza. Read a line repeated in every stanza. What effect does repetition have on the poem?
2. Explain how in each stanza what the people did was a fiasco.
3. *To embolden a craven bull.* Is this possible? Explain how.
4. What advice is given in stanza 5? Why are the elders called upon to do this?
5. What situations could you relate the poem to?

NYUMBANI'S TALE   37
by Zondiwe Mbano

Trappist went to the river
In the heat of early afternoon

There he came near a burrow
With footprints of monitor lizard

He examined these footprints
Showing monitor was in the burrow

Then he said as if to himself
Yet shouting for monitor to hear

I will bring and set my trap
Before monitor crawls out today

Meanwhile he quickly set the trap
And tip-toed to under a shade

Monitor had overheard the plan
And reasoned from inside the hole

I must run out of this grave
Before he brings his death tools

He crawled out of darkness
Hoping he was going into light

The trap was keen for his neck
It snapped and throttled him

Dangling he gasped for breath
His eyes and forked tongue out

From his shade under a katope tree
Trappist dashed towards his catch

How quickly I have got him today
See his double tongue flickering

I have got the skin to make a drum
That will call everyone to dance

Panted out monitor in a dying voice
It's you who have the double tongue

From your lips shine out hope
From your heart creeps out death

1. How did Trappist know that monitor was in the burrow?

2. How do stanzas 4, 5, 6 and the last
   one show that Trappist was a liar?
3. What was this darkness that monitor
   was running away from? Did he find
   light? What happened to him?
4. What do you think double tongue
   symbolises? Who has it?
5. Why did trappist kill monitor? Do
   you think it was fair? Why?
6. Do you know people who have a double tongue? What suffering do they
   cause to innocent people? What can
   you do to stop such people causing
   others suffering.

LEADERS   38

by Bridget C. Mhemedi

Remember you climbed high up
On the scafford of the people

Now you wax yourself with wings
Spitting as you look down on them

Beware of the heat from the anger
Of the hungry barefoot and sick

1. How can a scaffold be used for building or destroying?
2. What two things are the leaders said
   to be doing?
3. What thing mentioned in stanza 2 is
   susceptible to heat?
4. Can the condition of being hungry,
   barefoot and sick be blamed on the
   leaders? Explain.

5. What warning to leaders does the poem present?

SONGS FROM THE CLOUDS 39
By Francis Moto

I sat at Chingwe's hole
and heard songs from the clouds.
Songs bathed in blood
the blood of a people
sacrificed to quench the wrath
of bloodthirsty gods.

I sat on the shores of Malindi
a cold wind rode
on the rippling waves
to break on the sand,
pebbles and lake shell.
Again I heard songs from the clouds.
Songs of children sacrificed
to feed the stomachs
Of starved gods

Sitting on concrete slabs
Sipping a cold beer
The clouds broke into song,
A song wailing for women
Beautiful, young and ignorant:
Live women hand-picked
To be the king's pillow.

Chingwe's hole, a big dark hole, like a crater, is on Zomba Mountain. Stories are told of how people were sacrificed by being thrown into the hole. Later their bodies would float down the Namitembo (corpses) river.

1. Pick out a word that has been repeated three times in stanza 1. How does this help to introduce the theme dealt with in the poem?
2. Why were the people killed? Was this justified?
3. *..Songs bathed in blood...* Imagine how such songs would sound. What mood would they convey?
4. Describe the metaphors of calm and beauty presented in stanza 2. What contrast do the last three lines present?
5. Why were the women killed in stanza 3?
6. In each stanza how does the persona get the information about the murders that took place?
7. Are there modern practices that sacrifice women to men in power? Explain. What can you do to make sure such practices are stopped?

RIDING A LION 40
by Hellen C Kachala

When the leader rides a lion
Followers silently edge away
Fearing how the journey will end

When the leader rides an elephant
Followers tiptoe from a distance
Marvelling how he will dismount

And when the lion and the elephant
Graft themselves into siamese twins
We wonder whose blood is flowing

1. Why are the followers afraid?
2. Can a person ride a lion? What real life situation do you think this refers

to?

3. What political situation can be likened to what is described in stanza 3 ?
4. The last lines show that the people fear, marvel, and wonder. Do you think the leaders described in the poem involve or consult the people in major decisions of their party?
5. Would you say such leaders are good? Explain.

DRIFTING SCUM   41
by Max Iphani

Arm in arm
Tattered shirts and wrinkled faces
Striding along the streets
Stumbling over potholes
Towards cold slums
Surrounded by drifting scums
And yellow maize

Vendors voices grow hoarse
Only flies and mosquitoes answer
Their shrill cries in swarms.
Pedestrians merely salivate
Shaking hornless heads.
Selling turns into wrestling
As wares are shovelled
Onto peoples' bosoms and mouths

Widows dangle
Their hindquarters
And wear potent aphrodisiacs
But not even cassanovas
Want to act playboy, so
So children loudly whimper
With hunger pains

Walk about barefoot
Bottoms on display
Feet treaded
Bellies distended
Skulls on shoulders

Asians flount smiles
And beckon to customers
Who contort faces
In response to the affection.
No amount of screaming
'Sale, sale, sale!"
Brings any bargains
Speaking Gujerat only scatters

Automobile salers doze on counters
Textile factories wear rags
Second-hand clothes heaps
Are crowd pullers
And cause market stampedes

Education goes commercial,
Even graveyards are Etons of Africa
Where mandrax and hashish
Are consumed with gusto

Winds from the western hills
Blow morals afloat into the air
And hospital superintendents
Tread over dead bodies
When mourners collect loved ones.

1. What kind of people are described in stanza 1? Describe their houses, surroundings and locations.
2. What kind of income generating activities are they involved in? Do they make

much money? Explain.

3. *And wear potent aphrodisiacs.* Why do they wear these? What 'business' are they in? Are they to blame for this?

4. What signs of extreme poverty and malnutrition among children are described in stanza 3?

5. What kind of business tricks do the Asians employ? Are they sussccessful?

6. List indicators in stanza 5 and 6 that show:
   a) that the economy is very bad,
   b) that education quality is very poor,
   c) that the country is overwhelmed by death.

7. What has happened to traditional moral values? What has caused this?

8. Who are the people referred to as Drifting Scum? Are they the poor living indecent lives in slums, or the leaders whose policies have brought extreme poverty and suffering? Explain.

MODERN ADVERTISING   42
by Steve Chimombo

"Wake up to the world of Leonex"
The song gyrated across the mind
elbowing out reality
Pirouetted onto the corners of the soul
Bounced against the walls
And curtsied to a crash of cymbals.
It landed outside
And parrot-like chanted to the world:
Leonex! Leonex! Leonex!

The soul erosion exorcised truth
And replaced it more permanently with:
"Life is richer with Leonex!"

Now I use Leonex after-birth lotion-
Thanks to Leonex.
Wash my brains in Leonex liquid.
Thanks to Leonex.
Gargle my soul with Leonex mixture.
Thanks to Leonex.
And dry my tears on a Leonex towel.

The cleansed spirit yearns for the big name:
"Life is indeed better with Leonex?"
As I walk down the street
Breathing rarefied Leonex air
And see other Leonex faces
I give my thanks to Leonex
New York

1. What messages does the song convey?

2. What expressions show that Leonex messages are presented as if they were evangelical messages?

3. What toiletries has the person been enticed to use?

4. *The soul erosion ...Life is richer with Leonex.* Does the writer want us to believe that this message about Leonex is true? How can you tell that the writer is using irony?

5. The last stanza seems to suggest that the person has been converted and now worships Leonex? Is this so? Why?

6. What characteristics of modern advertising does the poem parody? Why?

WAITING FOR THE RAIN 43
By Felix Mnthali
Black faces smile and nod
Above limp hands
Clapping their automatic
Soundless and unintended
welcome

It has been done, before, done
Under every shade and colour of sky
From overcast, dark red to very clear

The robust and sweating poor of our sort
Clap hands, sing and ululate
For Land-and Range-rovers
Mercedez Benzes and Toyota Crowns
Six-O-Fours and Datsun B's
Forerunners of forerunners
With multi-coloured flashlights
And whizzing sirens
On their rooftops

It's been done, before, done
This ululation of the dispossessed
For the tired smile
And the tired nod
Tired and sad
From praying for the rain

The poor and sweating of our sort
Have been here since dawn
Clapping their hands
For every moth that frets and shouts
Its hour upon the stage
Blinking at the multicoloured lights
And wailing sirens
Taking them
Into the land of milk and honey.

THE NEW YEAR 44
by Anthony Nazombe
The seasons have run their course:
Marrow-chilling June
Gave way to blazing August
Which in turn yielded
To sky-rending November
Heralding the greenery of January

Water flowed from its source
To return with the rains,
Trees surrendered their leaves
To regain them green
And the moon waned
Only to wax again

And now life hovers
Between what has been
And events to come,
Night marking the end
Dissolves in the light of the beginning
And the snake casts away its skin

The cock sings a new song
To the rising sun:
Sweep the house clean
Of last year's dirt,
Empty pots of yesterday's beer
And wash them clean of insipid malt

Then we shall brew new *masese*
For the New Year throats
Clad in crisp wrappers
While women sing new Chioda tunes
And men stomp and dance
To the rapturous Ingoma rhythm

A PRAYER   45
by Zondiwe Mbano

Blazing sun
Staring from above
Wink at times;

Let your eyelids
Rain down
Tears of pity.

Green in fields
Green in the wild
Stoop under you

1. Which two words in stanza1 show that the sun is hot?
2. How does the sun wink? How is personification used here?
3. What human organ is the sun likened to in stanza 2?
4. What is referred to as green? What exactly has happened to the green? In which months does this normally happen?
5 What is the persona praying for? Explain.

Sick Child 46

by Owen Kandeu

Look at that child
His stomach full of emptiness
Safeguarded by ribs you can count

Look at that child
His face older than his age
A big head spinning on a thin neck

Look at that child
How does he walk
On the legs of a mosquito

Look at him now
In a swarm of green flies
And a dog cleans him with a lick

1 Is a stomach full of emptiness, small or large? How does the contradiction in these lines help clarify the message of suffering?
2. What evidence is there that in stanza 1 the child is thin?
3. Describe his face, head and neck?
4 *Walk on legs of a mosquito*. Is this possible? By using such exaggeration what does the writer want to emphasize?
5. In stanza 4, what has happened to the boy?
6 What would you say the child is suffering from? Explain the causes of this? How can the child be helped?
7. Look at the first line of each stanza, what do you notice? What effect does this style have on the poem?

A WIDOW   47
by Zondiwe Mbano

An old widow walking to the market.
She must keep on her head a heavy basket
To keep her children in school

I saw her down the road
Going to sell her maize
Her face

where many sorrows brood
Is cracked and scratched
  with claws of the cruel cold;
Her hands
  the dirty and coarse hands
  for those whose are clean
Have grown thick and callous;
The soles of her feet
  without hope for shoes
Have grown thick tissues

An old widow tramping
  her neck deep into shoulders
Down the road to the market

But suddenly an eardrum rending
hoot,
Helter-skelter to surrender their
road
  but near the edge she stumbles;
Then in a slouch she stands
  enjoying the heat radiating
  from her nail off bleeding toe;
Her maize scattered on the dust

Just then, a Benz zooms past;
On the backseat , a mastiff:
  the type that eat money a week
  enough to keep her children in school

Submerged in the dust, she slits
her eyes;
Then suddenly opens them
  to a big bang sound!
Hobbles to see, though
  what ill can befall them ?
Then walking some yards, she sees
  the triumph over terrain

the luxury of travelling
Crushed against a huge trunk   /

All around
  smashed glass scattered

Inside squashed steel
  man and dog locked
  in a death hug

1. Explain from stanza 1 the relationship between the basket on the head and the children in school?
2. How does the woman look like? Do you think she is successful in her income generating activities?
3. Describe briefly what happened to her on the road to the market? How did it happen ? Was it fair to the woman?
4. Describe the accident that happened to the Benz? Who were involved?
5. Would you say what happened to the man is poetic justice (instant justice), or it is one of those unfortunate accidents? Explain?

VIPYA   48

(*Ooo Vipya, Vipya wabazungu*)
by Zondiwe Mbano

Ooo Vipya
Vipya of the whiteman
Conqueror of the lake

Welcomed *machona*
From the bowels of gold
To bury them in the lake

Ooo Vipya
Heavy roaring iron
Ironing the waves

Vipya of the whiteman
Mass iron coffin
Deep under the lake

*'Vipya' was a passenger ship on Lake
Malawi. It sank in July, 1946. 'Vipya
wabazungu' means: Vipya of the white man,
or made by the white man 'Machona' are
people who go to work faraway from their
homes, and do not come back until they are
old. Most of the machona went to work in the
mines, in South Africa and Rhodesia (Zimbabwe and Zambia).*

1. Which two stanzas have the
   metaphor of the greatness and
   power of Vipya? Read the three
   words from these stanzas which
   show this.
2. How does stanza 1 and 3 show the
   power of the Vipya over the lake?
   Why is the metaphor of an iron
   appropriate in describing the
   ship?
3. What are bowels of gold? Why is
   the drowning of *machona* a very
   sad thing?
4. Why is Vipya an iron coffin? Why
   would a coffin be appropriate
   metaphor for the Vipya
5. In the final analysis would you say
   that Vipya had power over the
   lake or vise versa? Explain.

DEATH   49
by Rosemary Ulemu Mkumba
You come picking one by one
Like a bird picking grain
Leaving only songs and tears

Flooded rivers soon dry up
How long shall I mourn
Before my tears run dry

1. Who or what is being referred to as *you*?
2. What do the songs and the tears refer to?
3. What is it that is symbolised by:
   a) a bird, (b) grain?
4. When will the person's tears dry up?
   Does the person happily look forward to this time?

GRAVE MATES   50
by Steve Chimombo
We meet again at the same
Graveyard, familiar grave-mates.
The mounds like tumours of grief
On the ground's face separate us.
Misty eyes moisten the dust storms
Raised by the shovels and hoes
Refilling the freshly dug hole.

Today it is Tatha's turn.
Yesterday we mourned Malizani's end.
His bougainevelia wreaths are still fresh
As if watered by frequent tear drops.
Last week it was Ndatsalapati.
His flowers are yet less shrunken
Than his brothers' and sisters' before him.

Heads heavy with haunted thoughts
We retrace our steps, eyes locking
And grazing over the question:
When shall we meet again
In laughter, sorrow or in pain?
October 2000

1. What word used in the first two lines shows that they meet almost daily?
2. State common charicteristics around the grave.
3. *Mounds ˙separate us.* How do the mounds separate the grave-mates themselves, and the grave-mates and the dead?
4. List the three people in order of their deaths. How do their names emphasize the frequency of death?
5. Identify words or phrases that show the grave mates do not take frequent deaths lightly?
6. *...meet in laughter, sorrow or pain*? Does this anticipate three different meetings or one meeting? Explain.

DEATH   51

By Edward SA Moyo

A savage storm that sinks vessels
Roving shadow whistling at night
Sharp axe raised on innocent trees

You wriggle quietly into the home
And draw tears to caress the cheeks
For mourning is your victory song

1. What three things are likened to death in stanza 1? What common characteristic do they have?
2. Who or what is referred to as you in stanza 2?
3. *And draw tears to caress the cheeks/ For mourning is your victory song*
State the contradiction contained in each of the three last lines?
4. Pick out words in the poem that present death as if it were a kind of person? How does this affect your appreciation of the poem and its theme?

MOTHER _52
(In memory of my mother;
Dedicated to my daughter, Judith)
by George Chatha

In the night journey home,
Sleeping, waking, and sleeping
Yet I still hoped
To find you blinking
But I met grave-diggers tramping
Towards your final lodging.

I remember your frail face
Gazing but not recognizing me.
I thought you would open your mouth
And spit a good-bye blessing
Yet you slept on
Not welcoming me as before?

A year before, in the hospital, doctors
Assured us you would be fine.
Judith, Sylvia and sisters
Waited to see you walk home
Mother, gone down the insatiable belly
Where shall we find comfort?

1. Was the journey home a short one or a long one? Explain.
2. Was the person's hope fulfilled? Why not?
3. Did he have a chance to see the mother when she was very ill? Explain.
4. What assurance did they get? Do you think the doctors were deliberately misinforming them?
5. What is the insatiable belly a metaphor of? Why is it described as insatiable?

DON'T CRY 53

by King Norman Rudi

At the confluence of reality
Life shakes hands with death

When water runs to the lake
The earth dries up and cracks

Oh my children do not cry
The rain is coming again

1. What is a confluence?
2. Is the imagery of life shaking hands with death a happy or sad one?
3. How does the natural cycle of the land from green to brown to green symbolise life and death?
4. Is the confluence of reality a physical place where death meets life? Or is it a kind of mental balance that makes us understand that death is the other side of life? Explain.

SONG OF SORROW 54
Fanny, Alice and Solomon

by Zondiwe Mbano
(Pacali patali pasirya pa nyanja)

It's still far
It's still far across the river
  Lay the ropes
  for me to cross

It's still far
It's still far across the lake
  Many have gone
  but none has returned

It's still far
It's still far across time
  How can I sing
  and dance alone
  when my heart
  is sinking in many a tear

'Pacali patali pasirya pa nyanja,' is translated in stanza 2.
In the village, rope, extracted from bark, is used in making a bridge of poles, and in lowering a coffin into the grave.

1. Between the river and the lake which is more difficult to cross? Why is the author using these two images together?
2. Can a person go across time? How? Is it possible to come back?
3. Why is the persona alone?

4. ...*sinking in many a tear.* How does the heart sink in tears? What does this imagery refer to?

SILENT PALACE 55

By Sophie D Nambazo

Silence in the ghosts' palace
Many curtsey and enter it

When will the place be full?
When will you say enough?

We have cried day and night
We have prayed day and night

Lord when will you hear us
And remove this silent palace?

MY SWEET ROSE 56

by Kenneth Mtambalika

What wrong did you do them
To remove you while so tender

They came flocking as admirers
Hiding their motive in smiles

I am the loser, sweet Rose
But what have they gained

1. What happened to Rose? Did Rose do anything wrong to these people?
2. How did they come? What was their motive?
3. Why is the persona a loser? What has he/she lost? Have the other people gained anything through their action?

SILENCE RETURNED 57

by Zondiwe Mbano

i

Machine of men
With fossil power
Puff slow, slow

Up the green hills;
For though the road be bumpy
And the engine loud

There's silence up the hills;
There's dryness
And the memory of rivers

Memory of cool pools
Where ripples
Deface all serenity

ii

Machine of men
Puff slow, slow
On the road to Madisi

For the yellow sun
Stares at us, crouched
Around whiteness.

255

This stripling
Went to school
But silence returns;

Only yesterday
Fully agile, today
A cold presence
          iii
Power of fossils
That rolls the world,
Push us gently

Along sandy tracks
Through farms and forest
To that forlorn hill.

Our heads reel
As questions search
The wilderness of knowledge:

Is beauty tinder
For burning youth;
Is love autolytic?
          iv
Machine of men
Squandering the treasure of fossils
Puff slow into Sungeni:

A huddle of huts
Below a gold-crowned hill.
Now the reality of sorrow:

Hearts of stone melt
As men shake their heads
In silent agony of sorrow;

And the tears of children,
Of mothers and grandmothers
Erode all fortitude

(*A form 1 boy was beaten to death by a village boy while escorting a primary school girl-friend of his. There was an eclipse of the sun on the day we took his body to his home. Salima, February, 1978.*)

1. What is referred to as machine of men, and what is the fossil power which it uses? Does it use this power efficiently?
2. Identify words or phrases that convey a mood of troubled calm and silence?
3. Where are the people going, and why are they going there?
4. ...*the yellow sun stares at us*... Why is the sun described as yellow?
5. Identify words used in stanzas 6 to 8 that are metaphors of death?
6. The poem is made up of four sections, each with four stanzas. What is repeated at the beginning of each section. What effect does this repetition have on the whole poem?
7. Why did the entry into Sungeni village mark the reality of sorrow? What is it that eroded all fortitude?
8. *Autolytic* means self-destroying. For example the process of ripening in a fruit leads to rotting.
   How are the questions in section 111

stanza 4 relevant to the situation in
the poem? What answers would you
give to the questions?

HOW LONG LORD   58

by Patrick H M Kwalimba
Old parents bury their only child
Orphaned children wail in the night

Countries spend millions of dollars
Perhaps someone may find a drug

Lord how long shall You watch us
Being slowly wiped from the earth?

COMING FOR GOOD   59

by Tobias T Chidzalo
Is life mere smoke
That three years work
Simply blows away?

We endured long years
When you only came
Briefly during holidays

Did we wait for this
Your coming for good
Now cold and silent

1. How did three years work blow away?
   What was being pursued in the three

years?
2. *We endured long years.* Were these
   years different from the three? Why
   are they called long years?
3. They surely must have waited for
   his/her coming for good. What does
   this coming in stanza 3 refer to: the
   coming for good at the end of the
   studies, or the coming for good refer-
   ring to death? Explain.
4. Which two words in stanza 3 are
   metaphors for death?

IN MEMORIAM   60

by Anthony Nazombe
You disappeared at dusk
To be found at break of day
Dangling from a branch of a tree.

Athlete snapped in mid-leap
Arms poised and muscles taut
You would not reach the ground alive

Umbilical cord prematurely broken
Young shoot so soon hacked
Unfinished phrase...

Was that torn short,
Hangman's rope,
Your farewell?

257

THE NEW HOUSE   61
by Steve Chimombo

We came home to this:
Rats scuttling under the ceiling
Cockroaches pullulating in the pantry
Fruitflies hardened against the cold
Multiplying in the refrigerator

We came home to this:
Owls' mating calls on the roof.
Clawtops skidding on the corrugation,
Nightmares chasing each other
On our pillow jolting us awake

We came home to this:
Mambas slithering in the backyard.
Scorpions connecting across doorways
Guard dogs dying of rat poisoning.

Between the kitchen and the bedroom,
Between the births and the burials,
Between the spaces created by the silences.
We have to build in our own time
A new home we came to, you and I.

EARTH   62
Mercy F Longwe

Solid, deep and rich
The broad back that bears
All creatures big and small
Fixed, walking or flying

You receive the seeds
From the hands of the wise
And give them back in plenty
In the season of harvest

Those who cannot bend
Their backs in sun and rain
Will later crawl in the dark
To snatch the reward of others

1. Mention two things that are fixed, and three that walk on the earth?
2. How does the earth multiply seeds planted in it?
3. Why can't some people bend their backs: are they physically challenged or lazy?
4. Why according to the poem do some people resort to crime?

THE WAY   63
(Ndilongorani ntowa)
by Zondiwe Mbano

Show me the way
Show me the way

Show me for I am tired
And I want to go to sleep

I took a little porridge
And now it moves in my eyes

Wherever I have to go
Across the river or forest

The song I love to sing
Is show me the way

'Ndilongorani ntowa ' means: show me the way.

1. Why does the persona want to be shown the way?

2. What kind of porridge is this that moves in the eyes?
3. What things show that the persona could be drunk?

LITTLE FROG   64
(*Kacule ka mdambo*)
Zondiwe Mbano

Little frog of the river
Saw cattle grazing patiently
   Low dewlaps dangling up the valley

Little frog of the river
Wondered why he did not have
   Long horns pointing up the valley

Little frog of the river
Splashed some water, to rouse
   Long tails whisking up the valley

Little frog of the river
Started bellowing, to stir
   Calm humps undulating up the valley

Little frog of the river
Puffed up his belly, to frighten
   Blank eyes blinking up the valley

Little frog of the river
Burst like a puffed-up balloon
   Unheard by ears flapping up the valley

Kacule kamdambo   means: little frog of the river.

1. Four body parts of a cow are mentioned. Which are these?

2. Which line is repeated in every stanza. What effect does this have on the poem?
3. In each stanza there is a line that describes what frog did, and another line that says what the cattle did. Identify these lines
4. What three things did the frog do in order to make cattle notice it? Which line shows that the cattle did not notice the things frog did?
5. Would you feel sorry for little frog? Why? What do you think is the message from this poem?

MY MAN   65
(*Omunaanga nchiyani-
—song from Dowa*)
Zondiwe Mbano

What is this?
My man, what is this?
What is this now?
The shirt is tight

To the other wife
You went yesterday
And you return today
The stomach swollen

What is it?
My man, what is it?
What is it now?
The shirt is tight

1. One line says *what is this*, while another says *what is it ?*. What does each of these refer to? (the tight shirt, swollen stomach, the illness)
2. Why do you think the man's stomach is swollen?
3. Would you say the woman is a loving and caring wife, or a jealous and nagging wife?
4. Can you sing the song in vernacular?

REMAKE THE WORLD   66
(for Jimmy Cliff)
By Felix Mnthali
Need we wake up naked
in the sacred hour of a neutral dawn
to dance at the graves of our forefathers and
trample on the shrines
in which gods had spoken to men
and the men had vouchsafed
their future, their past and their present?

Is this earth, then,
infinite wisdom
shunting men and materials
to village sidings
where grasses overrun the rails
and snakes sneeze in the noonday heat,
leopards doze beneath the brambles
and owls chant eerie dirges
over corpses yet to be born
while hyenas heap their dung
on graves yet to be dug?

For us too the sun will rise
trailed by the iambic pentameter
of children marching to school
of hens cackling beneath the nkhokwe
and marbles crackling on the bawo.

We shall sing lyrics
not to the semblance of a dream
that might have been
but to the labours of man
who dresses mountain-slopes
with man-made forests and gardens for maize
who tattoos valleys and plains
with acres and hectares of tilled land
and triumphs over leopards and hyenas
lurking in the dark.

DAY OF NEW BABY   67
by Constantine E. Masala
A day of song and dance
Seeing a new shoot on the tree

A day of celebration
As new baby enters the home

A day of bad tempers
When others vie for mother's love

A day of new anxieties
As thin budgets stretch further

SIGNS 68

Steve Sharra

Marauding hyaenas fight at night
Sending people's hearts cold with fear;
They say it's a bad sign

A lonely owl hoots in the dark
And a toddler cries in sleep;
They say it brings bad luck

A sparkling fire lights the hearth
And a drunkard steps on his toes,
Following a path to the graves

Cats do not mate in daylight
While children point and watch
Or death visits the compound

1. Examine each stanza. What do the first two lines state? What does the last line add?
2. ... *a bad sign*. Why are the people afraid? What do they think will happen?
3. *They say*...Who are they? Do you believe what they say? Explain why?
4. Why do owls hoot? Do they have needs different from those of other birds?
5. What might happen to the man who follows the path to the graveyard? Are there people who sometimes hide at the graveyards. What motives do they have?
6. Cats are mammals. How do they reproduce? Have you ever seen cats mating? When do they do this?

BEADING 69

(From Part Four of Breaking the Beadstrings)
by Steve Chimombo

All beads are circles with holes
for the strings to pass through them.
Big or small, round, square or oval,
all the beads are circles encircling me.
I am a bead on a string circling me.

All the women are circles of beads,
necklaces linking one to the other,
bracelets holding each other's hands,
anklets with feet joined at the base...

We are the new colours of the rainbow
of our own beading, each to each.
This is the new healing circle.
Hold my hand as I hold yours:
together we form a magic circle.

HOME 70

by Chawanangwa BC Banda

I am on my way to the land
Of rivers of love and mercy

Land where peace is bread
And justice a drink for all

Where the wind sings poetry
And sunshine heals all pain

VILLAGE LIFE 71

by Esme Kusauka

Waking up before sunrise
Cutting, digging, pounding
Staggering under weights

Smells from kraals and pens
Cackling, bleating, lowing
Calls for food and freedom

The evening is for feasting
Singing, dancing, story-telling
Then resting for the next day

1. Why do people wake up before sunrise?
2. The middle line in each stanza has
   verbs in the progressive tense [-ing].
   What does this signify?
3. From the words in the second line of
   the second stanza, which animals are
   kept in the village?
4. What freedom do the animals cry for?
5. What activities bring relaxation and
   enjoyment after a hard day's work?
6. How would you compare life in the
   village to that in the town?

CHIKANDA BEACH 72

Austin Chiwindo Chirwa

As far as your eyes can see,
On the left is Thowolo Port
On the right Bandawe Port
And in between, Chikanda

In the hazy south-eastern horizon
Is Likoma and Chizumulu Islands,
And behind you, bordering a long
Lovely sandy beach, is Chintheche.

Canoes quietly sail on the blue
Sheet swaying up and down
As fishermen come from Chikanda
Singing about their large catch

OUR JOURNEY 73

By Charity Ndhlovu-Chinkono

It seemed so easy at first
Years seemed like weeks
We left spouses lamenting

On the hot valley of Domasi
Days, weeks, months, years
We spent drawing water

Phones rang and letters came
Intimating illnesses and deaths
The long road still wound on

Now that we walk the last mile
How do we thank the dear ones
Who endured the pain and worry?

SUNSET OVER MPARAYI 74
by Zondiwe Mbano

Now shadows elongate
Reaching towards the lake
That gives birth to the sun

Cattle slowly shuffle
And dust rises high
Like an oblation for rain

Boys riding on cattle
Chant the glory of their bulls
And whistle nostalgic tunes

Girls balancing pots
Yodel wistful songs that
Fan their secret fire

Men shouldering their kill
Cross fields to the idyllic welcome
By women and children

Hungry fires on verandas
Lick pots that flavour
The home and absorb fatigue

The sun crowns Mparayi
And drapes ribbons of gold
Over the slopes to Lukonkobe

Behind Mparayi a velvet
Cloud stretches upwards
To welcome home the sun

And now darkness stalks
Children and covers shadows
Skulking around the fires

FIERY BALL 75
by Albert Kalimbakatha

See that fiery ball
About to fall
Down that hill
To a world so still

The glimering west
In its best
Gold shade
Will slowly fade

Darkness returns
To take turns
With the light
And reign with might

1. Work out the rhyming scheme in this poem. What effect does it have on the poem?
2. Make a summary of what the persona is trying to say.

FORMULA FOR FUNERALS 76
by Steve Chimombo

The formula required is not mysterious:
a few famines, droughts and pestilences;
one or two *napolos* and HIV/AIDS, also
to control pullulation, create depopulation
and make room for more burial grounds.

The anguish of the bereaved gashes
the sunken flesh of cheeks like gullies
left on the land in the Great Rift Valley,
as tears gush out of eyelashes and sockets
enough really to refill the lake of storms,
razing to skin any moles and pimples
flash-flooding poles and flattening the hairs
or uprooting them in the wake of their passage.

The lamentation of the mourners furrows
the foreheads like the combined contours
of the Shire Highlands and the Kirk Range
as sorrow terraces the drained temples high
enough to cause the envy of the *mwera*
yet sufficiently deep to be hiding places of
Mulanje, Zomba, Viphya and Nyika mounts
when the heart's heaviness rises to the head.

Indeed, only a few ingredients are required:
the *mfecane*, slave trade or the *mchape*
and one or two world wars in between
to mobilize spears, poisons and explosives.
The results make more room for grave mounds.

1. By what means does death come, according to stanza 1 ?
2. Apart from reducing the fertility rate and bringing about depopulation, how can death make
    room   for more burial ground?
3. Stanza 2 and 3 describe the face of a grieved person, using geographical terms. Which features
   of the face are described here? What emotion do all the features convey?
4. Why does the poem show the face of the mourner extending to the whole of Malawi?
5. According to stanza 5, what were the main causes of death in the past? How does this compare with present deaths.
6. By seemingly joking about death, the writer makes statements about the extent and devastating effect of death. What is the overall message about death in the poem?

CHAMELEON 77

by K L Lapukeni

Basically, he started lean
and weak. Moths facelifted
him. Up one branch,
his first, he swallowed them up
segment by segment, then thoraces,
heads and antennae.
Stronger,

he heaved himself along
a sturdier branch,
foxing into birds' nests. He
swallowed fledglings: beaks
feathers and all.
Heavier,

he took a branchlet, along
which his eyes discovered more insects,
centipedes and hoppers/
It snapped, and he fell to the ground,
his belly open as a book,
releasing the young, mid-aged
and Machipisa alive.

We gaze at him now, breathing
relief, seeing no reason
why we are interested in him.

But we live.
Old, he is dying

NOTE: Machipisa Mnthali was Malawi's longest serving prisoner. He was in Kamuzu's jail for 27 years.

THE ROAD TO EMMAUS 78

(Luke 24: 13 -35)

by Zondiwe Mbano

On this winding road
A shadow is close by me

On this lonesome road
A shadow trails after me

Extending from my heels
East to the sun's cradle

And now the sun is setting
Slowly into lurid clouds

Spread behind the ridge
That sends out darkness

A shadow is close by me
On this wandering road

Yet darkness attracts me
As flames attract a moth

Oh my Lord, draw nigh
On this road to Emmaus

ANOTHER FOOLS' DAY TOUCHES DOWN: SHUSH   79

(for Mercy, Judith, Lunda, & Lika)
by Jack Mapanje

Another Fools' Day touches down, another homecoming.
Shush. Bunting! some anniversary: they'll be preoccupied.
Only a wife, children and a friend, probably waiting.

A Ph.D., three books, a baby-boy, three and half years-
Some feat to put us...Shush. Such frivolities no longer
Touch people here. 'So you decide to come back, eh?

Rhetorical questions dredge up spastic images. Shush
In the dusty, brown-grey landscape, the heat unrolls.
Some wizard has locked up his rainbows and thunder again.

Why do the gods hold up the rains?
Don't we praise them enough?
Shush. There are no towers here, no domes or gothic windows.
Only your children, friends nestling up for a warm story

*April 1st. used to be celebrated as Fools' Day before it was abolished during the Kamuzu's era.
Jack Mapanje was detained for years during the MCP government.*

1. 'Shush' means silence. Why is shush repeated many times? What atmosphere does this give to the poem?
2. Why are only the wife, children and a friend waiting for the persona as he comes from overseas? What has made the other people preoccupied?
3. What 3 things have happened in the years he was overseas? Why do the people at home not seem to appreciate these important achievements?
4. What warning to the persona is contained in the questions: *So you decide to come back, eh?*
5. What traditional explanation is given when rain delays?
6. *Why do the gods hold up the rains*? Is this natural rain or rain as metaphor of freedom?
7. Who is the wizard holding up the rain now? Why does he hold up the rain?
8. This poem was written during Kamuzu's era. Would you say the rain has come now? Explain.

266

WHO IS RESPONSIBLE?   80

by Steve Chimombo
('Kamuzu's Grave in Ruins'
The Nation, 8th November, 2000, p.3

A cenotaph of all cenotaphs
was built in the centre of Heroes Acre
by solemn presidential decree.
In this cenotaph was interred
the life president of all dictatorships.
Around this cenotaph heavy security
paraded and brooded day and night.
But, mark this, that was once upon a time.

The newsman nosed about responsibility:
Who tends to cenotaphs now in Heroes' Acre?
Why the desertion of the camping guards?
Who gave instructions for turning cenotaphs
into ruins so soon after the burial ceremony?

"It's not for us," said the security spokesman
"to explain the withdrawal of the guards men.
It's in the hands of other powers that be:
the Ministry of Home Affairs, for example;
talk to them, they can answer that."

"It's not for me," negated the former minister
for Home Affairs and Internal Securitiy:
"I've changed portfolios since then.
"I'm now in a different ministry altogether.
talk to the chairman of the Heroes Acre."

"I'm not the right person," chided the chair.
"I'm out of the Committee for Heroes' Acre.
"I'm no longer in government, even,
"I'm in the legislature, which is different.
Talk to someone who is able to comment."

The newsman wondered who to turn to next:
The city assembly? The national parks?
Someone surely issued instructions somewhere
for the lights around the cenotaph are off,
the security men's tent empty and draughty.

Meantime the cenotaph still sinks lower
lamenting over the weight of abandonment;
gathers mould and insomnia of desertion,
weeds and shrubs tickling it over the ramparts
as nature reclaims the corner into a forest.

Meanwhile more promises and decrees
wrapped in oily rhetoric are dispensed:
a project here and an appeasement there;
a scam here and a cabinet reshuffle there.
Everywhere fiascoes by someone responsible
as everyone scrambles for power or position,
being busy to be the next worthy candidate
fit to be in a cenotaph in Heroes's acre
November 2000

1. What personality did the man whose remains are interred in the cenatoph have?
2. How was the cenatoph treated at first?
3. What three things about the cenatoph does the newsman want to investigate?
4. Where did he/she start his/her investigation, and where did he/she end?
5. What common response did he/she get at each stage of the investigation? Why did the people respond this way?
6. Would you say the system described in the poem practises openness and accountability or suppression?
7. What other problems in the system are highlighted in the last stanza?
8. ...*busy to be the next...candidate fit to be in a cenatoph...* Do the people scrambling for power think in this way? What does this irony reveal about the people's preoccupations in life?

MLAULI'S MUSINGS   81
by Steve Chimombo

Mlauli said he had foreseen
all these happenings before;
and indeed his predictions
came to be , in our life time

-1-

The fields will no longer be ravaged
by locusts because they're radioactive.
Instead the army worm will invade
and eat away the hearts of the stalks.
Fake fertilizers will be fed to the soil
making fools wonder why there's famine.

Rivers and lakes will be exhausted
or emptied because of over-fishing.
Jungles will be silent because of poaching;
forests will be bare because of burning.
The air will become foul for breath,
the water poisonous because of pollution.

Commodities will not be homegrown
but imported at great expense
so that local produce soars in prices,
thus enriching the man across the border
as we do our shopping by mail order
or fly to our neighbours to buy our stuff.

-2-

The youth will no longer be initiated
by the riverside or in the bush shacks
but from sitting room watching videos
soon to be banned for explicit pornography
when the watchers know really
what goes on in bedrooms or resthouses.

Public exams will no longer be private
but secretly photocopied and then sold
in the streets, bars and even school rooms
by teachers arbitrarily transferred or not paid.
And still the man will convene committees
to find out what's wrong, why low standards.

Ministers, MPs and even entire cabinets
will in broad daylight siphon off funds
meant for the common good or the masses
into their own private accounts or companies
but the man will pretend not to see all this
and will ask for more evidence and proof.

-3-

We will no more be afflicted with
common infections like syphilis but
Acquired Immunity Deficiency Syndromes.
This we will pass onto our offspring
out of love for each others' partners
until we learn to stop illicit sex.

Limbs will not sprain walking in gardens
nor bones break falling in bathrooms
but be mangled by maniacal minibuses
snarling round corners meeting us head-on
with our saloons, cycles and scooters
or in derailment, crashes or flounderings

As much as we die from engineered war
or genetic manipulations gone wrong
we will still multiply at a rapid pace:
huts will be emptied because of poverty
concrete houses be filled by the unemployed
and pavements made impassable by vendors.

Mlauli had seen all these events before
and many more terrifying ones to come.
These, indeed, will also come to pass soon.
It had been decreed and will not be diverted.

ZOMBA MOUNTAIN   82
by Steve Chimombo

Great grandfather, founder of the clan,
baskets of spirits under each arm
claimed your slopes for our village.
We spread between the green banks
of two rivers: Naisi and Naming'asi,
planted and reaped in the fields,
played and prayed in the forests.
hurted and hunted, lived and loved
under the giant gaze of your granite face.

I, too, laden with a packetful of poems
under each arm, staked my claim
on your plateau, peaks, pools and all,
to wrest the wisdom of the ancients
from the myth-infested forests and rivers.

I read your visage like verse:
savoured your similes,
mined your metaphors
wrapped in the roaring rivers
or buried in the bowels of boulders;
deciphered symbols of import
in crags, crannies or crevices;
scanned cliffs clad in clouds
or rain-laden for fresh inspiration.

Now, great grandfather resurrected
would not recognize your visage.
They blasted your boulders down,
smashing myths to smithereens.
They graded your undergrowth,
mashing watermaids underwheels.
They pulverized the wood spirits,
flattening out their sighs and songs.

Napolo no longer bursts the banks
of Naming'asi, Satemwa or Naisi;
no myths meander down Mulungusi;
no lore slithers down the Likangala
past pawsteps of lion, leopard or lizard.
They all vanished into the valley below.

Now the crows fight ants over leftovers
of crumbs of cake from the cottages
or canned beef, beans or bottled water
from the backpackers on the camping site.
Concrete, steel pipes, plastic and bricks
sprout in banks, boulders and pathways.

Still, the cliffs cleave the skies,
split the sunset into shafts
of red, orange, purple and blue
doing a dying dance on your brows
sending the slopes to early sleep,
blanketing the town and villages below
in a premature foliage of darkness.
This you will never surrender to man.
This my great grandfather would recognize.
October 2000

Zomba Mountain is seen as a goddess, a great mother, like Makewana, who supplies all the needs of the people and spirits.

1. What did great grandfather get from Zomba Mountain? How did this benefit his sons and daughters, grandsons and granddaughters, and great-grandsons and great-granddaughters? Read a line from stanza 1 that shows that Zomba Mountain saw all these developments.
2. *Great grandfather ... claimed... I ... staked... to wrest.* Looking at the verbs used, how did these people get the items from Zomba? Why did they do it in this manner?
3. *I read your visage like verse:* What intellectual items does the persona get by contemplating the different facets of Zomba Mountain?
4. What desecration done to the face of Zomba Mountain do stanzas 4 to 6 describe?

5. *They blasted... smashing... They graded... mashing... They pulverized...flattening...* How does this manner of gathering resources differ from that of the persona (I) in stanza 3 ? What are the consequences of this?
6. Describe how a crow would fight with ants. What action by humans leads to this unnatural fight? How is this part of the desecration wrought on Zomba Mountain?
7. What role has Zomba Mountain, as mother and goddess, maintained in her service to the people. What evidence is there that the community in Zomba has been transformed so much that they resent some aspects of her role?
8. How would you use this poem to teach others about proper management of the environment?

SONG OF A CAR 83
by Dorah Mwase
I came to you sleek and new
Beyond the reach of many
Yet many were my adorers

Daily polished and perfumed
And adorned with embroidery
You gave me a caressing touch

Now that potholes and humps
Have rattled and warped my back
You turn me into a chicken-house

1.To whom does the *you* in the poem refer?
2. Describe aspects of beauty that attracted many adorers?
3. List four things marked by verbs in stanza 2 which demonstrated love and caring?
4. ... *rattled and warped my back.* In your own words describe what has happened to the persona's back? Who is to blame for this?
5. Would you say it is right to turn a car into a chicken-house like this?
6. Would you say '*Song of a car* ' is an allegory describing a human problem? If so what is the human problem being described?
7. What is the overall message of the poem?

STRENGTH FROM UNITY   84
by Alfred T. Y. Nkhoma

Rome was not built in a day
Nor one soul volunteered to build alone
How brave, wise, rich dedicated he was
But by forming unbreakable mass of unity
Of honorary noblemen, kinsmens, slaves and aliens
The magnificicent city of Rome stood.

Even a lichen plant hanging on a Mbawa tree
Deeply rooted and strongly attached to it
May be blown away by light chiperoni winds.
But a mass of lichens on a paw paw stem
Can surely resist the great hurricane storm
As simple as Dutch dykes in halting floods.

The united Chinese built the great wall
Division collapsed the once feared USSR
United we stand erect as a City of Rome
And divided we will fall as Berlin wall
Should we fail because of disunity
Surely birds of the forest will laugh at us.

WHEN THE METRIC CAME 85
To Brother Mhango C.C.
By Masuzgo Mhango

Dear Brother,
I wish we could take a look
And not only a look
But also a walk in
The glory of the junior past when
As it were
We could go to school
Walking long distances
Our fried maize in bottles.
We could learn and talk about
       the pint and the gallon ;
       the inch, the foot, the yard and the mile ;
       the libs (1b) and the pound;
       the dozen, the score and the gross ;
       not forgetting
       the fahrenheit ;
       the pence, the shilling, and the pound;
       and the MPHALA, the kingdoms and
       Colonialism;
then we could sing a song and go home.

But with the unfolding of the days
The metric came
Teachers did not know what to teach
And we (pupils) fell assunder
No say of our fathers, mothers, and grandees ;
Everybody was confused ; for
With it came a variety of things
The industrial world improved,
Class work hardened,
Incurable diseases began eating our flesh,
Corruption grew tap roots,
Rulers supped on bribes ;
And now deep is our sail in it
It's magnitude has increased
It's oppression wind is strong it's wave high
Quarter Masters have missed the course
Captains can not decide on their own
No one knows what to do
How do we survive ?

STILL ON THE MARCH   86
by Davie Nsewa

Still on the March
We are long this road

All these years marching
Not even catching a smell of our destination.
With quarrels, bickering
illnesses, grievances, mournings
We still keep on marching.
Forced by time we march, march
Never turning back

Years so innumerable
We have been marching
and still we are ;
Cursing, scorning, scoffing,
Despising, praising, weeping
All the way long.

Tired of we though desperate we aren't
Hopeful still that time to our destiny will take us
Though by fatigue we are conquered
With successes and failures
        Deaths and births, disapointments
                Appointments, engagements
                        Ever giving us a company ;
With unceremonious departures
        Promises unfulfilled, betrayals, debts
        We still march on
Hopeful however our destination we still reach.

by Macdonald *"Beverly"* Bamusi

Once again the big whilrlwind
Swirls round and round
Dangerously, ferociously turns
Shaking the black soot
Hanging on the rafter of one black heart
Persistently, doubling and redoubling
Forcefully, shaking the soot ....

There came another big whirlwind
Several moments ago
Rigorously swept through
Cleansed the black heart
Now of white sooty locks
That hang on the same rafters.

The two big whirlwinds
Coming one after another
From places afar
cleansing, the restless black heart
Of white sooty locks , and
Of carbon black locks
That hung on the rafters
Above the innocent but intimidated heart

ON RECONCILIATION   88
(THE HAWK, FROM THE CHICKENS)

by Alfred Tyson Nkhoma

You have been commissioners of death
More than three decades stopping our breath
But now let us all flock together
As birds of the very same feather

The manner of this diabolical fight
Would simply make the matter light
Once you cease to undermine our designs
With your special cheating signs

If you want the everlasting peace
We enjoy in this kingdom to increase
So that we all live in total happiness
Then you must truly stop your madness

By Wokomaatani B Malunga

Teach me teacher
The language of a responsible human
The metaphor of a constructive citizen
Give me teacher
The desire to build
And not the malice to destroy
Guide me teacher
To the benefits
Of sober reasoning
And not to the volcano of confrontation
Feed me teacher
With the sense of a balanced thinker
And never the recklessness
Of a drug addict
Develop in me teacher
The yearning for fairness
And not the quest
For sheer personal aggrandisement
Fashion in me teacher
The willingness to accommodate the views of others
And not the stubbornness
To deliberately ignore what is obvious
Straighten me teacher
So that I may ignore rumour
With spicy humour
And crave for correct information
The foundation of a good decision
Plant in me teacher
The seed of informed moderation
To lead me to the cultivation
Of a truly scholarly spirit.

STILL WE LIVE   90
By Immanuel Bofomo

Still we live, still we live, better than die ;
Though among countless miseries
Which wash our bodies.

The frequent 'which side are you'?
Endless harrassment ; torture, discrimination,
Just filled eyes and hungry bellies ;
Still we live
Though amidst countless miseries.

The 'I wish them dead' ; and wild threats
From unschooled mentors,
Perpetual slaps and wanton warnings
Still we live
Despite the innumerable shut ups ;

These rugs; these rents; and protruding bones;
Nitty hair; scary feet and swollen hands
These feeble knees and withering lips,
Still we live,
Despite the gaged mouths.

Thrown and neglected on the midden,
All this rubbish entering our ears,
Coerced to bend kneees on broken glass
Still we live
Though amidst countless miseries.

This blasphemy put into our holy mouths,
To call a pot the potter;
To clap at the air which is here now,
But no where so soon;
Still we live
Despite our pinioned wrists at times.
But how long shall we still live?
It pains me.

(From *Ring Freedom Bells, 1993*)

Democracy 91
By Khwesi Msusa

Democracy
I recall your inception in my country
which even after struggles accepted you as
you roared your way in
with loud shouts of words new to our ears
driving down hope into our hearts

they advocated you as a remedy
against the evils of that time
Some said you marked the end
of days of assault, nights of intimidation
mornings of oppression, afternoons of fear
and dusk of death
All these I despised and scorned

Others praise you for sparing
women clad in"National Wear"
singing with an air of authority
while husbands never complained
about wives who left sick infants at home

Boys welcomed you with smiles
for bringing in mini-skirts
so they could see beyond their mothers' knees
Girls cheered your coming
so they could wear trousers, smoke cigarettes, drink beer
just like their fathers
Mothers clapped hands in joy at your birth
so they could challenge their husbands in guise of gender
Fathers with brave faces took you in
hoping to reestablish order in politically shaken families

When I recall those days of Referendum fever
how the regime then opposed your coming
like old soldiers how they stuck to their old guns
and then the choice we made
devoid of knowledge
but full of emotion, high expectations, pleasant dreams
and great hopes
who wouldn't fall into your trap?

Suddenly reality has caught up with us
full naked reality like a shadow over our weak bodies
that thieves come at with guns
while guards guard with batons
that boys smoke herb in public
while the police pretend to be blind

A day has now come
when brother gives up brother
mothers cast their babies in latrines
while fathers rape their own daughters
Everything has now changed
hope into despair
dreams into illusions
expectations into frustration
and emotion into bitterness

You've turned Malawi into an archaic book
that exhales the dust of worries
as young men become prematurely old
due to hard work and low pay

Old men and women alike
in their monotonous struggle for survival
are full of sorrowful reflections on life
and lament for the Malawi of the past

Who can exercise your freedoms
on an empty stomach?
Who can enjoy your rights
while corruption and insecurity reign?
You promised riches but all I see are rags

You've blossomed where you were planted
I wish I could uproot you
Democracy
I hate you!
(Dedicated to my late brother and sister who never lived to see the rising sun of democracy).

92   *MONKEY BAY*
By Edson Mpina

I'll return to this harbour to
live my life; I have lived all my
life for others in the past.
I'll build myself a fortress over
the vast rock on which the ships Ilala, Ufulu
and Mtendere berth.
As I sleep in my fortress, monkeys from
Nkunguni Mountain will guard me.
Mphipe will fry my sweet chambo whose
calcium-filled bones will wave me passage
with a new method, letting the music
of water-refined air and air-refined water
refine the marrow coursing my senile bones.
Living here, I'll possess all my days.
Kakowa will lead me by hand to colonies
of hippos, sightseeing;
everyday I will waltz to Chilinda to sip lather
form coconut covers.
I'll have baths in the water falls of the sun here,
below an unbroken sheet of sky, a
sky without gaps. I'm longing for my life
next time
when I'll recline on my past blurred with jail.
and verse. My plans are packed.

93   African Child
by David Rubadiri

Why African child
Stand you dazed
Your eyes gazing
Far far into
The distance haze
And ask
Questions too silent
For answers -

African child
Your wings will grow
Then
You must fly.

1. Pick out two lines from stanza 1 which show that the child does not see clearly. In each line, which word in particular shows this?
2. Will the child get answers to his/her questions? Explain.
3. Why might some questions be considered *too silent/ For answers* ?
4. Can a child fly? What do you think flying symbolizes in this poem?
5. *Then/ You must fly.* Will flying be a natural result of growing wings or not? Explain.
6. Looking at developments in Malawi, would you say that you, as African children,, have grown the wings and are now flying? If so, when did this happen? If not, why has this not happened?
7. What would you say is the message of this poem?

94 Thoughts After Work
by David Rubadiri

Clear laughter of African children
Rings loud in the evening:
Here around this musty village
Evening falls like a mantle,
Gracing in all a shroud of peace.
Heavily from my office
I walk
To my village,
My brick government compound,
To my new exile.
In this other compound
I would no longer intrude.
I perch over a chasm,
Ride a storm I cannot hold,
And so must pass on quietly -
The laughter of children rings loud
Bringing back to me
Simple joys I once knew.

1. How many villages are described in the poem? Which one has more details given?
2. To which village does the persona go? Read the line which shows that he/she is
   forced   into this village.
3. Which words bring out images of happiness and dignity to the African village?
   Read two lines which show that the persona lived in such a village before.
4. Check the meaning of the word *musty*. What does it reveal about the physical
   condition of this village?
5. Do you think the peace in the African village will last long? Explain.
6. Check the meaning of *chasm*. From the images you get from the words *chasm*
   and   *storm*, what would you say is the situation the persona is in? Explain.
7. Between the two villages, where would you personally like to live? Why?

95   Yet Another Song

by David Rubadiri

Yet another song
I have to sing:
In the early wake
Of a colonial dusk
I sang the song of fire.

The church doors opened
To the clang
Of new anthems
And colourful banners.

Like the Beatles,
The evangelical hymns
Of conversion
Rocked the world and me.

I knelt before the new totems
I helped to raise,
Watered them
With tears of ecstasy.

They grew
Taller than life
Grimacing and breathing fire.

Today
I sing yet another song
A song of exile.

1. How many songs are described in the poem? What differences do you see between these songs?
2. *To the clang Of new anthems.* Do you think the new anthems were sang beautifully or not? Explain.
3. How did the persona help to raise new totems?
4. Give examples of *totems that grew/ Taller than life/ Grimacing and breathing fire.* during the previous one-party government. Are there such totems now?
5. The Beatles were a famous band from Britain. What two meanings do you think the word *rocked* has in the line: *Rocked the world and me* ?
6. Do you think this, *Yet another song/ I have to sing:* is a happy song or a sad one? Explain.

96   An African Thunderstorm
by David Rubadiri

From the west
Clouds come hurrying with the wind
Turning
Sharply
Here and there
Like a plague of locusts
Whirling
Tossing up things on its tail
Like a madman chasing nothing.
Pregnant clouds
Ride stately on its back
Gathering to perch on hills
Like dark sinister wings;
The Wind whistles by
And trees bend to let it pass.

In the village
Screams of delighted children
Toss and turn
In the din of the whirling wind.
Women -
Babies clinging on their backs -
Dart about
In and out
Madly
The Wind whirls by
Whilst trees bend to let it pass.
Clothes wave like tattered flags
Flying off
To expose dangling breasts
As jagged blinding flashes
Rumble, tremble, and crack
Amidst the smell of fired smoke
And the pelting march of the storm.

PART 6: EXTRA QUESTIONS

LOVE 1

1. In this poem love can mean two things. What technique has the author used to present this ambiguity?

2. In the first stanza the pronoun *you* has been used three times. How does this affect the meaning of the stanza and the poem as a whole?

3. Explain the use of imagery in this poem.

DEAR LORD 2

4. What would you say is the tone of this poem?

5. Compare this poem with 'Love' by Mambo.

MY LOVE 3

6. What message is the persona sending to his/her loved one?

7. The poem is full of hope. Find out the exact words and phrases which express this hope.

LOVE 4

8. Describe the overall message of the poem. In your opinion does the arrangement of the stanzas enhance the message? If you were the author of the poem would you arrange the stanzas in this order or you would change them?

THE LAST ACT 5

9. The image presented in stanza one is that of actors in a play. What comment does this stanza make on the experience refered to in this stanza? In each of the three stanzas, find out expression which amplify or justify the tittle of the poem.

BRING SUNSHINE 6

10. What would you say is the mood of this poem? Why? Compare the message in this poem with that in stanza 3 of 'The Last Act' by Nazombe

MY BEAUTY 7

11. The persona seems to believe that true beauty should appeal to the whole being. How does he/she express this belief. How does this tarry with the conclusion in the last stanza?

12. Read stanza two carefully and see how the construction of its second line affect the meaning of the stanza itself.

13. Compare this poem with poem 3. Which one is a richer poem in terms of human relationships?

14. In poem 6 and poem 7 the poets have used their visual senses to express feelings associated with love. How similar and different are these experiences.

EXORCISM 8

15. What problem is described in this poem? Compare the message in this poem with that in 'Bring Sunshine' by Luhanga

SONG OF NYAVITIMA 9

16. The poem has a pessimistic tone about the genuineness of love. How does this match with the title and the

last stanza.

17. Who are the children referred to in the last stanza? Among the 9 poems of love, which ones do you like most? Why? Write a poem of love.

MARRIAGE 10

18. In your opininon, does this poem truly represent marriage? Explain.

PILLAR OF LOVE 11

19. Describe the imagery used in this poem.
20. How are the "beloved " being talked about in stanza 3 ?

DEAR MOTHER 12

21. The poem starts and ends with *dear mother*. What does this tell about the tone of the poem ?
22. Describe the message of the poem ?
23. Discuss the theme of growing up in this poem ?

MAMA 13

24. Compare the theme of motherly love in this poem and "Dear mother" by Makhala-Nyamatcherenga.
25. Discuss the theme of growing up in this poem.
26. How is symbolism used in this poem?
27. How does the persona count time ? How does this affect the meaning of the poem as a whole?
28. How does the title of the poem relate with the experience in the poem? Do you think this is a suitable title? Explain.
29. This short poem summarizes a very long process of birth and growing up. Discuss the proceses in the poem.

WOMAN 14

30. If carefully studied 'Mama' by Khumuwa and 'Woman' by Mwawa complement each other. Explain how this is so?.

WHY THE OLD WOMAN LIMPS 15

31. Study the last line of each of the three stanzas carefully and see the conclusion which each makes. What does this tell you about the mood of the poem as a whole.
32. Compare this poem with "Mama" by Khumuwa and "woman" by Mwawa in terms of theme.

AUNT MAO 17

33. What is the tone of this poem? What does this tell you about the relationships between the persona and the audience ?

TRAIN TO BALAKA 18

34 In terms of themes, compare this poem with "Pillar of love "by Banda "Mama" by Khumuwa and "Woman" by Mwawa.

THE SPEAR 20

35 Though the authors are different and the title seem not to be related in any way, "The spear " by Matewere and "Leaders of Tomorrow " by Pungulani can be argued to be complementing. Discuss.

LORD HEAR OUR CRY 21

36. Compare the tones in the poems "Leaders of tomorrow" by Pungulani," the spear" by Matewere and "Lord Hear Our Cry " by Matope. How does this affect the theme of

responsibility discussed in these three poems.

37. Examine the structure of this poem.

SONG OF TEARS 22

38. Examine the setting of the poem. Compare and contrast this poem with "Song of Nyavitima " by Mbano. What messages of HIV/AIDS can you get from this poem, 'The Spear' and 'Lord, Hear Our Prayers'?

Songani Look Out 23

39. Discuss the description of nature in this poem.

CHASING PAGES 24

40. What experiences of education is described in this poem? Does the persona like school? Explain.

DOMASI COLLEGE 25

41 Assume you are the principal of Domasi College. Write a short poem in reply to this one.

42. This poem is a representation of the voice of a student. Study it closely and say whether you would identify with this voice or not.

THE SERPENT 27

43. Compare the theme of deception in this poem and "Honey Bird " by Mbano.

My uncle E.P. Mtungambera Harawa 28

44. Study the language of this poem and compare its language with "Songani Lookout" by the same author.

NYAMWEZI 29

45. The poet describes natural beauty. How does he approach it ?

LAKE KAZUNI 30

46. Compare the description of natural scenery in this poem and the "Nyamwezi " by Thawe. How do the experiences differ in the two poems?

SHIRE RIVER 33

47. How does this poem compare with 'The Lingazi' in terms of the experience. In your answer consider the characteristics of the two rivers and the opinions of the two authors respectively about them.

THE BEAUTY OF DAWN 35

48. This poem could be a commentary of the political situation in Malawi. Discuss the theme of freedom in this poem.

NYUMBANI'S TALE 37

49. Examine the style and structure of the poem. How was lizard deceived?

LEADERS 38

50. Think about a vernacular proverb that can summarize the theme of this poem and translate it into English.

SONGS FROM THE CLOUDS 39

51 The poem is a commentary on Malawian social and political history. What does it say ?

DRIFTING SCUM 41

52. Summarize the major themes discussed in this poem. Give examples from what is happening in Malawi at the present.

MODERN ADVERTISING 42

53. Would you agree that this poem is satirical. Explain

A PRAYER 45

54. Identify other poems in this antholo-

gy that are prayers.

VIPYA 48

55. Discuss the theme of death in this poem

DEATH 49

56. Which poem does this one remind you about in this anthology? Compare them.

MOTHER 52

57. Discuss the theme of separation in this poem .

SILENT PALACE 55

58. The persona asks two questions in a row in the second stanza but he/she does not wait for an anwer ? Why does he/she do this? What effect does this have on the mood of the poem ?

59. Read the last stanza carefully? What message does it carry?

60. Compare this poem with "Coming for Good" by Chidzalo in terms of language, theme, and structure ?

IN MEMORIAM 60

61. This is another poem about death? Examine the theme of suicide in this poem.

62. Look at different poems on death. Compare their treatment of the theme of death.

THE NEW HOUSE 61

63. What effect does the repetition of 'we came' have?.

64. What technique has the author used to impress upon the reader that the problem was intense?

65. Identify aspects of irony used in the poem?

EARTH 62

66. Study stanza 3 of this poem and relate it to the title. In your opinion how does this stanza fit into the structure of the poem?

THE WAY 63

67 Who does the persona address? What *way* do you think the man needs to be shown in his state?

DAY OF NEW BABY 67

68. Child birth brings mixed feelings. What does this poem say?

SIGNS 68

69. Identify other poems that describe people's beliefs.

VILLAGE LIFE 71

70. What is the tone of this poem? Explain.
Compare this poem with Rubadiri's 'Thoughts After Work'.

Formula for funerals 76

71. Comment on the manner in which the poem is presented. What feelings does this raise? Explain.

Another fools' Day touches 79

72. Compare the theme of this poem with that of 'Chameleon' by Lapukeni.

WHO IS RESPONSIBLE ? 80

73. Comment on the style of presentations in this poem. Imagine you were a journalist, what other problems would you want to investigate?

Zomba Mountain 82

74. What different senses does this poem appeal to? Give words or lines that describe different senses.

75. What are the main themes discussed in Rubadiri's poems?
76 Compare the treatment of problems of young people in' African Child' and `Leaders of Tomorrow' by `Pungulani.
77 How can you tell that most of Rubadiri's poems were written earlier than most of the poems in this anthology?
78 Identify the different themes covered in this anthology. List the poems according to the themes they deal with.

NOTES ON CONTRIBUTORS

Chawanangwa Banda, Jayne Banda, Guyce H Bvalani, George Chatha, Lackson J Chatha, Tobias Chidzalo, Irene Chipeta-Zimba, Sophie Jobe, Helen C Kachala, Ndekhane Kalumba, Owen Kandeu, Herbert B Kapota, Thomas Khumuwa, Esme Kusauka, Patrick H Kwalimba, Matilda Luhanga, Lydia Maideni, Elizabeth Makhala-Nyamatcherenga, Jullia Mambo, Christopher Matewere, Bridget C Mhemedi, Rosemary U Mkumba, Edward S Moyo, Kenneth Mtambalika, Dorah Mwase, Sophie Nambazo, Charity Ndhlovu-Chinkono, Louis Ngwira, George Pungulani, King N Rudi, Andrew Bwenkha Thawe, and Chris Zenengeya are secondary school teachers of English who graduated from Domasi College of Education between 1996 to 2000. While in college they participated in writers' workshop.

MacDonald 'Beverly' Bamusi, N Bisani, Cecilia Hasha, Peter Kalitera, Marvin Kambuwa, Masuzgo Mhango, Kwesi Msusa, Kondwani Mwangulube, Alfred T. Nkhoma, Patrick Nyirenda, Davie Nsewa were active members of the writers' workshop. They graduated from Chancellor College, University of Malawi, between 1990 and 2000

Immanuel Bofomo: Poet and Short Story Writer. His published works include *Blood in my Bathroom* (short story collection), *Ring Freedom Bells* (poetry collection), *The Best Partner for your Life* and *Ghost in My Bedroom*. Some of his works have been published in foreign anthologies including one, the National Library of poetry, Maryland USA. *Ghost in My Bedroom* and *Ring Freedom Bells* have been translated into French and Kiswahili.

Greyson Bongwe, short story writer and dramatist, is a lecturer in Language and Communication Skills at Chancellor College. His main interest is in children's literature and theatre in development.

Amos Moses Chauma is a lecturer in the Department of Curriculum and Teaching Studies at Chancellor College, the University of Malawi. Chauma taught in Primary Teacher Training Colleges and Domasi College of Education before joining the University of Malawi. He has published articles, short stories and educational books.

Steve Chimombo, poet, novelist, playwright and critic, is the editor and publisher of WASI, the magazine that greatly promotes the arts in Malawi. His plays and poetry, most of which explore Malawian myths and legends such as those of Mbona and Napolo, and his short stories have appeared in many local and international anthologies; and he himself has published poetry, plays,

and novels in English, Chinyanja and Chiyao. He is Professor of English (Literature) at Chancellor College, University of Malawi, and the patron of Writers' Workshop.

Austin Chiwindo-Chirwa is a teacher in Nkhata Bay disctrict. He did his teachers course at Mzuzu Teachers' College, and qualified in 1985. He writes poetry and short stories.

Benjamin Chunda is a teacher in Mzimba District. He did his teachers course at Mzuzu Teachers' College, and qualified in 1986.

Albert Chitsanzo Kalimbakatha is a teacher in Ntcheu district. He did his teachers' course through the Malawi Special Teacher Education Programme (MASTEP), and qualified in 1993. He writes poetry.

Andrew Tilimbike Kulemeka taught Linguistics and African Languages at Chancellor College before going to the USA where he lives with his family in Maryland. Kulemeka's first short stories appeared in Star Magazine in the late seventies. His other stories have appeared in various anthologies in Malawi and USA. He has also published two Chichewa grammar books and a bi-lingual Chichewa-English dictionary.

Ken Lipenga, poet, novelist and critic, is Honourable Member of Parliament and Minister of Tourism. As a student and lecturer in English at Chancellor College, he was an active member of Writers' Workshop. He was chief editor of 'Daily Times' newspaper.

Mercy F Longwe (Nee: Thindwa) taught English at a number of institutions, among them St. Mary's, and Chichiri Secondary School; and Lilongwe, and Mzuzu Teachers' College. She died on 30th March, 1993.

Ben Wokomaatani Malunga, poet and short story writer, is currently the University Registrar. Most of his poetry has been read on M B C, and published in magazines and newspapers. He has many times read his poetry on the local radio. His poetry collections <u>Kuimba Kwa Mlakatuli</u> and <u>Ndidzakutengera Kunyanja Ligineti ndi Ndakatulo Zina</u> are secondary school texts.

Levi Zeleza Manda, journalist, poet, and short story writer, is currently senior course manager at the Malawi Institute of Journalism and correspondent for Voice of America French Service. He has published many poems and short stories locally and internationally. The title story, 'The Unsung Song' won the 1984 University of Malawi Magazine fiction award.

Jack Mapanje, poet, is author of many collections of poetry published internationally, among them, Of Chameleons and Gods (1981), and <u>The Chattering Wagtails of Mikuyu Prison</u> (1993). He taught English in secondary schools before joining the staff of English Department, Chancellor College, and later was patron of Writers' Group and Head of Department, prior to his detention in 1987. He is Professor of Literature, and lives in York, England.

John E B Matope, graduated from Domasi in 1999, and taught English at Domasi Private Secondary School. He died in 2000.

Duncan Ngamanya Mboma, short story writer, is library assistant at the National Assembly. His short stories appear in national newspapers.

Francis Moto, is principally a linguist and also a playwright, critic, poet and diplomat. He is Associate Professor of Linguistics and African Languages, and the current Principal of Chancellor College, University of Malawi. As a student he was an active member of Writers' Group. His poetry has appeared in many publications, and in <u>Gazing at the Setting Sun</u>, a collection of his poetry. He has also published lots of poetry in Chichewa; and <u>Trends in Malawian Literature</u> is a book he has recently published.

Lupenga Mphande, poet, dramatist and critic, taught English at Dedza Secondary School and Malawi Polytechnic. Among his publications is <u>Namaluzi</u>, a collection of short stories which he co-edited. As a student, he was an active member of the Writers' Group. He is Professor of African Languages and Literature at State University of Ohio, Columbia, USA.

Edson Mpina, poet and novelist, was president of Malawi Pen and the first president of Malawi Writers' Union (MAU). His poem, 'Summer Fires' won the BBC poetry competition in 1981. Through Malawi Pen, he promoted writing in Malawi. He died in December, 2001.

Felix Mnthali, poet, novelist, and critic, was among the first Malawian members of staff of the English Department, at Chancellor College. He ran Writer's Corner, a Malawi Broadcasting Corporation programme in which stories and poems were read and critiqued. A collection of his poetry entitled When sunset comes to Sapitwa was published in 1980, after his release from detention. He is currently Professor of English (Literature) at the University of Botswana.

Mike Sambalikagwa Mvona, poet and short story writer, is a journalist and the current President of Malawi Writers' Union (MAWU). His poems and short stories have appeared in many newspapers and magazines, and anthologies such as American Poetry Anthology, and The Haunting Wind.

Christopher K Mwawa, Anglican priest, and lecturer at the Zomba Theological College, is currently pursuing post-graduate studies in USA. Before taking holy orders in 1991, he served as a soldier and teacher, after qualifying from Blantyre Teachers'

College in 1983.

Anthony Nazombe, poet and critic, edited The Haunting Wind: New poetry from Malawi, the second collection of poems from the Writers' Group, a forum that has produced most of the writers in Malawi, of which he was an active member who contributed many poems and short stories, as a student from 1973 to 77. He is Associate Professor of English (Literature) at Chancellor College.

Norah Ngoma (Lungu) is secretary of MAWU and one of the prolific women writers in Malawi. Her short stories have been read since the 80s. Former Malawi Pen Women's Chair, Norah has travelled as far as Finland on writing errands.

Dickson Vuwa Phiri, poet and short story writer, is Senior Assistant Librarian at Chancellor College. His poetry has appeared in many local magazines and The Haunting Wind: New poetry from Malawi. As a student, he was an active member of the Writers' Group.

Kingston Lapukeni Phiri, poet and economist, is a member of Lingadzi Writers' Workshop. He has edited Malawi Writing Today: a PEN Anthology of Recent Writing in Malawi, a collection of poems, short stories and essays.

David Rubadiri, poet, novelist, critic, broadcaster and diplomat, is Professor of Literature, and currently the Vice Chancellor of the University of

Malawi. He is the first Malawian poet to gain international recognition; has taught Literature at Universities of Makerere, Nairobi, Ife, and Northwestern University, USA; and was the first Malawian Principal of Soche Hill College, before taking up the post of Ambassador in Washington and New York. He is a trustee of Malawi Writers Union (MAWU). His publications include the novel, No Bride Price ; and selections of poetry: Guns of Gaborone, Poems from East Africa, and Growing up with Poetry.

Linda Chipiliro Saidi, graduated from Domasi in 1999, and taught English at Zomba Private Secondary School. He died in November 2001

Steve Sharra is currently pursuing studies in USA. After qualifying through MASTEP, he taught at Bilila before taking up the post of editor at the Malawi Institute of Education. His short stories have won national and international awards.